Other Works by

BETH BOSWORTH

*   *   *

A Burden of Earth and Other Stories

BETH BOSWORTH

Tunneling

A Novel

Shaye Areheart Books
NEW YORK

Published by Shaye Areheart Books, New York, New York.
Member of the Crown Publishing Group, a division of Random House, Inc.
www.randomhouse.com

SHAYE AREHEART BOOKS and colophon are trademarks of Random House, Inc.

Printed in the United States of America

Design by Lynne Amft

Library of Congress Cataloging-in-Publication Data
Bosworth, Beth, 1957–
Tunneling : a novel / Beth Bosworth.— 1st ed.
1. Girls—Fiction. 2. Authors—Fiction. 3. Time travel—Fiction.
4. Teaneck (N.J.)—Fiction. 5. Race relations—Fiction.
6. School integration—Fiction. I. Title.
PS3552.O795T86 2003
813'.54—dc21   2003008053

ISBN 0-609-61103-8

10 9 8 7 6 5 4 3 2 1

First Edition

For Sarah, Michael and Nora

ACKNOWLEDGMENTS

SOME THANKS ARE DUE. Thanks to Maggie Paley and Susan Wheeler for hosting our writers' group, to Harvey Shapiro for inviting me to join it and to all its members for encouraging me to go on. Thanks likewise to the Yaddo art colony, where some pages of the novel were written. And my very real thanks to my agent, Andrew Blauner, and to Shaye Areheart, Teryn Johnson, Sara Kippur, Sibylle Kazeroid and Katherine Beitner of Shaye Areheart Books.

I want also to acknowledge some of the novel's sources. The epigraph, composed by Tobias Wolff, owes something to John Keats and something else, we believe, to Fats Waller. The character known as The Assemblage and his dialogue derive largely from Billes Deleuze and Felix Guattari's *A Thousand Plateaus: Capitalism and Schizophrenia.* *Chinua Achebe,* the official biography by Ezenwa-Ohaeto, and detailed maps in the Brooklyn Public Library, provided what accuracy resides in chapter 5. Chapter 7 stems partly from Walter Pater's *Greek Studies,* a book I found in the Saratoga Public Library. Information on the successful campaign to desegregate public schools in Teaneck, New Jersey, came in part from Reginald Damerell's *Triumph in a White Suburb.* *Kafka's Prague: A Travel Reader,* by Klaus Wagenbach, traveled with me for months; DC Comics comic books, which used to cost twelve cents an installment, for years.

I would like finally to thank Dennis Nurkse for his constant support, my mother for keeping a shelf of my published works, and my children for their enthusiasm concerning this particular enterprise.

Beauty is Truth, Truth Beauty.

*   *   *

Rooty-Toot Toot, and A-Toot Toot Rooty.

—POSTED ON TOBIAS WOLFF'S OFFICE DOOR,
STANFORD UNIVERSITY, 1976

CONTENTS

Tunneling

Chapter One

Tunneling

I WAS WRAPPED IN HIS CAPE AND WE WERE FLYING
through the firmament, which was very beautiful and bright and yet
perfectly colorless and also great-tasting, and above us burned a flame
that shone white and yet not white, as all color had disappeared and
with it the desperate confused cruelties of humanity and meanwhile the
coelum empyreum and hoards of Angels hovered in an extremely celes-
tial fashion, the Seraphim Cherubim Dominions and Powers all hovered singing praise in perfect pitch and turning their perfectly illumined
faces up toward what I could just glimpse to be a fiery and variegated
Throne and below us breathed the more resolute perfection of the primum mobile, I really liked that primum mobile, the way it got things
going, and I knew I was safe in spite of being a human girl because he
had his ways of keeping me safe and then suddenly I was alone and sailing through that unalterable fifth substance, alone and bouncing
amongst the fixed stars, alone and crashing through one crystalline
sphere after another on which hung as if in some renegade sixth-grade
science project (I was going into seventh) the giant and terrible planets,
Saturn Jupiter Mars and Venus, also Mercury, and as the light waned
and the music of these spheres faded from my too-human ears I
smashed on through that last sphere and sailed on past the Moon into

mutable space, into this realm of mortal sin and all that festers, and I burst helter-skelter into a cold morning sky and went reeling above miniature fields and tiny thatched roofs, and went wheeling arms and legs akimbo into a flock of high-flying honking geese and an embankment of thick cloud, and went tumbling down toward stone belfries and the vaster monasteries and the massive Tower itself, and just as I plummeted toward Bridgegate with its weathered skulls and their mouths like *O*s, he caught me.

"Gotcha," he said.

"You must be kidding, S-Man," I said, rising and dusting off my britches. "What does the 'S' stand for anyhow?"

"Never mind," he said uneasily. "We're there."

"This isn't Prague, is it?"

I knew well enough from those weathered skulls; how often had I read about the remains of such prisoners, who dig tunnels by night and hide the dirt by swallowing! How often had I thought of standing before the gates of London Bridge! And yet—and this irked more than his having hurled me through an Elizabethan cosmos—I wanted above all things to fly back in time (not this much) and east in space (a little more) to Prague, where I hoped finally to make the acquaintance of the great Franz Kafka.

It was Kafka's "Metamorphosis" that had inspired me to write, or rather to pledge my young life to the cause of writing.

"*Patience,*" S-Man would only remark.

"That's easy for you to say."

S-Man shrugged powerful shoulders. His cape fluttered. His brown boots shifted on the cobblestones. Months before his world debut, S-Man was still experimenting with diverse workaday styles; on this occasion he wore an indigo cape spangled with stars and signs of the zodiac, a tight-fitting leotard on the bosom of which a slew of *S*s tore off into purplish oblivion and a thick pair of mustard-colored leggings above thick boots.

"You could apologize," I told him.

S-Man stood gazing out over the city of London.

I had never been to London before and was impressed in spite of my vocation by the breadth and sweep of the Thames. To either side of the covered bridge lay wharves and jetties, and seafaring vessels, and innumerable tugs laden with dried goods, tanned hides and the thick-spun cloths destined for this and that banks of the river. A fishwife waited on a quay, her arms bent and in them a wooden crate. S-Man could smell its contents from where we stood and he pinched his nose. He was always making me laugh, even when the doctor was coming. She was a grim woman of German extraction; I wondered what she would have thought to catch me out of bed!

A carriage hurtled noisily toward London Bridge; we jumped to let it pass. The driver, cursing, urged his horses on into the shadowy covered shops that spanned the river. The river sparkled. A yellow sun shone; a gray oak tree spread gnarled limbs; the world seemed composed of myriad levels of correspondence. "Shall we?" he asked. "Why not?" We turned and walked on and he filled me in on the details of our mission. *Shall we? Why not?* the very air, also the earth, the water, the flames flickering above a lone chimney—all seemed to sing softly, unless that was the music of crystalline spheres still humming in my ear. I hummed along a few notes and then stopped because even in Elizabethan England, I could not seem to carry a tune.

"Never mind," S-Man said.

"Is this the way?"

He pointed south. So we set off in the opposite direction of London proper, that is, toward the tannery and the bear gardens. We passed a tinker with his cart, a farmer on his wagon drawn by two stumbling horses. We stepped around patches of thick brown mud and avoided a heap of sunbaked straw in which several mice were spontaneously generating. We paused, for a moment or so, to observe a beaver at work; a doe lingering on the edge of a thicket; then walked on briskly, looking for all the globe like an Elizabethan player or perhaps a magician and his boy—a given of my travels with the superhero, who rearranged at will the fibers of his outfit, was that I disguise myself as a boy. That was fine with me! In fact I had recently taken a second vow, more private than the first. The mud deepened, the sky turned a bolder shade of blue. I couldn't sing but from the bushes a bird could and did, in piercing mellifluous syllables.

Upon reaching Southwark, however, we found our progress halted by a woman in muddy skirts who emerged to block the lane. She said something I couldn't understand. S-Man bowed low, his cape grazing the soil; then, rising, he shook his head.

The woman slipped behind a gate into the depths of a florid garden.

"What did she want?" I asked suspiciously but S-Man shook his head. He looked very fine in his cloak, with the blue-black curls at his nape peculiarly fetching.

Not for anything, I swore, stumbling after him; not for anything in the world would I become a woman.

"You think too much," he said, turning back. His eyes were the color of coal.

"Quit it."

With his superbreath he was making an _S_ of rustling leaves—the _S_ wound around my ankles, crawled over my Keds! "Just quit it," I said. His eyes narrowed. From somewhere a bear growled. My companion strode toward the theater entrance, an oaken door cut into a rounded wooden wall. I hurried after him and inside, where the long stage stretched emptily beneath voluminous wooden tiers.

"Where is he?" I asked, clambering after.

Already S-Man was scanning the Globe with his S-vision; I followed his gaze as far as my human eyes could, to the open roof above and the earthen floor below us; later I would learn more about what I was and wasn't seeing, about the heavens with their hidden dressing room and balcony, the trapdoor and hellish enclave beneath the stage and beyond it little rooms, alcoves and crannies where a man and woman might go to be alone.

"Well?"

He shook his head.

I picked up a largish pebble and tossed it onto the stage. Seconds later another pebble fell through the open roof and a faint smell of mold or earth wafted toward us.

"Uh-oh," I said loudly.

S-Man nodded.

Even my human senses could pick up the mildly unpleasant odors of certain villains. Worst by far was the odor of Malathion exuded by the archvillain Laff Riot, whom S-Man had still in real Earth time to encounter, and yet whom he detested and by whom he was detested and feared. Nothing of this temporal paradox passed through my mind as we stood beneath the open roof, surrounded by that inimitable if lesser odor of villainy, and beneath it the smell of old sweat and the ambiguous promise of rain. Sure enough a larger pebble fell; another; a veritable shower of pebbles and stones cascaded upon the great stage where a lone tree rattled its branches.

A similar tree—representative, I suppose, of Dunsinane—adorned the jacket of a book I read in New Jersey, when my parents were fooled into thinking me asleep. I was severely asthmatic and my nocturnal rasping caused them much concern. If they knew the life I actually led, not in bed but beneath it! I kept apples and canned juices stashed there and a flashlight under my pillow, and I would wait only for them to leave, the door to close, before climbing beneath my bed. There is a particular feel to cold hard floor against a girl's belly; meanwhile box springs reflected the flashlight's neat glow; books lay carefully stacked (I was otherwise a slob, although recent research into Kafka's life had turned up his Spartan habits) according to the intricate mysteries of their call numbers. Who doesn't love a call number? I would stay there, sometimes reading, sometimes not, until the dust motes swam like little fishes toward sunlight pouring through the window; later, at breakfast, my mother would touch my forehead and my father raise his eyes, and my sister, Elaine, get sent once more for his stethoscope. "I can't understand it," my mother would sigh, meaning that I seemed to go to bed healthy only to wake up exhausted and wheezing.

"It happened just like that to the Bubble Boy," Elaine would say darkly.

The Bubble Boy, as we schoolchildren all knew from our *Weekly Reader*s, was a child whose allergies so threatened his life that he was obliged to lead it inside a translucent plastic bubble-shaped dome. He lived in a hospital in Arizona and only saw his family during visiting hours.

But now S-Man leaped onto the stage and bounded into the air. I stood my ground and breathed deeply of the year 1609. I knew my part in our mission—we were here to save Shakespeare from himself, a notion that made total sense. Already we were experiencing terrific mental communications. A veritable avalanche of pebbles tumbled through the open ceiling onto the great stage and a black hat sailed down after, its lone feather fluttering loose and a tiny man darting to catch it as S-Man plunged through the roof to stand, legs parted, arms folded amid rocks still crashing around him.

Mr. Stick, that telepathic imp, sat on the air, arms and legs folded in bold mimicry!

"I give you thirty seconds to get off this planet," S-Man said.

"Ha-ha!" said the tiny man.

My companion's face flushed.

"Twenty seconds," he said.

Tunneling

"Ha-ha-ha!" said the tiny green creature. He darted here, there, hovering in the branches of the lone tree. S-Man took a deep breath and folded his arms. No doubt he was counseling himself to be *patient.*

"Make that fifteen," he merely said.

At such a rate I might never meet Mr. Kafka! I vaulted the stage, dodging the last rock or so as I raced into the players' room, grabbed a quill and an inkwell, scribbled the blocky letters of a word (backward) onto a scrap of parchment and ran once more into daylight.

"Hey," I said. "Can you read this, mister?"

The imp flew near to get a better look.

I held my breath as he whistled in my face. I would have pitied him, had it not been for his exhumations. In the months before my asthma, I had often felt the urge to display my reading skills to teachers and classmates. I had felt it like another scourge: *Look at me, listen to me. . . .* But I knew that Mr. Stick, with his pixie face and green costume—he looked a little like Peter Pan—was not to be trusted; unlike Laff Riot, who had no sense of humor, Mr. Stick tended to find the cruelest jokes funny. The harder he laughed, the immenser his tele-empathic powers grew; the only way to exile him to his own environment—I shudder even now to think what that must have been—was to trick him into admitting the tragic nature of this universe.

Sure enough: just as recklessly as he had flown down, he pronounced the letters *D-E-A-T-H* and was gone.

"Well done," said S-Man.

My companion motioned for me to hold on as we flew off again toward the bend in the river. Was that a trick of the era's light, or a young cupid stretched upon a cloud? Even now, these years later—it is four centuries or thirty years later, take your pick—opening *The Complete Pelican Shakespeare* to its frontispiece, I feel that subtle shock of recognition. The cupid wears only a fluttering white cloth and its thighs dimple and it doesn't seem the least concerned with being a girl or a boy. Even now its sheer cuteness, head to toe, recalls that other zone, the firmament my companion and I had traversed, and the music of those revolving spheres and the notion or hypernotion of a perfection that knows no color, nor divisions of class nor age nor even, as I say, gender. But we have spiraled down the air. Clouds puff white against a background of river and sky; houses proliferate like skunkweed on the opposing shore. How distinctly I recall each detail of our voyages; if only I had time to tell you all!

Soon enough (a group of sightseers, countryish, pointed up) we came in for a landing, frightening a herd of pigs into a stampede through the crowded Drury Lane. A boy there was selling pamphlets with the latest shipping news, and at my powerful friend's suggestion we stopped long enough to buy one. I proffered one of the Elizabethan coins—"Tuppence," the boy said—that S-Man had minted before we set out. Curling the pamphlet and tucking it into a small drawstring purse at my waist, I hurried after my companion to the wooden door of Blackfriars, where he broke the stiff iron lock and, once we had slid inside, remolded it with his S-vision. He turned to show me the repaired lock, his zodiac-spangled cape swirling, his coal-black eyes piercing, for all I knew, right through my boy's disguise. For the first time that thought vexed me and I shoved past him into the dim hall.

We passed a low door, another. I heard a quill scratching parchment—a groan—a chair scraping floorboards—another groan and the sound of something slammed violently against a wall. S-Man touched my shoulder. I wondered why he hadn't led me here in the first instance. I thought of my vow, etcetera and so on. Why this goose chase? I heard a goose honking as if in response, and looked about. *Honk honk.* It was Mr. Stick's specialty to read minds and to mock them, but hadn't I sent him, or rather hadn't he sent himself through the mirror-reading of the word *death,* into his own dimension for thirty days? Sanguine about that much, I opened the door.

Tunneling

*　　*　　*

I admit to you, reader, I was disappointed.

At twelve, one has notions.

S-Man, with his cape continually a-flutter and his boots so bright and his chutzpah, satisfied some urge in me so totally that had it not been for my desire to meet the great Franz Kafka, that is, to unearth some significant work (I had an inkling of its size and shape, and knew furthermore that it would have an appendix), I might have stayed forever in his company. The sun might shine, the moon glow, stars zoom in and out of view; across the world a tribal people carved niches for itself, in the event of colonial invasion, in the hollows of cloven pines. What of it?

In those last weeks before his world debut, it's true, S-Man sometimes seemed nervy, self-preoccupied, even mercurial—he appeared on my windowsill in New Jersey wearing this lightning-bolt emblem or that animal insignia on his broad chest, and sometimes his S-cloak gleamed yellow and sometimes white, and sometimes purple and now starry and so on; and I was to say what I thought of this or that design and color scheme; and today, I confess, I suspect him of refusing to share his whole name not only for my sake, but because he had planned all his youngish life for his debut and couldn't quite share it even with me, his twelve-year-old companion. And yet his excitement was infection, so that to this day a special quality adheres in such liminal moments, when everything is possible, everything just starting out and changeling and *now.*

As for Shakespeare with his bleary gaze, his speckled blunt fingers spread across both knees, his belly and too-high pate—Shakespeare seemed and still seems diminutive. I put things badly. Perhaps, sensing my own propensities, I feared the disorder of his room. Cheese rinds and brown apple cores dotted the one shelf and floor straws lay in rotten clumps. Books, wine sacks, parchments and scraps of parchment were strewn everywhere. Their owner glowered at S-Man, at me, at S-Man, on whose cloak the signs of the zodiac—bull, crab, infant twins—twinkled starrily.

"O," said Shakespeare.

"We've flown from the future to help you in your time of grief," I explained.

He nodded, as if some suspicion had been confirmed, and sat up.

"My wits begin to turn, then," he said at last.

"Please, Mr. Shakespeare, don't be afraid," I said.

"Down, earth" was his only response. He touched his temples.

Then, freeing a hand, the playwright gestured as if to say that we should make ourselves comfortable. S-Man nudged me. I sat, trying not to notice the rumpled sheets, next to Shakespeare. The window wasn't even a real window but a hazy cloth through which no air filtered. Silence filled the room. I thought idly about the lack of oxygen and how I never seemed to suffer asthma in the past and why that was and if it was so, as S-Man had recently maintained, that there was an inexhaustible supply of universes and if so mightn't we all just go to the best one—then even those idle thoughts died out.

Shakespeare sat hunched, head leaning on one hand, eyes following the fingers of the other. They were tracing shapes like crosses on his knees.

"Name something you'd like," I said finally.

But Shakespeare only slid a slippered foot across the torn parchments. The silence grew almost audible, like the buzzing of an insect, and then even the buzz ended. Minutes, hours, an afternoon and part of an evening (so it seemed) passed. Aeons passed. Wars were won and lost. Women cried out in their sleep, dreaming of childbirth. A dozen or so Jews worshiped in secret; a lone black African, living in a small stone house behind Westminster, stirred in his sleep. I thought I heard muffled laughter and the sound of a grave being dug.

"Nothing," Shakespeare said. "Nothing, nothing, nothing."

Tunneling

"There must be something."

S-Man walked over to the greased cloth and peered through. Had he caught the room's melancholy? This was the time of day he disliked, I knew, when shadows lengthen and the disadvantage of total recall makes itself felt. Frankly, I still don't understand why we waste so much time—entire lifetimes—learning things about ourselves that would only have been useful a year, a decade, a generation ago.

"How about a window," S-Man said, turning.

"Great idea," I said. "Why didn't I think of that?"

Already S-Man had flown through the greased cloth and streaked across the city to the river, where he found sand to melt and sculpt into a glass pane that he installed haste-posthaste. He wiped his palms. Shakespeare shuffled through the straw. He placed a fingertip on the smooth pane and gazed upon the discarded greasy cloth where it lay among the thatches. And so I explained again, S-Man joining in, about how we had flown back in time and east in space to succor him in this grievous time. Shakespeare's eyes gleamed. They were odd eyes. They were nothing like S-Man's eyes, for instance, which were a bit small for his fine head and set deeply beneath those massive brows. Shakespeare's eyes shone yellow and he squinted. He looked like a sailor or gangster. Were there gangsters, I wondered, in 1609? *Yes and no,* whispered a voice—again I looked around and thought to mention the voice to S-Man. I wish I had!

"Your work is very important," I said. "You have to finish that play you started. You just have to."

Shakespeare looked down.

A moment ago I had heard the sound of shovels striking dirt; now a sort of picture formed in my mind of a little cemetery and two graves, one smaller and the other larger and more freshly dug. Rain began to fall on these graves in my mind and also on the city. Drops pelted and slid down the glass pane and Shakespeare followed their virgin trail with one blunt-nailed finger. S-Man whistled. I saw him draw his breath and several things seemed to happen at once: the fetid straw (and a family of brown mice) were sucked into his mouth and then he was gone and then he wasn't, and sweet yellow straw lay in neat spindles above the gleaming floorboards and the glued parchments were placed side by side on the newly made bed. *Cymbeline, a Tragedie*—but the glow in Shakespeare's eyes had died.

I reached to whisper into S-Man's ear about the graves, lesser and greater. I couldn't have told him how they had appeared to me, or why I assumed their authenticity.

"We can't do that," he said.

"We can try."

"You don't know what you're talking about."

"We've never tried."

"Because it can't be done."

"Please."

"Please yourself," he said, and scooping Shakespeare and me up in his two strong arms (it was a sign of Shakespeare's mental state that he didn't struggle), he flew us out the door and down the hall and, like a giant swooping bird, through the courtyard. I pictured countless players in brown doublets and white hose, streaming out across the city—leaping like bobtailed deer across the countryside—then felt only the wind in my face and the flutter of the cape and the usual butterflies in my stomach as we rose. The moon shone yellow. The clouds drifted this way, that. I glanced at Shakespeare, whose yellow eyes matched the moonshine. He looked like a child. Years later—but why bring up the sorrow of these later years? He was the only Elizabethan S-Man ever carried at the same time as me. How odd that felt! He filled up a lot of the cape, for one thing, and for another his warmth was distinctly male. I couldn't tell what he was thinking. I myself was thinking hard about bridges. There was London Bridge with its storefronts and terrible skulls. There was the Comstock Bridge, which we could dimly see in the moonlit distance. Then there was the George Washington Bridge, beneath which my grim doctor lived in a tiny lighthouse when she wasn't paying house calls. Just once I wished that my mother knew where I was, where I had been, where I was headed; then we landed on the northern side of the Avon.

"O," Shakespeare said for the second time.

"Close your eyes," said S-Man.

I considered telling him about the voice but it had ceased during our flight and I did as he commanded.

One thing I don't miss, mind you, is stationary time travel! I would describe the feel if I could. Imagine walking through a forest with cobwebs so that you rub your face and instead your features come off. We must have gone back another twenty years in the space of a night. I could see no change in any of us but the Avon looked different beneath the rain. You have seen rivers under steady rainfall, I imagine, and can figure for yourself how water (churning) may seem complicit, how an Elizabethan or a young girl might imagine some elemental need on water's part to mingle with air or even—poor water—ether. I began to hum and desisted. S-Man sighed. Shakespeare murmured something unintelligible. The sun had been up, albeit behind the clouds, for some while. It was delightful to return to the normal passage of time. A woman approached the bridge from the far shore; she crossed slowly, milk pails glinting, wooden shoes clickety-clacking. A man sat atop a wagon at our end of the bridge. He waited until she neared him (and us), then jumped down and reached for her pails. He lifted them gently onto the wagon, where other tin pails glistened, and lifted her up to sit beside him and he clucked to his horse and the wagon rolled on.

We stood by that bridge for the better part of the morning, S-Man keeping off the light rain (the drops falling toward us, entering the range of his heated vision and melting clear away; it was beautiful to see) and Shakespeare watching the slow but steady traffic of his past across the bridge. We felt no inclination actually to enter the town and S-Man, who knew more specifically what we were here to circumvent, didn't press us. A church bell rang once, twice, thrice; a goose flapped heavy wings as it fled past; a boy about my age stepped onto the bridge. Shakespeare gasped.

I have declared my intention simply to record the events of that morning; let me do so and have done.

Like me, the boy wore short pants and a sort of white tucked blouse. He advanced slowly, rolling a hoop. The hoop dawdled, wobbled, fell. He leaped to right it and gave it a good push.

"It's gone," said S-Man, narrowing his eyes on some point beyond the river.

"What's gone?" I asked, but I knew. He meant the little grave. A flat grassy patch lay, he said grimly, where the little mound would or wouldn't. Either it would or it wouldn't.

"I could have told you that much," I said, but I knew as well as S-Man that what we were trying to accomplish went against nature. The hoop skittered toward us. The boy clambered toward it, us, the far bank. He had no business being on that bridge on a rainy Friday morning at the beginning of Lent. The hoop rolled on out of his reach and toward the bushes where we crouched. I knew from Shakespeare's eager catch that he was indeed this boy's father. The boy looked puzzled; from a few feet away he must have seen the hoop whisk itself out of sight. He paused. He scratched his ear. He felt in his pocket for something and held it on his palm.

S-Man, the only one of us who could see from this distance, said it was a frog. The frog lay on the boy's palm until it had recovered, I suppose, from the shock of a dark pocket and a sudden clear light rain. Then it hopped off his palm onto the bridge and in spite of the boy's efforts (he stumbled, sank, sprawled across the slats; Shakespeare would have cried out but the superhero covered his mouth) leaped into the rushing Avon. What next?

The boy shrugged and kicked the side of the bridge. Rain began to fall more steadily. I wonder even today about the boy's life, his feelings for his father, who came home rarely and usually in summer with other players. A hundred knights; fifty knights; perhaps he also lay in bed, listening to his parents' quarreling over certain houseguests. All conjecture, all fancy. Several things happened at once but I can only write them down one at a time. The boy climbed onto the railing of the bridge and stood defiantly, arms outstretched. The playwright stepped forward to warn him. We heard a sound like the shattering of glass and the sky opened. A round white face peered down. Not Mr. Stick this time, nor Laff Riot, but the terrible Assemblage himself!

"Damn you!" cried S-Man.

Can you blame him? The intelligence collectors dotting Assemblage's temples glowed more brightly than ever. The voice in my head rang more loudly: I understood only one word in five. Assemblage, the most inhuman of S-Man's enemies, was rapidly absorbing energy from all our minds, including Shakespeare's, and jamming what remained of our think tanks with what I would later recognize (with that same intensity of feeling, if not the same feeling, that I would recognize the flying cupid) as Intergalactic Discursive Prose (translated from the French). Shakespeare blinked. The boy tottered. The world winced. *"I is an order-word,"* the voice said, accents rippling with triumph. *"My direct discourse is still the free indirect discourse running through me, coming from other worlds or other planets. . . ."* At this moment a new shower of rocks commenced and I laughed a bit wildly to see them, thinking that we would combat this nuisance as readily as we had Mr. Stick's. I stopped laughing when I saw that they were rainbow colored.

"Holy Mother Planet!" S-Man shouted, clutching his abdomen. Rainbow-colored rocks—remnants of his self-destructed Mother Planet—were falling everywhere. A cross-dimensional communicator opened in the sky and again Mr. Stick appeared, imprisoned, it's true, in his own world of tiny people but keenly delighted, even overjoyed, to see the young hero writhing from the rocks hurtling through the intergalactic communicator. A terrible sound filled our ears, as if the hoards of angels singing God's praises had been replaced by gangs of impassioned cats.

"Run!" I shouted, meaning "Fly!" but even if he had still possessed the power, S-Man would never have fled. He wouldn't leave me; and Shakespeare, hands raised to his powerful brain, which was being simultaneously drained and filled with viciously abstract IDP *(There is no self. . . . There is no such thing as the existence of the self beyond the walls of language. . . .)*, wouldn't leave the boy.

The boy!

I turned too late; the boy stumbled, almost righted himself, and followed his frog into the rushing waters of the Avon. A bright rock landed on his bobbing head. I saw his pained expression and his terrible surrender to the waves as Shakespeare's voice rose in a shriek and the very cosmos seemed to shatter (but how could it go on shattering?) into myriad rainbow-colored shards and I did the only thing I knew under the circumstances: I dove into the water.

When I awoke, the sun was setting through a rounded window. A pigeon landed on the sill, clucked, peered in. S-Man, pale but alive, sat on the edge of my bed; a woman stood on the threshold, blond hair swept from her face, eyes blue and slitted. She looked Cornish or Irish.

"My wife," said Shakespeare, joining her.

Did she know? I tried to sit up, tried to tell her; S-Man shook his head quietly but firmly and I lay back, relieved to be spared another confession of my weakness. I had plotted to save her son from death and failed. I felt drained and useless and wanted my mother. But it would take weeks for me to recover sufficiently to withstand the physical hardship of space-time flight, and in those weeks my body would exact sufficient payment for my hubris. It was on April 4, 1609, in Stratford-on-Avon (foul river!), that I first got my period; it was not my mother but Anne Hathaway Shakespeare who frowned at the smear of brown blood on her sheets and took me into her arms as my tears flowed.

S-Man had filled me in on the outcome of our battle with his enemies. I wondered if he knew what had happened to me and, realizing that he had to know, looked stiffly out the window while he spoke. The voice of doom had belonged, of course, to none other than the terrible villain known as Assemblage, whose strangely multidinous brainpower might have triumphed had not Shakespeare, seeing my brave (I almost cried again when S-Man used the word *brave*) but futile dive after his drowning son, been filled with a righteous fury that swept like another river all doubt, all self-interrogation and the hopelessness brought upon him by the death of his old mother (thus the second grave)—thrust all this out of his mind. The sheer reconciliation of his furious mind with itself had jammed the intelligence collectors on which Assemblage depended. One by one the devices dotting Assemblage's forehead had turned from pink to red to red hot to white hot and exploded. The blasts had inspired Shakespeare to take cover; that essentially good if cautious man had dragged the already-unconscious superhero, who would otherwise have died from the effects of S-radiation, into the bushes. Mr. Stick was left to watch, aghast, as all this took place, and the only satisfaction he could take—that the boy died as foretold, that I also was swept downriver—was reduced as S-Man regained consciousness and swam to my rescue and eventually brought the three of us into 1609 again. I have often thought about the moment just before he yanked me out. It comes to me in dreams or I think it does: sometimes the water is dragging me down and sometimes I'm trying as hard as I can to cough up everything—water, earth, air—I've had to swallow just to crawl my way to freedom.

At any rate, said S-Man, I must understand that as far as Anne Hathaway was concerned, her son had been dead these twenty years; and as for Shakespeare, although still sad about his mother, he was once again writing the play he'd started for better or worse prior to her death. The playwright himself poked his head in just then. S-Man frowned and stood. An awkwardness ensued. I watched in silence his flowing cape and bluish hair as he retreated; I loved S-Man but I was mortal and he was not, and there it was.

Shakespeare was in a very good mood. He liked information, it seemed, above all things, and with S-Man around was acquiring it faster than a steam engine. "Steam engine?" he asked. "Marry, what be that?" I would have told him were it not for the sorrow still down inside me, coloring my insides like wet earth.

"Look ye here," said Shakespeare, unfazed, and he pulled up a chair and showed me a pamphlet.

It was the pamphlet I had bought for a penny on our first and last morning in London, but I thought the least I could do, under the circumstances, was to let him keep it. He showed me how it was all about Bermuda and a recent shipwreck off the coast, and went on to tell me about the half-men, half-beasts rumored to live there, and I laughed and told him there were no such creatures on that or any other island, but he persisted in talking about savages and exaggerative physiognomies so that I wondered if he wasn't racist, perhaps, but decided (who knows if I was right?) that he suffered from ignorance not of a willful but a cultural kind. Certainly he seemed eager to discuss just about anything, and asked if I had read any Montaigne, and what did I think about science and progress, and was it true what S-Man said about sheep that reproduced without haleking? I had to ask him what *haleking* was, and felt ashamed, but he reached to touch my forehead and I looked up into his yellow eyes and saw their benevolence and interest in this and other worlds, and I felt not so much reconciled to human nature as quietened. I told Shakespeare what I could recall about steam engines, which led to a discussion of air travel, and in the end I confessed my doubts about this double life, about flying with S-Man by night and using my Breath-a-Lator by day, and I told him about the doctor and how my parents and she were in cahoots, and he led me to see that my illness had become my family's and that I had to cure us all by going home.

I supposed when I sat down to write this that our chapter had an unhappy ending, because so much one might regret took place that day on the bridge and later in New Jersey, and my travels with S-Man were soon to cease. But really we were happy enough, he and I, as we flew away from Stratford with Anne and Will waving us on. We were quiet long after we had left Earth's atmosphere behind—we were newly shy with each other, I suppose, and conscious of our differences and of the end, which would be bittersweet. As the stars flashed past and the cosmos burst once more into song—who could follow that tune?—we were filled also with the sense of a job done not well but *well enough*. We hadn't killed anyone, after all, who hadn't already been dead!

We even took a detour through a bright new constellation, stopping at a planet about which S-Man had recently heard rumors, where the inhabitants have no ears and communicate via smoke rings. I wondered if I would be obliged to smoke, but he said no, of course not, and handed me a bottle of soap bubbles. I was too old to blow bubbles, I said, and handed the bottle back. This turned out once we had landed to be a mistake, I mean a real whopper, but that, as they say, is another story.

Chapter Two

New Friends

ODDLY ENOUGH, IT WAS MY SISTER, ELAINE, who precipitated my first encounter with S-Man. She and I had been arguing, as we were wont, about the contemplative and active lives. "When was the last time you went outside?" she shouted. She thrust open her bedroom window and, grabbing my book, hurled it straight across the porch roof!

"There," she said. She wiped her palms.

If Elaine's goal had been to prod me out of doors or windows, she succeeded; but I scrambled onto the roof after the projectile—a little red paperback of *Aristotle's Poetics*—only to witness its flapping trajectory over the roof's edge and the arrival through the air of still another missile, my stack of index cards. In vain I reached for them. The index cards, onto which I had so painstakingly copied the elements of the Dewey decimal system, soared en masse over the porch roof. The porch window slammed. My sister's grinning face vanished. A shivery gust sent me almost to my knees.

"Shoot," I said, rising. "She makes me so mad sometimes."

"Lose something?"

"I beg your pardon?"

An individual in tight-fitting leotards and billowing cape had apparently landed on the porch roof. He held the *Poetics* in one hand, my cards in the other.

"I'm, uh, S-Man," he said. "I can't tell you my whole name because there are people who might try to harm you. I use the word 'people' in its larger sense."

I nodded, surprised and yet confirmed, as Mr. Shakespeare would be (as Mr. Shakespeare was in the past that had not yet been experienced by us, I mean), in an old suspicion—in my case, not of madness but of something unusual happening one day. The S-Man handed me the rescued objects, which I reclaimed thankfully. Meanwhile clouds had grown even darker and currents of hot and cold air were sprinting past. The S-Man's cape shimmered; on his chest a series of dark letter *S*s snaked across a grassy field. (Although this was not his most memorable or successful insignia, it was the first in which I saw him.) A few strokes and a dash or two of color may complete the facial portrait: coal-black eyes set deep beneath a massive brow, and a longish chin punctuated with a cleft. The nose was nondescript. I had the feeling that I had seen his face before, and then again that I had never seen anyone resembling him ever.

"Do you like it?" he asked, gesturing. "I have others."

In a flash he had transformed his costume (I thought it was a costume) into a man-tailored version of the American flag, which item had sparked much sartorial debate among the members of my family and my school community!

"Neat! Are you a pacificist like Mr. Russell?"

"Yes and no."

Another bolt of lightning, further rumbles of thunder recalled us to the present danger. Not for long! My acquaintance (still a young man and a cipher to the general public) scooped me up and lowered me into the branches of the old maple tree, from which I could easily enough climb down and run, with a backward wave, toward the kitchen door.

"I'm Rachel! Rachel Finch! Me neither!"

Tunneling

What a violent storm—the last for some months—burst upon us as I scrambled indoors and rejoined my family! My sister and our parents and I had often gathered to witness nature's fireworks: we watched now through the kitchen windows as trees swayed, a telephone pole tilted and electricity scampered madly on slackened power lines. A family of squirrels fled pell-mell and chattering across the drenched yard. I realized with a pang that I had not actually thanked the flying man, who was nowhere to be seen.

"I arranged this show just for you guys," joked our father.

". . . just for us," our mother murmured, shaking her head.

At a particularly loud crack of thunder, she clapped her hands.

"You see"—our father gestured skyward—"how much I love you?"

Rain pounded the bent grasses; exhilarated, he reached to stroke her cheek.

". . . how much," Rose murmured, leaning back.

There being no further sign of the S-Man (perhaps *S* stood for "storm"?), I said nothing about him, not even to my sister, who stalked upstairs to her bedroom and slammed the door. As it happens, several months were to pass before rain was again to fall, and then I would recall my flying friend's words of caution and the sorrow that overcame him whenever we undertook the long journey home: "People will always be disappointed."

Who knows? Perhaps he foresaw our rupture, his and mine, and the hardships that would follow; perhaps he was reflecting upon the vagaries of his own career.

On our return from Stratford, the sky had grown rosy-fingered. Cloud bank gave way to cloud bank as I remarked sleepily on the strangeness of things: That was the roof of the NJ Savings & Loan! Look! Beyond the railroad tracks, our municipal park! Our junior high school, our houses, our lawns and trees . . .

All too soon S-Man had lowered me through my window and flown off, zodiacal cape and purple boots blending into the dawn sky; and I was creeping, an interloper to my own home, over the sill and into the room.

There was an emptiness to rooms after S-Man left me off, an emotion that had a distant cousin, it's true, in disappointment. Even the portraits hanging there seemed ordinary, compared to the manic aspect of a Mr. Stick, not to mention the more terrible physiognomy of Assemblage. Mr. Hemingway looked pained; Chekhov seemed overdelicate; even Mr. Shakespeare appeared pleased with himself, but that had perhaps to do with his frilly collar. (I knew him to be anything but self-congratulatory.) What's more, there was no apparent order to this gallery of literati. Over the years I had found a postcard here, a newspaper photo there. Some I had xeroxed for five cents each at the Teaneck Public Library, where I had become a member by inscribing my name, RACHEL FINCH, on a library card at the age of four. In spite of this promising start I had actually read only a few words by each author and, with the noted exception of the great Franz Kafka, my preferences changed more often than fashions in clothing. Before meeting up with S-Man, I had admired, each in turn, Dostoevsky for his recklessness; Dickens for his generosity with women; Rimbaud for his looks; Fitzgerald for his drinking; Thurber for his kindness to dogs . . . As for Bertrand Russell, his dry turtle face dominated the wall nearest my bed, where I had hung his *New York Times* obituary. It was upon reading this obituary, now curled and fading, that I had developed a fondness (not quite so short-lived) for the philosopher.

No poster of Franz Kafka hung on my walls; no tome of Kafka's rested on my shelves. No one, entering my chamber, would have suspected my feelings for the great Czech writer. No one, that is, who didn't think to look under my bed.

There, where (as I have mentioned) I crawled many afternoons and some nights, I kept a collection of *The Complete Stories.* I thought of this book as mine; its actually belonging to the library—*The Complete Stories* was six months overdue, like the Brod biography of its author—never diminished this pride of ownership. On the contrary! Between stories or during descriptive paragraphs (I had used to skip those, but was now sworn to my vocation), I would lean my chin on my hands and survey my little sunken world: a barely illumined stretch of wainscoting, an old doll's shoe. At night bedsprings glinted in the flashlight's glow, above books more legitimately borrowed from the public library. How I liked to press my hips against a cold hard floor, my cheek to a cellophaned cover! Then I would return to my reading; or rather, rereading. I very much enjoyed the story of the ape and also the one about twelve sons. Nothing thrilled me like "The Metamorphosis," but I recognized that high-pitched frequency, that insistence on exact detail that amounts to a cry for justice. I would not have known to express myself in those words; I would have said that the same man had written the stories.

The gallery of literati aside, my secret underworld aside, my room as I stood there seemed an unstrung medley, a cacophony of furniture and clothing and the occasional toy abandoned in some anterior time. In the morning light, I scrutinized these artifacts. Had I ever been the girl who played with this soapy-haired doll, that plastic horse with its chipped hoof? Since the last days of June, everything felt changed, changeling, and not only because I had left our old school behind. No. I had a secret to keep even from my family, most especially my family, because if they knew that I traveled the cosmos with S-Man, terrible harm could befall them or him or me. He had made that clear as the danger of my learning his full name. I felt a surge not of curiosity—that would threaten later—but of something more like pride at the thought of time travel, sky travel, any travel. To the best of anyone's knowledge, I preferred to stay home and read! If only they knew! And the faces on the walls seemed to kindle but that was only imagination, which was different from what transpired, what translated into the real!

And yet.

And yet the last Wednesday before the first Monday of seventh grade had dawned; the air lay thick with the leisures of summer, the swelter and yearning of it all. Every day promised rain that never came. Down the hall my father expostulated and my mother sleepily echoed. Were they arguing? My sister, I realized with some anxiety, was stirring.

"Is that you?" she whispered.

"No," I said.

"Come here."

"What is it?"

"What do you mean? We're going swimming today."

"Now? You and me?"

"No, Santa and Mrs. Santa," she sniggered.

I had stepped cautiously into the hall and passed now over the threshold of her room.

Elaine sat up. She wore a short, low-necked nightgown over her hourglass figure, and a sort of bonnet on her head that she removed—the bonnet, I mean—to reveal carefully curled locks stuck to her temples with shiny Scotch tape. Elaine hated her hair, which she called "Jewish hair," and she had terrific ways of punishing it.

"*Now,*" she scoffed. "No, not *now*. After breakfast. As soon as they *leave.*"

"We're not allowed."

"It's our last day of freedom," she said, touching her flattened curls, "and if *you* think I'm going to spend it home with *you,* my dear, you're mistaken."

"It's not good for me to swim on hot days," I whispered.

"So don't swim," said Elaine upon reflection.

"Listen," I said. "Are they fighting?"

We turned our gazes to the door of Elaine's closet, through which, we had discovered as younger children, our parents' intimate conversations could be overheard. It sufficed to crawl through the dark interior and to place your ear against a rear wall. My sister and I hesitated; we could listen, we could not listen.

May I take the liberty, while she and I consider our options, of describing to you her own bedroom?

Our mother, generally a distracted woman, had focused her creative energies on designing a boudoir worthy of Elaine's aspirations. The vanity table and little chair shone pink. The rolltop desk gleamed aquamarine. From the middle of the floor rose the bed, a pink-and-blue neweled four-poster concoction *à la française.* As for the walls, they reflected nuanced shades of egg-white, off-white, creamy white, beige. The faces of singing actresses—Elaine planned to be a singing actress— looked out from innumerable framed posters of Broadway shows amid more informally displayed magazine cutouts and advertisements for musical comedies and their leading ladies. Central to these last and encircled with loops of gold Magic Marker bloomed the truly beautiful face of Ann-Margret, whose names Elaine hoped someday to make famous in reverse. It was my sister's intent to become known not as the third-generation Jewish-American Elaine Finch, but as the elegant, passionate Margret-Ann.

"I didn't say come in," she informed me. "I said come *here.*"

"I want to know what they're saying."

"Do you even own a bathing suit?" she asked, but I had passed safely through her pink-and-beige boudoir into the closet, and pressed my ear to the wall.

The room next door seemed quiet at first.

"You aren't joking?" our father asked.

"Not joking," our mother murmured.

"Something is fishy here," he said suddenly.

"Uh-oh," I told Elaine.

They say that even self-made men are formed by wars; if so, my father was shaped by World War II. Drafted in 1940 into an elite corps of cryptanalysts, Francis never saw combat, but he did contract potentially fatal tuberculosis, did languish on a "terminal" ward for an entire year before medical advances and a VA bill got him to Paris and did encounter his "favorite code" during a violent thunderstorm. As it happened, said code, a doctor's daughter attending literature classes at the Sorbonne, had ventured out to watch the sky show. As it happened, so had Francis. Rose stepped to the end of the rue Rollin, a little elevated cul-de-sac; Francis looked up from the rue Monge and caught sight, as lightning flared, of slim clapping hands and a pale oval face.

"*Et voilà.* My project for life," he thundered.

Years later, over breakfast, Francis liked to remind Rose of that first Parisian encounter: the diamond-shaped stone steps leading from the rue Monge to the rue Rollin and the one lamppost glowing. "Remember?" he would shout.

". . . remember?" she would whisper. Francis, whose shortness of breath was the cause of his shouting, had by then been appointed head physician of the Children's Ward at our town's Holy Name Hospital; Rose, whose hardness of hearing resulted from childhood mastoid surgery, had by then become "nothing," as we used in those uncertain times to say. That is, she was his wife and our mother.

"My destiny," he might say. "My tiny doppelgänger. My diminutive albatross."

". . . diminutive . . . ," she would murmur sotto voce.

That my father believed my mother somehow fulfilled his destiny, I don't doubt; like some couples, they seemed matched if not in strengths, at least in weaknesses. And yet "destiny" seems the wrong word for such a man, even when the man applies it. The truth is that my father, Francis, taught me what little I understood about making your own life, that is, about heroism—certainly I didn't learn it from Rose, who remained in spiritual hiding all the years of my childhood. If I sound harsh, perhaps I am with cause. I have hinted at a familial rift; it was the wound that would not heal; and it was my mother's fault because she would not love him enough.

Tunneling

That wound, deep as it went, found temporary salve in the social upheaval and struggles surrounding us. Crisis seemed to bring my father's behavior to the level of performance. Through the streets of Teaneck, of New York City, of Washington, D.C.—the year was 1963, 1965, 1968 and the struggle for racial equality—Francis strode (it seems still) like a ticker-tape soldier: shoulders back, chest lifted, hands swinging or holding firmly to those of his daughters. When I was very young, my father would lift me onto his shoulders. I could breathe easily up there! I liked the pattern of sunlight through leaves, and although I couldn't sing, I held tight to my father's ears and thrilled to the sound of many people singing. We marched in those years with the Fosters, Dr. and Mrs. Foster (Dr. Foster, a children's cardiosurgeon, worked closely with my father) and their two young twins and Collette, who was my age and who shared with me an appreciation of correct spelling and Milky Way bars and certain songs. *"We shall overcome . . . ,"* sang Collette and Elaine in their lovely sopranos, and my father responded in his basso profundo and even my mother and I murmured as the crowd surged forward.

"We shall live as one someday. . . ."

Thus was my own family united for a time through appreciation of another people's struggle. Only rarely—once when Rose received a raw egg smack on her cheek and the woman who had thrown it from the blue barricades shrieked and went on shrieking terrible words at her and at Mrs. Foster—did I fear an evil beyond even my father's control.

Now it was morning in New Jersey. Rose and Francis had been married for twenty years. In the silence after songs die out (how quickly that happens, and with what little reason!) he had just stated his plan to gather us girls after school, each afternoon, now that we would be studying in the same school building. I pinned my ear to the closet wall (so to speak) and motioned to Elaine, who hugged her comforter. Our mother seemed caught between two impulses.

"... easier," she said in her habitual fashion, then added tersely, *"Good. Because I'll be busy."*

"Then it wasn't a joke?" he went on.

She shook her head, uttered the one word, "... wasn't ..."

"Just what are we going to teach?"

"... we're going to teach ... remedial reading. I mean, *I am.*"

"We're not serious?"

"... we're not serious. I mean," she said, *"I start Monday."*

"What"—he must have crossed the floor and returned to sit on the bed—"makes you think you can teach?"

"I've been thinking I can ... all summer."

"Summer school was bad enough," he said. "This would be all year."

"... all year ..."

"Why are you doing this to me?" he asked. "I've worked so hard to keep you. Dear God, just tell me where I've failed!"

Rose must have slid from the bed then. I heard her light patter, and her slight frame sinking into the maroon leather chair with the one worn arm. It was morning, and Francis hadn't had his coffee, and she should have known, I thought bitterly, not to bring up anything. It was too late now. The Board of Education had no idea what they were getting into, he said. "... no idea ... ," she agreed. I pictured her gazing out the window, her face too wan to be loving, too vacant to be trusted. He hulked, no doubt a ridiculous figure in the big rumpled bed, but the only father we had, the only one to drive searching for us time and again in case of trouble. Time (speaking of that devil) passed. Elaine stood staring through the closet door. I shrugged and she crept closer and also pressed her ear to the wall. Francis was rattling on full-speed about Rose and life and past and future events and God; and he didn't leave out our neighbors, whose dangerously "lax" habits were why we girls had, for some years now, been forbidden to enter their homes; and meanwhile Rose had abandoned her efforts at self-expression and was repeating catchphrases as if to refute them through her very toneless-ness. Again, against my will, I pictured our parents: he clenching and unclenching his fists and she shaking her head and wiping away dumb hot tears.

"What an idiot," hissed Elaine. "What a complete total moron. Why doesn't she divorce him? I'd never let a man talk to me like that."

Our father's voice deepened. His talk shifted to students and the germ theory of disease and other health dangers Rose would encounter. She would undo everything he had tried so hard to achieve for us ("Undo . . . ," she sighed); and why, for the love of Abraham ("Abraham . . . ?"), couldn't she ever come out and say what she meant? There was something she wasn't saying, some code he would break and she ought to know that. Eventually he would figure her out.

"I mean, I mean," she cried.

"What about the kids?" he asked finally.

". . . what about the kids?"

"Have you?" he asked. "My dear sweet woman, have you given any thought to Rachel's condition? She needs you here."

There followed a silence and then the sound of Rose's harsh weep-ing: ". . . I mean . . . I . . . I . . ."

"Get out of my room," Elaine said just as suddenly, turning. "Get out of my room before *I* cut *you* to pieces with the nail file I keep sharpened just in case. Get out before I do something *we* regret. You aren't ever going to be kissed by a boy. No one will *ever* love you. You will die the way you came into this world—alone, ugly and *unloved.*"

"I was just going," I told her, and faltering to my feet I tiptoed out of her closet, and stumbled across her room and the hall and into my room, where the obituary of Bertrand Russell fluttered. I sat at my desk. It wasn't quite breakfast time, but the thought of breakfast and of our parents' faces mushrooming above the kitchen table threatened to take my breath away. Then too it was summer in New Jersey, where toxins abound.

*   *   *

"Well?" asked Elaine.

Her face in the mirror was staring at me. She stood brushing out her tamped-down curls. Breakfast had ended as it had begun, in taut bright cheer interrupted by my labored breathing. We knew everything they weren't telling us. We knew their false camaraderie, their too-hearty offers of more syrup, more pancakes. We knew our mother's too-cheery farewell; she was off to her very last session of summer school, our father explained loudly as she kissed us on our respective pates, and he told us to behave, as if that were another joke, and instructed Elaine to call him at the ward if she so much as wondered whether I was having an episode.

"That's right," said our mother too airily, "so much as wonder."

"We have three hours," Elaine said now. "What are you waiting for?"

"What about your suit? They'll know."

"It'll dry," she said. "What are you, a *complete* moron?"

She tossed her hair, flat except for a stubborn curl spiraling from either temple, and stomped downstairs. I followed, then ran back upstairs for my Breath-a-Lator. Casting a longing look at my bedroom and the faces of writers adorning its walls, buoyed by the thought of the good work I might accomplish even poolside, I grabbed my index cards and hurried after Elaine through the porch door. We descended the little slope of our lawn, the door lingering like an open question on its rusty hinge.

We moved rapidly down Bowdoin Avenue. No one spoke to us. The trees themselves wore a stealthy look. One was a linden; its round leaves shifted this way, that. Another was a quivering birch.

"Hurry," Elaine said, frowning. "Do you need a whiff?"

I shook my head, savoring the strangeness of the moment: Elaine might sometimes ride her bicycle through our streets, but I rarely ventured beyond our yard. The sun hung low. A freight train hooted. We had almost reached the end of the block, where houses looked brighter than ours and newly planted firs, tiny, dotted expansive lawns. Since that last violent storm, rain hadn't fallen for weeks; lawns grew green only in patches where people had used their water allotments. And yet—and this was the grimness of that season—the air lay so thick and wet upon us that we were never spared, not an instant, the dream of water.

We walked on. We passed a pink house, a white house and a red-brick house where a freckled Irish boy named Patrick had once shown me a bloodsucker. *"They only suck the blood of Jews,"* he had whispered hungrily. Now a man stood motionless by a mound of azalea bushes, purple against yellowing grass. Beyond him lay more houses, whose inhabitants had raised families before we had even moved in. The cat woman—every town has its keeper of cats—stared through her latticed bay window and we quickened our pace.

We had almost reached the park, at whose far end lay the municipal pool, when Elaine spoke.

"There's a new kid like you, a total loser. You could trade index cards or something."

"You don't know the first thing about me," I said, and in that moment I experienced another thrill of pride, such terrific pride that I ducked my flushed face, as if to consider a waving hollyhock. Because of my reading skills (why else?) S-Man had chosen me, Rachel E. Finch, to fly to the aid of troubled writers! How much good might we do humankind, given that he could travel time (in my mind's eye I saw Time like a giant watchband), and I might develop, through the Dewey decimal system and other modes of learning, what my father called the universal outlook?

"*Now* what's wrong?" Elaine demanded. "I just said there was a new kid. You could be losers together. You could memorize the yellow pages."

I smiled at her. "I know why you're in such a hurry. His initials are HL."

"You're hopeless," she said mildly.

But at the intersection of Bowdoin and Tudor, I reached for Elaine's hand and she let me hold it. We walked across Tudor Street and alongside the junior high, which redbrick building huddled against a little hill until, halfway down, the hill leveled off. A raised Venetian blind dangled above a windowsill on which lay a lone glass beaker.

"That's *Mrs. Carlsbad's* classroom," Elaine said darkly for the *n*th time. "She's such a *witch*."

Soon enough I would meet the teachers of whom Elaine had so often spoken: *Mrs. Carlsbad,* whose husband, Charles "Chuck" Carlsbad, had come home so changed from Vietnam, and who herself exacted such discipline now that each year a select few became her willing *slaves;* Miss Bauer, the music teacher, who had lost a breast to *cancer* but went on waving her baton; Mr. Bogardus, the liberal-minded English teacher who lived with his mother and stuck the little finger of his left hand into his ear and twisted the finger slowly, then took it out and shoved its shiny tip right at you!

Then there was Mr. Franklin, the school principal. Mr. Franklin's shy, affable smile—he was a widower—almost made up, Elaine snickered, for the fact that he always gave the same speech. *"Tradition,"* mimicked Elaine, *"AND! Progress!"*

In the distance the overpass, impervious to our concerns, rose in an ever-widening arc; beneath it, rendered invisible by wild orange blossoms, stretched the railroad tracks.

Who knows what reversals constitute the life of a town? Beyond those iron tracks rose a little shopping plaza dominated by the NJ Savings & Loan, a Grecian sort of establishment visible from where we stood. It sported white pillars and a high gold-domed roof beneath which (we knew) gleamed a delightful array of fish tanks. Goldfish, redder than gold, swam with the calm dignity of bankers. Would I might halt this narrative—for that matter, this descriptive passage—while those red-gold fish still swim! But beneath the railroad yawns the underpass, haven for the disenfranchised, the desperate, the unwashed; and not far from those dank walls gape the underground vaults of the Savings & Loan.

Tunneling

Nearing the pool, we heard the cries of younger children and the guffaws of teenagers. Elaine dropped my hand. Her chin set and her eyes glared.

"Whatever happens, you deserve it," she said.

Fortune, reaching a long capricious finger to part that summer's cloud cover, sent light scalloping across the aquamarine water; Destiny crept nymphlike up the green ladder rungs. Elaine had insisted that I lag behind. She sat poolside, her long tan legs dangling. She wore cutoff shorts and a pink bathing-suit top and a towel around her shoulders. She reached her hand up to flatten a wayward curl. I stood in the shadow cast by the lifeguard's tower and recited to myself the first ten subcategories *(10 Metaphysics; 20 Epistemology, Causation, Humankind)* of the Dewey decimal system.

"Ha-ha," Elaine laughed. "Ha-ha."

Her school friends, Doris and Hester, shouted as they bobbed and treaded water. "Do it!" they cried coyly, their faces like bright ovals in the scalloping water.

(30 Generalizations, 40 Phenomenological Doubt . . .)

"Don't you dare," hooted Elaine.

The high school boys, Hugo and Sid, were threatening to drag Elaine into the water!

A word or two about Hugo and Sid: Hugo stood squat with unusually hirsute shoulders, while Sid lounged tall and gangly. Hugo had a broad hirsute face, Sid a thin hairless one. We called these two "high school boys" but in fact neither Hugo nor Sid had attended any school in many years. Instead they held down night jobs: Sid delivered brick-oven pizza and Hugo drove a cab. Their only academic interest, as far as Elaine could tell (giggling), lay in their study of foul language: Hugo expounded on it, and Sid used it.

"Come on in," Doris called, splashing eagerly at Elaine's toes.

Elaine smiled in a way that I could have explained, had anyone asked, was dangerous. "Um. Don't wet my hair," she murmured.

"*Merde alors,*" said Sid.

"Not *merde alors,*" said Hugo. "*Merrrde alorrrrs.* Keep those *R*s in the back of your throat. Pronunciation is important, Sid. I told you that."

"You're always bothering me," said Sid.

"Don't get moody now," said Hugo.

Sid hung his long pale head. Then he wrapped his hand around Elaine's ankle and yanked.

"Ouch," said Elaine.

"Leave the girl alone," said Haywood Lofty, who had until now been swimming laps.

"You heard the man," said Elaine. "Get your cotton-picking hands off me."

"I don't have to," said Sid, releasing her.

" 'Cotton-picking' is racist," said Cynthia, surfacing. Until that moment she had been practicing underwater headstands with Mindy Glueck, in the watery vicinity of Steward Blumenthal.

Like Mindy Glueck, Cynthia Lacey went to my school, or she would now that seventh graders from all over town were entering the newly centralized Benjamin Franklin Junior High. As for Steward, who used to be fat, he stood at the water's edge, gazing down neither at Cynthia nor at Mindy but at his own changed reflection.

"Well, I'll be," he said, resting his hands on his hips.

"What do you mean?" my sister asked Cynthia.

"Where do you think an expression like that comes from?"

" 'Cotton-picking,' " said Hugo, stroking his beard, "an expression first used by plantation overseers in the antebellum South."

"Actually," Haywood said coolly, " 'cotton-picking' is a term we Black Americans came up with ourselves, down South, to distinguish between our house- and field-workers."

"It's still racist," said Cynthia.

"I see," said Hugo. He smiled at Haywood, who nodded.

"Oh," said Elaine. "I just never thought about all that."

"Yuk," said Sid. "I guess he showed you, Hugo."

"In any event, the expression," said Hugo, his face reddening, "is now in common usage—"

Haywood, spotting a half-drowned stray hair ribbon, rescued it and held it out to my sister.

"—as in, 'Keep your cotton-picking hands off her,'" called Sid to no one.

Cynthia made a ticking noise in her throat. Sid dragged his foot out and stretched it long-toed and dripping across Elaine's lap. "That boy's pretty smart," he remarked, twisting toward Haywood. Hugo frowned. Cynthia put her hands on her bony hips. Elaine shoved Sid's leg so hard that he stumbled against Hugo, who shoved him beneath the water, from whence Sid arose spluttering.

"Hoo," laughed Cynthia.

"Ha," said Doris.

"Ha," said Hester.

"There," said Elaine.

"There," said Haywood after a while. My sister and he tugged gently on the pink ends of the rescued ribbon.

I had assumed and rightly that HL—Haywood Lofty—would be here; once (in fifth grade, I'll grant you) he and my sister had loved each other with a fierce and tender love; even now their two faces seemed reflected in each other's; but Sid, splashing around, cried out and Elaine turned her head.

"Did you say something?"

Flipping the hair off his long face like a goat, Sid called out, "Wench, will you marry me?" and Hugo burst into wild laughter.

"Wench!" Hugo laughed. "That's a good one!"

"I mean it!" Sid cried. "I'm a goner!"

Haywood resumed swimming laps.

*   *   *

Couldn't Elaine see, I asked myself, what her old flame must have seen—that Hugo and Sid were not *proper* boys? In truth they were more like the ne'er-do-wells S-Man apprehended on flights toward larger destiny: the charlatans and petty thieves who evinced such shock when he swooped down out of the air. What, I wondered, drew her to them? Even now Sid was thrashing around. "I'm a goner," he cried and Hugo, rubbing his own hairy chest and expounding loudly, lunged after. They shouted and flopped and were joined by other shouting boys. The lifeguard raised his whistle. A little boy, swimming underwater into the zone of their ruckus, ducked his woolly head and frog-kicked hard after Haywood, who had a way of attracting younger children.

The afternoon sun beat down steamily. One by one, my fellows leaped into the swimming pool. The air danced hot and yellow and the world shimmered. I narrowed my eyes and the scene "swam" back into focus.

There indeed floated the new girl, her eyes closed and arms crossed and her long-sleeved shirt (for some reason this new girl wore a long-sleeved shirt) billowing above the water's surface. Then there were the unusually fraternal twins, Edward and Edwin Morse, who took turns diving after pennies; and Steward Blumenthal, who used to be fat and stood gazing now at his bobbing reflection; and Cynthia and Mindy, and Floriana, and Susan Kolin, whose father was old and whose mother slapped her about laundry; and Robert, who knew how to blow his nose projectilely (he swam past, nostrils flaring), and his sister, Carol, who suffered from such low self-esteem that she hugged her own bosom. Collette, my old friend, was executing her rather neat breaststroke. "Hey Collette!" I called. "Are we walking to the Plaza after school?" but she swam past. As for sad-eyed Louise, crouching with fascinated care in the water, she lived with her sister, Mary, and her parents, Tom and

Tunneling

Muriel Bigelow, in a big brick house. The Bigelow girls were famous for having gotten their periods by the end of fifth grade; the Bigelow parents for missing home. They would wait one more year, Louise had told us, and if the town council didn't rescind its vote on busing, they were going to pack up and head on back to Birmingham, Alabama. "Gosh," we said, "your parents are really horrible." "Oh no," she sighed, "I love Mom and Dad. I'm glad we're leaving."

All the Bigelows pronounced that word in a special southern way: *Ill-eaving*.

Now Robert flew through turquoise water onto his sister's back; now she collapsed squealing and flailing beneath all that H_2O. Louise stood alone in the wading section. Around her the mothers, White and Black (as we said then), Occidental and Oriental (as we also said), made tugboat sounds and drew their babies' rounded limbs through the water. It had been, as I say, a season of some lasting drought, and the pool would be drained Monday morning, when we of school age returned to the halls of learning; mothers dragged their babies that much more attentively through it. "Water!" they cooed, and the babies, wrinkling their brows or slapping at the shiny rippling stuff, understood precisely what their mothers meant by the sound *water*.

And it was an odd decorum of the swimming pool that mothers of younger children swam them together and chatted about this one's newest tooth or that one's recovery from cradle cap, but cast a watchful eye (several) on the deep end, where older "children," teenagers like Elaine and Haywood and Cynthia and Mindy and Steward, splashed and disported; and that, once out, these parents grouped as if by prearrangement so that like sat with like, lounging on bath towels or sitting prim in cloth-and-metal chairs, from which they went on surveying the activity at the pool's deep end.

"I tell you what," said Sid to Hugo. "You can be our cotton-picking best man."

Hugo grinned.

"Geronimo!" shouted a boy, joining them.

"You say that again," said Cynthia, surfacing inside Steward Blumenthal's reflection, "and I'm going to pick your cotton all right."

"Watch your language, Sid," said Hugo, smiling.

"Sticks and stones," said Sid.

"Some people are always making trouble," hissed Mindy Glueck, loud enough to be heard.

"Hey," said Steward. "Now I can't see myself."

I was trying to figure out whom Mindy meant by "some people" when Elaine inched forward. She whispered to Doris; Doris whispered to Hester; Hester whispered something that made all three laugh. Sid lifted himself out of the pool, dripped all over my sister, tottered, twisted around and dove back in, oblivious to the lifeguard's shrill whistle.

"Aw," Sid said, rubbing his stomach. "Belly flop."

"Serves you right," laughed Elaine.

"That does it," said Hugo and Sid.

Within seconds they had dragged Elaine into the water. She clutched a blind hand to her hair streaming around her. "Shoot," she hooted.

" 'Shoot,' a euphemism," chortled Hugo. "From *shite,* old English for mud or offal, also *sheist,* Indo-European."

"Who the hell cares," whispered Sid to my sister. "Someday I'm getting the hell away from here. If you marry me, you can come too."

Haywood Lofty rose to the water's surface, brown eyes attentive, powerful shoulders moving neatly toward Elaine and Hugo and Sid and the deep end.

Sunlight beat down. The air smelled sticky sweet. I sat on the grass and put my forefingers in my buzzing ears, then, remembering Mr. Bogardus, pulled my fingers out hurriedly. I picked a blade of grass and positioned the blade between my thumbs. How the afternoon dragged! If only I had asked S-Man for a signal! I tried blowing into my cupped hands but nothing happened. As if Elaine were trying to shake me loose, I reminded myself of all that pointed home. I had a secret life. I was different from other children. I had met Mr. Shakespeare and other famous writers. I was going to meet the great Franz Kafka, who had spent the years of his childhood alone, if not lonely. I suffered from a potentially fatal condition but was not going to die of it yet. What famous writer hadn't suffered? I reminded myself that Franz Kafka, in his last months, had been rendered speechless by tracheal tuberculosis. I cleared my throat and lifted my head. The great Czech writer had possessed a prodigious memory; no doubt he would enjoy hearing about the Dewey decimal system. For all I knew, S-Man was at that moment flying past, perhaps even looking down on us and seeing with his S-vision how I endured the end of summer.

"I'm Rachel Fish. You're Rachel Finch. Your sister told me to be nice to you. Why don't you come in?"

The new girl's brown hair lay plastered to her head, atop which her bathing cap sat like a rumpled white crown. She was peering up at me. Her eyes seemed myopic.

"Didn't she tell you? Cold water isn't good for me on a hot day. I have asthma."

"Oh," the girl said. She clambered out of the pool and sat down beside me, her sleeves spilling across my top card *(60 Logic)*. "Oops! What's that? I'm sorry!"

"It's the Dewey decimal system."

"I just love the Dewey decimal system," she said. She picked up the card and shook it free of moisture. "I memorized the whole thing this summer before we moved here. I even memorized the appendix."

"There's an appendix?"

"There's an appendix to just about anything. I might become a librarian when I grow up. I mean in addition to becoming a writer. I've lived in six towns not counting Teaneck. How about you? What do you want to be?"

"I don't know," I lied.

"I'll get you a new card," she said. "Watch this." She slipped again into the pool. She sank beneath the water to emerge once more on her back, hands crossed as before over her thin chest, eyelids fluttering. Her huge brown eyes stared off-focus into the sky.

"Dead man's float," she said. "Get it?"

"Finch doesn't even know how to swim," said Robert, paddling closer.

"I do too. You poor boy."

"Says who," said Robert. He sniffed happily.

"Says me," said Rachel Fish, who couldn't have known whether I swam or not. "It isn't kind to tease a person with an illness. I expect you to apologize to my new friend this minute."

Robert stared. He had close-set eyes and his mouth hung open. I had meant it when I called him a "poor boy"; his parents had fled Nazi Germany, and for this and other reasons his father insisted that Alice Wurner sew slipcovers onto their furniture and wouldn't let anyone even set foot on their living room rug. "Remember," he would warn Alice and the children. "No matter what anyone tells you, in the eyes of the Nazis you are a Jew first. You must be prepared at all times for disaster."

"Well, I'm not Jewish," I would tell Robert and Carol. "I don't even believe in God."

"You are too," Robert would grin.

"Why are you wearing your shirt?" she asked now.

"None of your business," Rachel Fish said. "You should apologize."

"Actually," I said uneasily, "I don't swim very well."

"That's neither here nor there," she said.

"You girls are unbelievably dumb, especially Finch," said Robert. He swam a ways off.

"Don't worry," said Rachel, but I was clutching my index cards and thinking about her words: *my new friend.*

T u n n e l i n g

"Well!" she went on. "Where were we? Do you like to read? Would you like to come over my house sometime? My second-favorite writer is William Shakespeare. After him I like the Enlightenment. I really admire Voltaire. Actually, he's my third-favorite writer even though he didn't like Jews because he was opposed to slavery. You can't just not read everybody, can you? My rabbi, with whom I have struck up a voluminous and possibly fundamental correspondence, says 'Noah was a good man in his time' means you can only be as good as your time allows. But I think if you do something wrong it's one hundred percent your own fault. I hate lies, don't you? My brother, Hegel, is a math genius. Do you think the earth is shrinking? What are your thoughts on the space race? You could go to the moon and you'd be looking at stuff from ten years ago. If you could go far enough you'd be looking at when Voltaire was alive and if you had a good telephone which they will soon you could tell him he should think twice about tolerance except for Jews, women and Blacks. Especially because he was extremely instrumental in the development of our own Declaration of Independence written by Thomas Jefferson, who spent considerable time in France. And they say he kept a mistress there but I never, ever want to know about a writer's private life. I only want to know what they think or what they wrote or what jobs they did. Do you believe in God? What are your sincerest thoughts on pacifism? I think if you're Jewish, you should come right out and say so."

I had listened, mesmerized, to her words. Now I was at a loss for my own; because heat and sticky air and the confusion of events had caused my chest to constrict, and because I had never experienced, not even with S-Man, this kind of connection to another. Luckily I was spared the necessity of responding. Robert Wurner swam closer, and once he had gotten our attention—I pointed him out to Rachel Fish, who swirled with the look of someone preparing to do battle—he lifted one hand, held a finger over one nostril and blew a stream of yellow mucus in a high arc across the water.

"Oh my God," said Louise, treading nearby.

"Leave those girls alone," said Cynthia, surfacing. "Didn't your mother ever teach you hygiene?"

"Sure," he said and covered the other nostril.

"Oh my gracious," said Valerie, who had just swum up too.

"Get him away from me," said Carol, wading.

"That is nasty," said Collette. "That is so nasty."

"Oh, I don't want to swim here anymore," said Louise, fleeing.

"What happened?" asked the mothers, and the toddlers, diapers soaked and variegated faces shining, burst into anguished tears.

"What happened?" repeated the mothers, lifting the toddlers out. "What is it? What have those teenagers done now?"

"Look," I told Elaine.

We were walking home from Votee Park. The air shimmered. A bee buzzed and zoomed off. A caterpillar inched across our path and didn't even know that we had left its furry anatomy behind. At our backs and atop its hill slumbered the NJ Savings & Loan, whose eventual ruin lay in its own steel vaults beneath the steaming earth.

"Over there," I said.

Elaine paused to gaze happily across the playing field. I leaned closer. She had a lovely chlorine smell and that just-washed look about her. Her T-shirt twisted into a knot above her waist. She looked much prettier with her hair naturally curly and I wanted to tell her so. I had accompanied her. We were on our way home. We were going to get away with it.

Elaine followed the vector of my finger to a spot on the playing field. A ball flew into the air; someone shouted; an airplane droned. A woman sat slumped, head bowed, on the ground. From this distance we couldn't see what she was doing. We continued on our way, abandoning swing sets, the cries of swimmers, the arching overpass; soon we saw a man running, followed by another. Elaine and I stopped. There isn't really any mistaking one human being for another except in the case of true love, and then only for an instant do we think to see the man or woman in question: a blink, a step, a clearing and we find ourselves alone.

"What is he doing?" shrieked Elaine. "What the hell is that bastard doing here?"

That "bastard" was our father, Francis, running on long legs after another white-clad man. Francis was shouting and racing toward the woman, who sat limply on the playing field. I saw her touch a hand to her forehead.

"Don't run," I told Elaine. "Don't do anything unusual. Just keep walking."

Elaine bit her lip. We advanced past the half-hidden windows of the junior high and climbed the sledding hill. Elaine was flushed; I felt dry-mouthed and queasy. Halfway up, she had to wait for me to use the Breath-a-Lator. Its mouthpiece got stuck and I twisted it loose. Elaine sculled the air. We climbed again, she offering me her hand and I refusing it now that my infirmity had betrayed me. Flowers, insects, the moisture that accumulates—all conspired (so it seemed) to usurp my inalienable right to breathe. I knew something about citizenship! I ought to have insisted on staying home; I ought to have told on my sister. What would happen now? Etcetera. I tried not to think of our mother as we climbed past this patch of torpid grass, that clump of rocky earth.

We crested the hill and hurried, Elaine allowing for my slower pace—we hurried slowly, as it were, past houses where children had grown and past the house where Susan Kolin's Cuban mother slapped her once about the laundry and past the yellow lawn where the man stood motionless, dry hose in hand—we rounded that last corner and raced toward our screened-in porch and its four creaking steps and the screen door that slammed shut and shut again.

*   *   *

That night, while the vaporizer sent up curls of steam, I lay surrounded by the portraits of men who had devoted their lives to the writing of prose. I thought about our town and how it seemed to be changing. There was Rachel Fish, whose huge brown eyes seemed to join those of the authors staring through the dim light. *I hate lies, don't you?* There was Collette, whose father still worked with my father, and who wouldn't walk to the Plaza candy store with me anymore but would still defend me at the swimming pool. *That's nasty, that's so nasty. . . .* There were categories and names for things. Everyone was a swimmer because I wasn't. Everyone was an atheist or a Jew or something (I lacked the word for *heathen*) because Collette was a Baptist. But no sooner did Collette or Haywood or Cynthia swim past (in my dark room they seemed to swim past) than Louise, Steward, Susan, Robert, Carol and Elaine and Sid and Hugo and Doris and Hester and Mindy Glueck, and I, became White people. In my mind I saw Collette's long neck and her sober visage and behind her Valerie, whose father was a famous singer and a Muslim. I didn't know anything about Muslims except that they made women wear veils and stay indoors. My mother stayed indoors—had always done so, until this summer, when she had insisted on volunteering at the summer school. Now the wound on her forehead would leave a whitish scar. For a long time she had sat on the playing field just crying her eyes out, our father had said.

I heard his footsteps treading heavily on the old floorboards.

"She's asleep," he said.

"I'm sorry," I said tentatively.

"Sorry for what?"

I shrugged. Elaine's towel lay buried in her closet, where it would remain until we could safely wash it. I imagined that the chlorine smell was seeping toward us. It wasn't our fault that a boy had hit Rose with a rock, or was it? The boy, our mother had explained sleepily, just didn't want to learn. He hadn't meant to hit our mother, the boy claimed, but he had made her collapse with a head wound that went on bleeding. "I warned her," my father said. I knew from his tone that our mother wouldn't venture to teach reading again. There was some argument between my parents, concerning safety and danger, that he was always winning.

When she wouldn't get up, my father went on, the assistant teacher had run inside to tell the teacher in charge, and he—none other than Mr. Bogardus, the English teacher—had used his long index finger to dial for help. The ambulance driver had alerted Francis, who rushed out of the hospital and through the busy streets. The injury Rose had sustained cut deep enough for five stitches. Five stitches! I wanted to climb from beneath the bedcovers and run to her, but remembering how Elaine and I had avoided her prone figure, I twisted my face to the wall as my father bent to say good night.

Out of habit I touched his cuff links. Beyond the one long window the old maple tree stirred. Was that a bird in those convoluted branches?

I decided it wasn't, just as it spread broad wings and flew off.

Chapter Three

Son et Lumière

"WHERE TO?" I ASKED.

Salt air stung my cheeks; morning light was blinding; so
we set out across the sky while below us the Statue of Liberty watched
over her island and the city where my grandparents became Americans.
The statue looked very grand and knowing, but it troubled me to think
that the French had built her. The French! A heartless people, from
what I had read—inclined to cruel monarchy and bloody revolution
and mistaken identities! I liked, however, the fact that another tiny
statue (tiny as a golden key S-Man had given me just that morning)
stood on a bridge in Paris. "They stand for freedom," I said.

"Not yet."

"They do too," I said, annoyed.

He stuck out his chin in a familiar gesture. He had informed me
that an emergency demanded our immediate attention, and that the
trip to Prague had therefore once again to be postponed. It was such a
nice morning, I almost didn't care!

Where were we going this time? I asked, touching the tiny key on
its chain around my neck. If not Prague, then where? New York? London? Copenhagen? But S-Man said nothing until we had left statue,
city and continent behind.

We had already seen London, he reminded me.

Just for a moment, I told him; and besides, that was *then*. "This is now."

"So it seems," he said playfully and dipped toward the water. He darted this way, that; he trailed one purple boot across the spume, wetting my face, my clothes also; sea salt stung my eyes; I wanted to tell him that I was going to be very patient from now on, that if he had delayed our visit to Mr. Kafka for me to learn patience, there was no longer any need. I understood about artistic and other emergencies, but I was ready. And so on and on we flew, he using his powerful vision to spot vessels before their passengers spotted us, and I being entertained by the ocean itself: its green-and-purple sheen, its splash and porpoises. Porpoises!

"S-Man!" I said.

Directly below us, porpoises were chattering on the brine or nosing about jagged rocks. We circled; descended; the horizon fled like a cormorant across the water and a sea lion yelped. It was a mother lion, I saw. Three pups sat, ludicrous in their caution, above lapping waves. Or was that a shark? Danger follows so soon upon the heels of family! I looked to S-Man for something—information, if not moral support—but he didn't seem to notice the triangular fin slicing toward the little group. The mother yelped again. I could hear bravery in her tones and also a kind of reproach or appeal. We were still circling and slowly. The shark disappeared, resurfacing on the far side of the rocks. The sea lions were safe out of water, but how long could they remain there without starving?

"Or drying out," S-Man said, and I realized that we were circling for a purpose.

"No, a porpoise," someone said.

I looked down. Telepathic jokes can be frightening, as you will recall from our visit to Stratford; in this instance, a man had surfaced on a sleek shark's back. The man had bright blond hair and wore a turquoise costume accentuating his nautical good looks.

Tunneling

"Aquaman!" I cried.

He bowed.

You will think me fickle, perhaps? Just as the surface of the ocean shifts—bear with me, reader, as I tug this turgid analogy across those choppy waves—so I felt drawn from time to time to certain of S-Man's associates, heroes like himself who had not waited for his world debut before befriending him and, really, offering him in this and other ways a unique respect. He had his own life, in any event, with women whose buxom professionalism (and he had yet to meet his future bride) left me breathless. Well! In my heart I made room for him and a few others. There was Elongated Man, for instance, whose equanimous relations with his own wife (they were intellectuals) and whose lankiness cheered me; there was Green Lantern; and there was Aquaman, whose vulnerability to time—he could not live away from the ocean more than a day—touched me. It touched me.

I felt for the key around my neck as S-Man flew the rest of the chilly way down. In New Jersey just that morning he had handed me the key on its chain, and watched attentively while I clasped it around my neck. "Keep that with you at all times," he had insisted almost sternly. Now he skimmed the surface of the water, cormorant-like, horizon-like; we landed and sat on the rocks, Aquaman astride the shark and chatting with us.

He could not have been many years older than my companion, and yet there was something beautifully doomed about him. His hair shone yellow, his shoulders gleamed in the sea spray, but his subjects and his vast kingdom itself were dying. Already my friends were deep in conversation. Was there nothing to be done to save the seas? If not the seas, then the sea lions? If enough people were informed, I heard Aquaman say, it might be that the sea lions, whose worst enemy was not, as people might have thought, the shark, might survive. The sea lions; the haddock; the purple finback. The giant turtles! There was a book by Miss Rachel Carson, I told him eagerly. Perhaps if enough people read it!

"Look," said Aquaman.

The sea lion had perched on the edge of her rock and her pups were slithering cautiously after her. They yelped as she slid over the edge; she was gone; her whole family got very upset; she reappeared with a fish between her teeth and threw it at the smallest pup, who lost it to his raucous brothers. She didn't seem to notice or care but went on catching fish and tossing them silvery onto the rocks. This was at a longitude of thirty-six and a latitude of forty-seven, just beyond the coastal waters of the Atlantic Ocean, which, as everyone knows, is the coldest ocean by far.

"What about him?" I asked.

The pup hadn't given up trying to grab a silver fish, his eyes growing rounder and the gray fur around his snout ruffling. Aquaman whistled. I saw his thoughts like a net cast out upon the water. I was incapable, of course, of such telekineticism (as was S-Man), but I could follow its intricate designs and understood the inevitability with which a lone fish hurled itself onto the rocks just below this littlest pup, who swallowed it whole. To be so young and so bloodthirsty! Something in the natural order contributed to Aquaman's doom. He would go through time like this: infinitely pleasant, gorgeously talented, an Orpheus of an underworld whose splendors would pass unmourned by land dwellers.

The friends talked some more while I played with the pup, and I caught only some of their discussion, but I knew it had to do precisely with the problems elucidated by Miss Rachel Carson: I heard the letters "DDT" and the words "sonic," "mercury," and "warming." Meanwhile I scooped a strand of seaweed from the foamy water and drew it invitingly across the rock. The pup shied and leaped and we played until he lay finally panting, his fur surprisingly oily to the touch, his brown eye rolled back in mock wildness. As the sun rose hotter against a whitish sky (somewhere a conch sounded), Aquaman told us the story of the birth and life of oceans, their constant swirls and sudden drops, their mountains and volcanic regions and the deep flat surfaces, and we listened carefully, although my companion did suggest, coal-black eyes twinkling, that he had understood me to say that I had no actual interest in history.

"Oh no," I stammered.

Aquaman frowned then, leaping to his feet, and exclaimed that he had lingered long enough away from his subjects; he was needed elsewhere; and so he dove in and the sea lion dove after and the pups, one after another, plopped in. We could see something emerging from the water: Aquaman aboard his mother-of-pearl chariot. Six proud porpoises arched six silver necks. Aquaman reined them in—telekinetically, I mean—and tossed something that tumbled slowly over itself, flashing colors on its way into my palm. He disappeared beneath the waves.

"Where is he going?" I asked. We had resumed our own trajectory, higher and faster and drier, across the ocean.

"That's just a loan," S-Man said, meaning the shell that his colleague had thrown me. I turned it over and over, catching the light. What was the word for such a shell? Diaphanous. Pearly and diaphanous; and when I held the thing to my ear, I could hear the ocean below us and other oceans and voices and I knew that each spoke in a different tongue and that my job was to concentrate on their words as we flew on.

"Japan," S-Man said. "Italy. The Gulf of Mexico. Wherever he's needed, and he's needed all the time these days."

I nodded, not knowing what to say.

"Ready?" he asked.

Pocketing the shell, whose properties I had only begun to explore, I steeled myself for departure. Time travel is odd in many ways, but in one particular it resembles airplane travel: you never know when you will encounter turbulence. And so when we landed in the year 1764, after a particularly turbulent flight—we were actually thrown off course into 1865—the glow (it was a sad glow) of our stopover in the ocean had faded and I felt tired, ignorant, ashamed—in short, human. I would not deign to ask again where we were or what we were doing. What did I care? We had not landed in Prague or any other city but outside a long, perhaps even a one-thousand-foot-long structure of some kind. A palace or perhaps a museum? That setting sun was Sol, all right; but the trees seemed alien in shape. As we caught our breath (as I caught mine) I saw that the nearest tree sported the dark-green leaves of a chestnut but that this tree and others, planted at exact intervals along the borders of an expansive lawn, were shaped like upside-down bowls or even saucers. S-Man motioned me to follow; slowly we descended to the next level of landscape, where statues of men and women and mythical beasts dotted an arbor and the setting sun filled the easternmost corner of a purplish sky. This was Versailles, of course. I mean never to mystify but somehow to communicate what a time traveler might feel. I had already learned something about patience; how I would come to regret my lack of interest in history!

In 1865 we had been blown off course onto a battlefield. We had heard cries for mercy and seen men lying facedown in the dust and men lying bloody faced and vacant eyed on their backs while horses whinnied or rose on hind legs or careened past, shaking their manes, baring their teeth, gliding and bleeding into the hot sun, and some of these men had worn blue and others gray and their faces shone bright red or very dark and the horizon also had been shot full of red flames and huge smoldering monuments and here and there the hills had been littered with men who had died or were in the hollow-eyed and raving process of dying and from some vantage point a woman's voice rose keening on the hot southern wind. Enough! A lone cannon fired. A horse's flank, struck, exploded into wild flesh; another cannon fired and another; S-Man tucked my head into his red cape and we bucked the concentric rings of the time tunnel as they resisted our reentry (a time tunnel looks a lot like a tornado and has been mistaken for one) and we were taken up again by the backward flow of history, and to this day the smell of gunpowder sickens me as it would no doubt you.

In these late years I wax sufficiently mystical to think that nothing is useless; the turbulence that day may have prepared me to battle evil in New Jersey; just as, since our sojourn in Versailles, I have always hated kings.

"Explain something," I said to S-Man.

I had so often trekked, you see, through the streets of Teaneck to the leafy public library. I have—I *had* since earliest childhood gone there with my father, who seemed another man as soon as glass chimes above the opening door rang our arrival. The man who picked us up from school each afternoon broke into a cold sweat if we so much as asked to walk home alone; the man who strode through the library doors held calm faith in the future of mankind. There were signs, after all, of our longevity: night skies, public parks and lending libraries. In the huge reading room stood a grandfather clock and many giant potted plants and an armchair where Francis would sit while I went to choose my books. He enormously enjoyed reading about the world. The arch, the wheel, the wing—how my father loved to read about invention! But encyclopedias? As far as I was concerned, encyclopedias—*encyclopediae,* S-Man corrected—were dry and incomplete reference materials. In school we weren't even allowed to cite them in our reports. "That's where you're wrong," said S-Man. "Encyclopediae are the mirror of their times. History is everything," he insisted.

"But science makes things happen."

"History is things happening," he said (mistakenly, I think), "and science is one of them."

He picked me up; I feared that we were taking off into time again, but he carried me to a small secluded wood (I could see the white expanse of a château through trees) and under the sheltering roof of a cupola, where he disappeared to return *aussitôt* with a small bundle. He handed the bundle to me. I was to put those on, he said, and if anyone asked, my name was Jacques and my mother was feeling much better, thank God; I had gone home expecting the worst, and finding her restored in large measure to her usual sturdy health, was hastening to my post—I served as valet de chambre to the Marquise de Pompadour—at Versailles.

"I don't even speak French," I said and recalled the shell Aquaman had thrown in parting.

Of course!

Nonetheless I sighed when, the question of language resolved, S-Man drew from seemingly nowhere, as he was capable with his stupendous speed, a pair of jagged shears. As many times as he had cut my hair, and as many times as my hair had grown out again in our return flights to the present era, I hated how those shears flashed and how my dark hair lay like a helpless person on the floor. But there was no time to lose; within seconds I was shorn and there he stood, staring as if he didn't know what I was waiting for.

"Right," he said and turned around.

"You know what?"

"What?"

"That's what," I said, having stepped into elegant breeches and pulled on a pair of high black boots and struggled into a white sort of buttonless blouse. What did I care, after all, about my hair? Now I could climb trees and curry horses; now I could whistle through my fingers. S-Man motioned for me to walk with him across the grassy lawn toward the château. He wore yellow boots, a purple costume (*uniform*, he would have called it) with a giant sun splashed across the chest. As we walked, holding hands, then feeling odd for some reason and letting go, he filled me in on the nature of our mission. He had reason to believe that an enemy of free thought had infiltrated this *siècle* (which

meant "century") and schemed to spoil things not only for Denis
Diderot but for many philosophers of these last monarchical years. *But
how?* I wanted to ask, meaning that history cannot be changed; then I
remembered that textbooks and other scholarly volumes never mentioned, for instance, our visit with Mr. Shakespeare. There was never
any knowing when the story between the lines, as it were, involved vis-
itors from other times or time dimensions or solar systems. I found this
disconcerting (I still do) and only half-listened to what S-Man told me
about the court at Versailles and the king's favorite and her recent
expenditures, amounting to hundreds of thousands of francs, on items
as trivial as chocolates and fake moles and hairpieces made of human
hair. Those steps there, S-Man went on (pointing beyond a pale fountain to a narrow wooden staircase), belonged to the marquise. She was
missing me, he said, and gentled me toward it.

"Hey," I said. Stars twinkled; I recognized Orion and his belt; I saw
several Pleiades; I was no longer a child to be sent on a child's errand!

There are eras and there are eras. Since my first encounter with
Shakespeare I have felt at home, at least in the Keatsian sense, in Eliza-
beth's England; I cannot say that I have ever felt the same, not that
evening and not in retrospect, in Louis XV's France, an era best known,
after all, for its furniture. I like furniture as much as the next woman,
mind you—the puppy's gnawing at couch legs fills me with righteous
fury, just as his more intimate nips as I bend to clean after him (he mis-
takes me for his mother, *figurez vous!*) fill me with a certain sorrow. We
are quarantined here, the two of us, until the end of his rabies watch.

Have I neglected to mention the puppy? I found him in Votee
Park—precisely where my mother was once struck with a rock, he managed to land a dead bat. I who have grown squeamish felt obliged to pry
the bat from between his teething jaws, with these two fingers whose
open cuts (from the rosebush that needed trimming) have still to
heal. No stitches were necessary, this time. My Germanic doctor having passed on, a dour Hungarian assures me that I will have plenty of

warning should dander awaken my own long-dormant syndrome; meanwhile the veterinarian insists that although the puppy's rabies watch is a formality, Boomer (so named after a generation) is not to frequent children or other animals for six more days. So we wait out the time together, and keep watch for our respective disorders.

Perhaps it is this business of waiting that puts me in mind of Versailles. Can you smell the suffering of a people on the night air? Yes! I wanted badly to see him, this king, and wondered if he belonged to that small set who comprise our better selves and wondered what he would have thought to see us: S-Man, who bowed to no king, and I, who would have, I thought vaguely, if only he would give largesse and suffrage to the populace. As for Voltaire, just as soon as he and I came face to face—for some reason, I never doubted this encounter—I would tell him how wrong he was about Jews, and no doubt he would revise his opinion and his writings.

"Will we meet the king soon?" I asked.

"He hates new faces," S-Man explained. "Madame de Pompadour is a very old friend."

Now she was dying, and I was lucky or unlucky to bear a resemblance to the valet of whom she had grown fond in these sad months.

"Sad? Why sad? You mean because she's so sick?"

A war had been fought and lost, he said; a treaty had been signed here in Versailles; in the streets people shouted *"Pompadour, Pompadour,"* as if she were to blame for defeat, bankruptcy and dishonor.

"Is she?"

"She's a patron of the arts," S-Man said. We had neared the fountain, where a curly-headed man sat astride a curved dolphin and I was reminded of Aquaman—but already S-Man had leaped onto the fountain's rim and pressed his heels together in the gesture that presaged flight. A trick of evening sunlight made his long shadow also poise for takeoff. For a moment there were two of everything: two of him, two of me. One of us was a girl crying not to be left behind.

He zoomed into the air, his shadow scrambling across unlevel grass.

"Will you be gone long?" I called casually.

"Just make sure Madame la Marquise gets to dinner."

"That's all?" I hollered, as he grew tiny and tinier and his voice floated down toward earth.

"Keep your eyes peeled for anything out of the ordinary," it said.

"Jacques."

"Oui, Madame."

"I am cold."

"Oui, Madame."

"You will stoke the fire," she said. "Then you will leave me to die."

"Isn't it almost dinnertime?" I asked.

"I am not hungry. I have the galloping consumption."

"Oh," I said. "That's too bad."

"I am going to send word to the king that once again I am ill. Perhaps he will be displeased. I cannot help that! Misery has taken its toll on my body and would have my soul, had it not been for God. I welcomed God into my life in 1754, the year Louis tired of my regrettable *froideur*. It has plagued me all my life, although not as terribly as have those Jesuits. Jesuits, Jansenists—fanatics every one! I love God as much as I hate his lackeys. I didn't mind it until I tried to keep a king. Do you know, Jacques," she said, eyes trailing over my freshly shorn head and my figure, "you've changed. Is it the court? You remind me more and more of my poor daughter."

"Changed, Madame?" I asked, cursing S-Man in my heart.

"Stay still," she said. "You will take all the air if you move so much and then I will ask you to leave. I don't want to be alone. Soon enough will be time for that. Never fear; I will make *une belle mort* . . ."

As her words trailed on I looked around. Having passed through an antechamber with wooden panels where sheep and damsels (I thought they were damsels) stood out in bas-relief, I stood now in a decorative bedroom with an alcove and a large hearth. The bed was wide but foreshortened, as it were, and several pillows propped Madame de Pompadour, who lay on her side, her ruffled gown (pink taffeta) exposing her thick neck and shoulders and her hair rising in a soft high wave above her mobile face. A face is most itself, I think, in motion, even the motion of prolonged thought. Madame de Pompadour looked now like a butcher's wife and now like a nun. Her eyes, large and dark as my mother's, moved restlessly from the hearth to the high windows to me. She crooked her bejeweled finger. How I hated rich people and how I felt shamed in their presence!

Someday, perhaps, I will return to Versailles and see it again with my own eyes. As it is I have read up a little on the subject of *la grande bourgeoisie* and have in my possession a guidebook that shows the room as it looks now: the cordoned bed, the quilt whose existence seems italicized by age. The Pompadour spent the last hours of life alone in this room, the guidebook says. *Regardez!* They have even rebuilt the little mechanical lift that Louis ordered for his tired friend. An elevator in 1764! Is love not a miracle? If not a miracle, an anomaly?

"You must eat, Madame," I said.

"How is your mother?"

"My mother is much better, thank you."

"You are a good son to show so much concern," she said. "With us it is different. My own mother sent me at eight years to the good sisters. They treated me well but I missed my mother, a woman of such vitality! We spent such cold winters in the convent! She is not to blame but I began to suffer of the throat and heart. If you like—" she said, patting the bed and half sitting, only to be taken by a fit of coughing as I stood not knowing what to do. Beneath the sweetness of her perfume, I smelled a familiar too-sweet odor as of very sick people or dying animals.

Tunneling

"If you wish," she said, coughing into her handkerchief, "I will mention you in my will. I have just been drawing it up. Shall I?"

She didn't wait for an answer but, with the restlessness of melancholia, rang a silver bell. Through the low wooden door came a footman. He wore innumerable white ruffles on his shirtfront and spurs on his boots. He bowed very low, boots gleaming.

"You will bring me the will," she said, waving him off. The footman glanced at me and walked out backward. She seemed to rally (at the thought, no doubt, of altering destiny from beyond the grave) and pulled her feet (she had surprisingly large feet) around to the side of the bed. I squatted by the open hearth. Where was Jacques anyhow? What if he returned? I picked up the heavy bellows and squeezed them experimentally. A few red sparks flew. I fanned the sparks and a reddish flame spiraled. I picked up a stick of kindling and paused, wondering where precisely to lay it. She was paying no attention, I saw, but the footman, who had brought a parchment and a feathery quill, was watching with a curious look on his face. No matter! S-Man and I would be gone (I hoped, tossing the kindling on) before dessert! *Just get her to supper,* he had said.

"You may go," she told the footman, who went.

Madame de Pompadour pursed her lips; tilted her tired head; dipped a quill's nib into an inkwell. She looked like a doll with her legs outstretched.

"My husband and I had everything to live for," she said. "But when I was eleven years old, my mother took me to a soothsayer who said, *'This child will be the king's mistress.'* Tell me, Jacques, what I should have done when Louis fell in love with me? *Vive la France et la gloire de la France!* In any event," she said, taking out a fresh handkerchief, "if the English keep those American provinces, my name isn't Poisson. What do you think of this William Shakespeare, by the way, and how do you think he compares to our Racine?"

I had never read Racine or even heard of him. A good thing too! I

would have been obliged to lie or, worse, to tell the truth, which was
that I preferred the English with their cruelty to the French with theirs;
that I had read up on the French Revolution and that people like her
were going to get their names knitted into sweaters; that she would be
remembered only as a patron of the arts.

Her footman returned just then.

"For the love of God," she said, laying down her quill—so that poor
Jacques mightn't be mentioned, after all, in her last *testament,* which
S-Man would cite as one more proof that you can't change history. In
that case (I would have argued), what were we doing here, or had it
been foreordained that we play precisely the roles we were playing, and
if so by whom or what, and why was it that we never could know
whether we had been fated to prevail or lose? Etcetera. I remembered
the battlefield and the smell of gunpowder and the severed heads on
London Bridge and, for some reason, my sister Elaine's hunched shoulders as she hurried toward our father's Buick most afternoons. There is
no God, I decided all over again.

"What is it?" she asked impatiently.

A certain gentleman was here to pay his respects, he said.

"Who?"

The gentleman in question did not wish to be recognized, he said,
but begged use of the little staircase—

"Let Him in," she exclaimed, lifting a hand to her high wavy hair.
Her eyes scanned the fire and me and the huge wooden wardrobe and
the little table and two high-backed ornate chairs and the other, even
daintier table where her toiletries were laid out. "It's Him," she whispered. "Bring me the mirror." She pointed at an oval mirror leaning
against the wall and I fetched it for her. "Careful," she murmured, "or
we will have seven years' bad luck," and began to laugh as if what she
had said were terribly funny.

"I had a daughter," she said, wiping her eyes, "who died. You know
this. Sometimes it is hard. If not for my promise to Louis, I would—
Well," she said. "Never mind all that. Get in the closet. Hurry!"

Tunneling

I stared uncomprehending at the wardrobe, whose doors she had flung open (she had more energy than heretofore), and, seeing no better choice, I stumbled toward it. Once inside I was surrounded by crinolines and dust and perfumes and *de la naphtaline,* which means some but not all of the mothballs in the world. Phewee! Putting my eye to the keyhole, I saw an old man with a hooked nose and a bent spine. He clattered across the stones, knelt, swept his black hat off his head and bowed low, kissing her palm.

"Voltaire?"

"You are disappointed, Madame! You expected another!"

"What are you doing here?"

"You will have forgiven me our quarrel," he said. "I intended to please!"

"Your flattery almost cost me my position at court," she said. "What got into you?"

"I said what everyone knows, that you are here to stay. 'The belle of our hearts, the *fleur* of our pockets—'"

"François." She enunciated his given name: "François, I am dying."

"Never!"

"I was just now making out my will."

"I see," he said. "I had no idea. I have written a new poem in your honor, as it happens."

"Tell me something, François."

"Yes?"

"How is it that you have come? Surely you are needed in Ferney?"

"Ferney!" he cried. "Ferney is beautiful in springtime! The villagers prosper. The Protestants and the Catholics swallow their differences like castor oil. We make the best timepieces this side of the border, whose proximity I recommend. I recommend also the air. Only my niece is a holy terror and would have my land. As the years pass I recommend, *à vrai dire,* only one thing: not love, not riches, not"—he shuddered—"family. Work! Work, work."

"You are a bourgeois like me," she said.

"Do you remember, Madame, how you spoke—I should say *misspoke*—when first you arrived at court? Who took it upon himself"— he stiffened as he bowed, which sent him stumbling against the bed— "to clue you in?" She interrupted him with a titter that turned into another fit of coughing.

"There is a gentleman to see you," the footman said, returning. "The gentleman does not wish to be recognized."

"Quick! In the closet!"

The closet door flew open; the old man and I stared at each other. "Hurry," she cried and he gestured for me to make room and leaped in (he was surprisingly agile) as if accustomed to such requests. Then I couldn't see anything beyond the round white dome of his head, because he was pressing his features against the inner door. It was grow- ing hotter and increasingly sartorial in the closet. And who knew? Per- haps supper was even now being served!

"Jean-Jacques?" she cried. "I never expected you!"

"It's that bastard Rousseau," Voltaire hissed. "He's come to beg for money, I promise you that. No doubt he's heard about the will. What do you expect from a *converti?*"

"Madame," Rousseau began. There was a moment's silence; he must have bowed. I wished that Voltaire would relinquish the keyhole and, what's more, my lifelong dislike of enclosed spaces was speaking. It is not a dislike so much as a voice, more inner and urgent than the voice I once heard in Stratford. *Get out,* it tells me in our private language. *Get out while you still can.* Sometimes I regret the loss of the shell, which might have rendered the voice comprehensible to others! Just the other day, dining on the Hudson, watching a clear blue sky and two small jets advancing, I asked my mother, "Are those warplanes?" She laughed del- icately, as if it weren't commonplace for a day to turn out wrong!

"You are the enemy of the theater," Madame de P. said. "I am at heart an actress. What have we to say to one another?"

"You speak of enemies," he said simply. "I also have many. They have misinterpreted my words. I am too confessional perhaps by nature. *La nature!* Then too I say what no one will for another fifty years. The day I left Geneva *(Genève!)* I saw the city gates close on one future as the moon rose on another. For weeks I wandered through the forest eating nuts and berries. I saw a boy and a girl at tender play. They lacked a tutor to develop those faculties that had been denied. I suggested that they remove their clothes. I am constantly misunderstood."

"Madame," said the footman.

"Quick!" said Madame. "In the closet! It is He!"

"Yes of course, Madame la Marquise," said Jean-Jacques. Voltaire lunged to the rear and I clutched at a velvety gown as Jean-Jacques dove in. I barely glimpsed Madame de P. and her new guest before the doors slammed, although I heard clearly enough the urbane tones of another philosophe. I tried to remember how many there had been and wondered if we would all fit. Voltaire's elbow was wedged against my side. Rousseau's shoulder was forcing me to lean hard against the wardrobe door. Through the keyhole I managed to eye the latest *suppléant*. This one had brown eyes and dark skin and a white blouse and dark trousers and he was bowing low to kiss her large hand and I only saw him for a moment but I would recognize him anywhere from the sound of his voice.

"Denis," said *la marquise.* Her voice sounded deeper, more sensual. In a play we had read in school a terrible black crow, invisible to others, was said to fly about a room and into rafters where it perched. I recognized the too-sweet odor suddenly: it wasn't disease; it was Malathion!

That could mean only one thing. Laff Riot was hiding here in 1764 and not far and, no doubt, disguised as someone else! As Diderot perhaps?

"At last we meet again," said Diderot. "Aha-ha-ha."

"How did you persuade them to let you out of Vincennes?" she asked. The words were unkind but her voice had grown throaty, even feline.

"I suffered a religious conversion," he said, lowering his eyes.

"You! I have also suffered a religious conversion!"

"All France knows of yours," he said.

"France," she sighed. There was another silence. Perhaps she was thinking about the crowds that jeered; perhaps he was also, unless he happened to be Laff Riot. In that case I would take action. I didn't like Madame de Pompadour; a certain artifice about her struck a wrong chord, so to speak, in my democratic instrument. Nonetheless I had been entrusted with her well-being by S-Man and his instructions: *Just get her to dinner.* Easy to say!

"When I was eleven years old," she said, "my mother sent me to the convent of Les Oiseaux du Bon Dieu. A charming environment, but a bit chilly in winter! I have always been delicate of the *poumons*— Is that a wig, by the way?"

"Jean-Jacques," Voltaire whispered cautiously. "Is that you?"

"*Diable,*" said Jean-Jacques.

"I have been meaning to speak with you," said Voltaire.

"What is it now?"

"This *Contrat* of yours—"

"Don't start with me," said Rousseau.

"Try to have some perspective," said Voltaire. "No personal offense is intended. You just don't *get* it. The nature of man—"

"There can be no society without responsible and free individuals," said Rousseau miserably. "And I do too believe in God."

"Yes yes," said Voltaire. "Let us leave your nonsensical *croyance* aside for now. As for the governing and the governed: '*One thinks himself the master of others, which still leaves him more slave than they*—'"

"Precisely my point of view," said Rousseau.

"I know," said Voltaire. "I'm quoting you."

"Well, cut it out."

"Let me ask you one thing," persisted Voltaire. "Who is master of this situation?"

Tunneling

"She is, I suppose," said Rousseau, shrugging.

"My point exactly. That makes her, according to your little dictum—"

"There's nothing little about my dic—"

"—more slave than we, no?"

"I suppose."

"Then what are doing in this armoire?"

"Hark! He comes!" cried Rousseau because, the footman having returned to announce in an altered voice the imminent (also eminent) visit of none other than He Himself ("At last!" she groaned), Diderot had been enjoined to hide and had thrown open the doors and thrust a well-turned leg in. Voltaire and Rousseau also groaned. Diderot was perhaps, if only momentarily, taken aback; then he pressed harder, his leg bearing down on Voltaire's thigh and causing the old man's abdomen to jerk back and his head to strike me in the chest. There was a terrible moment during which Voltaire, Rousseau, Diderot and I tussled in the dark: "What's this?' someone said, grasping my forearm. "Perhaps a Jesuit!" someone hissed. "So long as it isn't a Jew!" someone else responded. Then, while I was thinking that perhaps I should explain that as far as the Wurners were concerned I was a Jewish person—a recommendation that would have meant nothing to the philosophes—from Teaneck, New Jersey—a place to which I would have given anything to return—I was thrown onto the flagstones, where I cringed, expecting beheading or banishment or I don't know what. "Quick," was all Madame de P. said, "under the bed!" Something in her tone made me understand what Rousseau had meant by what Voltaire had quoted him as saying on the subject of masters and slaves. Of course, I thought; then (shell or no shell) I didn't know how to put what I understood into words although it would have changed my life to do so. "Under the bed," she hissed. I crept on my hands and knees across the cold floor and slid beneath the bed (Louis XV), where I tried to quiet my breathing and to quell the nausea brought on by mothballs, perfume, dust, etcetera. A gong rang; a personage entered; Madame de P. rose magnificently (I have been told) from her pillows and stepped from the bed and curtsied (I saw the purple-white sweep of hair) to the floor.

"Will you come to dinner, Madame?" asked the Newcomer. (I nodded violently, striking a box spring coil with my head. A kind of noise came from the wardrobe.)

"I have lost all appetite," said Madame de P., sadly. "Besides, from what they tell me you have plenty of company."

"I always have plenty of company," said the king. The odor was stronger now than ever and unmistakable: Malathion indeed! Black insects hopped behind my eyelids. I mean that figuratively. I understood what S-Man wanted me to do: protect Madame de P. from the impostor! I had only to ascertain *who it was.* Not Voltaire and not Rousseau, I was certain. Diderot or the king? If Diderot, the other philosophes had placed themselves in deadly peril; if the king, Madame de Pompadour had to be warned. In any event she had to be warned. But how? I crept to the edge of the bed only to receive a swift shoulder kick from a spurred boot. *Was the footman in on it too?*

"The marquise will perhaps be interested to learn that the Bouvais, endowed as she was with innumerable and extremely pleasing attributes, has been sent back to Poitou," said the king.

"I see," said Madame de Pompadour.

She coughed tentatively.

"What happened?" she asked.

"She bored me," he said.

"What's for supper?" she asked. Once more I crawled toward the light. The king was playing with her combs—drawing one through his own thick curls, tilting his head this way and that as he examined his reflection. He had a handsome-enough face, with a high nose and a lot of teeth.

"Pâté de foie gras and frog's legs," he said, humming his finger along the comb. A murmur had arisen from the wardrobe. I waved at the philosophes to keep silent, but no doubt they couldn't see me, and what if they could have?

"*Liberté,*" someone said.

"*Fraternité,*" said another.

"Ouch," said a third—Diderot, or Laff Riot posing as Diderot? "I will tell you who is master," he—whoever he was—hissed from inside the wardrobe. "The master is the one who does all the talking."

"In my opinion," said Rousseau suddenly, "there should be no theater in Geneva."

Someone—Voltaire?—hooted. "Don't start that again," he said.

"Did you hear a noise?" asked the king (or the impostor). He had lain down her comb and was sorting through a pile of letters in the offhand manner of an old friend or an ex-lover or an archenemy.

"Frog's legs. My favorite," Madame de Pompadour said wistfully.

"I see you've gotten another one from d'Alembert," said the king. "Those philosophes of yours drive me nuts. If I so much as hear another peep out of them, I will chop off their heads for the fun of it."

The noises from the wardrobe ceased.

"*You see what I mean,*" exclaimed Voltaire.

A loud crash sounded and through the open doors tumbled the three men, their hair disheveled and their clothing awry (Rousseau had lost a shoe) and their voices raised—I heard the words "noble savage" and "cheap romantic" and "*assistance publique*" and "low blow" and "Cultivate your own damn garden"—and then the king's voice exclaiming, "*Nom de Dieu!* Save us!" and the unmistakable sound of smashing glass and a great whoosh of air and S-Man saying, "Okay Laff, the jig is up," and I wriggled out from beneath the bed and readied myself for action.

"Oh no it isn't," the marquise said, her wig flying off—it was a wig!—and her caked face with its look of resignation transforming into the hate-filled visage I knew and still see in my dreams. "Oh no it isn't," she cried, her voice—that is, *his* voice—shrill as he whipped his Projecto-Ray out of his bodice and aimed it in my direction. "You lay one finger on me and the kid spends the next millennium on the Planet Laff."

"The Planet Laff?" asked the king, frowning. "Is that one of my provinces?" He looked around for a response, but the philosophes had backed up against the wall and, in unconscious imitation of one another, stood with their arms folded and their mouths agape.

"What does a situation like this call for?" asked Voltaire, recovering.

"Your question for once is well timed," said Rousseau.

"I can tell you what it calls for," said Diderot.

Everyone turned.

"I said I could," he went on, palms outspread. "I didn't say I was going to."

"Your Majesty," Laff Riot sneered, "they named the Planet Laff after me. You want to know why? Not a damn thing grows there. I saw to that!"

"Your Majesty," said S-Man, "please step back."

"Step back?" asked Louis XV.

"I mean it about the kid," said Laff Riot. He leaned closer and I could sense the cold nose of the Projecto-Ray against my head and, more sickening even than the odor of Malathion, his free hand stroking my close-cropped hair.

"It's all right, S-Man," I said. "I always wanted to see the Planet . . . Laff. Really. Just do what you have to and don't think about me."

"What is it you want?" asked S-Man.

"I want this," said Laff Riot, and he squirmed until he had drawn a piece of paper from his pocket—"in their precious *Encyclopédie*." He glared wildly around at the philosophes (or I think he did). "I knew you deadbeats would come crawling as soon as I broadcast that bit about the will," he said. "Well, you're going to get paid all right. You're going to publish this or else."

Tunneling

"What is it?" asked Diderot.

"It's a recipe for a special shampoo," said Laff Riot.

"A special shampoo?"

"Let's just say it influences hair growth."

"Or else what?" asked Diderot.

"Or else my friend here"—and Laff jerked his bald head to indicate the footman—"gets hired as a shredder. I mean right now. And the three of you mice," he sneered, "get your tails carved."

"Well," said Rousseau.

"If it's scientific—" ventured Voltaire.

"You betcha it's scientific," said Laff Riot. He was sweating profusely and pressing the nose of the gun harder against my cheek. I closed my eyes. Elaine, I thought. I love you, Elaine. I did too; I was filled on the *treize juillet mille sept cent soixante-quatre* with love for my sister, who was sitting in a car—not my father's—with her new friends. These friends were exerting a bad influence over her. I ought not to have cared, given our history, but from this distance even her threats on my life seemed less important than kinship. She was my sister, who had once carried me on her handlebars up and down our tilting sidewalk; who had, in case I was allowed someday into the street with other children, rehearsed me on the rules of spud; and who had tried to teach me, in spite of my inadequate lungs, to play music with blades of grass. You hold the blade between your two thumbs, she said, and blow into the hollow there.

"This is most annoying," said the king.

"Your Majesty," said S-Man rapidly. "I apologize for all this," he said, waving his hand, "but I must ask you under the circumstances to remain still."

"You must ask *me?*"

"How about us?" asked Voltaire.

"Do we have to remain still too?" asked Diderot.

"Thérèse is expecting me," said Rousseau.

"Theresa is always expecting," said Voltaire. "How many does this make?"

"Very funny," said Rousseau. "Five."

"Let me ask you something more," said Voltaire suddenly. "If the nature of man is essentially good, how is it that the Jews—"

"Why," said the king, "you must be those awful men Jeanne-Antoinette is always talking about. You have written something scurrilous, I believe—some sort of enormous document, full of atheism and so on. I don't like atheism. Where *is* Jeanne-Antoinette?"

"I mean it," said Laff, as S-Man was about to step forward.

"Don't," I said, meaning that S-Man shouldn't bother about me, but he must have misunderstood because he stopped himself.

"It's agreed then," said Laff Riot. I felt his teeth on the nape of my neck.

"But I don't like the shampooing and I don't like the atheists," insisted the king. "I don't want them to write bad things about God. God loves everyone," he explained, looking around, "and he loves me best of all. Doesn't he, Jeanne-Antoinette?" Then he appeared to be thinking hard because this bald plebeian was not the Pompadour on whom he had come to rely for that rarest commodity, that is, colloquy—

"No one has agreed to anything," said Diderot firmly. I heard the Projecto-Ray zoom around toward him and felt rather than saw how S-Man tensed for an assault.

"Well," said Diderot.

"Say something else," I begged.

"It's like this," extemporized Diderot. "Either there is a God or there isn't. Either I'll wake up tomorrow morning myself or I'll wake up another person. I may sleep in a convent tonight; I may sleep in a ditch; my horse may bolt any number of times before I'm finished telling the tales of, say, young Jacques"—he pointed at me—"and his amours—"

"What is he talking about?" asked the king.

"Your Majesty," said Diderot, "I am talking about freedom."

"Freedom of belief," said Rousseau.

"Freedom of action," said Voltaire.

"Freedom of speech," said Diderot.

"Freedom of religious belief except for Jews," added Voltaire.

"Freedom to have your heads removed," the king said. "See to it," he directed the footman.

"Who needs freedom?" said Diderot, shrugging.

"Not me," said Rousseau.

"Not them," said Voltaire.

"I do," I said and took a deep breath.

"And you shall have it," said a voice.

And so it was that Madame de Pompadour—the real Madame de Pompadour—entered slowly. I saw the difference between disguise and identity; with her darkened eyes and rouged cheeks and the cane on which she leaned, this woman (a woman of what? forty-two years?) was ill.

"You have kept me waiting," said the king. He sniffed. "What is that odor?"

"Death," she said, "and there he is." She pointed at Laff Riot, who grimaced. "That man, there, is Death. He came into my quarters two nights ago and tried to sell me something; a hair tonic, I believe. When I wouldn't buy, he wrapped me in a terribly scratchy blanket and carried me into darkest night and he made me sit outside, and you know how easily I catch cold, while he plied your gendarmes and that *crapaud* over there"—she meant the footman—"with expensive liqueurs. I couldn't scream because of the handkerchief he had stuffed in my mouth. I tried but he still carried me into the depths of the dungeon and threw me in an empty cell and left me to catch the rest of my death. Do you know? I felt somehow comforted by the cold! *You will be a king's mistress,* the soothsayer told me—I was younger than Jacques—

but in my dreams I have returned so often to such cold cells, and in my waking hours so dreaded them! Now at least the wait was ended! You will not understand such comforts until later in life, Your Majesty. I must leave you sooner than planned. You must remember everything I told you. The Jansenists are not to be trusted. The deists—"

Voltaire leaned forward to catch her words, but she had begun to cough not as Laff Riot had coughed but horribly, her face turning white and red and white again and the bones of her neck distending. Frightened for her, I turned to S-Man, so that Laff Riot pressed the Projecto-Ray harder into my nape. She looked at him, at S-Man, at the three philosophes, at the king, at me—she looked long and hard at me.

"There is something here I don't understand," she said softly.

"Release my valet," she said to Laff Riot.

"I'll release him all right," he said, and laughed so cruelly that even S-Man and I were taken aback.

"What," asked the king, "is so funny?"

"I'll tell you, Your Majesty," said Laff Riot. "In about thirty years a lot of guys like you are going to be *kaput*"—he ran his hand across his neck and pretended to drop his head—"and there isn't anything you can do about it. This place"—he swiveled to indicate the room, the palace, the grounds—"is going to be a prison. I don't mean like the amusement park you got downstairs. And you jokers"—he pointed to the philosophes—"you're going to be left in the dust. The future isn't anything like you pictured. Reason! Logic! Ever heard of world wars? I don't think so. How about atomic bombs? How about six billion people and some shrubbery going up in smoke? Not to mention, before that happens, there isn't going to be enough water. People will be dying for a glass of water."

"Death," said Madame de P. with an odd look, "are you also a soothsayer?"

"I'm telling you," said Laff Riot with a terrible vehemence, "we're all three from the future. We came to tell you guys you might as well pack it in. If I were you, Your Majesty, I would spend every red cent in the treasury. And as for you, Madame de Pompadour," he grinned, "you're going to be remembered for doing just that. Congratulations. *La gloire de la France,* my size twelve foot."

"What," asked Rousseau, "will I be remembered for?"

"Exposing yourself in public," said Laff Riot. "Abandoning your children. A few good lines."

Rousseau punched himself in the forehead. "Even in posterity!" he cried. "Misunderstood!"

"*Ce chauf,* he is a madman or charlatan, *sans doute* hired to discourage our pursuit of knowledge," said Diderot soothingly.

"Knowledge," said Laff Riot. "This is what knowledge will get you." He ran his hand over his pate as if in actual sorrow, but when he looked up, he was grinning more horribly than ever. "Give it up," he said. "Go home. The Enlightenment Project was a stupid idea."

In the ensuing silence, the king took out a gold watch from his breast pocket and swung it. Everyone, myself included, followed its trajectory. *Useless, useless,* it ticked.

"I can see you still don't believe me," said Laff Riot. "I don't blame you. How about this: I can predict what each of you will say on his deathbed. You too, Ma-*dam,*" he said, mispronouncing the word purposely.

The men winced.

"This is nonsense," said Diderot.

" 'The end. Let us pray for a sequel,' " said Laff Riot, pointing with a jerk of his double chin at Diderot. Diderot looked startled, as if his secret thoughts had been read, then somehow pleased.

" 'Light, more light,' " he said, indicating Voltaire, who smiled modestly.

" 'Thérèse, where did you put my socks?' " he said, indicating Rousseau.

"You see," Laff Riot said. "You might as well listen. There's no point in anything you're doing. The future doesn't want to hear about your cockamamy ideas. We have microwave ovens and digital toothbrushes.

We have things you guys haven't dreamed of, and even if we don't blow ourselves up, the universe is getting colder. Can't you feel it?"

"Yes," said Madame de Pompadour.

"I'm telling you," he grinned, "your encyclopedia isn't going to matter a damn. Not to anyone. You might as well let it burn."

Useless, useless—

"If it doesn't matter," I said quietly, "then *why do you care so much about it?*"

"The boy is right," cried Diderot, brown eyes flashing. "Unless he's wrong!"

Several things happened after that. S-Man leaped into the air; Laff Riot cursed; he swung me around and the three philosophes dove to the floor; then Laff Riot must have pushed the button on his Projecto-Ray because I was alone on what I can only describe as an empty planet for perhaps a second and then S-Man was smiling anxiously into my face.

"It's so cold," someone—a shadow?—whispered.

S-Man took off his cape and covered me. "I can explain everything," I thought I heard him say. Then I was lying on a wide bed and the door to a wardrobe stood ajar and shards of glass sparkled on a cold stone floor and a haggard woman (I thought her haggard) and a man (I thought him supercilious) were hugging each other as if they had also experienced the cold of the Planet Laff. I had; it was worse by far than anything I had or have since imagined: a cold that enters your bones and becomes you for a long while, decades even, although you sit up and try to behave like other people.

"Gotcha," S-Man said, and in an unusual gesture he bowed his head and I put my hand to his steely brow, thinking he meant to apologize, but instead he explained in a whisper everything that had transpired. In the second—not even a second, he insisted—that I had been blasted onto that empty planet he had blown the three philosophes ("Who?" I asked drowsily) right back where they belonged: Voltaire was even now arguing finances with his redoubtable niece only a few safe meters from the Swiss border; Rousseau was rowing his boat in the *jardins* of Luxembourg; Diderot was hurrying to hide his manuscripts and their illustrations from the King's Men, who had instructions from Malesherbes not to find what they sought. I shook my head. Planet Laff seemed to have robbed me of certain memories. I could recall the three men who had thrown themselves onto the flagstones and, what's more, renounced their most-cherished beliefs; but I couldn't remember much beyond that. Today memory plays a different trick on me. I waste hours searching for my checkbook, my house key or the name of the person whom I have promised to call about selling this old house; but only mention "François" or "Didier" or "consumption" and whole peopled vistas open before me.

I am sure of this much: with the total accuracy that could come upon him, S-Man grabbed Laff Riot by his shining pate—"Tell the kid we're not finished!" the archvillain shouted—and hurled him through the smashed window and the cold blue sky and several centuries and a certain amount of geography and some cement so that the villain landed in 1969, in Arizona, in a federal high-security prison cell, just as the warden was making his last round of the evening.

"Back so soon? Nice togs," the warden commented, or so I am told.

Then S-Man went looking for me and found me and brought me home to Earth.

"All is lost," the king intoned. "The universe grows cold and the people despise us. What is to be done?" He looked about the room and his eyes rested on Jeanne-Antoinette, who stood very tall beside her cane.

"Some things are best forgotten," she said, which, like most aphorisms, sounds better in French.

"Just one minute please," said S-Man, and, having knelt to pull a hunk of coal from the hearth, he squeezed the hunk into a diamond, which he displayed to cries of general delight; he twirled the diamond slowly, hypnotically, and the cries faded on the air as S-Man disappeared from sight and memory. Only I saw his yellow cape fluttering from behind the brocaded curtains, and I knew to keep my peace.

"What is to be done?" the king asked again with a different inflection.

Perhaps he meant the empty treasury; perhaps the loss of his taste for *aventure*. He had forgotten, you see, everything else.

"Dinner is served," I said in a loud voice.

They looked at me.

"Of course. Now we go to dinner," said Madame de Pompadour simply.

And handed him her arm; and winked at me as they two departed as if in a solemn processional march (but really so slowly because of her illness), so that I have always wondered if she at least still knew that I wasn't Jacques, and wonder for that matter what happened to poor Jacques when he returned; although you could say that I did him a service of sorts, since he does—I mean, did—figure for a small but meaningful sum (twenty louis) in her will. You can see it for yourself in the Académie d'Histoire Française, where the originals of such documents reside, or at Versailles, where the present government has placed a copy of her *testament* on permanent display.

In any event, the odor of Malathion having subsided, we thought it best to leave Versailles and the Enlightenment behind, although we did circle above the palace dining room windows and S-Man had me lift the shell to my ear so that I could hear faintly through the glass. The king had forgotten all about Laff Riot and S-Man and the encounter with the philosophes; that was the nature of our interventions in the human history. Although I have lately begun to question that nature, I will say no more but watch with you, perhaps, as the king walks at the head of a small parade of ministers and courtiers (violins are playing) with Madame de P. seated to the right of his remarkably carved chair and flanked by various ladies with high white hair like hers and bright gowns and shoulders that seem to gleam; and the chandeliers shine with thousands of tiny lights that bounce off tall gilded mirrors and a woman, passing, stops to examine her proud doomed reflection.

Au souper at last, a man with a pointed nose wondered how gunpowder was made (I shuddered); another how silk was spun; a third suggested it was a pity not to have a reference book for such questions. Madame de Pompadour looked levelly across the bit of space (it was a small bit of space) that separated her from Louis and said if He hadn't banned the *Encyclopédie,* they could have found out even how the Bouvais's red garters had been sewn, and the ladies tittered and Louis said, "Well then, by all means let us end the ban and have the damn book brought in," which caused a stir. As we were lifting off I saw the same footman (he was not a bad man, S-Man explained, but one whose financial burdens had grown fearsome) and several servants rushing to carry in volume after encyclopedic volume, which is the true story of how Diderot's lifework was saved for posterity. It made me sad to see this splendor and inquisitiveness and to think in a few years they would be gone. I think it made S-Man more angry than sorrowful; as the sky parted and we dove into the time tunnel I could see the lines of his nose etched, as it were, which was his face's signal that I should keep quiet until his mood had shifted.

We made it home without any hitches, arriving in 1969 just in time for morning; we even paused at the same outcropping of rock where we had met the sea lion and her pups. I looked for them and for Aquaman, but he was more time bound than we and needed elsewhere. Too bad! I had questions about our journey and decided I would ask S-Man on another occasion, and then when we met again the occasion demanded our full attention and I never did get to ask. I might not have known how to phrase my doubts. It seemed that a philosopher was someone who dove into a closet, that science brought about the death of oceans, that love led inevitably to subterfuge; nor could I forget the battlefield and the stench of a dying and unspeakably evil institution; and yet I wanted to believe—I did believe—in progress through rational discourse and the free trade in ideas. As for Voltaire's not liking Jews—well, Rachel Fish had been right about that, and I remembered her words, "You can't just not read everybody," and wished I'd said something to him. Then I forgot the matter. It was, after all, a beautiful morning; the sun rode the waves, the rocks glistened with innumerable snails and barnacles, and a barn swallow beat a solitary path across the sky until S-Man blew it thankfully home, and we followed.

Just thinking of home made me yawn, and I must have fallen asleep because when I opened my eyes we were approaching the jagged coast of Long Island. I still had the shell in my pocket, I realized; and sliding it out and twisting its pearly ridges, I thought to tune it like a radio dial to the voices of immigrants and other patriots down below.

"That's only for emergencies," S-Man said, and I meant all the while we neared Kennedy Airport and the bright flags of so many nations waving proudly, as if cheering us on, to ask him what precisely constituted an emergency.

Chapter Four

The Other Rachel

AFEW INTRODUCTORY CRACKLES, THEN THE
voice of our principal, Mr. Franklin, poured over the loudspeaker
system. As he would every morning until Mrs. Carlsbad's nervous
breakdown, Mr. Franklin delivered an inspirational address. "Our town
was founded on . . ." His words flowed through the speakers ("All rise!"
cried Miss Bauer) and his affable blue eyes might have been beaming
down upon her and us, only he wasn't in the classroom. ". . . dreams of
permanence; dreams of plenty and slow progress; dreams also, my
young friends, of benevolence and brotherhood. Our friends the
Lenape . . . the Dutch, the English . . . The covered wagon, the steam
engine, yes, the railroad . . . as my dear departed wife, may she rest in
peace . . ." At whose mention Miss Bauer, standing musically by her
desk, laid her hand across her fabled half-bosom (I was reminded of
S-Man's saluting gesture to the Elizabethan cosmos; how long ago that
all seemed). Mr. Franklin's voice led us in the Pledge of Allegiance. No
sooner had our solemn voices trailed off than Miss Bauer's seemed to
gather vigor. "Everybody," she cried. "For the love of God and country,
everybody sing our national anthem!"

We looked at one another, abashed. There was an unfortunate
earnestness to Miss Bauer that had to do, it seems to me, with Mr.

Franklin; with her own real closeness to death; with, perhaps, some desire on her part for a choral perfection few attain in the modern era, and fewer in relation to our anthem. In elementary school our teachers had often enough settled for "America the Beautiful," which made us cry although no one was sure what "amber waves" were. And of course there was "My Country 'Tis of Thee," which stood in unofficially for the anthem itself. No one could quite master the tune of that latter, excepting Collette; moreover, its mention of bombs bursting had sometimes seemed untimely, in those years when some of our own parents were busily building underground shelters. The Wurners, for instance, had a terrific bomb shelter. Robbie and Carol weren't allowed to play in it, but they told us all about it, and we all knew where the entrance lay and we liked to stand aboveground, figuring to ourselves a life of canned foods and artificial light, beneath the earth.

"More feeling!" Miss Bauer called. "That's in the key of G, not A-flat minor, Mr. Duffy! You seem as tone-deaf as your brothers!" Rachel Fish, I was surprised to hear, had a clear, rather loud soprano. We sang on or made a show of doing so. Miss Bauer's bespectacled eyes passed over me. Had I possessed a voice, I would have rendered it gladly. The very harshness of *those bombs bursting in air*" seemed wonderfully softened by my fellows' singing, or standing there and listening to someone else's singing clear and loud over the racket, *"Gave proof through the night / That our flag was still there. . . ."*

Our flag was still there! Our flag still waved above Colin Duffy, whose father drank and whose brothers were all in reform school; it waved above Dwayne, who stammered with a fear, verging on phobia, of his English teachers; it waved over Valerie, with her Muslim father; and Rachel Fish, with her uneven home life; and Collette, with her vying loyalties; and Cynthia, who spoke so sharply; and Mindy, who also spoke sharply; and Steward, who had begun to grow; and Edward and Edwin, who were identical twins although one was Korean. Until we hit puberty (until puberty hit us) our plurality played as much part in our civic pride as anything, and only Louise, whose parents were *llll-eaving* as soon as her father could find a job back in Alabama, seemed to doubt it—there were Hugo and Sid, of course, but they weren't in our class or even our grade. Hugo and Sid used words, terrible words that Hugo would explicate and that otherwise we encountered only in their favorite haunt, the railroad underpass: words for soft parts of the body and other terrible words like *kike* and *chink* and *nigger* and *nigger lover*. Tiptoeing through that dank cavern, in fact, I had recently come upon my sister's name scribbled in conjunction with Haywood Lofty's. The "conjunction" had been the most ludicrous-seeming activity—something I couldn't imagine two human beings, let alone two fifth-grade children, doing to each other. But Hugo and Sid, as I say, didn't really count.

The rest of us knew, along with everyone in Bergen County and perhaps the entire state of New Jersey, that our town's school board had been the first all-White school board in the United States of America to vote for racial integration, through busing if necessary, of our public schools. As second graders we had thrilled to find in our Scholastic *Weekly Reader*s a photograph of our own town hall and of our "Schools Chancellor, Dr. Harvey B. Scribner, Instrumental in Producing Change!" In those days, the inhabitants of the only slightly more affluent section of town, West Teaneck, included no Black people; although the northeast section, predominantly Black, was distinctly middle class, most White children's contact with Black people was restricted to the women who cleaned their houses. (Or, in the case of Elaine and me, the young southern students we had met through our father's volunteer teaching at Tougaloo College, during what our parents called Freedom Summer.) Within weeks of the school board's decision, however, we schoolchildren had witnessed history and knew it: on September 8, 1965, forty-five Black children walked off two yellow buses and entered our school building and sat down beside us and became part of this word *us*. By springtime Elaine and I and our classmates would sum our difference (we knew something about race now and almost nothing about class) by comparing ourselves to the names of Crayola crayons. Peeling back the topmost layer of the TAN crayon, we would point out that no one was White, any more than anyone was really Black. In elementary school, if only for a time, we became TAN and BLUSH and MAHOGANY and BROWN.

The last chords of our anthem fading, the last loud voice also finally fading, Miss Bauer instructed us to become acquainted with our lockers and their combination locks, and to proceed from there to our academic classes. "Go forth and learn!" she enjoined us, while the fingers of her left hand crept across the fabric of her blouse.

My classmates and I fled into the swimming-pool-blue halls.

"Excuse me," said the new girl, Rachel Fish. "I think that's my locker."

"Excuse me!"

"That's all right," Rachel Fish said. "It's just better not to touch other people's things."

"I didn't mean to."

"Of course not. You're not the sort who would."

Around us milled our fellow students: seventh graders scuttling, eighth graders hailing old friends, ninth graders perambulating like some taller nobler species. I waved at Elaine but she shook her fist and passed on. By day's end I would have fallen, as it were, from a certain height; now, charmed as I was by the beginningness of things, even my sister's behavior seemed not so much outlandish as familial.

"I have too many books," Rachel Fish sighed.

Settling onto my haunches, I began to work my own combination lock. Who doesn't recall the mystery of such a lock: black dial, silvery indices, neat pointer? Eventually the dial clicked; the door yanked open, revealing a slip of paper on the locker's metallic floor. I turned the paper over as my loose-leaf binder slid from beneath my arm. Two boys hurried past, the nearest knocking my binder into the flow of student traffic.

"Hey!" Rachel Fish's eyes widened.

I scrambled to my feet.

"Hey you!" called Rachel Fish. "You could at least excuse yourself."

The boys paused.

"You could at least excuse yourself," Rachel Fish insisted. A dark-red flush crept up her neck and deepened across her face.

"What's the big deal, shrimp?" said the nearest boy.

"It doesn't matter," I said hastily.

The boys turned and sauntered on.

"It does too matter," Rachel Fish called after them. "You shouldn't pick on her just because she's different."

"Some people," said a gentle voice.

Before either of us could reach my binder, Haywood Lofty had stooped to retrieve it and placed it in Rachel Fish's hands.

Haywood Lofty had wide-set eyes behind bifocals and an almost prim mouth. Around his neck he wore a small medallion.

"Thank you," she said, her cheeks entirely crimson.

Haywood smiled, winked—which innocent gesture, I sometimes think, sealed my friend's fate—and strode on, his athlete's step transporting him down the hall and around the corner. Haywood had been selected by the school administration to squire the sick or wounded between periods into the one elevator there.

"Gosh," Rachel said. "Who was that?"

I told her.

"He seems so . . . nice. I have a lot of books, don't I?"

I felt compelled to explain that I had special permission to take out ten library books at a time, and that I meant to go right after school and do so.

"Me too! Actually I have special permission to take out fifteen but you can borrow some. I went last week during New Residents' Orientation. I like the public library best but I look forward to reading these excellent books and also to making use of the reference section. I love to read but am concerned about pressing social issues such as the Vietnam War, pollution and racial prejudice. Sometimes I get so mad at God I could die. How about you?"

"Well," I stammered. "I'm an atheist."

"Of course you are," said Rachel Fish. She patted my forearm comfortingly.

I glanced at the book titles in Rachel's overflowing locker, and I suffered an emotion akin to what my father, wooing my mother, might have called the lightning bolt of destiny. There was the coincidence of our names, and Rachel Fish's interest in the Dewey decimal system, and now this: she was reading *The Problems of Philosophy*, by none other than Bertrand Russell!

"I just adore Bertrand Russell," she said. "I have hung numerous of his pithy quotations on the walls of my room. It's much nicer than my last room. I've moved six times in six years. I sure hope we get to stay in this town."

"Bertrand Russell was a pacifist."

"I am most definitely not a pacifist," she said. "But I am a positivist. I believe that the world exists whether or not we think so. The way I know is, I bump into things."

"Neither is my sister," I told her, ignoring this last remark.

Rachel Fish removed her eyeglasses.

"Do you have bad sibling rivalry?" she asked, blinking. "I have terrible sibling rivalry but it's my mother's fault. She favors my younger brother, Hegel. My rabbi says I'm remarkably well-adjusted considering the injustice. My father is a traveling psychiatrist. He's why we move so much but I just revere him."

She had begun to scratch absentmindedly at the skin beneath her long sleeves.

"I am so proud to be an American," she went on. "I am absolutely opposed to the Vietnam War but I salute the flag. I noticed that you do too, which is a consummate relief. Did you know Bertrand Russell had four wives?"

"Yes."

"That is neither here nor there," said Rachel hotly. "I would much rather know nothing whatsoever about authors or thinkers or other accomplished persons. I don't mean you," she added. "You and I have to tell each other everything."

The bell rang and we both jumped.

"I'm a Girl Scout," she whispered, rushing off.

Pacifists, atheists, patriots: the world divided into so many categories! I hurried after Rachel Fish toward my first-period classroom, then, recalling the note in my pocket, slowed my steps. It was a jeering note, worded to make me fear for my well-being: "We'll teach you." Well? I was inclined, on this first day of school, to take the note lightly. For one thing, Elaine had often used such hyperbole in discussing her role in my future. For another, Rachel Fish suffered also from *"bad sibling rivalry."* And for still another, Elaine had good reason to resent my proximity! My father's concern for his daughters was severest where I was concerned. He would drive up today and every day after school and wait, anxious, sweating, idling that gray Buick, for us— for *me*.

"It's bad *enough*," Elaine had hissed just that morning, "that I have to put *up* with him *at home*."

"Oh no," Rachel Fish exclaimed. "Mr. Bogardus, that can't be true."

Mr. Bogardus had just said that William Shakespeare was the only writer in the world who could write about what he didn't know.

Mr. Bogardus, before launching into his paean of Shakespeare, had read all our names aloud from a shiny green roster and noted that we had two Rachels, also two Edward Morses, apparently twins. ("No, excuse me, one is an Edwin, isn't he?" he corrected himself pleasantly. "Raise your hands, if you wouldn't mind, boys. As my mother would say, 'Like as two peas.'") He then spent some minutes going over the rules of the classroom, which, he said, were benign compared to some of his colleagues'. He wasn't naming names.

Now he stood before the green chalkboard, holding his long, very clean palms upward, as if waiting for something to land in them.

". . . oops," said Rachel. "I guess I called out."

Mr. Bogardus smiled. "Calling out is bad because we need to listen to one another," he said, "but in my classroom, you won't get detention for calling out unless you give yourself detention."

We would start the year off, he told us (we were silent, contemplating what he had just said), by reading the abridged version of *Great Expectations* by Charles Dickens, then other great books about convicted people. In fact, Crime and Reform ("Above all, reform!") were the dual themes of the revised New Jersey seventh-grade curriculum, he said proudly. The Board of Education, after much reflection, had chosen these themes because of their relevance to young people. In Social Science, we would study the British and American prison systems, and in Science we would study theories of the criminal personality. We would have guest lecturers and we might even take a field trip to the infamous reform school, Bergen Pines. "A sense of place is so important," he said, emphasizing this word *place*.

Had anyone ever been to Bergen Pines? he wanted to know.

"Actually," Colin said, blue eye and brown eye unblinking, "that's where my brothers live. You might remember them. The Duffy brothers."

Mr. Bogardus seemed to reflect a moment. "Ah yes," he said finally. "The Duffy brothers. Come to think, there's a family resemblance. Which reminds me. You see, Charles Dickens himself as a young man . . ."

He trailed off for so long that we wondered if he had forgotten who Charles Dickens was.

"All novelists are limited by what they don't know," he resumed pleasantly, sticking a long finger in his ear (the left one). "Even, as we will see, our friend Dickens. Only William Shakespeare had what my mother would call true 'negative capability,' that is, the ability to imagine lives not his own. It's as if there were some very powerful, almost otherworldly telepathy at work in the Elizabethan era! Because of Shakespeare's influence on English language and literature, it remains the most inventive and humane literature in the world. That's why, in my opinion, efforts to 'abandon' the old New Jersey seventh-grade curriculum are misguided. More diversity, by all means; these are, of course, the United States of America. I'm for reform, yes; not, ahem"—ear-swivel, sniff—"'upsetting the whole applecart'!"

Which remarks occasioned two hands' swift rising into the air.

Mr. Bogardus removed his finger from beneath his nose. "Ah ha. Yes."

"I have two things to say," I gasped.

"Excuse me," called out Rachel Fish. "I think my hand was up first."

"This is not a bakery," said Mr. Bogardus pleasantly. "As my mother would say, the world of criticism is not first come, first serve."

"Oh dear," Rachel said. "Everyone has a right to be heard as much as everyone else. I'm extremely penitent. Would you like me to stay after school and clean your erasers every day? Great!"

"The first—" I said, then, because Mr. Bogardus had placed his shiny finger on his pink mouth, I paused. I saw no reason to give up, however. Nor did Rachel Fish. In fact, we began more wildly than ever waving our hands and following Mr. Bogardus with our straining bodies, a little like heliotropes will the sun, only faster. Our desks were those one-piece, top-heavy hybrids of desktop and chair.

Mr. Bogardus strolled to his desk—we swiveled—he picked up the green roster and, running his finger down its page, walked beyond to the window, where he stood leaning on his elbow. "Rachel Finch," he said, staring hard at my new friend. "I know your mother, don't I?"

At that moment, perhaps reaching too far, I fell over my desk. Or rather, my desk fell and I fell with it, landing in a sort of forward roll that unrolled. "Ouch," I said.

"Gosh! It's not all that funny when someone falls flat on her back, is it?" called out a clear loud soprano.

The ceilings in Benjamin Franklin Junior High School were low. The floor was hard. Usually I sat nearest the teacher's desk but on this morning of mornings, having found Rachel Fish sitting in my accustomed place, I had slipped into, and now reclaimed, the place behind it.

"Charles Dickens could have written about jungles in Africa," Rachel Fish was insisting. "He could have written about pyramids in Egypt. My father is a psychiatrist. But when I grow up I'm going to publish a book about things I never even heard of. I'm on the second draft of my first bildungsroman already."

I raised my hand.

"Yes, Rachel," sighed Mr. Bogardus.

"I read *Great Expectations* this summer," I said. "Can I read *Anna Karenina* instead?"

"No."

"Can I read *Hamlet?*"

"Did anyone else read a good book this summer?" asked Mr. Bogardus hastily.

Louise raised her hand.

"I read the beginning of a sad book about slavery," she said. "It was called *Uncle Tom's Cabin*. My mom threw it out because it made my dad angry. My dad wishes we could move back to Alabama tomorrow."

"That's too bad," said Mr. Bogardus. "Yes—?"

For some reason he had called on Steward Blumenthal, who stretched out his long legs and took a while to remark, "I used to be a lot heavier."

"I see," said Mr. Bogardus. "Yes—?"

"Huh," Cynthia said, twisting her head so that her beaded braids clicked. "My mom threw that book out too."

Mr. Bogardus seemed happy to have people talking about books they had read. "Yes—?"

"I read a new book called *I Know Why the Caged Bird Sings,*" Collette said. "It is by Maya Angelou and my aunt gave me it. Because of this book I know that I can be anything I want to be. I might become a doctor like my father or a lawyer or a singer like Maya Angelou."

"That is precisely right," said Mr. Bogardus.

"I read that book too," said Rachel Fish eagerly. "And I read *Great Expectations* the summer before last but there's always more to be learned from a classic. That's why teachers like Mr. Bogardus can go on reading the same books year in year out without getting boring. I mean bored."

"Excuse me—" began Mr. Bogardus.

"I did it again, didn't I?" said Rachel. Once more the strange blush spread across her features. "My repentance is total. I could wash your chalkboards too."

"If one more person calls out," said Mr. Bogardus with a smile that belied his words, "that person will seriously consider giving herself detention not with me but Felicity Bauer. And by the way"—the smile fell away—"if anyone has read *Great Expectations,* it is that person's responsibility *not to give away the plot.* We must be respectful of other people's right to find out what happens. Is that clear?"

I was reminded by Mr. Bogardus's last remark of, of all people, my flying companion and what he had once said on one of our return flights. I had been pestering him for details about the future, and he had declared something very like what Mr. Bogardus had just said about respecting other people's rights! Thinking of S-Man, and of the bluish air through which we had so handily plummeted, and of the well-lit landmarks of nocturnal New Jersey, I forgot myself and sighed aloud.

Collette raised her hand.

"Yes—?" said Mr. Bogardus, glancing at me.

"What if someone saw the movie?"

"Have you?"

"No."

"Has anyone seen the movie?"

We all shook our heads.

"That's a relief," he said. "If there's one thing I can't stand, it's when someone gives away the plot."

Mindy Glueck, who had red hair and red freckles and eyes that disappeared when she smiled, put her hand up.

"Yes—?"

Mr. Bogardus had called again on Steward Blumenthal. "It happened over the summer," Steward explained. "One day I woke up taller. Now girls like me."

"I see. Yes—?"

"I'm Mindy," she said. "Mindy Glueck. Is that *Uncle Tom's Cabin* as in, 'You're such an Uncle Tom'? An Uncle Tom is a Black who tries to act White—"

"Yes—?" said Mr. Bogardus, pointing.

"There's a difference," said Cynthia distinctly, "between an Uncle Tom and an Oreo."

"For instance," Mindy said, "Black girls who try to be like White girls are Oreos, but Black girls who try to hog a certain tall White boy are Uncle Toms."

Mr. Bogardus seemed to have forgotten the rule about not calling out. We watched as he closed his eyes. When he opened them, he examined first his long palms, then the backs of his hands. They were pale hands with lots of knuckle hair. "The question of an author's biases is finally very painful," he said. "Yes—?"

"I think people should just stick to their own kind," Mindy went on. "Don't you? My mother does."

Tunneling

"My mother hates it when these girls call our house," explained Steward. "When I was going out with Cynthia, that was one thing. But now it's Mindy one minute, Cynthia another. It's too much for her."

Mr. Bogardus squinted. His hand floated dangerously close to his ear. "I don't mean to avoid controversy," he said. "Ah ha."

Robert Wurner, squirming, shot both hands into the air for good measure.

"Yes, Mr. Wurner," said Mr. Bogardus, glancing at his roster.

"Can you explain about the criminal personality, please, and also do you think Hitler was a criminal or a madman?"

"This," said Mr. Bogardus, "may be your Social Science teacher's domain. But I can trespass, ah ha, this far. The criminal personality cannot be mistaken. The criminal personality is drawn to those weak, colorless individuals who have no existence independent of stronger, more ruthless companions. I doubt that anyone here has ever met a true criminal personality, but if you have, you'll know it almost from the smell"—here Mr. Bogardus's nose quivered and his fingers rose again on the air—"of an overripe French cheese."

"I know exactly what you mean," breathed Robert, casting a glance at Colin Duffy.

"So do I!" exclaimed my friend, then in the same breath whispered loudly, "Oh darn. You don't even have to ask me to give myself detention, Mr. Bogardus. I just volunteer to ask myself."

Still recalling that pleasant flight through the night air, I sighed again. "Yes?" said Mr. Bogardus, calling on me with apparent reluctance.

"The second thing I was going to say is—" I began. As if S-Man hadn't sworn me to secrecy! I had almost told Mr. Bogardus about the pamphlet that I'd "loaned" Shakespeare on my last morning in Stratford! What was wrong with me? "The second thing—" I stumbled on. "Right. Well. Actually, I prefer the published ending of the book, where Estella, who turns out to be the daughter of the convict and of a murderess with very strong hands, and Pip, whose benefactor turns out not

93

to be Miss Havisham but the very same convict, fall in love and get married. I mean, what's the point of reading a book if it's just going to make you miserable?"

"I couldn't agree more," said Rachel Fish. "Not to mention the author makes fun of people for the way they look. How cruel is that? In my *opus maximus,* which I'm just now revising, nobody even gets described. Period."

"Detention," he said, pointing the finger not at her but at me. "Three o'clock sharp. As my mother would say, 'One bad apple *can* spoil the whole bushel!'"

"Oh," Rachel Fish said, "I couldn't agree with your mother more. Doesn't that mean I should get detention too?"

Rachel Fish got detention all right, but not from Mr. Bogardus, who seemed to have taken as sudden a liking to her *("You don't mind if we've already memorized* Julius Caesar, *do you, Mr. Bogardus?")* as he'd taken a dislike, I'm afraid to say, to me *("Detention? Me? There must be some mistake, Mr. Bogardus!")*. Rachel Fish got it from an altogether different sort of pedagogue.

"Of course!" Elaine commented later.

Rachel Fish had arrived a heartbeat late for Science; had grabbed the seat behind mine; had listened (I saw her jaw drop) as Mrs. Carlsbad mapped the "forced march" she meant to take us on. "My young Americans, men and women of tomorrow, do you see *this?"* Mrs. Carlsbad asked. She picked up a book. It was actually more of a tome.

We, boys and girls of the then present day, nodded. Collette crossed her long white kneesocks. Margarita closed the little notepad into which she scribbled. Colin Duffy leaned across Margarita's desk and tugged on a stray thread in her sweater. "Detention!" shouted Mrs. Carlsbad. "Me or her?" asked Colin. Did Margarita blush? The classroom was brightly lit with the same false ceiling and desk-and-chair sets and the same high windows as other classrooms, and yet how different this one seemed! A lone beaker stood at attention on the sill. Beyond it lay the low hill where Elaine and I had hurried once, twice, a zillion times; and beyond that sprawled the scrubby fields of Votee Park and the drained municipal pool. And beyond that gaped the underpass! But never mind; the world is bright, the day young, and I prefer not to navigate that passageway just yet.

" 'New Jersey State Revised Seventh Grade Curriculum Outline,' " Mrs. Carlsbad read aloud. She looked up. "For ten years, no one has complained about my teaching. Suddenly they want relevance! It's enough to drive a woman crazy! Not me, though. Watch this."

Mrs. Carlsbad paused a theatrical moment—she was an extremely gifted teacher—then tore a long swath out of the NJSRSGCO's front cover.

"Ha!" she said, eyelids glittering.

"Neat," whispered Colin Duffy.

"Eyes on the clock," Mrs. Carlsbad thundered, her own blue eyes glaring from beneath eyelids frosted equally blue and her hands reaching for more pages. What big hands she had! What zest! Who can explain the nature of devotion? I loved S-Man well enough, although I knew our paths had soon to part; I loved my sister in a pained way, and my parents, and I was close on loving Rachel Fish; my feelings for Mrs. Carlsbad were other. From the moment of her big hands' straining at our state-determined curriculum, to our last moment together while destinies played out fathoms beneath the earth's crust, I would have done anything for Bev Carlsbad.

"So much for fetal pigs," she sneered. "And never mind snails or those disgusting sea monkeys. Relevance? Men and women of tomorrow, there has always been one and only one topic worth studying, one frontier worth crossing. I'll give you a hint. This," she said, chalking a high-pitched arrow clear across the board, "represents what we'll call the first dimension; your math teacher might call it the Change in Y. Now,"

she said, as she screeched a horizontal line through the first. "Can anyone tell me what this line is called?"

"The Change in How?" called out Rachel Fish. "Gosh. I'm sorry.
Can I slap your erase—"

"Detention, with, Felicity, Bauer," said Mrs. Carlsbad. She rolled
up her sleeve.

I gasped. Had she heard me? She yanked her sleeve down again.

Pointing to the shreds of the NJSRSGCO scattering like oversized
snowflakes, she began to talk with a certain excessive sarcasm (I
thought) about changes in *why* and *how* and *where* and *when,* and asked
if one of us wouldn't be so kind (did her blue lids glitter dangerously?)
as to deposit the state's efforts to control our minds in the trash can? I
raised my hand. I was chosen. I walked across the room. I gathered and
deposited, gathered and deposited, all the while recalling what had been
an unmistakable bluish gash above our teacher's elbow. Had anyone
seen? Perhaps even Rachel Fish, in the seat behind mine, wasn't close
enough. Rachel Fish was gazing soulfully. She was expecting me, perhaps, to speak up for her, as she had for me several times that morning.
I reclaimed my seat. I opened my notebook and folded a page and penciled a neat line down the central crease, which crease, Mrs. Carlsbad
said, had sure as shooting better appear on our homework.

"But," called out a voice—it was Rachel Fish's.

Luckily Mrs. Carlsbad was launching into one of those spicy personal anecdotes with which she would pepper her year's lectures on the
one topic worth studying, the one frontier worth pioneering, etcetera.

"Once upon a *time,*" she hinted broadly. "Which reminds me, my
husband was a Green Beret. Talk about relevance! We were married on
a Tuesday in the middle of his first tour. There wasn't a cloud in sight.
He kept his revolver in its holster the whole *time. . . .*"

And so—gloriously, relentlessly on!

"Some days," she would conclude, "I think I'm losing my mind.
Other days, I think maybe it's him, not me."

"Who is she kidding?" wrote Rachel Fish later that day.

Tunneling

By then we two sat side by side in Detention Hall, working beneath Miss Bauer's determined gaze on our first English assignment—"What Contacts I Had with the Criminal Element During My Summer Vacation"—and scribbling to each other (or rather, Rachel scribbling to me; I was too mortified) in the margins, *"Why does she tell us all that stuff? We're not grown-ups! We're kids!"*

Rachel Fish, as you may have surmised, had an unerring sense of boundaries. She meant what she had said about a writer's life. She didn't want to know anything about Shakespeare or Charles Dickens or even Margaret Mitchell, whose *Gone with the Wind* she had once adored and now despised on humanitarian principle. She felt differently about characters.

"That Scarlett," she might say, or "That Pumblechook . . ."

In my heart, which had begun to beat a strange new rhythm, I didn't envy her acumen, her allowance of library books, her privilege of slapping Mr. Bogardus's erasers (my allergies would have prevented me), but I did envy her ease with people, barring Mrs. Carlsbad. What communal instinct did my friend possess? It was in Rachel Fish's presence that I began to think hard about error and pardon. Indeed, I thought hard about everything she told me, that day and the subsequent fun-filled days before I was recalled to global duties.

Every day at lunch, Rachel Fish and I met in the cafeteria. I had never experienced the pleasanter aspects of friendship with a human peer and for whole moments forgot my life with S-Man; at other times, I reminded myself that even Franz Kafka had made the all-important acquaintance of—Max Brod! Well! There was the way my friend awaited me on the lunch line; the way that I might, having raced out of class, reach the cafeteria first and save her a spot in the line. The expression for this was "frontsies." I would have given her anything—or

almost anything—but was learning one of the finer aspects of friendship, namely that "frontsies" may sometimes suffice. We grabbed our
plastic trays, we surveyed the foods offered for general consumption.
How I had hated lunch for the regimen it imposed! Now two Rachels
accepted meals prepared by the school's capable medical staff; two
Rachels passed by peanut-butter-and-jelly sandwiches and whole milk
in small cartons (they would have given anything, the Rachels admitted, for a single bite of peanut-butter-and-jelly sandwich), then reached
for a waxed bag of carrot sticks and went out into the loud hall and
claimed their favorite table by the windows or moved up well-lit rows
to the emptiest table they could find and, chattering, dashed down their
trays. They—we—ate rapidly (mostly of soy), sat back and conversed.

The conversations we shared! At times, as I say, I even forgot my
travels with S-Man. I would not have known to lead my life, it seems
to me, if I hadn't forgotten it. At other moments, through my dialogue
with Rachel Fish, I began to weave a kind of private tattered cloth, to
acquire a more "universal perspective" (as my father might have called
it) of the voyages S-Man and I had undertaken.

But perhaps I recall those conversations as more coherent than they
were; ours must have suffered the inevitable fits and starts of any sincere
colloquy. Rachel, possessing the knack of friendship, had gathered
around her a small group of a cappella choir members. "Sopranos, give
it your all!" they would sing, mimicking Miss Bauer. That intrepid con-
ductress had determined that the a cappella choir would inspire the
whole school before year's end with a rousing and perfectly harmonized
rendition of the national anthem. Once, as the girls warbled (Cynthia's
was a husky alto), I tried to chime in; even suggested, their song dying
away, that we try next an old family favorite.

" 'We Shall Overcome'?" crowed Cynthia. "Are you kidding?"

"I hate that dumb song," agreed Collette, who had often sung it
with me.

On other occasions also I would fall silent, not always out of
unhappiness, and certainly not resentment, although Mindy Glueck

and Cynthia Lacey and even Collette Foster had a way of fake-puking whenever I mentioned our science teacher. I fell silent because I liked in their presence to watch how Rachel was made happy; how her hair cascaded, how she tossed her head or made prettily to pout. Her teeth were white and her lips chapped. She had a way of trying new expressions. For an entire week she fake-puked constantly.

In that first week of school we were called upon by Mr. Bogardus to write another composition, "A Comparison-and-Contrast of Yourself and Another Guilty Party." I kept my own effort for many years, and lost it only during this infamous flood-ridden year; I have since uncovered a once-sodden draft of Rachel's beneath my bedsprings, where I once tucked documents and other objects that I might lie near them during hours of private study. Although the handwriting has blurred, some words can be deciphered and the reconstructed whole gives some sign of my friend's temperament:

> *Rachel Finch and I share a love of literature. We are both going to be writers. We are studying very long works of literature such as* Bleak House *and* The Problems of Philosophy. *We appreciate these and also shorter works such as* Of Mice and Men, *which by the way sounds a lot better than* Of Men and Mice. *We like the same things, such as books that have an appendix. Not the operating kind. We aren't guilty parties at all, Mr. Bogardus. I am a Jewish Girl Scout and I always salute the flag. My mother was born in Latvia and my father in New York. I am opposed to the Vietnam War. Rachel Finch doesn't believe in God yet. Her father used to be a soldier. Oh yes, we both have siblings but hers is a holy—*

The draft, which ends there, offers only a suggestion, really, of my friend's acumen and powers of judgment, although it may point to a certain structural weakness in her mind's function. She seemed to go everywhere at once and never to remain long. Perhaps she was—I hesitate to think so—scatterbrained not only in relation to the material world (we shared this trait) but also in the realm of ideas. Nonetheless it was through Rachel Fish (the name had been shortened, she explained, dark eyes swimming across the lunch table, from *Magdovitz;* amazed, I told her that my grandfather's name hadn't started out as *Finch* but Ezekiel *Finkelstein!)* that I awoke from the long dream of childhood to a sense of history, and subsequently to the realities, as she helped me to perceive them, of contemporary life. It is not too much to say—nor to say very much—that my friend's awareness of politics, her commitment to the Democratic Party in its most liberal aspect, constituted the primum mobile of my moral and political awakening.

The year was 1969. There were, it seemed to Rachel Fish, good and bad people in the world. The good ones often got shot in processions or hotel rooms. A war was in fact being televised. Its cruelest weapon was napalm, its tiniest victim an infant whose mangled limbs and surprised expression aired after the Four-Thirty Movie. The Independent candidate for mayor, a Black man, categorically did not beat his wife—that vicious rumor was spread by people like Louise's parents, the Bigelows, who were worse than Scarlett O'Hara. If they had their way, Teaneck would again become a place of terrible racial injustice. Rachel had met the Democratic candidate and assured me that he was a decent man who would see that the town kept its civic promise. As for drugs, she was against methadone because it meant replacing one addiction with another.

And so on; I listened, half-dismayed, half-mesmerized by Rachel Fish's chapped lips as she licked them. Her white teeth gleamed. How could I hope to keep her friendship? If I felt tempted to speak of London or Stratford, or Versailles—I had learned something about progress there—I had only to recall her dismissive *"I would much rather know nothing about a person"* and her forgiving *"I don't mean you"* (the kindness in the latter statement was particularly disarming). Rachel Fish claimed an aversion to gossip of any kind.

Tunneling

One exception to this rule, I realized quickly, lay in matters concerning Haywood Lofty, or rather Haywood and Elaine. Rachel never tired of hearing about their star-crossed courtship: how, in that first hopeful season of our school's integration, Haywood had often declined boarding the yellow bus after school, how he would end up walking over a mile home, beneath the railroad tracks and on into the northeast and "Black" section of town, so that he might first accompany Elaine (and me, dawdling obediently) to her own tree-lined street, a few blocks from John Greenleaf Whittier Elementary School #4, and stand with her on the little slope of our lawn. They two would look not at each other but out at the street and the occasional passing car, as if for them love were this soberer matter of learning about the world. And yet how carefree Elaine had seemed in those months! How much kinder she had been to me, her sister! And how delighted I had been at the interruption of those troubling bold-faced notes! Once I even invited a classmate, Margarita, home. Or rather she invited herself, and wanted only to discuss the kiss that Colin Duffy had bestowed upon my cheek; which cheek was it? she wanted to know. I showed her and we both shuddered, and yet even that first recalled embrace partook of the season's beginningness.

At the end of that year, Haywood's father, a retired medical officer who had served in Vietnam, developed brain cancer and died. Haywood's mother needed her son to watch over his much-younger sister. The school bus became his vehicle too; no more walks, no more dawdled afternoons, no more learning together about the world. Haywood's mother did not, it seemed, approve of his friendship with Elaine; my sister was never invited to their home on Stuyvesant Street. It was a very pleasant-looking home, with a smallish front yard and a separate garage and a blue front door, Elaine had told me; she had trekked all the way across town and down Stuyvesant Street to see for herself one day that June. Our father had been beside himself with worry by the time she returned, silent and red-eyed, from her trek into what was already the past.

All this I explained to Rachel Fish, who listened, huge eyes swimming in her pale face, fingernails chewed to the quick and clawing at anything but her own flesh—stubborn, stubby nails tapping tabletops, drumming textbooks. For each of us, some story makes the conjunction of history and the present era tangible; for many, that story features our own self in some definitive role. Rachel Fish's defining narrative seemed not to figure her own person. As she saw it, the tragedy of my sister and Haywood Lofty was the larger-than-life tragedy of our times.

But such seriousness would have tired anyone without some leaven! I remember once walking down the hall and hearing a plaintive song. There stood Rachel Fish, arms extended, eyes pitifully glazed. "Alms for the poor," she sang out in her loud soprano. "Alms for the poor / *Legs for the rich* . . ." Another time, looking up from *Bartlett's Familiar Quotations* (one of her all-time favorite books), she mused, "The pen is mightier than the swordfish," a joke whose success depends, I admit, on the listener's being there.

We were there all right!

"Who will lead us now?" she once cried out.

"You'll see," I assured her, and wished for the thousandth time that I might confess all.

But I begin to wax where I ought to wane, that is, to let our story tell itself. We are sitting in the lunchroom. It's the third day of our meeting and already Rachel Fish has invited me to her house on the following afternoon, that is, she says, if Mrs. Carlsbad doesn't land her in the clink again.

"I don't think so," I tell her worriedly.

"We could walk home together," she persists. "We could roast soy dogs or eat soy cupcakes in my backyard. We could read books or work on our bildungsromans. I am writing mine in the fourth person, which is why it's taking so long. Sometimes I wish I could just go back in time and see for myself. Have you ever met a Brahman? I just love Mr. Bogardus, don't you? Even though he's wrong about revolution. Wrong,

wrong. I just read this really great book by the universally acclaimed Nigerian author Chinua Achebe. My mother gave it to my brother. I get his books after he's read them. Except my library books of course. The Teaneck library is much nicer than the one in the last town we lived. Chinua Achebe is my favorite writer of all time now except for someone else. Do you think books should ever be banned? Did you see what Mrs. Carlsbad did to that book? Have you ever been to Africa? From now on anytime I read a book by a White man I'm going to read a book by a Chinese person. Or a Nigerian. How about you? Are you in favor of universalism like Voltaire or are you a particularist? And what about imagery? Is it racist to talk about 'seeing the light'? When you write, should you talk about everybody's skin? You can't just say Mr. Jones was a Black man or a brown-skinned person if you haven't said Mr. So-and-So was a White man or a tan-skinned person. What time will you have to go home?"

"I'll ask my parents," I tell her worriedly. There are rules within rules in any household, composed of necessity and habit. As we stare across the lunchroom table, it occurs to me—oh earth-breaking revolution!—that I have never asked, never been asked, to go to a friend's house before.

"I have asthma," I point out.

"I know," she says. She leans, careful to avoid our trays, over the table. I feel her soft breath against my ear and abandon myself to hope: "I have eczema."

Eczema, ecstasy; at three o'clock I spun so giddily toward my father Francis's car that he must have feared another health crisis. I flopped into the backseat and flipped my Breath-a-Lator into the air and caught it and pocketed it and spread my big old books across my knees. What a day! I prattled to the air about Mr. Bogardus, about Mrs. Carlsbad. What a *witch* indeed! Just that day she had made the twins, Edward and

Edwin, stand in opposite corners of the room, which she now called the Occident and the Orient; and when the new girl, Rachel Fish, had objected, Mrs. Carlsbad had tried to slap her with another detention. "Anyone else?" she asked, blue lids glittering. "Oh I would, Mrs. Carlsbad," the new girl said, "but today is the first annual meeting of the Clean Our School Committee." Omitting from the history of Mrs. Carlsbad's cruelty only the thrill that left me helpless against it, I went on to describe the gymnasium with its long braided ropes, the music room with its padded walls, and the fact that Rachel Fish was urging me to try out for the Girls' A Cappella Chorus.

"A cappella?" my father asked. He knew better than anyone, having carried me on his shoulders through march after march, that I couldn't carry a tune.

The car door flew open. "Guess what. I have to stay after school," Elaine said.

Francis twisted around.

Elaine's face was splashed in sunlight. Behind her slouched the two "high school" boys, Hugo and Sid. Hugo was stroking his beard and gesticulating to Sid, who was inspecting something with a largish rock. He kept dropping the rock and lifting it and peering and dropping it again.

"Track team," Elaine said.

"Track doesn't start until spring," my father said.

"I thought so too," Elaine said airily. "Mrs. Handler says she needs people to help her get ready."

Sid hurled the rock over the low wall onto the lawn, then grabbed a stick and poked until he'd lifted something (it resembled a large cockroach) and sent it sailing after the rock. Sid pulled out a cigarette and tossed the empty pack. As it happened, Haywood Lofty, Collette Foster, Rachel Fish and other members of the Clean Our School Committee were passing just then. Haywood speared the very same cigarette pack and shook it into a billowing plastic bag. Rachel speared a pinecone. I giggled affectionately—she looked so serious—and, leaning my chin on his headrest, reached my hands into my father's hair. This was an old gesture with us.

Sid took a crumpled tissue from his pocket, made a launcher of his first and second fingers and let the tissue fly. Haywood speared the fallen tissue and shook it into his bag. Sid shoved his hand into his pocket. He brought out a handful of dirt and spare change and shreds of paper and let it fall.

"Lot of dirt around here," Sid remarked.

" 'Dirt,' " said Hugo, looking up. "A word with an interesting etymology. Do you remember it, Sid?"

"Huh," guffawed Sid uneasily. "I just said. Dirt."

"From the Middle Teutonic for 'underneath,' " said Hugo. "Underneath, below, less than."

Haywood frowned, forehead rippling, and walked on.

"Looks good with a spear," said Sid.

Haywood froze in his steps.

"She wants me to help with uniforms," said Elaine.

"What time would I get you?" asked Francis.

"She says she'll give me a ride."

This was such an obvious lie that I sucked in my breath; Elaine bent to show me the whites of her eyes. Francis's hands gripped the steering wheel.

"That's very kind," Francis said. "Make sure you thank her very kindly."

"Don't you have to go back to work?" Elaine asked.

"In the name of sweet Jesus," Francis exclaimed. Elaine's face flinched. Sure enough, as Haywood walked on, Francis expressed himself more fully. His own words seemed to incite further words. He discoursed on the danger inherent in late school dismissals. He discoursed on tardiness, which strikes a blow at empire. Empire led to America; and democracy; which wasn't a very good form of government, only the best there was. Only the best there was. Hadn't he done enough for us? Why, he asked, taking out a white handkerchief and wiping his nape, which was sweaty, *was she doing this to him?*

"And tomorrow you don't have to pick us up either because I have volleyball," Elaine said.

"Tomorrow I'm going to Rachel Fish's house," I announced.

Francis's knee jerked a lever. The windshield wiper began opining in a smooth mechanical arc: tchuh-*tchuh,* tchuh-*tchuh.* "What about your doctor's appointment?" he cried.

I had forgotten my weekly visit to the allergist!

"She could go after," suggested Elaine.

Francis looked from her to my face in the rearview mirror.

Tchuh-*tchuh,* tchuh-*tchuh.*

"Daddy," I said. "It isn't raining."

"So can I go?" whined Elaine. But in doing so, she had made a mistake; although the conversation lasted a few minutes more, she had admitted she had no real obligation to stay.

"Well, can I at least tell her?" Elaine asked, her voice breaking. She flounced away into the school building. Francis flicked off the windshield wiper. He seemed to make an effort to control himself and then exploded with more discourse on the prevailing dangers to teenage health. I remember only that pregnancy and the Constitution and, for some reason, our next-door neighbors were involved. I watched a bug mounting the windowpane. The bug would crawl, lost its grip and fall to the narrow plane where window met door and then it would begin to crawl again. Going up, it was saying, *Sometimes I wish I could travel back in time. Have you ever been to Africa?* Coming down, it said, *But that would be cheating.* I was considering opening the window when Elaine reemerged, stumbling into Haywood, whose bag went whirling down the cement steps. She wavered; he scrambled after a sheet of newsprint and she after him; their two cheeks grazed each other; Elaine hurried on and Collette knelt to retrieve Haywood's pole. I waved to Rachel Fish, who brandished her own.

Tunneling

Elaine clambered into the backseat. She shoved at my books.

"Move this crap," she said as we drove off.

Elaine's eyes were smiling in a hard way, and I realized that in allowing her to sense my excitement, I also had erred.

Perhaps when you began this chapter, you expected it to conclude with some clanging note? Some portentous event; another vicious note in my locker or a poisoned apple? In life an old dove smooths its feathers, a lone dog howls. The train that rockets through Teaneck each evening, dividing this side of town from that, does so with its usual braggadocio. The NJ Savings & Loan, pillars illuminated, dome templelike, resides beneath a sickled moon; and if anyone other than myself recalls how its peaceful aura once occasioned our ruin, no one says so.

That night I was too excited to sleep. My mother (listless since her accident) perked up to second the motion of my visit to Rachel Fish's house. Francis suggested that Rachel Fish's parents, notoriously free-living (he used the word *vagrant*, as I recall), were unfit guardians; he went on in that vein, the pieces of some puzzle fitting increasingly into place as he contemplated them, including my having been given detention on the first day of school, which fact now seemed not humorous but sinister, very sinister, until my mother twisted her head like a faucet and out poured an unfamiliar tone. I wanted to warn my father, but of what? " 'Free-living'?" Rose said. " 'Vagrant?' " Finally it was agreed that Francis would drive me to the doctor's office and if all went well—I would wait the usual hour for my shots to absorb—Francis would drop me at the Fishes' house on East Laurelton Parkway and pick me up two hours later, in plenty of time for dinner.

The Fishes' house! East Laurelton Parkway! Two whole hours!

"Please, Daddy," I begged. "Don't look so sad."

My favorite codebreaker in the world didn't say it, but I knew he was thinking: Why are you doing this to me?

*   *   *

I was not to arrive at the house on East Laurelton Parkway, as it happens—the most serious of my asthma attacks necessitating the allergist's rushing me to Holy Name Hospital, where my father admitted me to the Children's Ward and sat by my bed as the oxygen unit was connected. There was a plastic tube from which I had to draw breath, and a window on one side, and a curtain beyond which lay other children. The curtain seemed, as my father held my hand, very thin. Indeed, when morning came (I passed the night and a second day and night in that hospital, before my mother and a subdued Elaine came for me), the nurses left the curtain open. The children (they were very ill) met my gaze with their own implacable ones.

Was it silence or the fact of my compeers' greater suffering that brought me to myself on the second night? Or news my father brought from the outside? Each evening before going home, Francis was in the habit of moving from hospital bed to bed. I watched through the slitted curtain until he arrived at mine, and in this manner learned something more about this man whom I called father. He spoke kindly to each child. He knew each of their names and what games they played and who they wanted to see and what they remembered best about life before the hospital. He checked their menus and their lesson plans—some had lived so long on the ward, which my father and Dr. Foster referred to jokingly as the Home Front, that it had become their school. Sometimes my father just laid his warm, remembering hand on a warmer forehead; sometimes he tucked bedcovers more snugly around a child whose eyes, huge from the last stages of illness, put me in mind of my new friend. Did she blame me or tire of my symptoms? What if she forgot? My heart seemed riven: one chamber despaired (Rachel Fish hadn't sent word); the other hoped (perhaps she would).

On my last night in the Children's Ward, Francis sat down and, as was his wont, began to read aloud from the *Bergen Record*. I felt none of the confusion that accompanied my new friend's recitation of current events. My father's voice had always narrated the world to me. Things had always been bad, although they seemed lately to have gotten worse. In Biafra war was being waged through the starvation of orphans; Vietnamization was another name for cowardice; and here at home, purportedly concerned parents demanded reevaluation of the busing of schoolchildren! My father shook his head. *"Never take anything for granted,"* he said. He went on to inveigh against bigotry disguised as virtue and was reminded of his months spent as a young man deciphering enemy codes. His voice wound on about the practical necessity not only of recognizing the enemy but the moral necessity of recognizing when the enemy is a fantasy. I had heard him speak once at a medical conference, about his life as a patient on a terminal TB ward, and had felt proud to be my father's daughter. When the time came, I returned his farewell with an old affection, and listened through the curtain for his diminishing footsteps.

I slipped from bed and crossed to the window. I knew now why I hadn't heard from my friend; the dolorous news of the outside world would have been sufficient. Rachel Fish hated famine and disease and war, but most of all she hated what these did to children. No doubt she was busily praying for orphans. I wished for a moment that I knew how to pray too.

A long square of yellow light shone in the brick facade of our town hall. Feeling the solemnity of the moment, which was only a moment among others, I swore to record it in my mind. I had played this game since earliest childhood, often around dusk when Francis called us inside and children's voices floated through the screened-in porch. It wasn't prayer but a kind of record-keeping.

First, I noted the dark lines of a nearby maple, the blue of a hedge and the darker blue of the air between Town Hall and my hospital window. Second, I borrowed my window's frame and drew one like it, as it were, around everything I experienced. I "put" the maple, the hedge and the air inside this invisible frame. I put the *bzz-bzz* of car tires on mildly wet pavement, the cool feel of glass against my forehead and a familiar hospital odor, like camphor or sugarcane, inside it too. A figure darted across the shadowy lawn; I added him to my frame (have you played such a game, reader?), before recognizing, as a passing car shed momentary light, the fleshy countenance and bald pate of Laff Riot and the little dancing legs of Mr. Stick.

They were here.

They had followed me here.

As I watched, they strode toward the rear door of Town Hall. Like S-Man, Laff had a way with locks; soon enough he and his cohort had slipped inside, leaving only a kind of hollow in the darkness outside.

Chapter Five

Hearts of Light

"**E**XCUSE ME, PROFESSOR," I SAID.

The man so addressed looked up from papers scattered across his desk. He must have seen a middle-aged woman of no distinction. Certainly he didn't seem to recognize me. Can I say that I did him? The little statue on his desk, yes; the statue was the color of chalk dust, and wore a familiar if yellowed cape, and a familiar if obsolete red emblem on its chest. As for the professor, he wore a colorful coat or gown and a round woven cap of equally bright colors, and his eyes beneath the cap seemed weary, and I saw deep lines etched into his hollowed cheeks. Even in his prime he would not have been called handsome. And yet his face made you look again, as if you had perhaps missed something in its features.

"Hi," I stammered. "I mean, long time no see."

"I beg your pardon?"

He wheeled back in his chair and waited unsmilingly for me to speak. Apart from the cluttered desk, his office seemed sparse, even Spartan. Metal bookshelves housed a variety of books—I glimpsed the familiar names of Wole Soyinka and the poet Christopher Okigbo—and on the opposite wall hung a poster of a blue-skinned woman pouring water. The sounds of college life floated through the open window;

a young woman called out a breathless trill; another responded with a high-pitched ululation. The year was 2003. My father having died in a room he once shared with my mother, I had obeyed a panicked impulse to board a train and journey upriver. I regretted doing so. And yet (as the little statue on his desk proved beyond a doubt) this stranger had at one time been the young friend with whom I had shared formative experiences until history parted us and we walked our different paths, he to government college in Umuahia and I once again to my first year of junior high.

Our story, as they say, goes like this:

A few mornings after my return from the hospital, S-Man sent me to change into appropriate clothing—this time a white shirt and baggy white shorts, such as a British schoolboy might wear in the tropics. I changed hurriedly, only to be sent again to fetch the shell Aquaman had given me. I ought, of course, to have told S-Man about Laff Riot and Mr. Stick and how the villains had skulked across the hospital lawn. Hadn't S-Man always warned me about the dangers of revenge at home? But I had been back from the hospital for some days, and chafed against my father's virtual grounding of Elaine (for lying) and me (for wheezing). I told myself that S-Man no doubt knew what had happened, and I crawled once more over the sill into my room, which looked odd without me, and fetched the shell from a white earring box beneath my mattress springs, and snuck once more to where S-Man, garbed in a brilliantly white cape and white "uniform" with a red slash across the chest, reached open arms.

I would mention the villains' appearance, I decided, once we had set out.

In Africa I would find the shell very useful, S-Man said. Of course, it was only a loan like a library book (I wondered if he knew about *The Complete Stories*!), but the key was mine. In fact, he said, I would do well to wear the key about my neck at all times.

Tunneling

"But S-Man," I said.

As we flew above the rooftops a streetlamp blinked on, casting a faint circular glow on the streets below. Wind whipped through my schoolboy's attire and, burrowing more deeply into S-Man's cape, I listened for the silence of his alien heart. Think of the difference between those old ticking clocks—you will perhaps have experienced them, as Elaine and I did in childhood—and the digital quartz machines that mark so seamlessly the passage of these recent years.

"There's something I have to tell you," I said.

"Don't worry. I have everything worked out."

Upon our arrival in the city of Enugu, he explained (purplish sky expanding; dark suburbs and highways shrinking away), we were to establish contact with a Nigerian author by the name of Chinua Achebe. "Oh yes. I've heard of him," I said, my words snatched by the wind. This man had recently, S-Man went on, after high-level officials had caused him to fear for his life and the lives of his loved ones, relinquished his position in Nigeria's Department of International Broadcasting. No longer the government-appointed Voice of Nigeria, and having delayed his retreat to the eastern region, he was at this very moment being interrogated at a checkpoint on the highway to Enugu. The irony (is there irony in war?) was that the gravest dangers awaited the Achebe family in their zinc home there. "Our mission—" said S-Man.

"Yes?" I asked, then, seeing the entrance to the time tunnel, braced myself mentally.

Anyone who has experienced it will tell you that even under normal conditions, time travel bears no comparison to physical displacement. During "takeoff," as it were, the gray fabric of the tunnel thins so that patches of other eras shine here and there, or rather now and then, like cartoonish squares across a bubble's turning surface. The sensations produced have led me to believe that time and the mind are composed of some identical particle whose nature (neither thing nor act nor notion) has yet to be defined. But others since that moment, so to speak, have experienced time travel and are no doubt better skilled in recording their impressions.

Whatever our plans, we had no sooner entered the tunnel than we were ambushed! Violet meteors rocketed in; S-Man cried out as we lost momentum; the tunnel stretched so thin that daylight stabbed through and the taut walls bled from gray to red to crimson and we slid horribly apart. Holy Mother Planet! Was that someone laughing? S-Man flew past, bathed in a strange violet glow and clutching his ears. As I crashed through the tunnel walls and on into temporal reality, I felt the presence of something not evil but inhuman in its proleptic calculus. Who or what? *Someday;* I who lacked prophecy foresaw in that instant how *someday* my superfriend's enemies would unite against him and all would be lost. Then I was tumbling downward through the various stratospheres; perhaps I ought to have grown used to such descents; perhaps it was someone else, then, who began hollering S-Man's name (what she knew of it) as she saw treetops soaring toward her, who shrieked as she felt branch after branch crackling beneath the *whoosh* and *whoosh* of her downward spiral.

When I came to, the sun was a fiery red disk. A moon hung like a white hammock between tall trees. I lay on some sort of mat. A boy perched on a wooden stool. He wore European clothes—white shirt, white baggy shorts like mine—and in his lap he held a book. He seemed to be reading, although from time to time he would slam the book shut or riffle fiercely through its pages. After a time he slid that book into his satchel, an old-fashioned schoolboy's satchel such as one might read about in *Oliver Twist* or *Pinocchio,* and took out a second book, more dog-eared and apparently more to his liking.

Behind the boy and his three-legged stool rose a large thatched hut and several smaller huts. These huts also were thatched except for the two smallest, constructed of mud and overlooking a flat earthen area. Beyond the last hut, or *obi,* gleamed another edifice, lit from within by a yellowish gas lamp. This last structure had three rather than four wooden walls and several stories linked via an exterior ladder. Innumerable clay figures filled each level. One figure displayed a grossly distended mouth; another an elongated neck; a third figure, that of a woman, extended bizarrely foreshortened arms and legs. The statues' shadows, lengthened by approaching evening, commingled into still more distorted shapes. I had heard tell from S-Man of the Hall of Superheroes with its waxen images and wondered if I had stumbled upon its secret location.

Enlivened, I sat up.

"Excuse me," I said. "Is this by any chance Prague?"

"Well," the boy said, looking up. "You are awake at last."

"Yes," I said. Reaching for the lingual shell in my pocket, I realized that the boy was speaking English.

"I have waited several hours. They sent word when the women took you from the tamarind tree. This is my uncle's compound. Like my grandfather before him, he is an important person in this village, having taken all but the last title and like my grandfather before him having been generous to a fault with his fellows. He is of course a heathen. My name, however, is Albert. I am named after the consort of Queen Victoria, who is Christian. My father is a preacher and an instructor for the Association of God but when I have completed my education I am going to live in a city like Ibadan or perhaps Lagos and I will write far better books than does Mr. Joseph Conrad. But if you look closely at this other book, which is very old, you will see that it contains drawings of the human body. And this thing that looks like an upside-down cooking pot is the soul. When you die again, your soul will leave your body and perch on your coffin on the way to the cemetery. You know this, no doubt. My question to you now is this: Who are you? Who are your people and why did they drop you from the sky?"

"That's three questions," I said.

"I think you are an *ogbanje*," he said. "I think you are in a hurry to leave this world so that you can return in another form. But you will find the door to this world locked when you try to come again. It is locked because Jesus Christ has ruled that every soul must rest in his bosom, which is large as the bosom of his Father. This great mystery cannot be understood in my opinion. A son is never so large as a father. What are your thoughts on the matter?"

"I don't know," I said uneasily. "I'm not a Christian."

"No," he said. "You are an *ogbanje*. Still while you rest on Earth you must eat and drink like other people. In time I myself will be sent to Ibadan, where I will be trained as a doctor, but it may be that my path lies elsewhere in which case I will tell my older brothers George and Reginald, who pay for my education."

"My brothers," he added proudly, "pay greatly for my education."

"I'm very thirsty," I admitted.

"My aunt has left you some water and some yam *foo-foo*. It was she who found you hanging from the tamarind tree to whom you owe your life. Afterward she sent my cousin all the way to Nwangene to fetch water. He is not happy, I can tell you. But he is to marry soon and must be forgiven his ill temper until her family has brought his bride for the second visit. At the first visit there were some who teased because he would not lie with her until marriage. He should pay these foolish and execrable people no mind. When I court I will not even touch my bride's hand, not even her littlest fingertip, until the priest has joined us in holy matrimony. I will have only one wife, of course, but she, an educated Christian woman, will bear me many children. All sons. Now drink."

It was, as I say, almost evening. The sun slid behind a rim of trees. Two bowls lay beside my mat. One brimmed with clear water; the other contained a yellowish substance that I understood to be *foo-foo*. I lifted the water bowl and, drinking too rapidly, choked. The boy shifted on his three-legged stool. He was a thin boy with a large head. His eyes were deeply set, quizzical; his nose broad and buttonlike; his mouth full yet prim. He wasn't handsome but something in his face made you want to look again.

"What year is it?" I asked cautiously.

"What year? It is one thousand nine hundred forty-four years since the birth of Jesus. Don't you know anything? I am just now studying in school the paths of digestion, circulation and respiration. Also lymph. You have not answered my questions."

"I was looking for someone," I said, aghast.

He frowned and went on as if he hadn't heard. "Last night the elders of the eight villages held a meeting. They meet again tonight. Already they have decided not to adopt you. One man suggests that you be killed. Others have reminded him about what happened many years ago in Mbunto when an English who descended also from the sky was killed. You are not yet a man and no one would risk the destruction of their entire village to be rid of you. If you were a girl things would be different. My uncle feels burdened by your presence. Many years ago he had Christians in his compound but they made him so sad with their music that he asked them to leave. He fears that any moment now you might start singing. For whom are you looking?"

"It doesn't matter," I said, still shaken. Nineteen forty-four! Twenty-five years earlier than S-Man had intended! How S-Man had howled, clutching his ears, as the tunnel collapsed! What was to be done? How could I get help or be of help to him?

"I think it does matter," Albert said simply. "Last night I had an interesting dream. I will tell you my dream if you tell me whom you seek."

Thinking to buy time, I nodded. The bulk of Albert's dream is recorded below. I listened to him while trying to make sense of my situation. An important counsel was about to take place during which my fate would be decided. To reveal myself as a girl would clearly be to court death. If I let the elders know, at the very least, that I spoke Igbo? Stroking the ridges of the shell, I considered that language with its dialects and vowels and aphorisms: "The man who builds his *obi* out of the rain should not complain about drought." "You do not stand in one place to watch a masquerade." "Wisdom is like a goatskin bag; every man carries his own." Such sayings had a distilled quality akin to a delicate or classical appreciation of form. This quality manifested in the innumerable clay figures, or *mbano,* whose house Albert and I had just passed, and in the masquerade of godly personages that we were later to witness. Or so it seems today and in this room where I endeavor to explain my life and times to you, and despair of doing so with accuracy or grace, and rise instead—the puppy lifts his brown-and-white head—to stroll into what was once Elaine's room, where I part her curtains. The puppy's nails click across the floor and soon his little muzzle also parts the curtains. The lawn, restored in some measure to its antediluvian borders, slopes toward a heaving sidewalk; and the sidewalk yields to a whitish street with crooked tar lines. The puppy, no longer quarantined, whines. But I know from experience that those lines lead nowhere, and perhaps that is just as well, as I am inclined to return to my desk and resume, to his long-eared disappointment, our story.

Albert had finished speaking. "What do you think this means?" he asked.

"I never had a dream like that."

"Of course not," he said. "I would do better to share this dream with my father, my brothers and my sister."

"If I were you—"

"What a strange thought!" he said crisply. "Never mind. Dreams are for those who can decipher them. Whom do you seek?"

"A special friend."

"You are a strange and irritating boy," he said. "Even for a White you are scrawny. And your eyes are too large and very ugly. Perhaps you suffer in your lymph system. Can you walk by yourself? I would like to find out about you and this friend. But the elders are waiting, as you can hear."

A loud gong had indeed begun to sound; closing my fingers around the shell, I could make out the gong's rhythmic message: *GONG GONG . . . COME YE COME YE . . . GONG GONG GONG . . .* Above the whistle and click and whir of insects, the gong was summoning the titled men of the eight villages. *GONG GONG . . .* A single yellow light flared against the dimming sky. This light was followed by another, and another; a slow procession of lights, glowing ever brighter, drew on; then the first was transformed, as it were, into a torch-bearing man traveling a path that wound behind an *obi.*

Albert jumped off his stool.

"I have been instructed to carry you if necessary," he said.

"I can walk just fine," I assured him, hurrying somewhat unsteadily after him and down the wide sandy path. Another *obi* stretched across one end of a large swept yard. This *obi* had two entrances: the first, like a clay tunnel leading into the forest; and the second, longer and wider, facing the yard itself. We crossed to where an elderly man stood surrounded by men also bearing torches. A lone tree stretched out an imperious limb from which hung a heavy gong. The elderly man adjusted the shoulder strap of his wide cloth garment and struck a last blow to the gong's sheen. *COME YE COME YE . . .*

I touched the innermost ridges of shell and knew also the name of the tree: *uzulu,* or tamarind. Was it this tree that had saved me, or another? How beautiful its leaves against the purplish sky!

From out of the bushes—or so it seemed—still more men emerged. One by one they walked across the sandy ground, until the last had joined what was now a brightly illumined half-circle. Each man wore a wide cloth garment tied at one shoulder, and by the torches' light I saw the glint of small machetes.

"Greetings to my brothers and kinsmen," the elder said. "I have called another meeting and welcome you to partake with me of this kola. *Kwenu Uluzu!*"

"*Kwenu Uluzu! Uluzu kwenu!*" sang a chorus of voices.

The elder passed a large reddish nut—I thought it was a nut—to another man, thinner and frailer than he. In the torch-lit dusk, the first man's skin shone the color of burnt clay. He knelt and picked up a large white chalk, then drew with it on his toe. What was he doing? He passed the chalk to the second elder, who also painted his foot but declined politely to crack the nut. Thereupon the first elder insisted, until the second lifted his machete and smashed it. He ate carefully from its shards, and handed on the rest to his host, who passed a shard to each guest in the circle.

Beneath the long open thatch of the *obi*, I noticed the shining eyes of many dark crouching figures—women! They were staring at me. I felt an indescribable confusion of sentiment; I was of them and not of them. I willed myself not to stare at their exposed bosoms and something else—an aura of superstition or an essence of female. I remembered Anne Hathaway's embrace and the purple stain I had left in her bedsheets. Had one of these women rescued me from the tree's branches? Mightn't she or another understand, through some gesture universal to females, that I belonged with them? I didn't want to sit under an *obi* roof while men made decisions! I told myself that such women were bound to stare at a strange English boy, and straightening my shoulders, turned my attention to the words of the elders.

"I, God-Delivers, greet the villages of Uluzu," said the first man. "In a moment official proceedings will begin and then only a man who has taken a title may address the eight villages. For now—"

"Why have you called us?" asked the second abruptly.

"Uncle—" began Albert.

"Official proceedings," said the first man, holding up his hand quickly, "have just begun.

"My heart," he went on, "is heavy. A responsibility has fallen upon

us. The Great Ulu would not have dropped it without cause. We have
not honored him sufficiently since the coming of the English with their
guns and their religion. Their guns we understand well enough, their
religion less well. Things are really falling apart around here. That is
why we have chosen since my grandfather's time to send among them a
child of our own, and why we have sent this son of my brother Blinded-
by-God, this Albert, and not as some would have others believe because
of his truly insufferable character. Still we have many questions. How
can a man speak such gibberish as the White priest speaks—"

I saw Albert tensing.

"—and wield such mortal medicine? God-Remembers's first boy
had the swelling disease but he went to the White man's hospital and
did not die. His brother Talks-to-God's wife carried twins into the forest and when the medicine man came the bodies were gone. There is
much to be understood here by later generations, but much also to be
forgotten. This White boy," he said, pointing beyond Albert at me,
"must be killed and buried in a remote place or returned instantly. We
have sent a messenger to those English over the Path-That-Leads-to-
There."

Sent a messenger!

My mind began to race. If the English were to interrogate me? I had
no doubt (having seen with my own eyes the weathered skulls atop
London Bridge) that the English would extract from me what the Igbo
had left untouched—namely, that I was no lost missionary's son but an
American girl withholding priceless information about the future.
What then? How might that future be affected? I hated to conjecture!
You can't change history, S-Man often repeated, as if quoting someone,
but what if we *were* history? What if, so to speak, we had always been
visiting—no, always visited—but my grammar, it seemed, was not up
to describing our paradoxical share in human events. I cursed my education, which had left me not knowing, for instance, precisely where the
Igbo stood on the matter of Jews. Perhaps, given their resentment of the

English, I might do better to "confess" my "true" identity! If only I weren't a girl!

Meanwhile several elders had begun more informally to converse. The man who had broken the kola spat between his hands and rubbed them on his thighs. Shifting his stiff cloth garment, he nodded around the circle, which quieted. The women's faces gleamed and a gust of wind made their torches flicker and smoke. Leaves rustled in the dark trees. The gong shivered. I remembered the thunderstorm during which I had first met S-Man (perhaps the *S* stood for "soon"?) and looked hopefully around. Another circle, formed of men's shadows as they darkened the grasses, obscured and died out. The moon sailed into view and those shadows were reborn.

"Uzulezu, kwenu!" said the man who had broken the kola.

"Kwenu, Uzulezu!" answered the others. "Speak, Talks-to-God!"

"My friend God-Delivers speaks truth. We know that much of what he tells us does come to pass. Who does not listen to the alligator when his eggs are set to hatch? We all remember what happened to the village that killed a White man. Of course we would not have that disaster befall us. The English have been sent for. The Oracle has ordained this. But let us now hear what Albert has to say. Remember that Blinded-by-God's fourth son can speak to this English in his own tongue. That is why we have sent for Albert in spite of his character."

"It is not customary for a male who has not taken a title to lecture his elders," said God-Delivers abruptly. "How do you know what language the white-skinned creature speaks? He has yet to open his mouth."

"It is not Igbo for a boy to fall from the sky," said Talks-to-God. "And you can see by his manner of dress and thinness of lip that he is an English."

"Or a leper," murmured someone, which in Igbo was a clever pun, so that everyone laughed and I tried not to show that I understood.

"It is not customary," repeated God-Delivers.

Tunneling

"Let Albert step forward nonetheless," said Talks-to-God, smiling. "Is it not said, 'When the harmattan blows, even a wise man is tempted by the kites of his youth'?"

God-Delivers motioned ceremoniously for Albert to step forward. Albert stepped forward.

"If I may," he said, looking around, "I will tell all that I know so that the elders in their wisdom can decide for the eight villages what is best. However, I must tell you that I have dreamed a dream . . ."

The women's whispering rose once more. The moon slid behind a cloud swell only to reappear on the other side. The tamarinds stood like guardians against the bluish sky. If help were to come, it would come from up there; but no. I stood below, earthbound, and obliged to keep my wits about me.

"A dream can reveal much," admitted God-Delivers.

"A dream is like a hot soup," said Talks-to-God.

"A dream is like a pregnant wife," said a third man.

"Doesn't-Believe-in-God speaks truth," said God-Delivers and Talks-to-God together. "What was this dream? Tell us now."

"I dreamed," said Albert, closing his eyes and beginning to sway from side to side, "that—"

His eyes shot open and, while one hand felt his forehead as if for fever, the other swept the air.

"God-Delivers, Talks-to-God, God-Remembers, Reads-God's-Lips, Doesn't-Believe-in-God and God-Awakens, heed me! I dreamed that my brothers and I were binding palm leaves and that my leaves towered over theirs and their leaves bowed down to mine. I dreamed also that the new moon came and at the Festival of the Yam even the priest of Ulu, Sing-God's-Praises, bowed down. My father, my mother, my brothers, Tom, Dick, George and Reginald and also my sister, Gladys, bowed down and then the moon and the stars came out. What's more, when the harmattan blew, the sound of my name could be heard in its howl and the dust itself was inscribed with letters: *A-L-B-E—*"

"Maybe they meant someone else," suggested a tall young man. He was standing near God-Delivers, who glowered.

"I think I have read a dream like this somewhere," whispered another young man behind them.

"The queen's lover was also an Albert," whispered the first.

"Inscribed," said Albert more loudly, "with letters that spell out the name of my mother too."

"Aah," whispered the first young man. "That is a different story."

"This I have never heard anywhere," whispered the second.

"As I was saying," said Albert, "the dust itself was inscribed, etcetera. And this is what baffles me truly, O son of my father's father—"

He bowed deeply and looked around the circle. I had the impression that in spite of the gravity of our situation, he was enjoying himself.

"The moon and the stars were also bowing down. This is difficult to explain, although I have found a book in the library at Umuahia. This book is a very small and powerful book in spite of its execrable lack of punctuation. I was telling, however, about stars. As if they perform a kind of dance in my honor, they go like this—"

But a murmur had once again arisen among the women and this time, although God-Delivers turned to hush them, it didn't die away. God-Delivers gestured severely at Albert. Albert paused in mid-sentence. A child laughed and clapped his hands. In unison the elders edged away, moving slowly at first and then more rapidly across the dark field, where they formed a huddle. "Uh-oh," whispered a woman. "I would feel sorry for him," whispered another, "if he weren't so ugly." She meant me, I realized. Things didn't seem to be going well. I considered running away and remembered the slim machetes. I might make it as far as the jungle—but then what? Which was worse, the fate I might suffer in the hands of the Igbo, or the English, or in the jungle itself?

"We have decided what to do with this English," said the elders, returning with surprising speed across the brushed yard.

Tunneling

God-Delivers stepped forward and raised his hand.

"Excuse me, Albert," I whispered urgently. "Do you think you could ask them where they stand on the question of the Jews?"

"What does he say?" asked God-Delivers.

"He asks, Uncle, where the elders stand on the Jews."

"The Igbo are the Jews of Nigeria," said God-Delivers proudly. "That is, we are the Christian Jews of Nigeria. At least some of us are. You two are more like goyim."

"Goyim?"

"Excuse me—"

"We will send Albert with this young boy to the English," God-Delivers said rapidly (and somewhat thunderously), "but we will send them along the Path-That-Doesn't-Really-Go-There-After-All."

"The Path-That-Doesn't-Really-Go-There-After-All!" cried Albert.

"Excuse me, please—" I said.

"O son of my father's son, you question the wisdom of the elders?" asked God-Delivers.

"No," said Albert. "Of course not. I just wondered if I could perhaps send word—"

"As it happens, you two will leave at daybreak. Tonight you pass in my compound. Your father-my-brother will in due course be informed of the elders' decision."

"In due course," said Albert. "Yes. I see."

"My brothers in Ulu," said God-Delivers. "When the tortoise doesn't speak, the snake doesn't ask why. I salute you."

"*Kwenu Uluzelu! Uluzelu kwenu!*" cried the men, vanishing into the brush.

"Albert," I said. "Are you sure this is the way?"

"Indubitably."

Still carrying his satchel, he glanced behind at the sand path, bordered like all carefully tended Igbo paths by leaves and tiny sticks. We had walked a similar path the night before, from the meeting place to the outskirts of Albert's uncle's compound. Thus I had learned that the leafy border would guide my feet through darkness. Now we had been traveling the Path-That-Doesn't-Really-Go-There-After-All for some hours and the sand had grown hotter and, as the path narrowed, the terrain had begun to shift. A by-now-familiar buzzing filled the air, and the tamarinds—I felt rather sorry to see them go—had conceded some argument to the mangroves, whose corky arms jutted out. A mosquito stung my arm; another and still another my swelling face. In the middle distance a wide brown river flowed. From time to time as the ground rose, we glimpsed those brown waters but never seemed actually to draw near. The trees grew rougher in appearance, their limbs knotted, their roots grasping more greedily at the hot uneven soil. The path had narrowed to a wavy line. I watched Albert's face as he paused on the verge of uncharted territory; why wasn't he frightened?

Entering Albert's uncle's compound, I had followed Albert to a low-thatched mud hut, the domain of his uncle's fourth wife. Albert, deeply upset by the elders' decision, had introduced me summarily. The woman—she had the tiniest build I have ever seen, and her palms and soles were the color of dust—instructed him to instruct me to squat on a corner mat. I did so, thinking perhaps to rest. Was I personally acquainted with Mr. Joseph Conrad? Albert wanted, however, to know. Was Mr. Conrad as truly execrable in life as in art? I frowned, trying to remember what I could about that author. I didn't think he was still alive in my time, but had he perhaps been alive in some other time I had visited? Rachel Fish would have known. Rachel Fish would have told him. The thought of her greater acumen, her generally greater worthiness, oppressed me, and then I felt the relief we feel sometimes in sheer distance from the ones we love.

The tiny woman spoke in a low voice. Her eldest child approached with a plate of yam *foo-foo* and another clay water bowl. This time I ate and drank greedily. Feigning inability to converse in her tongue, I asked

Albert to thank his aunt for the food and above all for having saved me. Albert's spirits lifted when he saw how impressed was his father's brother's fourth wife by our communication. He generously repeated his dream with further embellishments. The evening wore on as stars swayed, the moon danced and so on. Finally his aunt motioned for me to lie down. I knelt in ceremonious, if awkward, thanks; she laughed, tiny breasts swaying, and told Albert to inquire if something was wrong.

I crawled to my sleeping mat. As soon as I had lain down, a lone mosquito began to whine about my ears. I shifted, swatted, buried my head; sitting up, I caught the gleam of the woman's eyes and of her children's. Could they see in the dark? I lay down amid renewed whining and the *whir-whir* of crickets. That night I slept fitfully, unused to such company and the close air of the *obi* and apprehending the journey down a path whose name, I assured myself as the sun rose, had no doubt a metaphoric sense.

Now I stood with Albert at the end of the Path-That-Doesn't-Really-Go-There-After-All, fearing some more literal interpretation. The sky stretched dizzyingly vast. The earth rose hillocky or sank into fetid puddles. There was no egress to the river that I could see.

"Do you think we should turn around?"

"The elders have sent us for a purpose. Is it not said, 'A man who does not trust to his chi is like the sow who will not suckle her young'?"

A shiver moved like a giant snake through preponderant grasses.

We walked on, the sun hammering our pates. Soon my cheeks, my forehead, my lips began not only to itch but to burn. My mouth felt strange. I thought about the swimming pool in New Jersey and the swamp and other wet things. Once at the river, Albert had said, we could drink our fill. For now we must make do with what water we had. We would beat a path around the swamp, which was filled, he said, with execrable creatures. We would climb toward a higher slope and hope that it would descend eventually toward the river, where we might find transportation north and east. It was Albert's hope that once we had reached Umuahia, a hitherto uncharted river city, his father could be contacted and I returned to the English. I nodded, not telling him that I held very different (if uncertain) views as to what constituted rescue!

"Are you quite sure you know the way?"

"What does it matter? My chi is very strong. For this reason I have been chosen among the boys of our village to attend University College in Ibadan after I have completed my studies in Umuahia. No doubt you fell from the sky for some purpose. There is nothing to fear at this time."

"Of course," I said. "Hey. What's that?"

In the yellow grass before us lay what looked like a pile of bones, stripped by the elements of moisture and color. Instinctively I touched Albert's arm.

"That is what happens when someone's chi is not strong," he said.

"What happens?"

"Lion," he said briefly.

Are you wondering where S-Man has been all this time? On our way to Africa, as you will recall, we had been ambushed. This time S-Man couldn't save me because he was exposed through the machinations of Assemblage and also Mr. Stick (or so I believe) to a meteor shower of ultraviolet spectrum Mother Planet rocks. This form of meteor effected in S-Man each time a significant if temporary change. Once it had turned him into a woman and another time it had rendered his S-breath more flammable than igniter fluid. Still another time it had caused his beard to grow so profusely that his secret identity became impracticable for many hair-raising (no pun intended) weeks. On this new occasion S-Man had been instantly stripped of his powers, with the exception of S-hearing. As UVMP meteorites soared past, I had heard him cry out and peripherally saw him tumble as did I an instant later through a hole in the time tunnel into the blue-black night sky, and he would certainly have died moments later had he not landed by some stroke of luck ("My chi," he would later call it) on a cargo block being lowered from an airplane's hold.

Needless to say, his first thought, upon jumping down onto the tarmac, was to ascertain my whereabouts; but within moments he was swept up again in the tumultuous tide of human history. This was on August 17, 1967, at Enugu Airport in the self-declared and sovereign state of Biafra.

"Ouch," he said, lifting his head.

For a while that afternoon, after coming upon those bones, Albert and I didn't speak. Occasionally, glimpsing the river, we would turn toward it only to find ourselves mired once again in the mangrove swamp. Then we would veer off to the east—I had kept track of the sun's trajectory from east to west—onto firmer ground. Once I stopped to drink from the little gourd that Albert's aunt had supplied me. (I would have been pleased by her attentiveness, had she not seemed saddened by our travel plans.) The air danced beneath a hot white sky. The tall grasses made walking difficult and giant creepers sprang up to trip us. Or rather, to trip me in my thick-soled shoes; Albert walked barefoot, satchel slapping his thigh as he sang—he had been singing with gusto ever since we had come upon the bones. I thought with sudden sympathy of his uncle. Then I began to wonder whose bones we had seen and how long ago the lion had passed that way, and what lions thought of swamps, and whether they had any preference in human beings, or if most people tasted the same. My legs felt heavy and my stomach growled. In the compound we had breakfasted at dawn on more *foo-foo* and a kind of bean paste that stuck to my palate; the children had laughed as I tried to swallow. I tried to swallow now. I stooped to take a pebble from my shoe. The pebble had been bothering me for some time, I realized. What's more, the landscape looked familiar. Were we traveling in circles? To our right, tamarinds reappeared; to the left, a single mangrove stood against the horizon. Birds screeched and chattered and hooted; a bright-headed toucan poked furiously at the roots of a flowering bush; overhead, a giant bird circled. The words of Albert's song, to which I had begun to listen, added to my malaise:

> *This is my body, take of it and eat;*
> *This is my blood, take of it and drink;*
> *Because I am life and I am love*
> *O Lord carry me away in your lo-ove—*

"Hey!" I said, hurrying. "Wait for me!"

"For an *ogbanje* you are more than slow," said Albert. "Is it the redness of your face that distresses you? In Umuahia I will see that you receive proper medical care. For now you must exert yourself appropriately."

Irked and more uncomfortable than ever, I trudged on behind Albert. Beads of sweat dripped into his now-soggy collar. I was drenched myself, and insisted on stopping to drink.

"You have forgotten how to fly home," he said, when I had lifted the gourd from my lips and held it out. He shook his head, patting his own supply. "I understand. You have remained too long on this earth, and now you will have to wait a generation like the rest of us. No doubt the doctors in Umuahia will know how to ease your discomfort."

Forgotten how to fly home! If only he knew how close to the truth he was! Tears threatened to blur my vision and I shook my head fiercely, and at that moment we heard a low fauvish growl.

"Run!" I shouted; but Albert was racing toward the mangrove on the edge of the swamp. The ground became suddenly treacherous; once I slipped and heard the animal's growl. "This way!" shouted Albert. He had reached the first branch and was swinging himself up. I scrambled after, my breath coming in shallow bursts. "Hurry!" said Albert. I staggered across the mudflats and, holding tight to his outstretched hand, hauled myself onto the branch, which swayed.

"Holy cow," I gasped.

"Not cow," whispered Albert. "Look."

A lion, or rather a lioness, had stalked into full view. Her haunches were incredibly thin, and her triangular face as she gazed at us seemed both knowledgeable and devoid of—of what? Of something that I associate to this day with humanity, perhaps; something, that is, that might have spared us.

A high whine sounded in the invisible distance. Rising to his feet and stamping dust off his white boots, S-Man lifted his head and aimed his S-vision—no such luck! "Great Mother," he whispered, remembering the violet glow. He went through the inventory of his other powers: stared hard at the ground, which refused to heat, and breathed in the hot dry air, which refused to enter his lungs more than moderately. "By the Blasted Deserts of the Mother Planet," he said aloud, using the strong curse he reserved for such moments. Cautiously he tuned his ears to the world around him. They at least still worked! From some hundreds of miles away he overheard the first proud crow of a Ghanaian rooster. He heard the crackle of a Senegalese leaf. He heard the whistle and chatter of several Dahomean titmice. . . . What about his strength, then? Never a man to shirk action, he smacked his fist hard into the airplane's cold wing.

"Ouch," he said for the second time that day.

"*Ewuu,*" someone giggled.

S-Man wheeled and saw the group of shiny-faced boys, each holding aloft an oil torch.

He had arrived in Biafra, all right.

The boys had once been chosen (he knew) for physical strength. Their job, which was to illuminate the dark runway precisely one minute before a friendly cargo plane landed, required strength. Even so, he recognized the first tinges of the gold-reddish hair color symptomatic of kwashiorkor, or protein starvation. It would not be long before these boys, like so many before them, relinquished their torches.

They fled en masse toward the hangar.

S-Man assumed that the boys were frightened by his arrival, then realized that the whine he had been hearing for some time had grown loud enough for human hearing. The door to the hold opened. A man appeared; he held white sheaths that scattered as he leaped straight at S-Man and rolled him over and over beneath the wing. Schrapnel pelted the ground and *pang!* bounced off the metal canopy. Small dust clouds billowed around the writhing figures. *Ping pang!* S-Man struggled to free himself. His assailant was smaller but had the advantage of surprise, and his arms around S-Man's chest tightened. In the flare of an explosion the visitor could see his assailant's grimace; the two lay beneath the wing, staring into each other's eyes as the mortar fire retreated. S-Man felt the arms around his chest relinquishing their hold. He lay back, panting. Something unfamiliar trickled down his cheek. Sweat? *Blood?*

"I beg your pardon," the man said, sitting up.

Warily, clearing his throat, S-Man did the same.

On the far side of the airfield, beyond the distant trees, the fighter-bomber whined on. The man's papers lay here, there; one fluttered beneath the tarpaulin and he hurried to retrieve it. S-Man bent also to gather another sheath, which he wiped clean with his fingers.

"These fighters cultivate dust," the other said, accepting the page. "Not a man's crop. I must apologize again for retaining you. You would have died if I had let you walk further. But perhaps you hoped in this manner to meet Death?"

S-Man shook his head.

Tunneling

The man held out his hand; slowly, S-Man extended his own. He wished, without quite knowing why, that he had thought to change the fibers of his uniform before losing the power to do so.

"My name is Christopher Okigbo," the man said.

"Ogbanje," said Albert severely.

We were still sitting in the branches of the mangrove tree. The sun was a low red ball. First we had felt too hot; then, allowing ourselves to drink a trickle from time to time, too thirsty; and thirstier still when the lioness, leaping and causing me to drop my gourd, carried it off between her sharp-toothed jaws. Even now she lay pawing at its crumpled remains.

"I said I was sorry."

Albert shrugged. "You talk like a girl. I execrate not the loss of the gourd but your lack of faith. Have I not explained that my chi is strong? Would I have been given such a dream only to end in a lion's belly? Had She-Lion been hungry she would have feasted before we ran. We have only to wait until she tires of playing. Of course, if it were to rain—"

The sky, it occurred to me, had grown darker.

"What if it did? We would have water, wouldn't we? We could collect it in a leaf or something," I went on eagerly, "or in your gourd."

Albert shrugged. "There is a saying among us, 'When python sleeps in the mangrove, then is not the time to pray for rain.'" He pointed into the tree's branches; following their intricate gnarled lines, I saw the thick coils and triangular hooded head of something I had seen only in zoos.

"What's that?" I gasped, but I knew.

"Poor *ogbanje*," he said. "I begin to grow fond in spite of your unappetizing appearance and your shameful cowardice."

"Of course," he added, "you cannot help your nature. I will now share my interesting thoughts. Perhaps my chi does not belong only to me. The meaning of the dream is perhaps that I have been chosen to help my people. It has been thought that I might become a doctor or a priest. Now I think that I will be given another mission entirely. I cannot say more at this time. I know I will be married someday to an educated Christian woman who will understand all that I try in vain to explain to you, *ogbanje*." His eyes narrowed and he struck his palm so that the branch swayed. "The dream means more. The dream means also that many unforetold and wonderful things will happen to my people, and to the other peoples who will comprise the sovereign state of Nigeria. We are going to be united. We are going to be one country under God with a lot of electricity. You and your kind will be gone by then and we will learn to care for ourselves. We are not weaklings but people who have been robbed of strength. In my village I never thought about these things but in Umuahia at the government college certain individuals brought this and other matters to my attention. I confess also that when I first went there I admired very much your Mr. Joseph Conrad. This is because when I was a child I did not know the difference between storytelling and lies. I am almost a man now. The new era comes fast upon us. We will forget you. You and I are stranded in this tree but history journeys on. If I were you, *ogbanje*, I would remember how to go home—"

"Albert," I hissed. "Don't you think you should lower your voice?"

"There is an old saying—" he said.

At that moment, a largish raindrop splashed my forehead.

"You are an American. Red Cross, I suppose."

"Yes," said S-Man, who never lied but sometimes allowed a linguistic confusion to reign. Wasn't it true, after a fashion, that he was American? The man seemed to await further explanation; S-Man would have to furnish a name, an alias, an identity. He riffled his whitish cape.

"I'm Kant. Immanuel Kant," he said impetuously, then added, "No relation to the philosopher."

Tunneling

"You Americans have such a pronounced sense of fashion," Okigbo said vaguely. "The other Red Cross less so. Their lorry left several hours ago. I was delayed because of this manuscript, which has still to be delivered. Now I drive into Enugu City. Perhaps, Mr. Kant, I might give you a lift?"

"Yes," said S-Man. "I would very much appreciate a ride into Enugu. Can you tell me—"

S-Man had been about to ask the date, and decided instead to tune his one remaining power to the nearest radio band, Radio Nigeria. *"Rebel forces have been defeated. . . . The valorous Nigerian army has advanced several hundred miles in the direction of Nsukka . . . many hundreds of rebel soldiers slain on the road from Benin. . . ."* Meanwhile the poet had led him toward the hangar and the few parked cars; halting at an old Cadillac with rusted hubcaps and a crumpled side door, he motioned for S-Man to climb in. S-Man slid across the seat (on a bundle of clothes in the rear lay, he saw, a well-used clarinet) and the poet followed, slamming the door hard until it stuck. Soon he had sent the Cadillac in a wide jerky arc toward the exit. S-Man touched his cheek and stared at his fingertips; the blood was coagulated but unmistakable. "Mother meteorites," he muttered. "Now what?"

The poet glanced at him.

"Are you also a musician?" S-Man asked aloud. Okigbo slammed the accelerator; the engine sputtered and roared as he raced his car up the entrance ramp and onto a two-lane highway. The highway was thick with vehicles. S-Man clung instinctively to the rattling door handle. The wind blew hot against his temples. He had picked up the date with his remarkable hearing: *17 August 1967. This is the newly appointed Voice of Nigeria. . . .* He had arrived a day later than intended! Was there time? He groped aurally, as it were, through tumultuous streets of that city toward dawn, past still-loud clubs filled with "night fighters" and "area boys" toward the little zinc house on the quiet avenue. He heard the sounds of a woman gently breathing, and of straw faintly rustling, and of two children sleeping. From the sounds of things the woman was exhausted, the children very young and about to awaken.

"Do it," he whispered. "Wake up!"

Okigbo glanced at him again and S-Man, realizing that he was arousing suspicion, repeated his question.

"Yes," Okigbo said. "I am a musician of sorts."

"But you mentioned a manuscript," said S-Man, politely.

"Musician, poet, soldier—in wartime," said Okigbo, "we are many things. In peacetime too. I manage something called the Citadel Press, at home and abroad." He shifted gears, grimacing. "Shall I tell you about our work? I mean in addition to the wonderful things happening at the University of Nigeria, Nsukka. A young writer in London has just sent us a most interesting manuscript. It is a children's story. The Citadel Press will publish children's stories to ensure our African children a healthy reading life! This particular story has been through many revisions. At first it featured a dog who learns through various forms of suffering to obey his masters. We have, however, little interest in dogs who obey their masters. For this and other reasons we have collaborated with the author, an Igbo man studying at the University of London, to create a more interesting version. We call it *How the Leopard Got Its*—"

But whatever the poet was about to say, he didn't, because, opening his window and waving, he swerved so rapidly into the next lane that his bumper grazed the fenders of a Chevy. S-Man cried out. A Klaxon sounded. "Mother of Idoto," the poet shouted, pointing at a large van that careened from behind them into the lane they had just left.

"I see," S-Man shouted above the wind through the open window. "I was mistaken. I thought this was a two-way highway!"

"It is."

At that moment another fighter-bomber zoomed through the sky and from both lanes cars began rushing toward the verge, where they released their passengers to flee into the bushes; after a long minute S-Man's host pulled over. Pebbles flew. "Hurry!" Okigbo cried, leaping out his door and dragging S-Man once more after him. "Hurry!" he cried, racing down a steep embankment and then, with a sudden cry of "Clarinet!" bounding back up the embankment and into the car and waving the instrument over his head as he tripped and fell. S-Man by this time had hurled himself into the bushes while tuning his hearing to the cockpit of the airplane overhead, where the pilot, a Hausa man, was conversing in rapid English with his Yoruban copilot. Again that name, Nsukka . . . then the thunder of exploding bombs and the cries of men and women drowned out their words and S-Man was lunging to drag Okigbo, swaying upright with the clarinet, down into the bushes. Indeed, it wasn't until the plane had dipped once again behind the trees that S-Man could make out the pilots' dialogue, and by that time the shouts had turned to wails and the travelers, reemerging, had gathered around a man stretched prone.

"My wife, my children," the man said dazedly.

He said it again and again as if the words were not understood: "My wife, my children," in that order. His crumpled vehicle lay like a gaping wound out of which spilled like larvae—or not at all like larvae. The truth is that no comparison will do here. Nor was I there to witness this tragedy but only heard of it from my alien chaperone. The man had lost his thirty-year-old wife and their three children: two girls and a boy. How S-Man must have regretted his super powers! How he must have missed above all the power of flight! He had flown here to prevent a similar catastrophe: the death of a woman and her children. The task had seemed simple enough; he had only to get her and her children out of their house (it was a zinc house) before a wayward bomb exploded . . . and now his powers, with the exception of hearing, had been denied him!

At Okigbo's suggestion, poet and alien climbed into their vehicle and resumed their trip. S-Man scouted the area with his hearing; the bombers had flown eastward. Around him people were suffering and he couldn't think how to help them. He feared not failure, so much as the knowledge of failure; that he might overhear the death throes in that zinc house and still not be able to help.

Okigbo reached behind to pat the clarinet on its seat.

"Death used to be a much more personal affair," he said. "Today we are enlightened; we share it with everyone. I thank you for returning the life I gave you. I need it a little while longer. You see, we are going to start a creative writing program at the University of Nigeria at Nsukka. It is the most beautiful university in Nigeria and one of which we are especially proud. The creative writing program will attract writers from all over Africa. It will be very wonderful indeed."

"You're welcome," said S-Man, exhaling a rather human breath.

"In any event," Albert said serenely, "the rain has eventually to stop."

"What do you mean, 'eventually'?"

"Oh," he said. "About four months."

I let my breath out slowly.

"Albert, I am going to tell you something."

"By all means," he said.

We had been sitting in the mangrove tree for hours, and although the lioness had departed, the python had not. Every now and then a few raindrops fell. The python would lift its triangular head and blink. The sun was going to set soon enough; and then what? The more I thought about it, the less I wanted to spend a night in a mangrove tree, surrounded on one side by a dangerous snake and on the other by an unbearable intellectual prig of a boy. For some reason I thought of the one time in my life I had actually kissed a boy—Colin Duffy, the class dunce, in the dreaded underpass!—and that thought only added to my distress.

"You are not going to find the path to Umuahia this way," I found myself saying. "And I can tell you something else. They sent us this way because they don't like you."

"That's not true."

"It is true. And—I don't like you either."

"That is of minimal importance," he said quickly, but he ducked his head.

Not at all contrite, I stared past him at the surrounding vista. The rain and the end of daylight made everything different. The mangroves in the distance seemed menacing, the swamp an angry pool into which droplets shattered. The python lifted her head. I knew she could kill us whenever she chose; and yet I no longer feared her, nor Albert's learning my gender, nor S-Man's disappearance, nor anything. I think if my father had stood beneath the mangrove just then, and ordered me to climb down upon pain of his disapproval, I wouldn't have done so.

"And what's more," I said, "it's that stupid dream of yours that got us into this trouble. Didn't I tell you not to tell anyone?"

"You understand nothing."

"They sent us here to die."

"Nonsense. And I must do what is best for my people."

"Nothing is going to happen the way you think it is."

Albert closed his eyes. His lips were moving. I wondered if he was trying perhaps to cast some sort of African spell on me.

"Albert," I asked finally, "what are you doing?"

"I am forgetting you," he said. He opened one eye, saw me staring and shut it again.

"Well, I'm getting out of here," I said, rattling the branch we shared.

"Sorry, I have forgotten you."

I rattled the branch again. The python raised her strange head. I stopped rattling. Even so the python swayed from side to side. The rain seemed to increase; the python slithered slowly, very slowly, down the trunk. Her eyes blinked. She stopped a few feet above us and lowered her head. Either of us could have raised a hand to touch her coils.

"I'm sorry," I whispered after a long while.

"Oh," whispered Albert. "Is there someone here? I thought I was alone."

*   *   *

S-Man had just left Okigbo's car. It had taken some doing to convince the poet that he didn't owe the newcomer a meal and a bed. "Let me at least take you to the other Red Cross, Mr. Kant," he had called, and seemed angry when S-Man waved him on. Now S-Man stood deliberating on a broad avenue. Perhaps he ought to have accepted the poet's offer. The cement buildings on either border of the dusty street were intact but deserted. A cistern lay clumsily on its side. In one hand S-Man held a torn map of the city, in the other a slip of paper with a smudged address. According to the map, he should have found himself near a post office. Was this it? A formidable edifice stood atop a steep hill. The edifice was built after a certain British colonial style, which made the silence eerier; clearly the conquerors had vanished. Even the rightful inhabitants of the city, he knew, had taken to transacting business on its outskirts after nightfall. A kind of cart lay useless, empty sockets glaring where wheels had spun. Here and there a bomb had torn a jagged hole in an exterior wall. A child slumped on the back of its father, who wailed. As father and child passed, S-Man saw that the child was a boy and that he was dead. Turning his face, S-Man saw a street sign on the ground. The sign said OKPARA AVENUE. He followed that avenue blindly until he arrived at a low cement building. Most of the buildings here were intact. The streambed was dry. The air whistled or seemed to whistle. S-Man allowed his hearing to pick up sounds and then, sickened, tuned them out. He was sweating and his sweat smelled all too human. He had reached Garden Avenue, which extended into the northern reaches of the city, where he would find, he knew, Park Lane and the little zinc house.

At an intersection he paused; there should have been no market here, but one was being set up. Traders, women with brightly colored turbans, were going about their business as they pointedly ignored the sky. In peacetime, he knew, their voices would have been much louder. He also knew that these women would have sold all manner of goods in the open market near the railroad station, from cassava to juicy tomatoes to the great sacks of rice that could sustain whole families during the dry season. In peacetime Enugu was a sober hillocky city of five hundred thousand hardworking people. Now the traders displayed only a few sacks of grain in the corner of this makeshift marketplace and stacked other merchandise—a few leather purses, woven blankets, sets of knives—in the shelter of a clearly temporary mud wall. As S-Man stood there the women moved quietly into a group, their voices dropping; a child plucked at S-Man's cape and he smiled until that child was joined by another and another. Soon he was surrounded by a dozen children holding out thin hands and calling something like *gari.* *"Gari, gari."* S-Man shook his head; the children's hands held tight; he swung the cape free, a pitifully easy task, and ran suddenly away from the market toward what he hoped was the extension of Okapa Avenue and the junction there. It was his intention to continue north and east until he had reached Park Lane, where the zinc house, he hoped, was still standing. But the crossroad had disappeared. In its place sprawled great slabs of concrete and one forlorn overpass. The city was for the most part intact but this stretch of highway had been bombed. Beneath the overpass several families seemed to be living in the crudest conditions. Eyes dulled, they watched as S-Man ran past in his white-and-red uniform. A child—so many children—lay panting amid torn cardboard. S-Man cursed the fate that had deprived him of his powers, and he marveled at the irony of destiny, which had ordained that even so deprived, he would possess more strength than those around him, because they would be starving. Consulting the sun—it shone ten o'clock in the morning—he began to run faster and still faster. The event that he had come to obfuscate was to take place within minutes. Already his hearing could detect the whine of another fighter-bomber and low cries of traders and children. They were packing up and heading for shelter. He sorted other sounds of the city, its medley of voices and motions and considerations. He heard silences. He heard water meandering through a conduit and a woman's voice wearily singing to an infant. The woman went on singing, then stopped. S-Man was running at full speed now, past the *buka* and through a crowd of area boys, weary from their night on the prowl, who made as if to accost him and let him pass with an admonishment: *"I go chop—"* *"He no hear Igbo,"* someone snorted. *"O-ibo!"* a woman cried. "You want night fighters?" But it was daytime and he was running as hard and as fast as he could now, his cape stirring in the bit of wind and his boots impervious to the dust they roused in miniature fighter-bomber pattern.

In times of famine, such as these, a woman had to rise early to find *foo-foo* and *gari,* and so Clara had done, washing with water from a jug and dressing in her market dress. It was today that Chinua was to return home. She stood in the doorway, her hand on her belly, still somewhat swollen since the child she had lost on the ship. The voyage was terrible. They had left Lagos hurriedly to the sounds of their neighbors' strange laughter and only after the ship had left port did she notice the palm kernels it carried. The kernels added to the general lack of hygiene and also the odor had been most disagreeable in her sensitive nostrils. Whenever pregnant she smelled with such acuteness that excessive cleansing grew necessary. On the ship this was not a possibility and she had suffered stomach upsets, as had other passengers who had not been with child. She had forced herself to eat the food cooked in a drum of filthy appearance and stirred with a big stick even filthier in appearance. At night they slept on planks. Still she had counted herself lucky when she had heard stories of other women who had experienced rape and the marauding and killing of loved ones. Now she thought of Chinua and how he would be the last to leave Lagos, the last to abandon his dream of a united Nigeria. One thing in particular disturbed her: did he know that she had lost the child? He was not like some Igbo men who would blame the woman when this happened, she told herself. And she had been blessed twice with healthy babies. She would simply have liked to know if he knew.

Tunneling

Clara considered her two sleeping children. The little one had his father's full yet prim lips and the other, the girl, had her broader cheeks. The two children were thin but not terribly and with some luck Clara would find enough dried beef to make a stew this evening. Every day now was a day of luck or no luck. There had been fighter-bombers in the night, but she would follow Park Lane until reaching the wartime market and she would not listen to the cautions of traders who only wanted to raise prices. She had given up her position at the College of Saint Gregory, where she had been an instructor of English, and she was so busy with the children now that every day was simply a day of luck or no luck; she felt like a distant cousin of that woman who once stood at the head of a classroom to teach of subjects and verbs and agreements. It would be harder for Chinua. He would suffer every day that this stupid war went on.

Clara drew her red-and-yellow market dress around her and, unthinkingly, began to stroke the head of Chimaka, the girl. Chimaka raised her head and, seeing her mother in street clothes, began to cry. Soon the little one was awake and clamoring for milk. Clara would feed him and his sister and clothe them. Then what? She hated to take them into dangerous streets, even to go to market; and by the time she arrived, who knew what would be left for tonight? In normal times she would have left the children with the maid or with her sister, as she had once left the older one with Chinua's mother.

Clara half-smiled, remembering the old woman with her harsh voice and imposing manner. The old woman had died as she had lived, insisting on her deathbed that she be given an old-fashioned burial. That was before the war. And the first time Clara had seen his mother she had been not old but equally imperious. Back then Chinua had been the quiet earnest youth who would not touch Clara's littlest finger in spite of their months' acquaintance and serious courtship practices. She had even wondered if she was marrying a man who was not really a man! Now she shook her head and fingered a statue, a *mbana,* that he had insisted on giving her in those early days. Because it had come from him and because its head and garments were odd, she kept it. Chimaka leaned her head against her mother's shoulder. This was a rare moment of peace for them because of the little one, sleepily drinking from a teat of goat's milk. Clara told Chimaka to dress the baby, who was only six months old and of such decided character that they all feared, funeral or not, the return of the old woman's spirit.

But the sun was higher—Clara would have to leave for market if she was to acquire beef. Sometimes when the market was bad she walked through the fighting lines to the free territories, bartered for meat and vegetables and then walked the long way back with her goods hidden beneath her dress.

"Lazy girl," she admonished Chimaka, who sat there, the baby's bright cloth in her limp hands.

"What am I to do with a girl such as this?" Clara asked, hands on her hips. "Is there time in this life for this?"

"Albert," I said.

Dawn was breaking into shards of light. We had remained tree-bound. The rain had kept drumming. The python had disappeared into the blackness of things, but now and then I had heard her coils rustling, and once I awoke to Albert's tenor faintly singing about flesh and blood. Was that a growl? Had the lioness returned and was she hungrier? Albert just went on singing. This was the second night that we had spent together under difficult conditions. How much time had passed? I had felt irritated, even concerned, by the words of his song; now I began to feel comforted. Perhaps I closed my eyes—in any event Albert pinched me very hard and I saw the ground rising and knew to grab onto him. He put his arm around me; we sat together, my head tucked against him, and I thought of another heart whose alien silence I had heard so recently.

Tunneling

Eventually the sun appeared on a very far horizon indeed, then slipped behind thickening clouds.

"There's something else I have to tell you," I said. "Just in case we don't get out of here. It's about who I really—"

"I also have something to say. I have been thinking while you slept."

"I wasn't sleeping."

"It has to do with my uncle," he said slowly.

"Shh," I said; but the python, having lifted her triangular head, lowered it.

"You are right," he went on. "My uncle doesn't like me."

"What makes you say that?"

Albert blinked rain water out of his eyes; it trickled down his cheek. "It has also to do with my dream," he said. "It was a foolish dream for a boy to share. I am to be a man soon, and such a blunder would be unforgivable."

"Nonsense," I whispered. "Dreams are very important."

"Once," he said dully, "I would have agreed with you. I see now that I have only irritated good people with my incessant prating. I give up. Or rather, I am about to give up."

He stared into the leaves around us. Was he awake? He was staring, I realized, into the python's gleaming eyes, and she had, I thought, rustled closer, but perhaps I was inventing things. I recalled the words of the adage: *When python sleeps is not the time to pray for rain.*

"Albert!" I said. "Snap out of it!"

"Snap?" He was leaning forward, his head drooping, his arms beginning to collapse ever so gently beneath him. The python was motionless.

"Yes!" I hissed. "What about your chi? What about your path? Your destiny?"

"My uncle doesn't like me," he said. "He left us here to die. I am very sorry, *ogbanje.*"

"What about the woman? You were going to marry a special woman—"

"Well, yes," he said tonelessly. "I was, wasn't I?"

"Won't she be disappointed if you give up now?"

"Such a woman wouldn't want me," he sighed. "It doesn't matter. Nothing matters, does it?"

Nothing matters . . . it's hopeless . . . Where had I heard that before?

"I'm not what you think I am," I told him.

"I beg your pardon?"

"I'm not an *ogbanje* at all. I'm not a Christian either, although I've read a lot of books by Christians."

He shrugged. "If you said you *were* an *ogbanje,* I would know not to believe you."

I thought hard and despairingly. The python's left eye appeared to wink, but no doubt that was an illusion; as was also, no doubt, Albert's left eye's seeming to respond in kind as his hand relaxed around the branch.

"Joseph Conrad matters," I said.

"Joseph Conrad," Albert said. "Joseph Conrad? Joseph Conrad," he said, lifting his head, "is a most execrable person and an even more execrable author of novels."

"Oh," I said loudly. "I just think he's tops."

"You," said Albert, and his voice seemed to gather its old scorn: "I would expect nothing more from an impoverished spirit than such nonsense. Why—"

But at that moment three things happened, two of which I must take the time to tell you. The first was that the lioness did indeed return; what's more, she was indeed hungry. The second was that the python slithered straight at us.

"This is it," said Albert, releasing me and standing up on the branch, which bounced. Albert only stood taller and yanked a slim machete from where it had lain hidden in his waistband. He lifted the machete high. "Now my chi fights for us both or it doesn't."

*　　*　　*

Tunneling

Christopher Okigbo's automobile had attracted some attention and some shouts. There were beggars who clamored for coins or food, and an old woman who begged only to be driven somewhere else, and children who trailed in his wake. That was the worst. He considered abandoning the car and walking home; then, remembering his errand, he drove past the market and the abandoned warehouse and what had been a highway and now lay like some giant broken-backed camel on its side. Christopher had seen many camels once as a boy. They had been Hausa camels, hulking shapes. Now Hausa men rode on other animals and some armored vehicles to bring death to hundreds, thousands. What was civil war and how could it be prevented? He rounded a bend and cursed at a car driving toward him. One of these days he would catch his death, Clara had told him. He had given her a lift on the last market day. Whenever he was in town he did that. She was feeling much better now and there was never a word of reproach for her husband, who had matters, she said, to which he must attend. What matters? Okigbo had once joked. That had been a mistake; she had insisted on getting out and walking to market, which wasn't safe anymore. He would go to her house and drive her or at the very least watch the children. They were very fine children, such as he hoped someday to have if he was lucky enough to find a woman as worthy as their mother. He had said this also to Clara, who had smiled but not climbed back in the car. Now he turned into Park Lane. He heard the whine of the fighter-bomber before catching sight of the strange red-and-white caped man, Kant, who had ridden with him into the city. Kant's white face had turned as red as the red emblem on his chest. He was running. Okigbo waved until he had left the man behind and rounded the corner to the very quiet street where the Achebes lived. Then Okigbo heard the whine of the bomb and then he heard the explosion.

"Now my chi fights for us both or it doesn't!" cried Albert, flashing the slim blade and rushing the python, who moved so rapidly that I didn't see the knife go flying or hear the growl of the lioness, who, having begun to climb the tree, was flung earthward by the python's rushing past us and down the trunk. Albert leaped after. I heard excited shouts and felt a familiar *whoosh* of air. S-Man! S-Man at last! The lioness, turning from the python, who swayed to her full and terrible hooded height, snarled, then leaped upon this other creature whose flesh she would have devoured. When S-Man's skin resisted her fangs, she howled and took a backward step. The python chose that moment to strike or would have had Albert not leaped upon her long body and clung, swaying. She twisted violently and Albert was thrown to the earth. She towered above him. I heard more excited shouts. From my perch in the mangrove tree, I could see newcomers rushing over the yellow grasses toward the scene: Albert's uncle God-Delivers and the other elders, including Talks-to-God and God-Remembers and Doesn't-Believe-in-God and God-Awakens and another man whose priestly attire led me to believe that he was the man, Sing-God's-Praises, of whom Albert had spoken—only a day ago!

By the time Albert's uncle and the elders arrived, pointing and shouting, the lioness was nowhere to be seen, S-Man having lifted her in one hand (she tilted her head) and the python in the other (she blinked) and flown off with them, only to return seconds later as the Igbo elders reached the foot of our tree.

Albert lay sprawled. I sat on the tree limb. S-Man alighted on the grass. The elders stepped back in apparent surprise.

"Please," S-Man said in very clear American English. "I am not a god."

"What does he say?" asked Albert's uncle.

"He says he is not a god, Uncle," said Albert, leaping to his feet and looking wildly about. "Where is she?"

"Where is who?"

"She-Lion. She was about to eat us, except for Mother Python, who leaped to our rescue."

Albert's uncle, who had seemed relieved to find us alive, drew himself to his full height. He was relatively tall, although not so tall as a mother python.

"I see no lioness," he said.

"I assure you," I said in the clearest Igbo possible, "that we have spent the night in the company of a lioness. What's more, if it hadn't been for Albert, that python—"

"Python?" Albert's uncle asked. The others murmured excitedly, whether about the snake or my lapse into Igbo I couldn't tell. Later S-Man explained that the python was sacred to all Igbo people, and that her presence and intervention could only mean that the gods, even Chunkwo himself, wanted us preserved. And that was enough for Albert's uncle, who from that day forward put up with his nephew as best he could, only occasionally remonstrating him for some perceived display of arrogance. His uncle (it turned out) had never expected Albert to take his word so seriously, or to insist on following the Path-That-Doesn't-Really-Go-There-After-All for quite so long. Other boys, he explained jovially (the elders laughing but I somehow missing the humor), would have given up before lunchtime. I turned to Albert, who was busy translating for S-Man. The latter insisted with a light in his eye that he was no god but a mere servant of humankind. The elders looked somewhat puzzled, then their faces brightened.

"Tell him we are also not gods," said one of the elders, in an equally affable tone.

Later—because S-Man and I spent the night in Albert's uncle's compound, and what with feasting on goat's meat and *foo-foo* and cassava cakes and palm wine (which S-Man let me taste) and the flow of conversation and, after that, wrestling, which was a sight to see, and a storytelling contest, which I liked very much, and last of all the masquerade, which was awful and wonderful at once and followed by a parade of *mbana* statues, including one small but, it turned out, all-important statue of S-Man that had been hastily prepared for the occasion, we hardly found time to talk with each other—S-Man told me in a few words about his experiences in the wartime city of Enugu. They sounded very terrible. First he had fallen onto an airstrip, then he had been driven into the city by a madman, then he had almost been killed in an explosion that rocked the city.

"Not a madman," he said, in such a sad voice that I urged him to tell me what had happened.

He had arrived at number 37 Park Lane to find Christopher Okigbo ("Who's he?" I asked) weeping and digging through rubble. "They must be here," said the poet. "Please." S-Man had joined him in digging, although he doubted any good would come of their efforts. It was then that my friend had noticed the clay figure with the letter *S* on its chest and the cape flowing about its shoulders. Some days later, he managed to trace via a delicate and highly scientific process of fossil age determination my exact moment and place; then he had only to wait for the restoration of his powers before flying to find me.

Clara and the two children returned from market some time later to find the two men sitting amid the rubble of her home.

"Now how am I to make his dinner?" she had asked, then turned to address the older child, a girl, who had begun for the second time that morning to cry.

"Who's Christopher Okigbo?" I asked again, and he told me about that brave and inspired poet, a man whose energy and uncompromising nature and talent made his contemporaries call him *ogbanje,* that is, one who has been born before and is in a hurry again to leave this world. Okigbo, having ascertained that the Achebe household was safely ensconced with neighbors, and having heard from these neighbors of the ongoing attack on the University of Nigeria at Nsukka, had rushed off in his Cadillac (engine sputtering, roaring) to its defense. "And then what?" I asked, and reluctantly S-Man told me that the university had fallen to the Nigerian government soldiers, who had razed it and burned all the precious books and massacred hundreds of Biafran defenders, including the man who had given him a ride into the city that morning.

So then I didn't see how I could tell S-Man about my adventures with Albert, which hadn't been so very important or earth-shattering or tragic; but he teased me gently, as if the reason I didn't want to talk was that I had never spent a night in a tree with a boy before; he even began to sing an old song about a boy and a girl and a tree, which was so foolish of him that I had to laugh. I felt bad for laughing in the face of so much sorrow, and we flew on silently for a while through the Sahara Desert. I had asked to see it before returning to New Jersey, but what with the news I had just heard, and the events of the night before, and the fact that Albert hadn't quite forgiven me for fooling him (after my sudden lapse into Igbo, and knowing that S-Man would soon enough have hypnotized the whole tribe with more hastily squeezed diamonds, I had told him the truth. I don't think my being a girl bothered him so much as the lie itself), I hardly saw the white sands or Hausa on high swaying camels or the strange glittering mosques. I was thinking too hard about Albert; and the masquerade; and how women had danced and cheered and run howling in terror or gleeful mock terror from the masked elders, so that I wondered not for the last time in my life just what was meant by the term *oppression* when applied to one sex or the other; and how at one moment Albert had been carried on the shoulders of his age group; and how at another I had held the hastily constructed *mbana* statue of S-Man, only to have Albert reach down and scoop it from my hands; and how I had seen my flying companion paraded also on people's shoulders, and heard him protest, "I am not a god," and heard the jovial echoes of the elders, who had returned after the masquerade to their quotidian secular roles. "We are not gods!" they shouted happily; they seemed to think this an American form of polite address.

"For goodness' sake," I said after a while. "He isn't even cute."

*   *   *

Albert wasn't cute, although there was always something in his face that made you want to look at him again. I thought so then and I thought so when, thirty years later, I stood in his office door for a moment or so, and considered introducing myself and thought better of it. The little statue on his shelf had grown quite dusty with years, and what would we have said to each other?

"Can I help you?" the professor asked, glancing up.

I had determined, if queried, to reply that I was looking for someone, perhaps even a "special friend."

"What's that you're reading?" I asked instead. He seemed annoyed, then his face took on the slightly pained expression of famous people who expect to be disturbed by strangers during their office hours, and he wheeled around in his chair and lifted the book for me to read its title, which was *Heart of Darkness.* "I thought you didn't like that book," I said.

"Sometimes the most execrable of texts can save our lives," he said, and as I excused myself I wondered just what he meant by that rather pompous remark.

AN AUTHORIAL INTRUSION

Each semester I ask my students in Developmental English 92 at Bergen County Community College to write an essay on the following:

Tradition and progress are often in conflict with each other. Agree or disagree. Illustrate your argument with your own experience, your observations of others and your reading.

"Can we agree and disagree?" a student asks. His name is Antoine. He wants badly to correct his written grammar. He wants just as badly to tell the truth as he sees it; and he wants, perhaps, to impress me with his originality. He is older than some, younger than a few others. He has a family and a past.

"Just this once," I finally concede. I give him a complicitous look, as if we share an interest in the creative in-between, but in fact the semester will end and Antoine, like 60 percent of his peers, will fail the state-administered exam and be barred from further study. And I will return to my quiet home on leafy Bowdoin Street.

For a week or so I recall him: burly, West Indian, once prone (according to numerous personal essays) to violence but determined to make a better life for his children. Well? I imagine walking into the chairman's office and insisting that this one student dossier be reopened. On a chance free hour, I do. The man's test is reevaluated; his skills are no more appreciated by another impartial reader than before. Was I right about him? For a few weeks more I think of what might have been. I consider a further appeal. The semester ended, I begin to forget. Or rather I play a mental game, similar to and more sinister than the framing game I have played at twilight. I place big-shouldered Antoine in my own mbana *house, as it were; in that pantheon of distant stars and other familiars, where his memory is rendered painless.*

I have never understood history, because it is inconceivable to me that a person might belong to a group of people. I am most comfortable alone. Yet these houses surrounding mine resemble mine, and their inhabitants mean as well and not much better, I imagine, than do I. Other than myself, no one recalls S-Man's battle with Laff Riot and his ghastly cohorts, nor the explosions, nor the tunnels dug beneath the playing fields, nor the little heaped addition to the cemetery; but everyone recalls if not the loss of a loved one, then some betrayal, and in time of flood our losses dislodge and rise to the water's surfaces.

Just the other day, the flood having since receded, the drying and wringing and reordering all done—even the river returned to its customary bed—I set out to do my shopping at the West Teaneck Food Market, and there I overheard a couple talking. Like other newcomers to our town, the man wore the yalmulke, the woman the wig and fifties-style dress of Orthodox Jews. I didn't and so didn't quite exist for them, and could eavesdrop all I wanted as we stood at the checkout counter.

This couple, I soon gathered, had hired a Haitian woman to watch their children and clean their house. The woman had for some years worked for them, under their urging had attended night school (none other than Bergen Community), and had eventually left their employ for a job in computers. With tears, Judith (her name was Judith) had parted from her little charges, and yet no sooner gone than she had turned and sued the couple for severance pay!

"How could she do that?" the wife asked, eyes watering.

I left the market. I walked with my few groceries past the once-dreaded underpass to the wide cement bridge arching over the railroad tracks. Once a train, bound for Fort Knox, rattled down these tracks; once its passengers, representatives of that great warehouse upriver, carried glowing ingots through our dark streets to the NJ Savings & Loan. There the ingots were meant to lie safely until the government recalled them. Wasn't ours, after all, a model town? Be that as it may, on this morning the train tracks stretched empty. The sky stretched blue. Our world was come once again into its own; birds trilled above fields bursting with the pride of green growth. Crocuses abounded—we have been flooded all over again with such crocuses, yellow, white, purple! I walked at a leisurely pace. A woman walked briskly in the opposite direction. Nothing in this woman's dress (black slacks, open purple parka) or manner (impassive face, swept hair) bespoke any social class. She might have cleaned or nursed; she might have been a civil servant or lawyer; she might have lived in our sedate neighborhood or among the newer arrivals on Teaneck Road or in the northeast section. We two nodded, as if to acknowledge a crossroads, and walked on.

I was in second grade, as I say, when the first Black children came to school with us. The girls remain with me most clearly. There was Rhodina, who kissed boys and talked back and grew up to become Dr. Rhodina Johnson, and her friend Heather, who helped care for five brothers and sisters and later founded a children's publishing house like the one Christopher Okigbo hoped to found. There was Cynthia, who mocked people with the psychic cruelty of a Mr. Stick; and Floriana, who tended to do what Cynthia told her. All these girls were flesh-and-blood kin, perhaps, to children who had stepped off buses in our southern states! Thinking about that made us— made me—feel somehow clean. And yet there was the fear of using that old wrong word, Negro, *and the fact that our* Weekly Reader *had prepared us for poor people (these were not poor people); and then there was the difference I felt generally between myself and all children.*

But there was one new girl, Collette Foster, whose father worked with my father, and whose serious visage and long hands particularly drew me. I, who had only once invited a friend home, began to court this girl's friendship. I hovered near her at recess. I volunteered myself for hopscotch and even punchball games. One day our teacher read aloud a story about one Black and one White child who wish to play together, and about the White child's mother, who makes an issue of their friendship. In the story the children share snacks and imaginary games and quiet explanation. Afterward Mrs. Entenmann tested our reading comprehension. My hand shot into the air—Mrs. Entenmann was big-limbed, blond, even beautiful—but my heart sank. Perhaps I was not like the children in the story; perhaps I was more like that mother. One day I invited Collette to my house. We ate tuna-fish sandwiches, and later we sat on my bed and she told me about her church and I realized (that is, I sensed it then and thought it years later) that something far more significant than the colors of our skins—hers coffee, mine sallow—separated us.

Someday, I told her nonetheless, we would all be the same color.

"Ooh," she said. "That's nasty."

Once, she having slept over, I watched her getting ready for sleep: long brown hands clasped, long Cleopatra neck bent, dark head bowed. "Don't you have to say your prayers?" she asked. I shrugged. After that I made my mother buy me a flowered nightgown like Collette's. Some nights, I would crawl in my new nightgown to the edge of my bed—I had not yet developed the habit of slipping under it—and make as if to join my hands. "God bless everyone and help me to be good," I heard myself say. I hunted for more Christian words.

"What are you doing?" Elaine hooted—she had opened the door!

"Nothing," I said, dropping my hands.

"I saw you. You were praying."

"I was not."

"I'm telling," she said, smiling.

"I was not," I said again and still a third time.

For a time Collette and I remained united in our appreciation of

Tunneling

"sweets," as she called them. We would meet at three o'clock, and my father might trail after us and we wouldn't mind particularly, because it was fun to walk down Englewood Avenue toward the railroad tracks, and fun even to race together through the horrific-smelling underpass ("Don't let it touch me!" Collette would cry, mindful of her white kneesocks) and up the stairs into daylight.

As for the boys, White or Black, I hardly remember them from that first year, although Elaine spoke so frequently of one Haywood Lofty, whose academic excellence was rivaled only by his social acumen, that I tend to imagine him among the members of our own grade. In fact he was in Elaine's and would move on like her to the now centralized junior high; I see him in my mind's eye, strolling in his neat way always around the next corner. Even my sister, departing, would leave behind emptiness rather than relief. Perhaps we miss most the people who have hurt us, if only because we loved them at such cost.

Not one of our teachers was Black; it would be several years before change of that order was implemented. What I remember best is something else—an incident that had nothing to do with the arrival of the Black students yet remains linked in my mind.

Corporal punishment had been banned from public schools during our parents' lifetimes. Our parents regaled us with stories of teachers and rulers; but we had a song that mocked their former ability to harm us. We sang it (even I mumbled those lyrics) to the tune of "The Battle Hymn of the Republic" and crescendoed on the words "Teacher dropped dead and that's the end of school—YAH!" Then one spring day in 1965, Mrs. Zingenberg so lost her temper with Colin Duffy, who had begun giddily to laugh at his own bad grammar (Colin's only interests were kissing and cap guns), that she lunged past our desks, yanked him by the ear and dragged him by that ear across the classroom.

Had the incident involved one of us—I mean the secular Jewish children whose arrival in Teaneck seeded the growth of the school system—the school board would have been notified. But Colin Duffy played the class dunce and dressed sloppily, and his Irish brothers and father resembled him but for their great dull girth. Moreover, Colin Duffy had one brown eye and one blue; the latter eye tended to cry on its own, the result of his having been struck by a baseball bat (Colin having stood too near the batter and future entrepreneur, Douglas Rothstein). We watched him sail across the classroom. He slumped against the wall, his feet scrambling sideways, his blue eye crying. It looked up at Mrs. Zingenberg, whose face seemed to shatter.

She stood there, chest heaving, trying to collect the shards of her features.

"You're not allowed," Colin said, rising.

The majority of the newly bused children (a mere 9 percent of our student population) lived, as I say, in fine houses with parents who earned salaries in keeping with their homes, as they nurtured and dreamed for their children; that is, but for the facts of race and ethnos, these children were typical of what was once designated, in a 1949 report to the Office of the Undersecretary of the United States Army, a "model town." In those days nearly every face that peeped out of army photographs (displayed worldwide, and in particular at a Tokyo business conference called Our American Way of Life) was White, although the one Black student who attended John Greenleaf Whittier Elementary School stood in the front row. I noticed something similar in a photograph taken of Ms. Pitlak's second-grade class just last year. For divers reasons, including perhaps the Orthodox Jews' practice and (to a lesser degree) the Catholics' practice of sending children to religious day school, students in the once predominantly White Whittier Elementary School are now predominantly African American and Latin American. Perhaps for the same reasons, the town board has voted down school budget after budget. Mrs. Pitlak and her charges, hoping to raise money for the Whittier Elementary School library (once the pride of our county), now sell tea bags. They advertise their

Tunneling

"Teaneck Teas" in posters around town. In these posters the darker makeup of the class is obvious, but the child who stands smack center lends a distinctly Caucasian cast.

Well! I stray once more from our story; or perhaps not, as events that unfolded that year of strange weather did take place within a context. Call it, if you will, historical.

Chapter Six

Baldly Put

"F INCH," MRS. CARLSBAD CALLED. "WHAT TIME
is it?"

"I don't know."

"Are you sure you don't know?"

I considered the overhead clock. Answering any question in Mrs.
Carlsbad's classroom had become dangerous, particularly when the
question had to do with the passage of Time—*God's little* Joke *on all
of us,* as she called it.

"Time to get a new watch," she said. "Aha!"

"Of course," I said, trying to smile.

But my best friend and I had argued and the world was rendered
grim.

Mrs. Carlsbad had made good, *plus ou moins,* on her threat to teach us
about the one frontier worth crossing. There was Stonehenge, after all.
And there was Confucius, although she passed over him rather hurriedly. "Does anyone know who invented the first mechanical clock?"
she asked. I raised my hand tentatively, there being a good chance, it
seemed to me, that the answer was "the Swiss"; but my friend, being

called on first, offered the information in a loud clear voice that it was the Chinese who had invented the "water clock tower." "The Chinese," said Mrs. Carlsbad. "Aha. Anyone else? Yes?" Mrs. Carlsbad's taste for the apparatuses with which we log our lives was as insatiable as the apparatuses were various. There were sundials and, yes, water clocks (she frowned), and (her face lightened) there were nuclear-powered naval clocks and giantesque machines known as computers; there were light-years, nanoseconds and allowances constantly to be made for the earth's turning. To quote our teacher, *yikes!* One day, to bring home to us all an important truth, she made Edwin and Edward observe the big overhead clock as it ticked. Hitherto I had thought of school clocks as friendly, with their clear numerals and their human nomenclatures of face and hand; but as Beverley Carlsbad kept the boys immobile for ten, then twenty, then thirty minutes, so that their two faces, the one pale and the other paler—unless it was the other way around—began to glisten and their combined limbs to tremble, I began to see the inhumane aspect of that second hand. "Excuse me, Mrs. Carlsbad," called out a high loud voice. "May I ask what the point of this exercise is?" "The point? It has to do with relativity," said Mrs. Carlsbad, narrowing her eyes. "No relative of mine," Rachel Fish whispered. "Detention!" cried out Mrs. Carlsbad. "My eczema is killing me," whispered Rachel Fish— and so it must have been, because she almost never complained. "Two detentions!" cried out Mrs. Carlsbad, whirling. "Did you hear that? I thought I heard something."

Mrs. Carlsbad's blue eyes watered. Her hands shook.

"I didn't hear anything," said Rachel Fish boldly. The school bell rang.

"I heard *that,*" muttered Cynthia.

"Hallelujah," whispered Collette.

After which Rachel Fish did something unusual for a seventh grader. Gathering her books, she marched not into detention hall with the emphatic Felicity Bauer but on past into Mr. Franklin's office, where she demanded a transfer the heck out of Mrs. Carlsbad's class. When Mr. Franklin, whose widower's affinity for our science teacher was well known, only beamed, Rachel Fish appealed to Mr. Rizzo, the shiny-pated vice principal. The result—her parents, in a rare show of concern, came in to discuss the matter—was that Rachel Fish no longer sat in my Science class. The day of her switch into the other section, taught by the nondescript Mr. Biagini, she confronted me with my "citizen's responsibility" of defending the downtrodden in her absence. I pointed out that the matter of Mrs. Carlsbad's mistreatment of her seemed resolved. "You mark my words," she said, "that woman is having a nervous breakdown." In any event, Rachel Fish agreed, her huge eyes looming, we had more important evils to combat, such as a seventh-grade girls' conspiracy to divide our central stairs (there were two facing central staircases, and a third at the far end of school) into Black and White passageways. "Nobody takes Cynthia or Mindy seriously," I said—how could they?

"Collette does," she said, which seemed almost a low blow, given what she knew of Collette's distance from me. "There are people who would say bad things," Collette had explained, on the one occasion that I had suggested one of our old trips to the candy store. "Bad things?" "About your sister. You have no idea how evil people are." But when I reported this to my mother, she only echoed the last words, "how evil people are," and said slowly that perhaps Collette was embarrassed to be seen with a White girl. "But I'm her friend," I insisted. My mother only smiled. After that had come my father's decision to drive us to and from school, and so the question had become, almost, moot.

"*Whose side are you on,*" Rachel Fish began nonetheless to sing in her loud, clear soprano. It was our responsibility, she added, to walk wherever and whenever we chose.

"You think you know everything," I shouted finally. "They're just picking on people."

"You don't trust me," she shouted for some reason.

Two girls stared at each other. Two girls walked away.
"Whose side are you on . . . "

As the days passed, I had to admit (I admitted nothing) that Mrs. Carlsbad's agitation seemed to increase. Her blue eyelids glittered dangerously.
She would pace the classroom and point with her quivering yardstick—
at a canister, a textbook—and insist that the object had moved in the
night. She would make us change our seats and then make us change
again. "Emergency alert!" she called out and we would scramble into the
aisles and freeze. "She's having a nervous breakdown," my former friend
Rachel proclaimed to her circle of singing friends, and inwardly I would
deny the charge against my teacher. Sitting there at my own table (I sat
alone again, although not far from theirs), I would envisage the future as
I had before Rachel Fish's arrival in Teaneck. I remembered flying across
the ocean and back some years to my friend Albert's side. I was sitting in
a mangrove with him, surrounded by natural predators and having a
whale of a time. Or I was in Versailles, explaining to Voltaire that Jews
were like other people. Was I, then, Jewish? There were so many different kinds of Jews; Orthodox Jews and Reform Jews and terrible Jews like
Mindy Glueck with her staircase and other Jews like my father, who
eschewed all institutionalized religion. "Institutionalized? By all means,
lock it up!" he would joke to Dr. Foster, who shook his Baptist head but
who had an abiding respect for movements of whole peoples. Just what
kind of Jew, I wondered, glancing over at her, was Rachel Fish?

For that matter, I wondered that day and subsequent days, just
what constitutes a woman's nervous breakdown? How could you tell
when your favorite teacher was having one?

A bell rang. I walked toward a stairwell. "You can't walk here," said
Cynthia, and she imitated a certain look in my eyes by sticking out her
neck and gawking.

Tunneling

"You have to walk here," said Mindy, stepping into the main lobby and gesturing.

"Whitey," called Cynthia.

"Schwartzes," whispered Mindy, passing by.

The argument between Cynthia and Mindy had erupted, as such arguments sometimes do, over a boy—Steward Blumenthal, who used to be so fat! Unable to extract from him any hint of preference for either girl, Mindy had taken the measure of polling our classmates. With the exception of Rachel Fish and I, who refused to respond, girls in our grade had mainly fallen into camps: those who felt that White boys should only date White girls, those who felt that Black girls should only date Black boys, and those who felt that Cindy had a prior claim to Steward's affections as she had loved him chubby. Both girls had only grown more rancorous in their claims, which, as such claims will, had grown more general.

Later, finding me at the foot of the above-mentioned stairwell—I was thinking over what Rachel Fish had shouted during our unfortunate exchange—Mindy whirled me around and pointed once again toward the opposite staircase, where other White seventh-grade girls were now supposed, she said, to walk. Did Mindy expect me to object? I stumbled like an old woman in the indicated direction. The last I saw of her (until Science) was the glint in her green eyes.

One day Mrs. Carlsbad came into class wearing sunglasses and after that she wore them every day. One day her hands shook and the next, she didn't know how to finish her stories.

"That reminds me . . . ," she would say, her voice trailing off.

If a pattern emerged, it was this: the closer we came to learning relevant facts about the natural world and human progress (ostensibly the curriculum for seventh grade, culminating in a Spring Science Fair), the further Mrs. Carlsbad would veer into reminiscences of her own high school years. "He was so cute," she would sigh, meaning her husband before Vietnam changed him. She might begin a humorous anecdote—the last time Chuck Carlsbad sleepwalked, the time he forgot where they lived, the time he began digging with his rototiller in their neighbors' backyard—only to conclude her stories with that of his full-speed decline. He drank, he smoked, he ran around with women, he threatened people he didn't like with automatic weapons. "Life isn't fair!" she barked, startling us. "Reassigned seats," she would snarl and we would rise happily. "All rise. All sit. Now then. Yikes! *Remind me to tell you about the time—*" and we would sit, once more miserable. One Tuesday she pressed her ear to the laboratory wall, then tapped her yardstick at the ceiling, above which gaped the school's Assembly Hall. "Silence," she shrilled, as if we hadn't fallen silent! Sometimes she made us do more than switch seats; adhering to our earliest training, she might make us huddle away from the windows, or crawl under our desks and tuck our heads between our knees.

What was wrong with her?

"Why do you care?" Rachel Fish asked, exasperated, when I approached her; I shook my head and we two parted in the halls. I couldn't or wouldn't explain. Nor would I have shared the image of Laff Riot and his diminutive cohort Mr. Stick, darting across a municipal lawn. S-Man had never expressly forbidden me to talk about them. But to reveal that the fiendish duo had descended upon our town was to open a line of questioning that could only end, it seemed, in my friend's discovery of my other life.

I couldn't have told her—how could I, even if we had still lunched together?—that when Mindy Glueck had spun me around toward the other stairwell, her green eyes glowing, I experienced a visual confusion that would continue, on and off, growing ever more severe, until the night of our science presentations? The corridor grew thick and moist. Vegetation sprang from its walls, creepers dangled from the ceiling and all manner of tropical bird laughed in my ear. I had the acutest sense not of visiting another country (I knew what that was like) but of seeing it through alien eyes.

I wouldn't tell my friend any of this.

Tunneling

*   *   *

Shortly after our latest rearrangement (which left me sitting at the desk nearest the teacher's, and Edward and Edwin at diagonal poles of the classroom), Beverley Carlsbad remarked in a bright tone that someone's parents—I blushed for my absent friend—had actually complained to the school board about her teaching!

"I had every intention of getting to that etiolated curriculum," she said, biting off that last word: *curri-cu-lum*. "So I ripped it up. Now I have to see a shrink? Me, have a psychiatric evaluation, when that nut I'm married to just goes free? Unless, of course, I'm the nut. . . . I don't think I am. . . . Sometimes I am but not usually. . . ."

Like my father, Beverley Carlsbad seemed to thrive on adversity. She rallied now and went on to "throw us" a list of topics (we were to choose among them) she would have, before "this year of years," taught us in due time. Things being what they were, however, we would now devote valuable class hours reading up, and taking our own notes, on such relevant issues as biological misengineering, nutrient theft, Third World exploitation and the cruelties of plant courtship. The biggest crime in the world, as everyone knew (she said dryly), was the one we humans were perpetrating against Mother Nature.

"But Mrs. Carlsbad," asked Collette Foster, having raised her hand and duly been called upon. "What about the final frontier?" And Collette, who had taken careful notes all year, angrily riffled the pages of her notebook. They were filled with references to Time Past, Time Future—everything but Time Present—and to a series of anecdotes figuring one Charles "Chuck" Carlsbad.

"We've crossed it. Any other questions?" asked Beverley Carlsbad.

After some excited commentary, we determined—or rather she determined—that Collette Foster would study corporate responsibility for endangered species; Cynthia Lacey, the life cycles and eating habits of certain "bad" frogs; Susan Kolin, the deleterious effect of most name-brand detergents; Margarita, the nesting patterns of those thieves, the jaybirds; Robert Wurner, the ability of hamsters to learn avoidance of electric prods; and Colin Duffy—going rather against the spirit of the thing—the possibility of natural ingredients' combining over time into highly effective explosives.

My report would have to do with the misuse of insecticides—in particular, Malathion.

I hadn't made this choice lightly.

In so doing, I had presented to myself the philosophes and their faith in progress and knowledge and reason; had thought of Mr. Voltaire and Mr. Diderot and how they were curious, open-minded men, although not quite so open-minded as Mr. Shakespeare, who was perhaps something of a small-towner (I didn't know the word *provincial*) after all. Now I relied on my mental pictures of these great figures as I put my personal problems aside and determined to learn more about the lethal substance. I hadn't forgotten S-Man's promise to take me to the great Franz Kafka. Perhaps my next encounter with S-Man, I thought, opening my notebook, would be my last! I would tell him that I didn't want to fly anymore and he would understand, as he had always understood, and fly me one last time, to Prague and back. Then perhaps Laff and Mr. Stick would leave us alone and Rachel Fish and I could once again plan our literary lives together. The more I thought (pressing my pencil to the page), the more I was convinced that the evil archvillain and his tiny cohort were responsible for what was happening.

Everything was the same; everything changed. The hospital, the hall, the library—our town's three most imposing structures had always stood (at least since colonial times) at some distance from one another, across wide expanses of lawn and rhododendrum, and set back each in turn from Teaneck Road as it dipped and meandered westward. In spring, azaleas would bloom here; and the purple-and-blue hyacinths, and dark-green ivy and bright-red June roses; and all year the fir trees towered above the maples, which had only been planted, after all, the year the elm trees died. All this had been my childhood's unexamined pride. Now the air hummed with strange insects. The afternoon felt irrationally warm. I had spent a night breathing into a machine, and two more days awaiting my release to active duty. Leaving the hospital, I stumbled and my father reached his hand to steady me; how to explain that I shied now from his touch? His was a human smile, a human touch; and yet by sheer touching he recalled to me Laff's mocking smile in Versailles, Laff's hands on my nape and in my hair, as if he (Laff) and I both knew that I would never cross some threshold safely into womanhood. My period had come once in an Elizabethan era, and never since. I was flat-chested, ill-favored and bound someday soon for the bubble dome, where no one, as my sister had explained, would ever love me. Or so it seemed as I sat there, blinking in the fluorescent light of schoolrooms.

Imagine my horror, as I read on about pesticides, their names and laboratories of origin, to discover the widespread uses for Laff's favorite eau de cologne—that is, Malathion! "This chemical compound," ran an article in the *Scientific Monitor,* "is a non-systemic wide-spectrum insecticide."

"Non-systemic," I copied fast and quite furious: "Wide spectrum."

"Effective," the article went on, "in the control of insects in tomatoes, apples, oranges, pears, broccoli . . ."

I took up my pencil. In a newspaper photograph clipped inside my Malathion project folder, a duck lay somehow clownish in death, on the shore of a deserted New Jersey lake. Another duck floated with bedraggled feet sticking up. I felt a pang akin, I think, to that I once felt upon reading Bertrand Russell's obituary. Poor philosopher! Poor duck! Rainwater, it seemed, had drained from surrounding wetlands into this lake where ducks had used to swim, and with rainwater had seeped the chemical substance such that ducks, geese and the soft-backed turtles who make their homes in and out of clear water had ceased to lay eggs and one after another, in variegated clownish poses, died.

"Died," I wrote. My pencil snapped.

"Finch," said Mrs. Carlsbad, without looking up.

"Yes," I said reluctantly.

Her hand motioned for me to step forward. I thought I saw a teardrop slither from beneath her sunglasses. I would have done anything to dry it, etcetera.

"I need this note taken to the principal's office." She pointed to the ceiling, meaning the second floor. "Do you see what time it is? I want you back in five minutes. That's f-i-v-e."

I nodded wearily. "What staircase should I use?"

"Why do you ask?"

I heard Cynthia suck in her breath, and Mindy grunt.

Mrs. Carlsbad paused to scratch her head.

At that, her scalp moved forward and back to an unnatural degree!

"Did you say something?"

I shook my head and she scratched her head again, her scalp moving forward and back.

Wouldn't you have wondered? I did!

Could the real Mrs. Carlsbad, I asked myself, turning rapidly back, be *hiding* somewhere? Could she be in want of succor, as had been Madame de Pompadour? And if this wasn't Mrs. Carlsbad (whose own strawberry-blond hair, I was certain, was dyed but not replaced!), who was it? I sniffed for the telltale odor. Was it my imagination, or—? As I had in Versailles, I began to see myself in double. One of us watched miserably as Mrs. Carlsbad reached into her drawer for a tape dispenser; the other leaped across her desk and tugged like a maniac on her blond chevelure.

"Finch," Mrs. Carlsbad called. "Am I losing my mind?"

I turned. Whoever she was, she was holding out the hall pass. I took it from her.

"You've got three minutes," she called. "Tops."

"Holy Kamoly," I whispered.

The halls were deserted. My words floated away. I considered examining the note's contents, but the strips of tape discouraged tampering.

I walked quickly past rooms whose numbers seemed to boast of a still-functional world order: 1–2, 1–3, 1–4; 1–5 . . . I would have liked to have drawn Rachel Fish's attention to the square window of 1–5's door; she might have acquired Mr. Biagini's hall pass and crept with me into the girls' bathroom to exchange news of the hour.

Beyond the door of 1–5 lay the unclaimed stairwell. I hurried up several steps to a concrete landing by a largish window.

There, safely out of sight, I paused. Sunlight illumined specks of dust. They swirled and when I reached, darted away. Beyond the one large pane, green fields shimmered. The sod seemed to rise and fall like a man's (or a woman's) toupee; when I looked more closely, I realized it had never moved. People could not be relied on to be themselves; classrooms and landscapes shifted unaccountably. I was reminded of the terrible voice and its resounding words above the River Avon: *"There is no self. . . . There is no such thing as the existence of the self. . . ."* Just what, I wondered, cringing, was the sense of those words? When I say that I cringed, I mean that if you had come upon me in the stairwell, you would have found me doubled over. "I hate myself," someone said—me! Nothing heroic there! I had begun to wander into this mental swamp more often than I like to admit. "Who will guide us now?" Rachel Fish once cried. "Help me," I whispered. *"You can't fly home,"* said a voice. *"You will never be loved." "You think too much." "We're not finished with you, kid." "Who needs freedom?" "Not I." "Not I . . ." "Now my chi fights for us both or it doesn't!"* And I saw Albert in my mind's eye, recalled his own doubting moment in the mangrove tree and his subsequent leap onto the swaying neck of Mother Python, and I passed on . . .

. . . through a wide door onto the second floor and into the administrative offices where affable Mr. Franklin and his redoubtable assistant, Mr. Rizzo, administered to our lives. Mr. Franklin stood even now in the door of his office—his very aura (beatific) made me want to confide all—and yet it was Mr. Rizzo who opened Mrs. Carlsbad's note. Mr. Rizzo, as aforementioned, was bald. I wasn't naive enough to suspect every bald person. Still I felt a necessary estrangement from the people around me, even our school vice principal. I tried, in spite of S-Man's caution, to *think:* If I were a villain, if I were Laff or Mr. Stick or even Assemblage, what would I do next?

The elevator doors opened and Haywood Lofty appeared. With one hand he held apart the doors, with the other he steadied a girl on crutches. The girl hobbled, halting every few steps, down the hall. Haywood was about to disappear again into the elevator when something through the long exterior windows caught his attention.

The girls on the varsity track team were sauntering toward the open school door. These girls, shiny-faced, invigorated, slapped one another across the shoulders and shouted bold epithets. Among the girls strode Elaine. Her thick hair spilled out of her ponytail, her brown eyes flashed. She flung her sweater into the air (the sweater was white with the blue letters *BFJHS,* painstakingly emblazoned by our mother) and caught it. She tossed the sweater high; it flopped sloppily across her face; she tossed it higher.

She paused, looking around.

"Very funny," she said flatly.

Sid, dangling her sweater, stepped from behind the flagpole.

Sid was bald too! That is, he had entirely shaved his head! He looked like a cancer victim or convict. I reminded myself again that not all bald people were evil, that to presume evil in anyone due to their appearance was another form of what tainted our school. But Hugo, moving quickly out from the shelter of the building's overhang, sported likewise a shaven cranium. The two looked nightmarish (to me) with their naked pates, their khaki fatigues and black leather boots. Whatever suspicions I might have had about Mrs. Carlsbad disappeared as I examined the bold insignias on their jackets: shiny-headed rats sporting untied sneakers and wielding machine guns.

Sid carried a grease-stained pizza box.

"Hey babe," he said, balancing it on his fingertips.

"You guys aren't allowed here," Elaine said.

But she had begun to smile and, glancing around the hall, tucked a vagabond curl behind her ear.

"Who's here?" grinned Hugo. He held up a set of shiny keys.

"Wanna go for a joyride?" asked Sid eagerly. His long bald head gleamed under the fluorescent light.

" 'Joyride,' " said Hugo, "an expression first surfacing in the post–Great War years, when young people began to take advantage of the privacy offered by the automobile."

"Yeah," said Sid.

Elaine laughed. "I have things to do."

"She has things to do," said Hugo. Sid lay a hand on Elaine's forearm. The rat on his bosom sneered above the wicked barrel of its gun.

"Let go," she said.

"How come you don't come to see me lately?"

"I said let go." Elaine twisted free; I waited for her to walk through the double doors, but she glanced from boy to boy. A grave look had come over her features.

"I'm leaving," said Sid. "I'm coming into some money and I'm leaving this bloody town for keeps."

"For keeps?"

" 'Bloody—' " said Hugo, smiling.

Sid winced. Then he twirled the pizza box and slapped it between long hands.

"Where are you going?" Elaine asked.

"California maybe. Maybe New Mexico. Wanna come?"

"When?"

"Soon," he said. "Ever heard of the gold rush?"

"I thought you were busy anyhow," he added.

"—an adjective first heard frequently—" Hugo went on.

"I could keep you company," Elaine said quickly. I wondered (I had moved to one side of the glass doors) if she meant on the open road or on Sid's pizza route. How could Elaine imagine freedom of such an egregious type? Did she think our father would just let her go?

"Marry me," Sid said. "Last offer. I'll teach you how to bake a pizza."

"I have to go now."

"Hey," he said, stepping forward. He wrapped his arm around her and reached his lips to her ear. I saw him wink over her head at Hugo, who grimaced. Sid reached further, puckering, and would have smacked a kiss on Elaine's mouth had she not caught sight of Haywood. She jumped. The kiss landed on the tip of her nose. She wrinkled that organ and ran past her former beau, who stood very still until she had disappeared through the wide doors.

"You got a problem?" Sid asked.

Haywood shook his head.

"Good," said Hugo. "We don't either. Let's get a move on, Sid."

"You know what this is?" asked Sid. He glanced at Hugo as he emitted several words of what sounded like Italian.

"Not like that," said Hugo and pronounced the words with some difference. I thought regretfully of Aquaman's shell, lying in a white earring box beneath my mattress at home.

The pulse in Haywood's forehead began to beat.

"I'll give you a hint," said Sid. "There are too many in this town."

"Aha," said Hugo. He rubbed his stubbled pate again. In spite of his having corrected his friend, he seemed less at ease. "Come along, Sidney."

"Hold off," said Sid. "I got to ask this guy a few more questions."

Tunneling

"I'm sorry," said Haywood, glancing at his wristwatch. "I have to go now."

"He must be off," echoed Hugo uneasily.

"How about this?" grinned Sid. "You know what this means?" He shot out words in a foreign language—I thought it was Greek—as Hugo winced and Haywood abruptly headed for the elevator. He must have caught sight of me, standing as I was in the folds of the flag; his face masked all recognition as the elevator doors closed. When, some days later, I chanced upon Haywood punching hard into a sawdust bag hanging from the far end of the gymnasium, and he looked up so that his eyes and mine met, the same mask would slide over his features. "Who are you," the eyeholes in his mask seemed to say, "to think you know something about me?"

"Come on, my good man," urged Hugo.

I waited until Hugo and Sid's footsteps had receded. A moment or so later, their taxi stuttered to life. Somewhere a clock made audible note of the passage of time. What about Mrs. Carlsbad? I hurried downstairs.

I had almost passed room 1–5 when Rachel Fish stuck her head out of the girls' bathroom. "Finch," she hissed, waving her own hall pass. Had she forgotten our argument? I motioned to indicate my need to return to class; she beckoned more energetically until I slipped into the bathroom. Her eyes seemed huger than ever and her skin more mottled.

"I want to know," she said, "what's going on."

Rachel Fish and I had argued before, but never about anything so serious as our current conflict. We had argued, for instance, on the afternoon of my "audition" for the a cappella chorus (a fiasco, replete with Miss Bauer's surprised "Aren't you tone-deaf?" and my subsequent teary-eyed flight); argued on the day of her six-year-old brother Hegel's induction into the High School Math Club; and argued on the anniversary of the death of Robert Kennedy, when she had insisted that we dress in white, the color of Vietnamese mourning, and keep silent vigil all afternoon. Each difference had ended well enough, albeit with my excuses, explanations, promises. . . .

Was it my friend's fault that my character caved in so to hers?

"You don't tell me things," she said finally.

"I do too."

"Like what?"

"Never mind."

"Very funny," she replied, so dryly that we both laughed and, laughing, forgot to be angry! A faucet was dripping. The air smelled damp and close. She leaned to whisper; did I want to know something? Her tone suggested that there be no more secrets between us. But all she said was "Guess who my favorite writer is?" I didn't know. "I'll give you a hint," she whispered. "He's from Prague. I keep a book of his under my pillow. Can you guess? Good."

Good? Then why wasn't I pleased by this news, this further sign of our similitude? What excess, what corollary to love, makes us think we might own even a literary other? I had no right to possessiveness where Kafka was concerned, and yet I seem to have felt it.

"Now tell me what's going on," she said.

"What's going on. Yes."

"I'll die if you don't tell me."

For an instant, hard-hearted or no, I wavered. I abhorred lies large and small, of course, and I was delighted that Rachel Fish was speaking to me again. The second-floor bathroom had two stalls—both, we had established by ducking our heads down, empty. There were two sinks and two mirrors, in which I could see two girls reflected.

"There's something you're still not telling me," Rachel Fish said. "It has to do with why you don't invite me to your house."

"Don't invite you?"

Again I felt a certain hardening (of the heart), perhaps even the tiniest twinge of resentment. To expose to Rachel Fish's relentless if myopic gaze my mother with her distraction, my father with his too-pressing concerns? What could such a fierce patriot understand about the compromises of our home? Turning away, I twisted ineffectually at the dripping faucet and reflected on the fact that Max Brod's biography of Kafka had for some weeks been gone from our school library. Following a hunch, I had asked after the book; sure enough, the librarian had informed me, Rachel Fish still had it out.

"There's something you know that I don't," she persisted.

"It's about my sister," I said, fleeing.

Lies, however enthralling. Or worse: half-truths, intended to conceal as they revealed. And I, who abhorred falsehoods, who adored my friend, told them willingly to her. Trusting fool! Intransigent, fierce lover of justice and country!

Two things happened that afternoon, both of which had never happened quite the same way. The first was that Mrs. Carlsbad sent *me* to detention for returning late to class. The second? As a result of my being detained and my father's experiencing an emergency at Holy Name Hospital, I was instructed to walk home alone. In fact, I walked home with Rachel Fish, who acted so heroically upon hearing of my punishment that in spite of my having incurred the wrath of my favorite teacher, I warmed to my friend all over again. She walked right up to Mrs. Carlsbad as that personage was submitting her attendance slips to Mr. Franklin, and insisted in her clear sweet soprano that the fault of my tardy return to science class was her own. *Mr. Franklin gave her such a look then!* Rachel Fish said, and we smiled to think of that beatific widower giving anyone a look. What matter that my friend asked so many questions; that she had begun to intuit, with her remarkable empathic powers, the secret of my apprenticeship? She waited outside school; when I exited she was warbling the refrain of that old favorite of my family's, "We Shall Overcome" (Mrs. Carlsbad hadn't deigned even to respond, she exclaimed), and we two set off down the avenue together.

The sky gleamed that odd sad color it gets, and somewhere a lone ball began to bounce. Rachel Fish intoned a few more bars.

"It's too bad you can't sing," she said. I looked at her. She was carefully balancing on the sidewalk's curb, her nose in the air. I wondered if she had made the remark with malice; another child would have said it with malice; but she was incapable of such sentiment, and must therefore have uttered the words "It's too bad you can't sing" in an objective fashion. "And you can't even go to anyone's house," she added, one foot dangling. She went on to describe her house's wonders: how her parents, nomads though they were, gave every sign this time of staying put; how they had painted each room a different color, such that the living room shone chartreuse, the walls leading to the second floor orange, and each bedroom a different hue of red. There were rooms where every wall shone a different color and wicker furniture swung from metal chains. "You would love it," she said wistfully. "We got the color scheme from Oscar Wilde. Oscar Wilde is my second-favorite writer of all time. I just love the way he makes you laugh and all the time you know he's crying inside. I'm so sorry you got detention."

She began to scratch hard at the skin beneath her long sleeves.

"Stop," I told her.

She hopped away down the curb, birdlike, swinging her taut sleeves this way and that. "Oscar Wilde was such a terrific liar."

"I thought you didn't like lies."

"Oscar Wilde told lies but they were stories," she said to the air behind her. "That's different."

"He would have saluted the flag," she added, with such finality that I wouldn't have thought to disagree.

At the corner of Emerson and West Teaneck Avenue, we loitered. A flock of birds sat with marked aplomb on a telephone wire. There would be telephone calls, a flurry of them, to ascertain my safe arrival home—I knew that—but I was tired of bells ringing on me, ahead of me, because of me, and this was a moment my friend and I might not have again. The air felt very much like fall air. A lone leaf dangled down and a crow flew overhead. I slid my hand inside Rachel's jacket pocket, a game I used to play with my father and sometimes played with S-Man. "We're lezzies," she said, which sounded so funny that we both laughed.

"Maybe someday we could go to Prague," she suggested. She toed the earth and smiled sadly.

"It's about my sister," I panted.

Then and there, I lied. I told Rachel Fish that my sister and Haywood Lofty had not only become betrothed to each other in fifth grade, but had run away. I told her that before his father died (actually of a broken heart, I said) Haywood had been in the habit of escorting Elaine home, and that he had come into our house many times and spent many afternoons upstairs in her boudoir.

"How can you die of a broken heart?" she asked.

"He was so worried about them," I said vaguely. Rachel Fish nodded, then asked how Haywood could have walked Elaine home.

"They would wait for Francis to go back to the hospital," I explained, which was true enough. "Then she would meet Haywood on Emerson, and he would walk her the rest of the way. Our parents disapproved because—well. You know."

Rachel Fish sighed. If possible, her eyes grew huger. Some lovers will do just about anything, we knew from our readings on the subject; and the younger you are, the longer and more truly you love. I lingered, embellishing the courtship: telling her how Haywood would leave notes for my sister under a largish rock, how she would look both ways before squatting to grope under it. "He used to write these poems," I whispered. Rachel Fish nodded. "They were really dumb poems," I said.

"Then what?"

"Then what." We had rounded the corner and were walking uphill toward Kensington Avenue, down which broad street lay her family's house with its colorful interior. My father and I had driven by it many times. It looked like a gingerbread house, with white-peaked sloping roofs and the grass growing wild because her parents, socially progressive, didn't believe in mowing lawns. I wondered what she would do when we had reached that corner. I felt reckless. I felt capable of following her anywhere, even to the house with rainbow walls and dangling furniture. In my mind's eye I saw another house with a telephone and a thin figure of a mother rushing to answer; what of it? "Then our parents found out," I said. "You don't know how my father is."

"How did they found out?"

"Because Haywood's father died. There wasn't as much money in the family. Haywood had to get a job. He found a paper route three days a week, and the other days he helped take care of his sister. The lovers," I added, "began to feel desperate. Maybe they just wanted everyone to know. He started calling our house in the evening."

"How did your parents find out?" she insisted.

"I'm trying to tell you. Haywood and Elaine knew their parents would never let them get married. Elaine decided they had to run away. She needed my help, so she told me, which is how I know. They saved up Elaine's allowance, and she borrowed an old suitcase of my mother's and Haywood made some extra money helping other boys with their paper routes. One day they went to the Greyhound terminal and tried to buy two one-way tickets to Reno. The stationmaster told them they couldn't have tickets just like that, even with money. So before he could call the police, they set out on foot. They got as far as Hackensack."

"Wow," said Rachel. "What were they doing there?"

"Beats me," I said. "The police said they were just standing by the Hackensack River."

"I bet they wanted to drown themselves."

"No," I said vigorously. "They didn't know where to go. Even if they had gotten to Reno, no one would have rented them a hotel room. They were only in fifth grade."

"Then what?"

"Well, that's the terrible part," I said. "Haywood's mother wouldn't let him see Elaine once my father called her. She said her son was a good boy, and Elaine was just trouble."

"Just white trash," I added.

"What about your parents?"

We had reached Kensington. Rachel was walking slowly, positioning her feet in the cracks and lines of the sidewalk, a reversal of that childhood game.

"That's why I don't want you to come over," I said, lowering my voice. "They're terrible to her. They say terrible things about Haywood and his family. About people like him. They're the worst hypocrites in the world."

"So now you know," I said after a while. "My sister suffers from a broken heart, and she does things that don't make any sense. She can't be trusted. And my parents seem nice, but really they're terrible racists."

Rachel Fish freed her hand from mine in her pocket. She touched my sleeve and moved toward me. She was standing so close that I could see myself reflected in her eyes, and her breath smelled at once sharp and sweet. I had been hearing bells all afternoon and now another went off.

"We have to help them," she said.

Chapter Seven

A Breather at Reading

"**S**-MAN," I SAID. "THERE'S SOMETHING I'VE been meaning to tell you."

"What's that?" he asked.

We had been flying over England for some time, and I was beginning to wonder when we would land. There didn't seem much point in hovering forever above a landscape grown dreary, east of London; and yet S-Man seemed disinclined to approach the villages and fields still so tiny below us and rendered all the drearier by the approach of winter. The light glowed dull, unseasonably even for November—the date was November 21, the year 1895—and here and there patches of fog blinded the human eye to its surroundings. Perhaps to offset the effect of this environment, S-Man had chosen for the occasion a costume composed of multitudinous swathes of color: his cape gleamed vermilion, his cowl crimson, his leotard ocher; the *S* in the middle of his chest shone green and blinked on and off. I was tempted to tell him, but didn't, that from a certain angle he looked a bit like a traffic light.

"I know," he said suddenly. "Let's take a breather."

He dove down until we had reached the rim of a large white cloud bank. I expected him to continue on, but instead of the cold mist of a cloud's interior, I felt the sudden warmth of sunlight, albeit faint, on my face, my shoulders, my arms, and felt also the uncloudlike resistance of the substance beneath us. S-Man motioned me to sit; he took off his vermilion cape and wrapped it snugly around my shoulders and knees, and its warmth made me forget my petty objections to his ensemble. I didn't even ask how he had contrived to render the cloud solid enough to rest upon, as in picture books or old stories. (My companion had in fact manufactured it in the Citadel of Isolation, where, during his "time-share," he performed such experiments.) I was willing enough to sit beside him, his *S* blinking lazily on and lazily off.

This was to be, I had decided, our last detour. I was a little disappointed that we had made it to rescue Mr. Oscar Wilde, who seemed (in spite of Rachel Fish's enthusiasm) the antithesis of the author I had chosen for a mentor. Even now I meant to tell S-Man about Laff Riot and my fears for our town. Undoubtedly S-Man would help right the wrong, as he always had. There was no question that he would also terminate our adventures, once he realized the danger he had put us in. He would take me to Mr. Kafka, from whose advice I still hoped to benefit. Then he would return me to New Jersey and that would be that.

For just this while longer, then, we sat on our cloud above Reading Gaol and took a breather. We had seen heroism in our travels together, but we had also seen inhumanity and hypocrisy and selfishness. We talked now about the villains we had encountered and others still unknown to me and we talked also about the diverse weaknesses—S-Man called them "Achilles' heels"—of each opponent: Mr. Stick's I knew, of course; and I gathered dimly that Laff Riot's very technological skill might be used to his disadvantage; and as for that terrible Assemblage, said S-Man, one thing he couldn't stand was *harmony*. I reminded my companion of the day Shakespeare's mind, reconciled with itself, had caused the intelligence collectors on Assemblage's skull to burst one by one; but S-Man only repeated what he had said, as if Shakespeare's spirit and *harmony* were somehow indistinguishable. After that S-Man seemed content to let me follow my own trains of thought. Perhaps he also felt the dreariness of the season as it pressed upon us; then too, he possessed the power of gazing into the future. We who cannot prophesy have reason to feel grateful.

"What did you want to tell me?" S-Man asked presently.

I hesitated, the *S* blinking. Perhaps, I thought, it stood for "secret."

The cost of my avowal, like the fine for an overdue library book, seemed to have accrued. How to tell S-Man, who never lied, who so rarely suffered doubt or self-examination, that I had told my closest friend (my only friend, barring him) a series of blatant untruths? Even now, no doubt, she was preparing to aid my sister and Haywood Lofty to elope! With her there would be no hesitation until my fraud was uncovered. She was like S-Man in that respect: a born volunteer.

I told myself—beware such self-serving constructs!—that there wasn't any real hurry, because we had just come out of a time tunnel into another era. Whatever was going to happen at home couldn't possibly be happening yet; or rather, if it were, we could always catch up to it, couldn't we? There was no injunction, so far as I knew, against changing the future. Wasn't that what people, perfectly normal people, did every day of their lives?

A wisp of cloud drifted past. S-Man blew it on its way, then summoned it back—with his superbreath he arranged for it to spell the *S* of his name.

"Quit it," I said.

The wisp wiggled its nether end, so to speak, and dissipated.

"Did you ever feel as though someone was better than you?" I asked.

He didn't say anything for a while.

"Did I ever tell you about when I was a kid?" he asked in turn, and I realized that he thought I meant him!

I nodded, pulling the folds of his cape tighter.

Another cloud, white and puffy like ours, approached; S-Man blew it gently enough into several puffs that dispersed in the atmosphere. In spite of the season, my limbs felt toasty beneath the cape's otherworldly layers. Perhaps all was well enough. I thought how it would be when the writer from Prague and I met up at last. Rachel Fish's words ("Who's your favorite writer?") came to me but I pushed them away like so many clouds. A quality of authenticity, something bonelike, emanated from my friend; she would do important things; and yet hadn't I, and not she, been chosen by S-Man for this destiny? All I lacked, he had so often insisted, was *patience.*

But hadn't I learned something about patience from Mr. Shakespeare? From Madame de P.—the real one? And Albert? Perhaps Albert and I would meet up again someday (we would, as you know). Perhaps I would become a real writer! Since the onset of summer and the taking of my double vows, I hadn't actually put pen to paper. Something seemed each time to stem the flow of my words. But that would pass, no doubt, and I thought happily enough of my Igbo friend across the world, and of the harmattan and then of the photographs that adorned my bedroom wall and how their faces had seemed so pale, upon my arrival home from Enugu, and how I had begun to wonder even then whether the club of literature wasn't expanding and if it meant that no one writer would ever again achieve the fame of, say, a Shakespeare, because whatever he was, he wouldn't be something else—not a Hindu and not a Chinese person and not a Nigerian—and so there would always be something that he hadn't said, and then I couldn't decide if that would be a pity or not although, I was certain, Rachel Fish would have known.

"They're transferring him right about now," S-Man said. He didn't move. "I want you to remember," he said after a moment. "If you hear things—"

"Later on, you mean." Once again, I realized, he was talking about himself.

"—things that don't make sense."

"I won't listen to other people," I said. "I'll always know who to believe."

He nodded, apparently satisfied, and went on as if I hadn't just admitted to having heard the story of his arrival on Earth. There is a pleasure to stories we have heard before, and I wrapped the cape more tightly around my shoulders and folded its soft indestructible hem around my hands.

"I don't remember anything from before Pa Kant found me," he said. "Ma and Pa had wanted a son of their own for a long time. One day Pa was driving down the highway, on his way to the adoption agency, when out of nowhere he heard a whistling noise and saw something fall from the sky. This was before people started seeing UFOs."

"But it was a UFO," I said.

"Well. In this universe, yes."

"Wasn't he scared?"

"He pulled his car over and got out, and walked across the field to the ditch where my rocket had fallen, and what shocked him right off was that I was apparently unhurt. I was crying, but not the way a kid cries from pain. Pa had the presence of mind to wrap me in my blanket, the one my birth parents had given me, and then he carried me across the field and into his truck, and sat me on his knees and drove around so I would stop crying and Ma would think he had gone as far as the adoption agency in Columbus. Even so she was surprised to see us arrive home so soon. Later she admitted she was just so glad that she didn't ask too many questions. And then, after a few weeks, when they could see there was something strange going on, she made him explain."

"What happened to the rocket?"

S-Man frowned. "We never knew," he said. "She made him drive to the field where he had left the rocket, but it was gone."

"And you never—"

"—tried to find it? No. They had the blanket and that was enough. Put out your hand."

I did so; something dropped onto my palm: it was a sandwich, a peanut-butter-and-jelly sandwich, wrapped in the sort of translucent wax-paper bag that Rachel Fish and I had always coveted!

"Put out your other hand," he said again and I almost missed the eight-ounce Grade A milk carton that fell toward my palm. I tried to smile. S-Man and I had from the start frankly discussed my allergies to certain foods and how those allergies dissipated in the past. I will spare you the full explanation of this phenomenon and say only that as I understood it, I couldn't be allergic to something if I didn't exist yet.

"It's okay," he said, thinking perhaps that I hesitated for fear of an allergic reaction, even so.

"Wow," I said, miming eagerness. "Thanks. But how did they know you needed a costume?"

"Uniform," he corrected mildly. "All that was much later."

I held the milk carton on my knee. It had been nine years or several centuries (depending on your timepiece) since I had last tasted cow's milk. What's more, I knew without a doubt that had Rachel Fish been here to comment—what an odd thought!—she would have urged me to enjoy this treat. And yet, remembering the way we two had shared those difficult moments on the lunch lines, so that they weren't difficult but great fun, I felt something very like lack of appetite.

S-Man squinted; no doubt he was using his S-vision to observe the terrain.

From far below I heard the faint whistle and, reminded of my hometown and country and era, I peered over our cloud, but saw only a tiny gray smoke puff above two lightly penciled parallel lines. I unwrapped the sandwich, took out a triangular half (we liked our sandwiches triangled) and bit into it. White bread! Another extravagance, one of which Francis and Rose would not have approved. I chewed therefore as slowly as possible, and with each bite savored that sweet sticky mixture with its jagged peanut chips. I would drink the milk, I decided, sip by sip and only after I had finished my sandwich.

"I pretty much wrecked the place a few times," S-Man said. "I just didn't know my own strength. And by the time I was in high school, I was pretty full of myself. Pretty wild. There wasn't anything I couldn't do, you see—and yet I had this kind of hole inside where an idea of myself should have been. I shoplifted sometimes. I began to hang out with the wrong guys. Little by little I hinted to them about what I could do. Until one day Pa set me down and told me the agency wouldn't let me stay if I didn't shape up. He was telling a sort of truth: if people had found out what I was capable of, they wouldn't have let me grow up in a human household. I would have become a specimen or worse. Who knows? Without a stable family life, a lot of potentially good people go wrong."

"My sister has a stable family life," I said.

"That's what you think," said S-Man. I could tell he wasn't listening, or he wouldn't have made that remark. He never took sides in family squabbles, however fierce.

"I don't think you can understand how it is," he said. "To grow up knowing there's something you can't let other people know about. Something that makes you a lot stronger, a lot more dangerous. Something that might make them stop loving you if they find out. I had a terrible crush on a girl once."

"You mean—"

He shook his head. "Before her," he said.

"Oh ho," I said. "You never told me about that one."

"You never asked."

At that moment, quite by accident, I dropped my milk carton; down it went, spiraling toward Reading! S-Man trained his S-vision on it and it disappeared. A slight odor of burnt milk and waxy carton wafted back.

"Her name was Sarah," he went on. "Sarah Salem."

"What did she look like?" I asked, swallowing. Peanut butter stuck to the roof of my mouth and I poked it experimentally with my tongue. I still had the wax-paper bag; I busied myself folding it into smaller and smaller squares.

"She wasn't what you would have called pretty," he said. "But she had something about her that made you keep looking."

"I know what you mean."

"She lived on a farm not far from ours," he said. "I would stop at her gate on my way home from school. She wasn't even old enough to walk to school by herself and she still had chores—I mean hard chores like cleaning the pigs' sty or feeding them slops. She must have been about eight years old and she still didn't know how to read."

"She didn't know how to read!" I exclaimed.

"Nope. But she loved to hear about school. I would tell her all sorts of things, things I had learned that day or knew from my parents—I mean my adoptive parents, Ma and Pa Kant. The way I knew she liked it was that she would come down to the mailbox as if she were checking for mail. There never was any. Then one day there was a letter from the truant officer."

"Saying what?"

"I suppose it said her parents had to let her go to school."

"So?"

"So she went. And after that, she wasn't waiting for me by the gate. I would see her sometimes in the schoolyard, but we wouldn't speak."

"That's a sad story."

"No," he said. "It's happy."

"Isn't it time?"

S-Man nodded; I unwrapped the cape from my shoulders and handed it to him. He slipped the cowl around his neck, gathered me into his arms—I brushed crumbs off his neon-green sleeve and watched them recede—and we began our descent, S-Man blowing gently so that the cloud preceded us. He filled me in on this latest mission and

Tunneling

I listened carefully, understanding only to the extent that my twelve-year-old sensibility was capable and storing details away for future meditation.

Did I know about Oscar Wilde? S-Man asked delicately.

"What about him?"

As it happens, a book of Wilde's fairy tales had for some years stood on a shelf in my parents' home. This book held for me (it holds for me still) a fascination having to do, I think, with the sorrow that never quite engulfed the form of a story; what Rachel Fish might have called "the way he always seems to be crying but makes you happy." My fascination—it was not quite approval—had also to do with the book jacket, on whose whitish background stood a purple prince on a purple pedestal in a purple city square. His coat of mail—he wore mail, a bejeweled sword, a crown—shone intact but for an empty patch where a leaf of mail should have lain. Telltale patch! This, then, was the Happy Prince, on whose shoulder perched a bird, a sparrow who would espy a person in need and report to the prince, and at his suggestion pluck a gold leaf from the coat (purple only on the cover) and carry the leaf through the cold city to the person's rescue. The figures in this tale, with their acts of extreme generosity and self-sacrifice, had troubled me; more so did those of the infanta and the misshapen dwarf who dies of a broken heart, thereby spoiling, the infanta says, stamping her pretty foot, her birthday party. And so on. I had read this book early in life and gone on reading it, disquieted by these and other acts and above all by the disenchantment that crept from its pages. Were people truly so capricious? In my experience they were more likely to err out of mere self-interest.

In any event the Oscar Wilde of whom I now heard tell hardly seemed the author of a collection of fairy tales. He was in jail ("That's g-a-o-l," said S-Man) on charges for which no twentieth-century British citizen would have been arrested; indeed, in Wilde's own time, a British law forbidding "immoral acts between men" had been passed only

weeks prior to his famous trial and subsequent sentencing to two years'
imprisonment with hard labor. Hard labor! It wasn't the labor so much
as the diet, said S-Man; not the diet so much as the dysentery and the
ear damaged from a fall; neither the dysentery nor the infected ear so
much as the constant punishment for the slightest infractions, including speech; and none of these so much as the fact of being forbidden
pen and paper.

"So we're here to get him out?"

Reading Village and its environs lay below: stone houses and
swampy brown fields and sheep like white cloud puffs reflected against
a liquid brown sky.

"No," said my companion. "He hasn't arrived yet."

"We're here to give him pen and paper?"

"No."

"It's the train, isn't it. We're going to hijack the train."

On our way here and now from New Jersey and 1970, S-Man had
told me about this particular morning in Wilde's life, during which he
was to be shuttled from one prison to another. At this very moment, he
reminded me, Mr. Wilde, in prison garb (a gray sort of pajama with
great black arrows everywhere) and handcuffs—handcuffs!—sat aboard
a train chugging into this station where, due to an unfortunate delay, he
would wait hours for the prison van. S-Man shook his head. The
swathes of color in his uniform seemed to have dimmed, and the *S*
blinked more slowly.

"I give up," I said.

We had flown close enough to graze the treetops. Once again,
steadying our cloud with his superbreath, S-Man motioned for me to
hop on. I crawled to the puffy rim and looked over. The village con-
sisted of a square (deserted now) surrounded by a few white-and-brown
houses and tall bare elms, and a stone-gray station house. A small crowd
awaited the train's arrival. An automobile pointed its hood toward the
station house, where a horse stood tethered. The horse flicked its tail

and snickered; a hooting arose in the distance; the hooting became a blaring and the horse more agitated as the train pulled into the station. The cars—there were three—rocked forward and back. A door swung open and a police officer appeared, followed by a man who stumbled onto the platform.

This man bore little resemblance to the Oscar Wilde whose face looked out from the purple book jacket in my parents' home. That Mr. Wilde wore his long hair parted over a high forehead; that Mr. Wilde had strange sloping eyes and a hawked nose and full lips; that Mr. Wilde sported a thick-collared, fur-lined woolen coat. This man's hair was cropped short and combed stiffly to one side. He had the strange eyes but the look in them had altered. Overall he made a gaunt and unattractive figure, unattractive because his face had lost most but not all of its haughtiness. The struggle between pain, and fear of his situation, and this haughty remnant puts me most in mind, as I write this memoir, of the shards of Mrs. Zingenberg's face after she had struck Colin Duffy. This man, I remind you, had not struck anyone; I wanted, therefore, to like him. Rachel Fish (I couldn't help thinking) would have. And yet the pitiful figure he cut—rain had begun to fall gently, so that a villager lifted his head to peruse the sky, and S-Man pulled me lightning-fast from the cloud's rim—seemed to stop up whatever source of pity I possessed.

The villagers had began to murmur; someone called out to someone else; what if they happened to glance up? There was no real danger to S-Man or me if anyone spotted us, no doubt; but there was the usual question of the extent to which history might be altered should our interventions become known seventy years earlier than planned. In my then-numbness, with a chill settling around my heart, I might not have cared!

The villagers had begun to speak more loudly among themselves, and the same man who had peered up at the raindrops now exclaimed, "I tell ye who it is. That thar is Mr. Oscar Wilde!"

At which a gasp went up and a woman draped her arms around the shoulders of two young children, who shook free as villagers jeered. Mr. Wilde blinked. The corners of his mouth turned down. I wondered if he was about to cry.

Instead he vanished, leaving only a pair of manacles on the station floor.

"Holy Mother," whispered S-Man. "Not again!"

A tinkling like and unlike human laughter filled the air.

"What's going on?" I asked, clouds whipping past, birds squawking as they were swept along in our wake.

"Rash of disappearances," S-Man said tersely. "All in the last day or so."

"You mean—1885?"

He shook his head impatiently.

"Where are we going?" I asked. Ahead of us a gray time tunnel was taking shape and fabric from the atmosphere. I felt the first exposure to the weblike substance of which such tunnels are constructed, the first winnowing of my bones as the stuff (was it stuff, precisely?) harrowed me. "S-Man?"

"No time!" he shouted. I closed my eyes and allowed him to tuck me more securely into his cape. We flew off again! The gray walls loomed, pulsed, enveloped us; all seemed colorless, perhaps even point-less; certainly, as Mrs. Carlsbad would have said, relative.

We emerged beneath an impossibly blue sky onto a white-hot beach.

"Stopover," said S-Man. "Cyprus. Greece is what we want. The year 490 B.C."

I nodded, eager to play whatever role destiny demanded and yet more affected than I liked to say by our rapid journey. Clearly there was, as S-Man had maintained, "no time"; we dove once more into the gray tunnel (I felt the harrowing in my thighs, hips, girl's womb; that slow relentless pressure of so many years) and reemerged over low tile roofs and winding alleyways onto a hill overlooking a quiet harbor. A little island sparkled in the sun. To our left stood a kind of open pillared temple—it looked a little like the NJ Savings & Loan—and below us, down the green rocky slope, nestled (if such a large thing could nestle) the round stone tiers of an open-air market. My spirits rallied. I didn't know yet what this visit had to do with Oscar Wilde, but like many schoolchildren I had studied the Parthenon and the Acropolis, and even without the shell (which I now slipped out of my pocket) I would have known an "amphitheater" or an agora when I saw one.

S-Man gathered me into his arms. We flew swiftly downslope.

No sooner had we landed on the highest circular row of that very amphitheater than the audience—by which I mean thousands of men in white togas and some hundreds of women in longer white dresses with high-swept hair and here and there a boy in the company of a man or a woman—burst into loud applause, and a tall person wearing what my companion described as a gold-trimmed purple-sashed toga seemed born of the resounding hullabaloo. "First prize," S-Man whispered. I clutched the shell but couldn't hear what the announcer was saying or see much from this distance. I still felt thirsty, then forgot my thirst. Near us a man sat examining a walking staff; he wore sandals that roped up his ankles and his hands on the staff were long fingered. A woman sat a few feet apart; she looked very beautiful with her hair coiled high and her lips brightly painted, but I wondered if she was sad to sit alone. And another woman wore a snake coiled right around her arm! What would Albert have said about that!

The first man had allowed himself to be carried offstage by two others who paraded him expertly around the central arena; each successive section cheered as they passed. The bearers seemed to be wearing very high heels. Eventually silence fell. The sad beautiful woman crossed one sandaled foot over the other. Then a second wave of clapping seemed to produce another pair of thespians and a second man, perhaps older than the first. "Here we go," said S-Man, "second prize." He scooped me into his arms and flew with me over the tiered crowd toward the central stage (really a low round arena with a few raised platforms and some sort of machine on giant wheels).

"S-Man!" I said, because I had heard the sad woman and the man with the walking stick gasp as we took off, and now we were approaching the stage in full view of some several thousand Athenians, but he flew on; and I suppose I wasn't surprised, given his recklessness, when this second man disappeared.

"Who was that?" I asked, but it was only after we had once again entered a time tunnel—in fact, we were to enter it many more times in what I experienced as an afternoon—that he answered briefly, "Socrates. I mean Sophocles."

"Oh," I said.

"Can't we rest a little?" I asked, but we were off again. Sophocles from the stage, the philosopher Socrates from his prison cell (on the morning of his last speech to the Athenian Council, S-Man explained), Euripides in the midst of a rather loud marital argument—just as I thought there was a pattern to the disappearances (everyone except Mr. Wilde seemed Greek), we dove into the time tunnel and emerged into the bustling, smog-ridden city of nineteenth-century London.

And so on.

Greece, England, Italy, Germany, France, the US of A—or rather I should say Athens, London, Rome, Munich, Paris and New York—and Algiers—in Algiers we floated, S-Man zooming this way and that, above white-clay houses and squat dwellings and European-style bars until from the last bar emerged a Frenchman whose eyes glittered above an oval face and who ran stumbling down an alleyway covering his eyes so that he must have been blind to the moment of his own disappearance—

"Who was that?" I asked, but the wind grabbed my voice away.

Tunneling

Well! Were the personal not quite so boring to others, and were nothing quite so personal as questions of one's health, I might be tempted to rest long enough to blame that afternoon, alas, for my youth's foreshortening. And yet—knowing what I know, would I trade normal female health for the sheer hoopla of that high-speed chase through time and continent? Once, rushing above rooftops (we returned often to London), I made the mistake of breathing deeply of the London fog and caught such a chestful of smoke and fog and tar, and something else I couldn't name that had to do with closed rooms and unavowed practices, that I shivered, remembering how in another life such air would have sent me to the hospital bed and the oxygen tank. I knew that something terrible had to be happening for S-Man to drag me through history and I clung with all my might to his cape and when next we emerged, panting, from still another gray pulsing tunnel, everything was very quiet. Or rather a kind of throbbing filled the air, such as one might hear if one were to take the sounds of a cathedral and play them back, amplified. We were nowhere near a cathedral but on a promontory overlooking a green landscape. This is a landscape to which I have often returned in dreams and each time with the best surprise, that is, one born of repetition. I should add that beneath the sounds to which I have referred ran the murmuring commentary of the ocean. Were we on an island?

"Keep your eyes open for a guy with mustaches," S-Man just had time to say.

"Greetings," said a musical voice.

"You! I mean, She!" S-Man said, whirling. "I expected as much."

A scent of earth and the earliest crocuses and the salt sea wafted toward us. The woman thus addressed—I supposed "She" was a woman, although she might just as well have been of another planet or order of being—cocked her diademed head. She had been on the verge of drinking from a large goblet. Instead she smiled and raised the goblet, as if to salute S-Man (She entirely ignored my presence). Again I felt thirsty. Hadn't we just chased all around the space-time continuum in the name of literature? Instead of grabbing She or scolding her, S-Man just stood staring, his arms folded mid-chest.

My American heart began to beat strangely.

The "woman" looked very beautiful, of course, although later I heard men say that She had looked one way and others another, and some even insisted that the personage who had ruled over that island kingdom was in fact a male figure, possessed not of a goblet of ambrosia but of red wine, and a staff that withered and bloomed, and an entourage of wild animals and women whose eyes bled the same wild color as the wine he carried. In my eyes, at least, She's blond locks flowed around a wide high brow and her eyes shone the color of wheat, and her chiseled nose could appear stern and her lips were full and delineated, and there was that firm chin. She also wore very little clothing, so that her ripe figure was exceedingly visible. She had in fact what Rachel Fish and I would have called a Class-A bosom. And yet there wasn't, I don't think, anything flashy about her. She seemed to satisfy rather than provoke. I expected a wand; she carried none.

"Where are we?" I whispered. S-Man seemed suddenly conscious of his appearance—running his fingers through his hair and adjusting the waistband of his colorful uniform.

"How lovely to see you again," She said.

"The pleasure is mine," he said.

"Where are we?" I asked more loudly.

The creature seemed for the first time to notice me.

"Do I know you? You remind me of someone," She said. She looked over my head at the hillside, as if hoping that the someone would appear. When She rather carelessly held out the goblet, I felt piqued enough to refuse.

"Welcome to paradise," she said lightly.

Just then a man walked over that same hill. "Mr. Sophocles! I mean, yes, Mr. Sophocles!" I cried.

Tunneling

But forgive me! I had ought to take a little more care in describing to you our environs! S-Man and I were never to return to the island—it was indeed an island—and in how brief a time we, you and I, will also take our leave! Already the waters heave, froth, dissolve; already that great horned bull, History, advances another shuddering step toward shore.

Imagine then that you were arriving not by air but in a more orderly fashion, perhaps even by boat. You dock your vessel at a long rickety quay, make fast its rope around the iron mooring and set out up a straight drive, past salt marshes thick with wildlife (it is early spring) to one side, and a small lake in which a rowboat dawdles, its inhabitants both familiar and unfamiliar, until you come to a fork in the road. A largish sign reads (on the island there is no need for Aquaman's shell; all languages echo with equal mystery) TO THE GARDENS, and were you to follow the arrow, you would find yourself among the most exquisite, because not entirely blooming, of gardens. Here the promise of rose and marigold and tulip makes itself felt, and vines begin shyly to rise from the soil only to hide their poking heads, as in Della Robbia's blue-bordered landscapes, among the white trellises that have weathered another winter. Then do you turn and face the just-green rectangular fields, and with the iron smell of young earth (and that other of brine) in your nostrils, set out once more toward the mansion on the hilltop some several hundred yards beyond. I say "mansion," but you must understand that everything here lies frozen in time, and so this and the outlying buildings give off a quaintness, even a mustiness, such as interiors of certain nineteenth-century novels may do.

Before the mansion with its stone face and wide windows, one pane of which even at this hour has been opened, lies a stone terrace where (even at this hour) a few figures, quite human and sleep-tousled (and all, I noticed, wearing white togas), gather to drink from smaller versions of the goblet She had proffered me. They gather, drink, discourse throughout the early morning, whose only fault is that it passes so quickly. Their colloquy would seem patternless, no doubt, to the new-comer; and yet what doesn't it touch upon in the course of an hour? *Generalities?* Yes. *Philosophy* and *Psychology?* Assuredly. *Religion, Social Sciences, Languages* (*200, 300* and *400*)? Indubitably!

Eventually the figures disappear indoors and all is quiet for a while.

In a high tower, perhaps surrounded by ivy, a lone man with trou-bled eyesight—is it our Frenchman, lately of Algiers?—labors on.

Let us take advantage of the calm to peruse also the outlying build-ings, which have their own charm, being that much remoter and home-lier. There are three, the largest facing west with a hint of bravado, and the most remote bearing the name of the tall pines that amplify its rus-tic charm. Even here some ill-expressed gloom, some subtle effect per-haps of the turning inward we associate with the artistic enterprise, makes itself felt: in the ivy, which takes advantage of the return of spring to creep skyward, or in the dark fir boughs. A wide circular path leads to each of these buildings, themselves set back so as to draw one's gaze toward the landscape itself.

The landscape! Bright green lawn slopes toward a sea that never ceases to remind the wayfarer of its ultimate presence; a kind of silent battle thereby declaring itself between the omnipresence of ocean and the more pressing, quotidian concerns of land and land folk. Silent? Not really; a lavish white fountain spouts and douses as if to express this same conflict and its musical resolution, and in the surrounding woods all manner of animal abounds: hare and red fox and the occasional defi-ant doe, and most striking in each is its resemblance unto and only unto its species. How very foxlike the fox's eyes and snout and body; how unmistakable the hare's startled lope and scut and bobbed tail!

As for the humaner—I mean more human—of creatures, they also surprise with their resemblance each unto him- or her- (mostly him-) self. The queen (later S-Man would insist that She wasn't queen of any-thing, and that he personally hadn't seen anything resembling a diadem but the sort of headdress that women on the Mother Planet had used to wear) led us away from the stone terrace via a short path through bushes still to bloom (I felt such an odd longing to stay there, to witness the arrival of seasons) to another hillock where, the sun having begun to shine in greater earnest, an elderly man stood leaning against a large rock surrounded by men and boys. I noticed that not only did the sun shine more brightly, but the flowers on this hill seemed to have bloomed in precipitous anticipation of the full season; as if high noon brought with it the actual shift into summer. Men and boys alike wore white togas, and even without S-Man's help ("This time it is Socrates," he whispered, eyes narrowing as his S-vision kicked in) I would have known the identity of the former.

"Is it really Socrates?" I asked nonetheless, meaning that perhaps the entire island was some sort of illusion, such as Mr. Stick might have created just to trouble us; but S-Man, squinting at the horizon—I suspected that he was looking back through time at ancient Greece— nodded. Both Socrates and Sophocles (also Euripides and Philogenes, Diogenes and Isosceles) were missing from their proper niches, he said. So, for that matter, was Sigmund Freud . . . and Bertholt Brecht, and Isaiah, and Langston Hughes, and Ferdinand de Saussure ("Who?" I asked again and again), and Galileo, and Einstein, and a man named Bohr and a slew of painters, sculptors, poets, rhetoricians and historians.

"And Dante," she said. "He's a bit miffed that we haven't implemented his architecture. All those circles." She shuddered daintily, then smiled. Everything she did seemed to end in a smile. "He's with the dissidents for now. We have a special house set up while they take the waters. And you must let me show you our plans for the Next Phase."

"The Next Phase?" asked S-Man.

"This is just the beginning," She said. She waved her arm. "You don't mean to tell me you think we've finished? We're expanding in every direction. Physically, mentally, spiritually, politically. The nice thing about the System"—here she cast a benevolent, if meaningless, glance at me—"is that it's so flexible. There'll be problems, of course. The interactions of cultures bring problems. But we've anticipated as much as we can, I think. I'd be more than proud to show you the Laugh Shack."

"The Laugh Shack?" asked S-Man, who seemed reduced to repeating himself after her. I was reminded of my mother and felt such an admixture of feelings then, such a desire to be in my mother's presence and such despair at the shrinking aspect of her nature, that I longed to share my confusion with someone, even with She. I felt thirstier than ever. I wished I had accepted to drink from the goblet, and instantly saw it in my mind's eye: crystalline, shapely. I heard S-Man, still scanning centuries, suck in his breath. This was just the sort of situation he most feared, the worst historical chaos. But I had heard a lot about this Mr. Socrates and, forgetting our various concerns, moved to observe him.

He stood addressing the small group and turning upon its members the flushed face (not at all handsome) of certain writers and heavy drinkers. He had a nose like a potato. But his gaze was piercing, and I would not have liked to displease or disappoint him. He seemed not to resent questions from one Xenon, who struck me, I must say, as a bit of a fool. Xenon would ask a question; Socrates would respond forcefully with another; this would set the boys to giggling and scribbling onto their styli; Xenon would blush and stammer another question, stupider than the first. I felt there was something unfair about this exchange but, fascinated by the dip and flash of styli, would have stayed to watch had not the queen (was She queen here, then?) linked arms with S-Man. He paused only to ascertain that I was following before allowing her to draw him on. "What do you mean, Next Phase?" I heard S-Man say again. "Don't be so literal" was the casual response.

"Mother of the Universe," I heard S-Man mutter.

"What's wrong?" I whispered.

"Can't seem to find Walter Pater."

"Is he the guy with mustaches?" I asked, needlessly—S-Man was gesturing to indicate not only mustaches but gigantesque, even grotesque ones.

"Yes," She was still saying. "We anticipate problems whenever newcomers arrive. It's only to be expected when the foremost minds of so many cultures around the world—later, it'll be the universe—interact. We started with the Western tradition but don't get me wrong. What's gender-neutral in one culture reeks of genderism in another; and you guys only have two basic genders. Wait until the Alphacentaurians get here. What's cliché in Europe makes no sense at all in the Australian outback . . . and still less on Calyx number thirty-four, fifth asteroid from Zephyr Omega. There's oral tradition, written tradition, telepathic tradition and everything in between. And of course the Western notion of the self either is or isn't outdated—that is, without our Greek friends"—she waved a hand—"it's perfectly true that there mightn't have been a democracy, but is democracy the answer on such a crowded globe?

"Then," she went on with apparent satisfaction, "there's the question of what constitutes a good joke and what, poor taste. I admit to you, S-Man, that one seemed insurmountable at first—you know how it is with Terrans. Then someone suggested we set up a committee. They've already begun to meet. Formally their meetinghouse is called the Center for the Investigation into the Moral Nature of Humor. We just call it the Laugh Shack."

We had circled the mansion and set off now downhill. The impression of chaos, lingering after our afternoon of flight, began to disperse, and I might have sensed without anyone's telling me that what struck the casual observer as haphazard was in fact a carefully disguised order. Ocean, swamplands, gardens, lawns leading to the mansion and the path with its outlying buildings—all were more representative, perhaps, than real, just as the numbers 100 or 200 or 500 (*Natural Sciences* and *Math*) stand for entities less and more real than themselves. I pondered this and like matters until, hurrying to catch my companion and his guide, I stubbed my toe (I had removed my sneakers) on a very real rock.

"Ouch," I cried.

"Oh, what is it?" responded a man, spinning around. He had a sad wild face, like a prizefighter or journalist, and when I didn't answer he shook his head as if embarrassed by his own alarm. He kept adjusting his toga at the shoulder. He had hairy shoulders.

The queen and S-Man stood waiting. I wasn't surprised by her expression (unperturbed, slightly impatient), but I was by his (unperturbed, etcetera). The man whom I had startled remarked in Arabic comprehensible even without the use of my shell (I had it in my pocket, but as I have mentioned, I found it unnecessary on the island) that it was hellishly hot this time of year. As if to prove his point, he pulled out a great white handkerchief and wiped his neck. "Isn't it?" he asked anxiously. I wanted to inquire if he was all right and had just found the words in his native tongue, when the queen motioned that I was to refrain from questioning him.

"Aren't you supposed to be somewhere?" She frowned.

"Why don't I have a bodyguard?" he asked. "Where is my bloody bodyguard?"

"You're safe here. I told you that," She said. "It's that way."

She pointed over the hilltop; when the man didn't budge, she leaned to whisper in his ear. Whatever she told him was enough to send him, in no time at all, scurrying up the slope and over it.

"Sometimes there's a period of adjustment," she said mildly.

"I should imagine so," said S-Man.

What had been wrong with the man? I wondered. And what was wrong with my supercompanion, for that matter? And what had She meant by "a period of adjustment"?

S-Man and She set off again beneath the trees, and I followed, querying S-Man openly and to no avail. He only said that the writer in question (like the Chinese prisoner whom we also passed along our stroll; he seemed excited enough to have been allowed in under the new rules, and wanted only to know, please, to whom he should address complaints concerning accommodations, and what form of decision-making adhered in this political body, and had we seen the members of his political action committee, who had arranged to assemble today to discuss these and other issues; I looked into his face eagerly because we had watched him disappear from a jail yard in the year 1998, which is to say, the future, while the queen went on smiling tensely, it seemed at least to me, and gazing out over the hilltop as if she sought someone) still had many free years left in our own real-world time, before he would write and publish a novel that would so outrage certain people, religious people who had allowed themselves to be led astray, that they would swear to hunt him down. Wouldn't the countries of the world resist? I wanted to know. Wouldn't our governments do something to protect his right to free speech?

By this time we had passed several authors whose faces I recognized from my own collection of photographs and from my schooling. Some, like the above-mentioned novelists, wandered alone or apparently in search of others; a few seemed resigned to sit by themselves, such as M. Gustave Flaubert, who sat looking uncomfortable in his toga but writing with a determined air into a notebook. He sat in his own leafy clearing, on an elegant iron chair next to which "perched" a rather awful stuffed green parrot. I wanted to ask him something but couldn't remember what, and I had in any event never read his books, and so I took off down the path after the others, who were conversing in urgent low tones.

"It just won't do," S-Man was saying, but he didn't seem inclined to do anything about what wouldn't do. Why not? It annoyed me all the more that he barely noticed my presence, and on a whim, I took a fur-ther detour down a path that hadn't appeared until now. I thought I heard the gurgle of a fountain and determined to drink unnoticed by the others. But I had walked only a few feet into the woods when I saw to my delight and consternation—"S-Man!" I cried, half-turning—the figure of none other than my friend Rachel Fish! "S-Man!" I cried again, as if to thank him or simply to include him in this most fortuitous encounter—but when I turned back, the slim long-sleeved figure must have walked off into the bushes, leaving only the echo of her footsteps and the odd pert way she held her head and the fact of her being slightly pigeon-toed.

"Hey!" I shouted, racing up the path. "Did you see that?"

I had begun, for some reason, to cry.

But at that instant we all heard a shout, and joining the queen and S-Man where they stood atop the hill (we had come almost full circle) I saw a smallish, newer-looking abode, a sort of prefab cabin; the shout, which as we approached became several howls of laughter, had arisen from it. For some reason the queen looked discomfited; S-Man, after training his S-vision upon the cabin walls, rather pleased.

(Later, when I asked, he said that the Committee for the Investigation into the Moral Nature of Humor apparently hadn't gotten very far; that Mr. William Shakespeare—"You mean Mr. Shakespeare was there and you didn't tell me?" I interpolated—had been called upon to speak to the committee, comprised of twenty African, Asian, North American and South American writers, and one Australian, but that Mr. Shakespeare had elected instead to demonstrate what can be done with one fat man playing dead on a battlefield, the result of which had been the hoots and screams we had heard. "Apparently," S-Man said, "one joke in poor taste could keep them entertained for the better part of a day. At that rate, they wouldn't have gotten very far.")

"It's almost noon," She explained stiffly. "Time for a break."

No sooner said than a bell sounded and, turning our backs on the Laugh Shack, we saw how the inhabitants of this odd paradise poured outdoors and emerged from bushes and strolled across patios, and each of them had his or her (but mostly his) lunch box, a quaint black affair with two metal hinges. The queen snapped her fingers and a man with a remarkably thick brown beard and a wild face, like a ferret's or wood-chuck's, appeared with two buckets swinging from either end of a wooden beam he bore upon his shoulders. He smiled nervously (I thought) at me, and I saw that on one bucket was the word *LETHE;* on the other, *EUNOE.* I hoped that the queen would offer me a drink again but she sat deep in conversation with S-Man. Who knows what would have transpired had I had my way? It was the particular enchantment of the island that the more you got, the more you wanted of it; and so, explained the queen, every day at a certain hour it was necessary to call off work. Occasionally it was even necessary to return an inhabitant to the other world, she said, frowning a little at the howls still wafting over the hill.

"No matter," said the queen. "We have all the time in this universe."

Something in her voice made me shiver. When S-Man spoke again, I was surprised by the grave timbre of his voice.

"You have no right," he said. "I am asking you for the last time to return them to their proper places in history."

"Proper places? History?" She waved a braceleted arm (the bracelets swayed, tinkled, shone; the flowers around us seemed no longer to bask in the heat of the day; their petals had lost that unmistakable glow of first youth, although I couldn't say what was altered in their brightness or sheen. And was it my imagination or did She also appear to have— aged? If not aged, to have grown wearier, as if our questions troubled her more than she wanted to say, or as if even her infinite patience was beginning to wear thin?). "Ask them," she said, a certain edge in her voice. "Ask them if they want to go back. If even one were to do so— but I promise you, S-Man, not one will. Thus far, not a single one." Actually she didn't call him S-Man but what I knew to be his given birth name, a word that cannot translate into any Earth language. I meant to ask him as soon as we were alone how it happened that she knew it.

She put her hands to her mouth and called out in a surprisingly loud voice, "Oh Galileo. Halloo."

A dark-eyed man of distinctly Renaissance extraction looked up from his lunch box. She beckoned appealingly; he grabbed his lunch and scurried over to where we sat. "How are things going?" She asked.

"Nicolaus and I have passed a wonderful morning, a morning *magnifico,*" he said happily. His white shirt opened wide at the collar, his leggings clung tightly to his bandy legs. "We had just been discussing the advisability, indeed the necessity, of empirical proof—in this case of the existence of sunspots—when Arthur chose to share with us his remarkable lens."

"I see," She said. "Tell me something. Are you happy here?"

"Happy? Do I seem ungrateful, O most beneficent of patrons?"

"My guests are skeptical," she said, her eyes resting lightly on me.

"Newcomers, perhaps?" he asked, and bowed low enough to kiss her hand, which seemed a popular activity around here. "Galileo Galilei at your service," he said to S-Man. "Are you a technical writer? I heard that a technical writer was coming."

"Our guests won't be staying," she said.

"I'm Rachel," I told him. "Rachel Finch. I've heard about you. You're the man who first said Earth turned around the Sun."

"Hardly the first," he said, smiling.

"Well, congratulations anyhow. Even if you did take it back."

A shadowy pain crossed his face; then his features cleared and he was once again smiling, urbane, eager to return to the little circle of astronomers and other writers excitedly discoursing over lunch.

"You'll notice," She said, "that they associate with whomever they like. At night he sleeps in his tower, but by day he does as he pleases."

We walked on, passing other small gatherings until, from the lowest garden tier, a last group emerged amid haughty, high-pitched laughter. What different kinds of laughter there are in this world! The group, still tittering, spread out around the fountain, where the first of its members pulled himself onto the low white wall surrounding the jet of water. I say "jet," but the fountain had *two* jets, a fact that the reader will understand, if you haven't already, to be of some significance.

"Galileo has forgotten, you see," she said. "I can't do everything, but I can do that much. Here on this island of mine, you remember what you choose."

"*You* choose?" asked S-Man, softly.

"*You, I,* what difference does it make? Would you have him remember threats of torture? Weeks spent alone or in the company of one corrupt priest or, worse, another who believed? Would you have him recall months, years after he had recanted and they kept him locked in his rooms until he went blind from loneliness? It's not just for them," she said, leaning forward. "I can help you too, my friend. It wouldn't take so very much. The choice is all yours. I rob most men of memory, but I can also render it."

I think her words had taken S-Man by surprise, because as he went on looking at her his half-smile faded.

"Don't you want to know what it was like?" she asked, her voice syrupy, overripe. I noticed wrinkles around her eyes that I hadn't before, and a fleshiness to the corners of her mouth. "The good parts, I mean."

Did he nod? Later he would insist that he hadn't. Did he lift the goblet she proffered to his lips? I know I licked mine.

"Look," She said, pointing.

We followed her finger toward the bottom of the hill, some distance beyond the fountain, where a line of trees indicated the border between the mansion and its environs, and the swampy lands that led to the rocky shore. S-Man swallowed loudly and handed her back her goblet. Something was sailing over the horizon. What? I had seen extraterrestrial vessels, of course; indeed, upon landing here I had wondered if I had somehow missed, given the stopovers we had made, our own passage right out of this world. This vessel, however, resembled none that

I had seen on any planet. It cut an undangerous slow path through the air. It shimmered. It must have had dimensions, but I recall only the rainbow shimmer and again a kind of humming that filled the air, as if we had entered a cathedral and someone were throwing its susurrations back at us. I felt an odd desire to lie down. S-Man, having stood very tall, sank to one knee. Did he see what I saw? A figure much resembling a man flew upright out a portal or door. Without speaking, the man stood to one side; the portal opened again and a second figure, that of a woman (of similar Class-A dimensions, I couldn't help noticing, but far more youthful than the now middle-aged queen), appeared.

"As you see," She said. "Nothing harmful, though much that hurts."

S-Man flew across the lawn; the queen and I caught up with him by the fountain, where he hovered, looking around wildly for the figures, who seemed to have blended into the dual mists.

"Mother," whispered S-Man. "Father! Wait."

"All you have to do is drink," She said, pointing. I saw now that the fountain was in fact split into two currents that spouted endlessly: above one, as on the buckets the brown-bearded man carried from group to group, a sign read LETHE; above the other, EUNOE. "Oblivion," She said. "Or partial recall. As you please."

Just then, looking beyond the fountain's round rim, I spotted a man whose most obvious physical trait was a pair of enormous waxed mustaches: was this the Pater of whom S-Man had spoken? Instinctively I stumbled forward, then stopped when I saw that among the little laughing crowd, surrounded by high-spirited people, each of whom flashed a goblet above the glittery reflections of the fountain, lounged Mr. Oscar Wilde.

"Oh Oscar," said a woman, waving a fan. She looked like an actress with her wide eyes and delicate features, but for her waistline distended beneath her toga.

"Oscar, I just can't believe that of you," she warbled.

Tunneling

"A lack of imagination of which I would not boast," came the response from the Irishman, whose help I might have attempted to enlist—S-Man seemed so beside himself—had it not been for Mr. Wilde's own goblet, which he twisted in the pale afternoon sun and then emptied in a swift gulp. He had exchanged his striped prison togs for a toga, and boy did he look happy! He whipped out a handkerchief, wiped his fleshy mouth and refilled the goblet. He proffered it to the woman, who drank, then, with a puzzled expression, asked just what it was they had been discussing. I saw the haughtiness go from his face, to be replaced with an inestimable look of something very like pity. The day had grown cold; he led her around the fountain to where the sun shone most heatedly.

The man with mustaches had slipped unnoticed (except by me) into the shade of a nearby grove. He stood watching the goings-on by the fountain, but when I moved toward him, he lifted a finger to what must have been, beneath bristling handlebars, his mouth.

"That's Lillie Langtry," the queen went on explaining. "She's pregnant. Shall I send her back too? She came with him, but I will if you insist. Back there she has to disappear for a year to convince the world of her respectability."

"What about the others?" asked S-Man quietly.

"What others?"

"The ones who aren't here. The ones that got left behind."

She shrugged almost irritably and adjusted the diadem (as I saw it) more comfortably on her blond locks, which were, I realized with some regret, dyed.

"You mean them?" she asked, waving her hand—beyond the fountain and the thick trees, I saw many figures waving at us. At first I took their waves for greetings, but as they swarmed closer I saw that their faces were distorted and that they waved objects—pitchforks in some cases, sticks and clubs and crosses and anything they could get their hands on, in others. "They aren't worth the trouble."

"Don't," said S-Man sharply.

She had been on the verge, I think, of passing some sort of spell, but upon his urging she lifted her slightly sagging shoulders, and the crowd seemed to rise of its unified accord and drift toward us through the trees, pitchforks and clubs and crosses and so on falling from their hands and landing with a *kerplunk!* in the low waters of the farthest reaches of the fountain, so that Mr. Wilde turned his head in their direction.

"Where have you taken them?" S-Man asked.

"What are they so mad about?" I asked eagerly.

"Sin." She sneered past me at S-Man. "They'll wander around for a while and then, if you insist, I'll turn them into flesh-and-blood people. I can't imagine why you bother. In every age there are people who would impose on artists a *système de pensée.*"

"A what did she say?"

She ignored me. "And in every age, there are artists who transcend the pettiness of the commoner's vision of things. And can you imagine, ———," she said, using his Mother Planet name again, "what a da Vinci, say, could do if he had all the time in his world? It isn't only trouble I'm freeing them from!"

"A what did you say? And what do you mean, why he bothers?" I asked.

Instead of responding, She asked me only if I wasn't growing thirsty.

"Listen," S-Man said. He lifted his hand.

"A small technical detail," She insisted. But had the air grown even colder and was her voice not quite so beautiful?

"There's very little time to lose," said S-Man, "if that's what I think it is."

"You mean—" I said.

"The space-time continuum is ripping," he said. "There's been too much disturbance. Too many people missing. Too many things that should have happened that haven't. Flaubert hasn't even written *Madame Bovary,* let alone withstood the trial for indecency. Socrates never drank his poison. Hemingway never shot himself. You heard Galileo; he's never even heard of the Inquisition. The closest I can come to what's happening is to compare it to a tidal wave. A sort of historic tsunami. It's the end of humanism."

"Who needs humanism?" hissed a voice—it was She's but sounded different.

"It's the end of a lot of other things too," went on S-Man.

"Oh!" cried the woman. "Oh Mr. Wilde!"

Was I mistaken or had a note of fear crept into her voice?

"Can't we do something?" I cried, leaping to my feet.

"We can try," said S-Man grimly; but even as he leaned to gather me into his arms and fly across the lawn toward the noise (which was deafening; which was everywhere), She, looking suddenly very old and terrible, stood up and did something to the dull ring on her finger, so that a rainbow-flecked gem was revealed and S-Man, gasping and clutching his abdomen, stumbled and fell right into the fountain. She seemed satisfied by this, and returned the ring to its former state (later S-Man said it was a simple-enough trick to cover the deadly gem with an alloyed locket). By the time I managed to reach S-Man, he had swallowed enough of the stuff—he had landed in Lethe, I think—to choke; and even after I had smacked him on the shoulder blades and he had brought up a mouthful, he went on shaking his bluish-haired head, and then an odd look came over him and he sat down on the rim of the fountain and stared into his two hands as if he had never seen them.

"S-Man!"

At the sound of my voice, he glanced up with pointed indifference.

"Somebody help me," I shouted. But the group around Mr. Wilde seemed intent only on laughter. "Do tell us more about your Mr. W. H.," I heard someone say, and I saw Mr. Wilde look puzzled in the way to which I was growing accustomed, and then he knelt and filled his goblet swiftly from the spout marked *EUNOE,* and so he must have recalled that moment when he had written a story about none other than Mr. Shakespeare and a young actor, because I heard him answer that in his next article, he would discuss whether the commentators on *Hamlet* were mad "or only pretending to be"; which made everyone roar and even S-Man grin vacantly. She (it wasn't my imagination, I decided; she was much older and the chill in the air quite real) seemed to have lost interest in S-Man. Glancing one last time at Mr. Wilde (whose help I despaired of enlisting now that he had mastered the trick of drinking first from one fount, then the other), She strolled up the lawn toward Galileo. That gentleman gathered his toga to bow for the thousandth time that day.

"Hey!" I called.

Had She turned, I would have joined ranks with her, so dismayed was I by the look on S-Man's face; I was left to approach Mr. Wilde and pluck his sleeve. "What's this?" he asked, looking down.

"A boy," said a person—this person had blond hair and a face that looked both wicked and very lovely.

"Can I be of service?" said Mr. Wilde.

"It's the water," I explained.

"I see," he said and then, although he had just drunk from the goblet, he added, "I never touch the stuff."

"Please don't make a joke of it," I said. "Not now."

S-Man, while this exchange was taking place (and the sky growing darker, and the figure who had reached the astronomer and his cohorts stooping with age, and the roar of the fissure in the space-time continuum blending with the wind, which tore a bough here, there, from trees beginning to groan beneath an autumn storm), was watching the play of light on the fountain's two sources.

"I joke about tragedy," said Mr. Wilde, eyeing S-Man. "This is merely tragic. Who, for God's sake, is that man's tailor?"

"You don't understand," I said. "They made his uniform out of a blanket." And then, because it seemed that the sound of the space-time continuum being torn had grown not only louder but closer, as if (were I obliged to find an analogy for that awful noise) many voices, many cacophonous voices were being piped into my skull, which was itself as large as a mansion, a lawn, an island, I told Mr. Wilde everything I knew about his life as rapidly as possible, beginning with the four names his mother had seen fit to bestow upon him and ending, sadly enough, with his own mysterious disappearance from Reading Station. "Don't you remember anything?"

"No," he shuddered. "I'm quite relieved to say I don't."

"They were taking you to Reading Gaol," I insisted. "You have spent a year in prison and now you have to spend another. By the time you get out, your health will be ruined. Your wife and your children will be forever estranged. You won't even write much."

"Not write much?"

"One long poem. Also a sort of nasty letter. That's it."

"I see. And the name of this poem?"

"What difference does it make?" I said. "There's no time to be lost. She said—"

"She?"

I pointed at that worthy, who stood clutching her staff in the midst of a lawn turned, I realized, quite dry. Mr. Wilde frowned.

"I tell you what, Oscar," the blond man said. "We'll take the boy with us when we ship to Paris. We'll have a wonderful time and then we'll toss him out and just be by ourselves for a while, and then we'll have a glorious battle over all the money I make you spend, and then we'll get ourselves another boy just like this one. Shall we?"

Oscar smiled. My heart sank.

"Mr. Wilde," I said. "Won't you at least consider it?"

"Consider it?"

"She said if one of you would sacrifice—no, that's not how She put it."

"Yes, that's right," said a voice. It belonged to the gentleman with the bristling mustaches, who stepped out now from the little grove. "You've figured it out too, I see," he commented and hurried off toward the mansion. "Time is definitely of the essence," he added.

"What should we do?" I cried after him; but really, I knew.

"Tell her you'll go back. Please tell her," I said, returning to Mr. Wilde.

The blond man began somewhat petulantly to shake his clothing free of the fountain's waters. I didn't blame him; as the wind swept the dessicated leaves from the trees, he and certain others, gathered here and there about the fountain and indeed about the lawn itself, began to shiver. I saw Galileo whisper to his companions and they all moved, as it were nonchalantly, in the direction of the mansion.

"I assure you, I remember nothing of the truly uninspired story you told me," Mr. Wilde said. He seemed to think that would clinch things. And perhaps it would have, had S-Man not lifted his head and begun to blow bubbles. Not the kind of bubbles that human beings would blow, but superhuman bubbles, such as might drift into air and hover, in spite of the chill and lateness of the hour; drift, hover, divide, reunite; chase one another like so many rainbow-patched baubles around the fountain; and then the air was filled with all the waters of the fountain poured into one stream, Lethe and Eunoe bound together and flying like a serpent around and around, and S-Man was smiling to himself as if he were doing something very clever, and I remembered what it was that Ma and Pa Kant always said to get him to behave, and although it hurt to do so, I said fiercely, "The agency will come and take you away if you don't behave," and the waters fell once more, and Mr. Wilde was drenched and even I, who knew better than to allow that liquid to reach my lips, felt a lovely sensation coming over me, as if only the good deeds in my life might be recalled, so that I was the sum of a series of pleasant and successful and above all moral performances, and I began to feel rather satisfied with myself and warm inside at the thought of all

I had done, and would have looked around for Rachel Fish and told her that I forgave her for being a better person had it not been for the growing gloom.

For gloom it was. The sky had grown quite dark and the clouds had moved in not as rain clouds will but with the ponderousness of clouds bearing snow, and in the midst of the barren field stooped an old woman holding herself upright with a staff, although later Mr. Wilde insisted (as we were flying him home) that a beautiful, willful boy had stood in her place, and that it was the boy's rage at being ignored that made him wither everything on the vine and everyone with it, and I was reminded once again of the infanta's fifteenth birthday party. S-Man always said that he agreed with both of us, which reinforced my belief that from beginning to end he had been under She's spell and in no condition to comment upon anything. We agreed that a terrible winter storm had rushed upon us; the figures on the lawn fled here, there, leaving their lunch boxes to flap in the terrific wind and the brown-bearded man to abandon his buckets of the mysterious twin sources, Lethe and Eunoe, and to race pell-mell toward the mansion, where windows were slamming open and shut, open and shut, and I assure you there was no more laughter that day, in fact a keening had risen so that I might have felt sorrow for the old bent woman, so desolate and so bereft. She seemed to be missing someone very badly. But there wasn't time to think about that because just then a thunderclap—the sort one hears once or twice in a real Earth lifetime during the winter months—exploded overhead so that even the old crone's voice was drowned and only because I was standing near him could I hear Mr. Wilde's words, expressed in a rather bored, annoyed tone, "Oh very well. But ask them if you please to leave my hair. I can't bear it short."

And that was that; we found ourselves, S-Man and I, flying above another island entirely, that of England on a dreary winter day, and with us flew Mr. Oscar Wilde, who grew sadder as we neared our destination, and stopped speaking as we landed a few seconds before the train had ever pulled into Reading. He shook hands with me, which made me feel very awful, and he took out a handkerchief and blew his nose into it, and began to cry in a way that wasn't at all haughty, and then he insisted on shaking hands with S-Man and then with me again, and he would have missed his train entirely had S-Man not gently insisted on returning him, at superspeed, to his seat and to his handcuffs.

There was nothing left but for us to fly home and we did so. The tunnel walls made me thirstier than ever, and there seemed no danger in my drinking now; and so, leaving the tunnel and finding ourselves once more in 1970, we flew into the parking lot of a 7-Eleven, and S-Man went into a telephone booth and came out looking very mild-mannered, and we bought some soda pop, and although my allergies were back (I could tell from the ache in my teeth) I didn't complain, and we sat on the curb and drank our pop. I asked him all the questions I had wanted to ask for some time, and seeming to recognize that this last adventure had differed from our others, he took the time patiently to answer me. Yes, the island had been real enough; yes, the danger to our world had been clear, although the crowd with pitchforks and angry faces had been a well-crafted illusion. But I was to rest assured (I didn't feel assured) that all the writers, and indeed a number of artists and musicians and scientists whom we hadn't encountered, had been restored to their rightful if painful moments in time. Mr. Wang Pei, said S-Man, very soberly, was soon to be released from prison. M. Gustave Flaubert had received just that morning a summons concerning the moral indecency of his novel, *Madame Bovary*. Mr. Joyce was returned to exile, Mr. Rushdie to a decade of hiding, Miss Lillie Langtry to the stage—

"I saw him, you know," I interrupted. "The man with the enormous mustaches."

S-Man looked skeptical—having scoured, he explained, the island with his penetrating vision—and then, when I went on to describe the huge forehead and diminutive stature of the gentleman who had stepped quietly into and out of a grove, he said, "Oh. That little Belgian," and I realized that I had mistaken one set of Herculean mustaches for another.

"But S-Man," I said eventually. "He didn't even remember."

S-Man knew that this time I meant Mr. Oscar Wilde, and we sat silently by the curb, watching as a station wagon pulled up and a young mother stepped out and walked hand in hand with her little girl into the store. The mother reminded me somehow of the queen as we had seen her in our first instants on the island, but of course that couldn't have been; we had left She an old bent crone, howling and hiding alone beneath an old blue hood from the humorless onslaught of wind and snow and time. S-Man agreed that Wilde hadn't remembered much at all about his life in Ireland and still less about Oxford, and still less again about London or Paris or Avignon or Algiers. "So why did he say yes?" I asked.

"He never cared much for autobiography," said S-Man, which statement I pondered for many years before understanding it in the following fashion: Mr. Wilde couldn't remember much, but he could imagine very acutely.

"I see," I told S-Man, not seeing at all. We sat cradling our soda bottles, and the dust had begun to make my eyes water and S-Man had just begun to say that it was time to get me home, kiddo, when the store door opened and a little girl walked out. She was the cutest little girl you ever saw, with dark-brown hair and light-green eyes set in her head like jewels, although the rest of her face was quite dirty from eating something that my parents would never have allowed me in a million years. No sooner had she seen us and stopped to stare, and looked around somewhat puzzled and then perhaps frightened to find herself alone outside, than the woman hurried out clutching a paper bag. "There you are," she said, relieved, and taking the child's hand in hers she walked quickly around a rainbow-colored oil slick to the far side of her car; we heard the door opening and then her cajoling the child, who, no longer frightened, was young enough to resist for the sake of resistance all the strapping and tugging that would secure her in the car seat.

"I've had quite a day, sweetheart," we heard the mother say, as if she were pleading with her daughter just this once to sit still.

Then she was stepping quickly around to her own side of the station wagon, and climbing in and slamming her door and turning to see as she backed her car out of the parking spot and, after a pause, drove forward to the exit, and as she passed us and S-Man stood and reached for me (we would take off with superspeed, thus avoiding being spotted) we saw her reach her own arm around, as if she just wanted to ascertain that the little girl was safely ensconced in her car seat, which she was.

Chapter Eight

The Underpass

WHEN WE GOT BACK TO NEW JERSEY—THAT IS, when I got back, since S-Man was obliged to hurry about his business—the first sign that the substance of history had been altered, by our own rescue missions or through some more sinister agent, was that Hugo and Sid's hairstyle (or lack thereof) had been adopted by innocents like Edwin and Edward Morse and also Steward Blumenthal, who was if anything taller and less attentive to Cynthia Lacey and Mindy Glueck in what should not have been, given that S-Man returned me to the precise nanosecond of our entrance into the time tunnel, my *absence*. I had not actually been absent, and yet there they were: the bald boys in mock army fatigues.

Take a Möbius strip and flatten it, or one of our old LPs (that's "long-playing" record) and scratch its vinyl; we seemed, in grotesque fashion, to have skipped a beat. I knew, without having to find it out, that I was no longer a model student in a model town. I was just Rachel Finch now, whose index cards had gotten shuffled. Even the weather was shuffled: one day autumn leaves fell; the next, temperatures soared. Insects we had never seen—locust, Asian hornet, vociferous tsetse fly— whirred overhead in late February. Some trees actually budded, while from others dangled, impossibly, last summer's green leaf, last fall's brittle but intact seedpod. One day storm clouds moved in to the sky and never left. Birds chirped hysterically. "Waddya doing?" they chirped. "Waddya waddya doing?"

I fear the time has come to fulfill my promise, reader, and tell you a thing or two about the underpass.

To this day the underpass figures like a lost relative in dreams from which I awaken drenched and sorrowful. In my dreams it is a dark, dank, fearsome, loathsome, decrepit, foul, abandoned, slime-and-rat-infested tunnel among other tunnels. In reality it remains the meeting place of our town's disenfranchised; of lovers whose parents disapprove, of friends whom the years and murky business deals have managed to estrange. Fights, one gathers from the *Bergen Gazette,* are enacted bloodily down there; trysts enacted tragically down there. Maturer lovers choose hotels or roads that lead out of town—the young make do with their cell beneath the earth, where fellow prisoners, as it were, scribble their own confessions on the lurid walls.

Shall we venture *down there,* you and I?

As you can see, this corner of the world—I mean here, above-ground—feels deserted now, perhaps because the thrift shop, the pet store, indeed all but the NJ Savings & Loan have relocated, and even that institution no longer draws business as it did, having once given the lie to our town's fabled peacefulness. And yet this late-winter picture (I have parked my car; we have sauntered, you and I, around to the curb) deserves a moment's reflection. As if someone were painting on a broad canvas: see how branches glow silvery or very white where sunlight falls on them, and the stuff of which man makes things, his brick, aluminum and glass, all glows.

Approaching, we might expect the whole to have shrunken since childhood, but the entrance gapes mawlike as ever. A car whizzes past. With a sense of trespassing on property once ours—once mine—let us descend! Bottles lie smashed against the walls and a sneaker, heel up, dislodges and bounces toward the bottom step. Urine stains impart an oddly intimate knowledge. Mold collects. The door behind which the conspirators plotted and dug and surfaced stands bolted and chained. Even the conspirators' voices have died out. A bit of sunlight creeps halfheartedly, it's true, down two opposing staircases; a single lightbulb hangs from the low ceiling. A bee, unlucky enough to have followed us, zigzags forlornly from wall to wall; a resident spider seems simply to have abandoned hope, and dangles listless in her own moisture-beaded trap.

The one bulb continues to shed its faint glow. . . .

To tell from what the door still reads—or has it been painted over and marked again?—wild and hideous appetites feed as ever upon the suburban world! Never mind! Return to daylight if you will; there; I wander on, and send you word that if the writing on the walls speaks true, women do still feed on men and men on women, and men on men and women on women; and Denise does it, apparently, with what looks like dogs or (the first letter being smudged) hogs; and if your God is in the details, then surely he is here too, where White women give real good suck and Black women have sweet hot pussy and Angelo wants it up the ass go ask his felching mother (*"Felching, an expression first surfacing amidst . . ."* someone has added in painfully neat script) and someone better give back my necklace that I left at Jonah's house; and there are too many Jews in this town (that last underlined) and someone else has written in blocky print THAT'S RACIST next to an advertisement (in sloppy red ink) for "niger [*sic*] lovers." And more; the door and moist walls say more, but by this time I've given up deciphering and begun to walk, briskly and more briskly, and then God help me I'm running as if life depended on my reaching daylight, but knowing that I have still to retrace my steps and resisting the impulse to return via West Englewood Avenue's Panama-graded bridge, if only because I've left my car unlocked, I run back down into darkness.

Darkness and the memory of darkness, and a shadow running for—what else?—dear life.

The bald boys gathered in silence before school. In the early morning they seemed exhausted and their dirty khakis hung from their spent limbs. Hugo would drive up and watch, idling his engine, as Sid brought out another steaming pizza pie. "Breakfast!" Sid would shout, or "Snack time! Hurry!" He was no pleasanter but walked with a springier step, and I wondered if he was nearing his goal of leaving town. Hugo and he took turns making loud allusion to the "gold rush" that would surprise a hell of a lot of people. " 'Hell,' " said Hugo, "a place-name of Ancient Finno-Ugrian origin," but Hugo spoke more rapidly than before, as if he feared Sid mightn't show the patience he once had. Occasionally they shared jokes of a strained nature: "You got a vaulting imagination," Sid said and Hugo guffawed. Perhaps Sid planned to leave after the gold rush. For now, whatever the hour, the bald boys stumbled forward to buy his dripping cheesy slices for one dollar each, which in those days was twice more than at the Cedar Lane Pizzeria.

"Hotter up here."

"Yup."

"Where's Douglas? Dwayne?"

"Still down."

"Not Colin."

"Colin got kicked out."

"What a Duffy."

Someone, perhaps my neighbor Robert Wurner, sniggered.

"A vaulting imagination," Hugo said. "Aha. A pun, a play on words."

Wiping his palms on his ample jeans, he tilted his thick skull to show a pockmarked Band-Aid. He had nicked himself, he said, shaving.

Tunneling

Perhaps this business of shaving accounts for the bald boys' awe; with their downy upper lips and fuzzy chins, these twelve- and thirteen- and fourteen-year-olds must have marveled at the thick curls on Hugo's forearms, dark tufts sprouting from the V of his T-shirt. By the following week several boys had also nicked their scalps while shaving, and also wore Band-Aids around which peeped fresh purplish wounds. These boys had dirt under their fingernails—as did Hugo and Sid—and circles beneath their eyes, which blinked in sunlight.

Grimly I recalled Laff Riot's words, "Tell the kid we're not finished," and his figure creeping into Town Hall. I could not deny the menace in those words, nor the evidence of my eyes, although the latter were afflicted with intermittent visions of such intense jungle flora and some fauna (the occasional water buffalo lumbering into view) that I shrank in my seat. "Is that you?" I cried once, to my classmates' amusement, but Mr. Stick, if it were indeed he, didn't answer. One day I heard the slightest chuckle, another, saw only the ghost of a feather, falling. Nor did S-Man return. As days passed and there was no sign of him, I told myself that his absence could only mean that all was well, or well enough. And what would my parents have said if I had tried to warn them? I was no better than Elaine with her prevarications; no more reliable than Mrs. Carlsbad, who informed us that our science exhibits were to be shown to the entire parent body on Back-to-School Night. Mr. Franklin would deliver a general address and then it would be our turn, as she put it, to wow the public. "They want va-va-voom, we'll give it to them!" she was heard to crow. "I only wish Chuck could come. Sometimes I think it's all a bad dream, but then I wonder, whose dream, and what if that person wakes up?"

By now we were as used to Chuck's entry into our classroom discussions as we were inclined (most of us) to forgive his wife's increased wanderings from the one subject worth studying and, for that matter, from the task of supervising us. The bald boys also wandered now—I mean quite physically—fingering this beaker or that dissecting knife, bullying this student or that, and eventually ordering us to close our eyes. When we opened our eyes, glancing sideways at Mrs. Carlsbad to see if she would stop this new game, the boys had vanished! Without a hall pass or anything!

Who could blame Mrs. Carlsbad for her inability to maintain even the rudiments of order? We knew all about it now: about Chuck's sleep-walking on the football field; his somnambulant appearance at the Tea-neck Bar & Grill, where he had to be dissuaded from tearing up the linoleum; his dressing in his own faded army fatigues and shouting for his knife and lantern; her having been obliged to hide his MK-37 from him and his "pestering" her to return it; and so on. He would swear and stride and do unnameable things in the name of his right to bear arms, she told us, until finally, as if the return of sunlight sapped his unnatu-ral energies, he would sink to the bed and hide his face (she showed us how he hid his pale face). *"Mo,"* he would murmur. *"We got all of 'em, Mo."* At this she would reach for the vial and pour out the pills with which, the doctors had assured her, she might keep him this side of sanity.

"If he's sane, then I'm crazy," she added.

Palm fronds quivered in a too-hot wind. The air grew thick with smoke. I coughed, clutching my throat, and stumbled into the hall and to the nurse's station, where I inhaled once and again the sickly-sweet essence of the Breath-a-Lator before returning to class.

"He isn't coming to Back-to-School Night, is he?" whispered Mindy Glueck. She wrinkled her nose and shuddered delicately. Susan Kolin shuddered too.

"He's not even allowed out then," Mrs. Carlsbad said, meaning the evening hours. "Detention for calling out," she added.

"Why not?" we asked, ignoring this last in our eagerness.

"He's in a target category," she sighed.

We nodded; we had known what she meant; that was the second sign of change.

Tunneling

*　　*　　*

Following the sleepy deaths of two elderly sisters—sleeping sickness
having hitherto been the rare booty of the war veteran—our town
council seemed impetuously to have elected to spray Malathion over
all neighborhoods where the tsetse might hatch in high weeds and
withered grasses. Posters had declared Malathion to be harmless to
most people, and yet we were advised to stay indoors between 6:00 and
10:00 P.M. Elderly citizens, house pets, people with allergies or histo-
ries of chemical exposure—we knew that Chuck Carlsbad had the latter—were urged to avoid inhalation by staying indoors. Spraying
would begin in the football fields behind the junior high and Votee
Park and would fan out northeast and southwest to cover all of Teaneck Township. On her way to school, Rachel Fish had encountered
several such posters, and others suddenly protesting the fait accompli
of busing schoolchildren; the latter seemed official with their Town
Hall stamp but were removed when my schoolmate, ever vigilant,
pointed them out to Mr. Bogardus and he called Town Hall (I'll grant
him a certain civic-mindedness) to inquire. Elaine and I had spotted
another such poster tacked to our maple tree. Thus far we had yet to
hear the spraying helicopters, but we had heard the curfew siren countless evenings.

"Stay indoors?" our mother repeated wonderingly, each time the
curfew sounded. And she would wander out to the porch, and gaze
through the slitted screen, and once I caught her leaning her head hard
against that iron mesh with its smell like cold earth.

". . . throughout Teaneck Township?"

Once, no doubt, such infringements on our rights to roam would
have instigated loud protest. What had happened to stem it, if not
some wayward, forward motion of the clock? Citizens obeyed what
wasn't precisely law, and eschewed formal and informal gatherings. They avoided gatherings and sunlight and grass. The drought

continuing, the grasses seered yellow . . . the municipal pool, for reasons of health and conservation, would not reopen come spring . . . it
was rumored that the library would cut its weekday hours. . . . One
day, the mailman ceased to deliver mail twice daily. The butcher, who
had long dreamed of retirement in Arizona, hung a sign on his freezer
doors and disappeared.

Only my father, at such peacetime odds with the world, seemed
invigorated by this atmosphere. Perhaps the curfew brought him back
to his youth. He was the first in our town to purchase gas masks, and
although only his younger daughter was clinically allergic, he kept four
masks, one for each family member, in the trunk of his Buick. Evenings
included the ritual of his blowing a whistle and our rushing outside to
don our respective masks (he had Rose, who pursed her lips, initial each
mask) within the time he deemed necessary to survival—about sixty
seconds. These years later, when seasonal Malathion Plus sprayings have
grown routine, such masks (as you know) have become common; at the
time Elaine and I felt deeply the indignity of their presence in our
father's trunk. There was always the possibility that Francis would be
moved to wear his when picking us up.

Plus ça change, plus c'est la même chose, as Mr. Bogardus's mother
might have said; by which I mean that the fifth day of the week was
still Thursday. I had somehow missed a week of school. It had taken
me all day to track down my teachers and obtain my missed assign-
ments. Mr. Bogardus in particular had been hard to find—he hadn't
been in the faculty lounge, where I was told to look, and even when I
did find him hurrying into the building, he only hurled a paperback
at me and rushed on. I stood in the lobby, clutching the book—*Crime
and Abridged Punishment*—surrounded by my peers: bald boys with
their strained silences and dirty hands and greasy mouths, cheerlead-
ers with their musculature and jackets, and the occasional Orthodox

Jew (there were Orthodox Jews now) who hurried as if apprehending trouble, as if the secular school hall and we who inhabited it were trouble. Certainly Mindy Glueck and Cynthia Lacey were trouble now. With other girls, even eighth and ninth graders who had joined them in my inexplicable absence, they loitered in the main lobby, they talked back to teachers, they smacked their chewing gum, they stood at their opposing stairwells and called out epithets to girls, Black girls and White girls and other girls who tried to walk past uncaring and who, out of hearing, heaved sighs. "What is she looking at like that?" Cynthia said of me on my first morning back; I saw Collette shake her head when, inspired by my friend Rachel Fish's example, I turned to retort. "What is she staring at?" Mindy demanded from across the hall; I hurried away. Things were different now, Collette's headshake had informed me.

Things were different. Everyone, it seemed, was more overtly something than before: more "Italian" or "Polish" or "Chinese" or "Korean" (with the exception of Edward Morse, or was it Edwin?), more "Cuban," more "WASP," more "Mexican," more "African" or "Jewish"—more everything. A step forward? A step back? Who is to say? "Meet me at the tracks" was the common-enough cry. There, not far from the underpass, our various arguments (there were many arguments) would grow into solemn dances, the slow circling of opponents who looked, more than anything, confused. Others among us were more overtly religious now too, which is to say that the manifestations (as opposed to the truer signs) of faith grew prominent. Italian girls sported golden crosses, as did the Poles. Margarita was heard to pray over her endless missives. The bald boys seemed immune, at least, to this show of religion; while Colin Duffy, who had dropped or been dropped from their ranks, squinted at the changed world out of one eye and then the other. Matthew Arnold, take a letter! We had waited too long, and the time when art might beat like the heart of culture had passed. It was a sign of the times, of my times, at least, that I might feel more in common with squinting Colin Duffy than with my true best friend, Rachel Fish.

On my first afternoon back from She's island, I called past the bald boys and students milling on the front steps to that very person. Rachel Fish stood on the school lawn. Her hair hung like a dark casket—I mean *casquette*—around her pale face. Hadn't she heard me? She was staring, I realized, at my father, who had driven up and was sitting in his car! She gave him such a singularly ferocious look that I retreated beneath the school eaves, but she saw me and hurried in my direction.

Tugging my arm, she urged me indoors, beyond the bald eagle atop its flagpole and past the wide-glassed office and across the long hall to the interior doors, which opened onto another long hall. It was empty.

"I've been looking for you," Rachel Fish said. "What you told me. That's just terrible."

I nodded.

"I have to go," I suggested.

"We have to help them," she said. "I've been thinking about how it must be. For your sister. For—" She gulped; was there a catch in her voice? Did she disapprove, in the final analysis, of the young lovers? Her next words belied it. "—for Haywood and your sister. They belong together. They make a perfect couple. They have so much in common."

That last being palpably untrue—Haywood Lofty's not being in the least homicidal, and Elaine's never having helped an invalid in her life—I didn't know what to say. A few girls sauntered chattering through the doors. They were, after a fashion, more pronouncedly "Jewish." They flicked wrapped hair off their shoulders, they rolled mascaraed eyes and wore gold letter Chais around their necks and toted their books with schoolgirlish glamour—arousing in me a sentiment not unlike that which Madame de P., or her impostor, had done. Rachel Fish seemed not to notice them.

"We'll arrange a meeting," Rachel said. "That's the only way. Your sister has to be jarred out of her negative thinking. She has to meet him face-to-face. Then she'll remember how she really feels. And he does too," she went on, turning her cheek. "He does too."

"Things are happening so fast," I ventured.

"That's exactly how it goes with star-crossed lovers," she said vigorously. "Look at Romeo and Juliet. Look at the Scarlet Pimpernel."

"Look at Bertrand Russell and his fourth wife."

"This is not a joking matter. We have to think of a place where your father won't look for them. A place and a time. Any ideas?"

"Well."

She had said the words *your father* with such vehemence!

"I know," she went on. "We'll do it the night of our science exhibits. Everyone will be distracted. Haywood will get a prize, I suppose, and his mother will be there, which is unfortunate. But there's no other time."

"I don't suppose there is."

In truth, I cannot justify the lethargy—the disinclination to act— from which I suffered in those critical days. It was as if in deceiving Rachel Fish I had set loose a monster—I don't mean Rachel Fish, of course, but this thing we were concocting—and now I watched its destructive growth. Occasionally I was tempted to tell all, but to whom? More often I was preoccupied with the increasing frequency of those flashing visions from another clime. Were they memories and if so, were they somehow *mine?* I would *remember* palm fronds and the baked earth accompanied now by the longest-living, most patient resignation (or was it vigilance?); and sometimes now there were little women, *remarkably little hatted women, bending over a tiled floor transformed into moistened earth.* "Are you all right?" my friend would ask, and I would cover my eyes and perhaps set my hand an instant on her shoulder.

In any event the letter we crafted was Rachel Fish's idea; the words, Rachel Fish's invention. That letter never having been recovered, I quote as best I can from memory:

Dear Elaine,

I have never forgotten our first kiss or our plans for lifelong happiness. Please meet me in the underpass on Thursday, March 15, 1970, at 8:00 P.M. Don't be late! I have much more to tell you, about everything.

XXXOOO,

Your secret admirer
P.S. As Shakespeare wrote, Love conquereth All.
P.P.S. Bring a suitcase.
P.P.P.S. My mother didn't mean the awful things she said about you.

Is it that we near the end of our story, or for some other reason that I experience this new lassitude, like and unlike my lassitude in those last days? In early morning a dog barks. A milk van rumbles down Bowdoin Avenue. *Onward,* its rusty motor sighs.

Very well . . .

As if I knew what to expect (I didn't and could never forgive S-Man for not having warned us), I clung to my dear friend. The more she enthused, the more I endeavored to forget my doubts. What difference could even an afternoon with Mr. Franz Kafka make, I tried to persuade myself, compared to the many afternoons she and I would spend together? We had determined not to wait for experience or maturity but to get immediately to work on our *opus maximus,* which was not, Rachel Fish explained, your rear end, and which would be, she suggested, a joint oeuvre. That was the meaning of a fourth-person narrative; so we had, after heated debate in the first-floor girls' bathroom and elsewhere, concluded.

"Think about it," Rachel Fish whispered. The bathroom door creaked open. A girl entered and went into a stall. We knew her vaguely from gym class and waited what seemed an interminable time. "Coast is clear," Rachel Fish hissed as the door closed again. Later, in Mr. Bogardus's class, we passed notes. Still later in the lunchroom, we sat at an empty table. Where there is a will to togetherness, there may be a way. "Well, what do you think?" she asked.

"What do you think?" I countered. We stood in the swimming-pool-blue stairwell. We had played with notions: my favorite was that if the fourth dimension were time, perhaps the fourth person had to do with it. "First, second, third—all have to be there, you know? And the other guy doesn't. So fourth," I said, "could be the other way around. They have to be there but you're absent. Like in another time zone or something."

"Forget about it," Rachel insisted. She was clutching a nubbly black-bound binder. "First person is me and we. Second person is you and you. Third we know about. That uses up just about everybody, doesn't it? Wrong. Fourth is like a group of people talking all at once."

I was put in mind then of Assemblage with his foul invective, words spewing across the Avon: *There is no such thing as the self . . . no such thing beyond the walls of language. . . .* But Stratford-on-Avon was far away and long ago. Versailles? Likewise. The little rock in the ocean stood alone, waves lapping. . . . Albert was a grown man with a family and a nation to nourish. . . . Mr. Wilde was long dead. . . . I could not seem to total my experiences; could not, at twelve, draw them into what my father would have called "the universal outlook," that is, what we today might call a narrative of the self.

"They can disagree like in a democracy," Rachel persisted. "Don't you get it?"

"Sure."

"Okay," she said happily. "You start."

"Don't we start together?"

"You're right!" she said, wrinkling her nose. The gesture was new to her. Mindy Glueck and Susan Kolin walked by and Rachel looked up, expecting them to greet us; but Mindy murmured to Susan K., who slunk after her biting her nails (her own, that is). A few seconds later and those two were followed by Steward Blumenthal and Colin Duffy; as the doors closed we could see Cynthia and Floriana walking pointedly on toward "their staircase," across the long main hall. Rachel Fish returned to our topic with an even louder enthusiasm. It was as if the more people erred, the more my friend aimed for a true vocation. Frequently now her cheeks grew splotched, always a sign of strong sentiment; even her knuckles, clenched, sprouted purple splotches.

"First we have to ask ourselves the five questions," she said, Mr. Bogardus having spoken to us, however uninspiredly, about journalism and the interrogative pronouns.

"*Where?* That's easy," Rachel Fish said, "where else?"

Again the strange lassitude came over me and, just as suddenly, I suffered an intense and tropical vision. It seemed as if I had formerly chosen to fly through time tunnels, and now I was dragged through them without my consent and without my companion to protect me. I was thrown *in memory* against the earth. My ears rang with the memory of something a lot like a helicopter descending. The earth shook. The hall grew narrow and dark and hot and loud. My ears roared, my eyes burned, bamboo sticks parted to reveal a dank earthen corridor. The helicopter's propeller roared above us. The earth was hollow, hollow and dank, and something slithered over my face as I was sucked underground and—

"Is something wrong?" asked Rachel, narrowing her eyes.

Just as I thought I would speak up at last, I felt the memory relenting, and I was returned (trembling) to our school hall as it had been built by the Bergen County Municipal Construction Co. Ltd. in 1958. The air in 1970 felt humid. The day, Thursday, March 10, was under way. Math, Science, English—subjects in which I might once have delighted—weighed like so many fates. I felt no chagrin at my fall from academic standing, but occasionally, catching sight of a former self (who was that girl who waved so hard in her seat she fell over?), I was tempted to creep home, and crawl beneath my bed, and ascertain that my once-prized possessions, *The Collected Stories* and the Max Brod biography of Mr. Kafka, were still there. I had lost the desire to read them, but I liked still to touch their cellophane jackets.

"*Who?*" she asked. "That's easy too."

"Rachel," I interrupted. She waited for me to speak.

"If anything ever happens—"

She nodded encouragingly, her huge eyes fixed on me and putting me rather in mind of Mother Python. What was I thinking? I shook my head. For a moment I had been tempted to tell her about the books beneath my bed! About the hidden key, and perhaps even my adventures with S-Man! I might have lost the reading habit, but I wasn't going to squeal!

"—to one of us, the other will finish it, right?" she said, finishing my sentence. She was still nodding, her eyes fastened, as it were, to my visage. Who knows? Perhaps she too was channeling information from Mr. Stick; more likely, she intuited my growing inner chaos. I have never known any human being quite so empathic. "I had a cousin once who had seizures," she said empathically. We stood in the long hall until the double doors opened—we had paused each on her way to class—then several students and a few teachers walked through, each and every one less himself or herself—each, that is, more a member of a certain set.

Later, from the backseat of my father's car, I watched houses and lawns and clusters of peers rumble into the past, and I thought of Assemblage and of the woman S-Man had called She and the island paradise She had hoped to establish where nothing was political. "Everything okay, girl?" asked my father. As we turned onto Trafalgar Avenue, I remembered what Laff Riot had ejaculated in our last moments in Versailles. Not "I'm not," but "*we're* not finished. . . ."

*   *   *

Back-to-School Night approached. Our parents, Rachel Fish's and
mine, would attend. I was curious to meet her parents. For once her
brother wouldn't hog them, she said bitterly—it was one of the few
times that I ever heard her express bitterness. Still she was excited about
our classes' Nature Exhibits, and not just her own exhibit (on the Dar-
winian advantage of kindness to all creatures, including slugs) or mine.
She felt that as students we had everything to learn from one another,
and was thankful to the school administration and her science teacher
for giving us this opportunity. I didn't point out that my own science
teacher, whom Rachel Fish continued to abhor, expressed fervent
enthusiasm about my class's Back-to-School Nature-and-Progress Program Exhibits.

Mrs. Carlsbad had told us how a singular idea had struck her after
a particularly confusing evening with Chuck. She'd found him in the
Chinese restaurant, ordering fortune cookie after cookie, the tablecloth
scattered with fortunes like white peels and cracked-open cookie bits.
She could tell he had been sleepwalking because of his eyes, which were
crossed, and the dirt shovel he carried. "Chuck," she said. "Do you realize how bad this marriage has gotten?"

"Pick a card, any card," he said. (She imitated for us the monotony
of his voice in such moments.) *"Watch out. Another trapdoor. Is that a
rat or a dead baby? What kind of name is Mo? All of them. Give me my
gun and I'll blow their heads to kingdom come. I'll blow yours too, babe,
if you don't hand it over."*

"What's confusing about that?" Cynthia whispered.

At that moment Mrs. Carlsbad had realized, she said, what each
person wants in life: *vindication.* "I mean," she said, "is he crazy or am
I? That's the fifty-four-dollar question!"

"Could you spell *vindication* please?" Collette asked politely. Collette was the only one among us still taking notes.

"It would be different," Mrs. Carlsbad went on, "if he took his
medicine. In the morning, he's so sorry! Something must have happened, something he can't forget. Either that or I'm losing my mind."

Behind the sunglasses her blue eyes blinked. "I don't even want to know from bank vaults," she said vaguely. "I'm going to make it up to you kids or die trying."

We didn't know what she meant precisely, although when I reported this to Rachel Fish, thinking to improve her opinion of our teacher, Rachel Fish snorted. "She means she hasn't taught you anything since the first day of school," Rachel said, which didn't seem to jibe with what she herself had said about how much we could learn from each other. But on the subject of Mrs. Carlsbad, my dear friend may always have waxed extreme.

During the days leading up to Back-to-School Night, I kept careful watch over Elaine, whose behavior was frankly puzzling. She seemed more at ease, more affectionate with our parents, even with Francis. His worried look had begun to fade. Evenings were pleasant enough. Our mother, Rose, it's true, seemed tense—once, hearing Elaine and Francis and me laughing over a story he told (it was a funny story, although, taking place on the Children's Ward, it ended sadly), she lurched to clear the table, which was Elaine's job anyhow, and her elbow knocked Francis's coffee into his lap. Francis leaped backward so fast our bench toppled. The cup shattered. He had banged his head against the wall. Rose rushed to gather the china shards as coffee streaked in brown rivulets across the linoleum. Francis stood rubbing his scalp. Rose was just huddled on the kitchen floor. I was used by now to Mrs. Carlsbad's sunglassed tears, but when my mother looked up, her eyes were dry. "I am sorry," she said. "I am too," he said. Still carried on the wings of his anecdote, perhaps, Elaine and I burst into high-pitched laughter. Francis's face twitched, at which Rose threw the china shards and sponge into the sink and stalked out.

"Rose—" Francis called. Elaine grabbed some paper towels and began wiping at the remains of the spill.

After a while Elaine stood. She cleared her throat. Perhaps she was about to ask to go out; just then we heard the telltale whine of a helicopter. It was probably a TV news helicopter, Francis said heartily. Elaine nodded.

But for the most part, as I say, life at home was unusually pleasant. It had been several weeks since I had received messages in my locker (a relief I still associated with the brief period of Elaine's first liaison with Haywood). Although I had masterminded the supposed current affair between them, I began to forget that fact in light of Elaine's renewed interest. I was walking past her room one evening when she exclaimed, "Here it is!" and, beckoning me into her boudoir, showed me the photograph of Haywood that she had once cut out of their fifth-grade class picture. "I always wondered what happened to it," she said in a nonchalant tone that didn't fool me: she took great care sliding the photograph into its frame. So Haywood once again occupied a certain, if off-center, spot on her vanity. What's more, she and our mother could often be found together in the evening. Sometimes they swung side by side on the front porch rockers; other times they sat like dolls, legs extended, on Elaine's big four-poster. I might surprise them in quiet tête-à-tête and, no matter how much I pried, not be made privy to its subject. Their voices lifted and fell in a quiet sustained pattern that would dissipate if I strained to discern words.

The evening of our catastrophe approaches. Is there no time to tell you more about our lives, and if not our lives—hardly our main concern—our other adventures, S-Man's and mine? Since 1970 his name has become a household commonplace. He and his compatriots roam this and other universes, and our world is not as it was. The NJ Savings & Loan may once again display its fiduciary goldfish, the playing fields have grown green, and the underground tunnels are blocked off; the change is nonetheless total, and retroactive. Even a woman such as I, who passes days without human speech, cannot help but note it.

Tunneling

For this and other reasons I make sure every few days to telephone my mother, Rose Finch Bogardus. Her second husband having passed away only hours after his own mother, mine lives on in the Bogardus house; it's a barn-red house overlooking Route 4, and although the house was spared essential water damage during the flood—was it only a few months ago that our town lay submerged?—time and the elements and the occasional determined porcupine have chipped at the chimney stacks. A pink brick poises to fall one of these days. I often muse, walking past with my dog, about seeing to that brick. Who else, if not I?

How extraordinary, I muse further (you may recognize the sentiment), that my life should have become so ordinary! Once, on a whim or bet, or because S-Man knew something I didn't, we—"we!"—traveled back in time to the palatial if financially strained residence of none other than Thomas Jefferson, where a lovely cultured voice spoke, unaware of our presence just beyond the pane, of her hopes for her sons. She was an old woman and (S-Man told me) the mother of men who had once been slaves. I never did see her face as we traveled on. To Saint Petersburg, and once to Belgrade, and twice to Saigon, and still another flight to the Mesozoic era (exceedingly uncomfortable), and one time we flew to prehistoric southern France (Not France again! I cried; and couldn't we at least go to a city?) and watched as a man and a woman painted on a dark cave wall. I was reminded of the story of Sophocles' (I mean Socrates') cave. I would have liked to have been granted time and strength to describe to you, reader, our visit to the universe where everything anyone has ever conceived exists, and, for that matter, continually bursts into existence. What was most striking about that visit was the sound of new things. It resembled indeed the sound of popcorn popping—and what was sad, agreed S-Man, was that the "kernels" had begun to slow. Here and there, now and then, something new came into the world—a three-toed elephant child, a square broccoli—but the pattern was unmistakable even to my human ear.

Over more time than I could fathom (I struck S-Man a playful blow when he said that) almost everything under the sun (and the sun) had been thought into existence. How could that be? I asked. It has to do with probability, he said. Just then the reason for our having flown through the time tunnel walked, or rather, slithered into view and our conversation was cut off. . . .

Later, approaching home, I did get to ask my flying companion some questions. Were there any planets in that universe where women ran things? I wanted to know. Why didn't we ever visit women authors? "S-Woman takes care of that," he said briefly. "Oh," I said. How about planets with racial harmony? World peace? You name it, he said, and pop! it has to exist; but so do entire planets devoted to male supremacy, bloodshed and other horrors of which I hadn't conceived. We were flying over the railroad tracks; S-Man glanced down and might have seen something that would have averted the entire tragedy (I beg to differ here with Mr. Wilde's definition) but for the passage down those tracks of the 4:45 Pennsylvania-Lackawanna-Detroit, loaded as ever with heaps of coal and coal-blue slate and fool's gold, huge heaps of gleaming fool's gold through which S-Man, as everyone by now knows, cannot see.

"You won't believe everything," he once begged me on a cloud puff, and I nodded, not realizing the cost of that pact. Sometimes when I pick up a newspaper or turn on the radio—activities in which I indulge infrequently, as I am often outside, weeding my newly planted garden or warding off the dog's foraging (why must he hunker on my marigolds?)—I get the feeling that I'm flying alone through the universe where anything exists so long as you imagine it. Pop! S-Man Caught Red-Handed. Pop! S-Man's Childhood Sweetheart Tells All. Pop! S-Man, Friend or Dictator? Pop! Pop! The world, so wary of its heroes and so covetous, has taken back what never belonged to me. I'm not surprised by this so much as the frequency with which I sense my loss. "I want to die," a voice says—I glance around, ashamed to claim it as my own. Then the dog jumps to lick my face or the telephone rings and I am asked to enter my beleaguered marigold or even my daylily beds (daylilies are difficult to time, but timing is one of my few on-the-job-trained skills) in the Teaneck Garden Show, and this much involvement in our mortal sphere reminds me how much, in that end-of-term paper "Life in This Era," I am inclined to argue *for.*

The auditorium sparkled. Our classrooms gleamed. The air thickened with some major impulse. Occasionally the air also thickened, it's true, with the humid undergrowth of some alien, heated clime. For the briefest intervals of consciousness, I saw *green . . . heard a woman shouting . . . as an infant was wrested from her arms and a man rose through a thatched opening in the earth . . .* and just when I thought I couldn't see any more, couldn't bear any more (never envy the tele-pathic!), I was returned to Bowdoin Avenue and the iron smell of the old porch screen and the days of the week like the names of old friends. I had learned from my mistake in Stratford, and resolved to tell no one until such time as I could distinguish matter from mind. In what I felt to be a stroke of genius, Elaine insisted on bringing a yellow suitcase to school. It contained *important props* for her class's *contribution* to the evening. As it happened I had spotted the suitcase in her closet and, feeling a certain obligation to mankind, peeked inside. She had bor-rowed one of Rose's best dresses, a pair of panty hose, a nightgown, a shell-backed hairbrush and a few other items. She had included a pho-tograph of herself and a smaller one of me, which I would have found touching had she not been intending to leave me with what would have become, by then, our brokenhearted parents.

Poor Francis! Poor Rose! Since Elaine's drama class had chosen to perform silhouette skits, and Elaine had volunteered with Doris to mime a well-known scene in which Ann-Margret, shot through the chest, delivers her swan song in her lover's arms, Francis saw nothing odd (there was everything odd) in my sister's toting the yellow suitcase to school. Nor, clearly, did Rose, who allowed her lips to part in a sad smile. In those last days Rose seemed to move as in a dream. Even when Mr. Bogardus motorcycled past our Buick and I called out, alarmed at the sight of my docile English teacher now metal-helmeted and leather-booted—although he at least, I was glad to see, had allowed his hair to grow—Rose stared out the window. "What's gotten into him?" I asked. I may have hooted. Elaine's sharp nails dug into my arm. "There's so much traffic," she opined loudly.

". . . traffic . . . ," breathed Rose.

In the school parking lot, car doors slammed. Families from our surrounding leafy neighborhoods would normally have walked to school; threatened by Malathion sprayings, all felt obliged to travel in Buicks and Chevrolets and Darts and the occasional foreign automobile. "There's that nice Haywood Lofty," murmured our mother.

I glanced at Elaine. Apparently oblivious to danger from the air, she stood holding tight to the suitcase.

"Hurry indoors," Mr. Rizzo called, glancing skyward.

Mr. Bogardus stood at the double doors; he was welcoming people in an officious way, reaching his pale hands out to parents and calling jocularly to my fellow students. He looked quite ridiculous, I thought, with his hair longer but slicked flat, and his aftershave was abominable; I pointed this out to my mother as we walked past. She only tilted her head and, at a word from Mr. Bogardus, fell behind. I looked back. She was wearing a very pretty floral-print dress and a white carnation in her own hair, and she couldn't seem to keep her hands off the scar on her forehead.

I took my father's arm as we walked on. His face glowed with the anticipation of hours spent in an educative environment. Rejoining us, my mother seconded my father's greeting to his colleague, Dr. Foster. We took our seats near him and his family. Elaine was staring hard at, I thought, Haywood Lofty's profile. Perhaps my fears for the evening—

they were various—were ungrounded! Beyond Haywood, Susan Kolin sat with her mother. Louise sat in the very front row with her parents. Steward Blumenthal wasn't here, it seemed. Nor were several bald boys. Colin Duffy slumped alone in his seat; his project on the natural ingredients of explosives having received only initial attention from Mrs. Carlsbad, he had lost much of his own enthusiasm.

As for Mrs. Carlsbad, she was accompanied after all, I saw, by a tall man with cropped hair and a thick leather jacket and a largish duffel bag—Charles "Chuck" Carlsbad! Husband and wife were apparently arguing. Beverley Carlsbad was waving what might have been (I suspected it was) a pill bottle, until Chuck, clamping his powerful hand over hers, squeezed hard. "Are you crazy?" she hissed loudly. "You aren't even supposed to be here."

Where, I wondered, was Rachel Fish? I scanned the auditorium, its emergency exits and eagle-tipped flagpoles and its folding and unfolding seats. Piano chords swelled over the loudspeaker system. The brocaded curtains parted in crimson scallops to reveal Miss Bauer's thin figure. "The Girls' A Cappella Chorus will lead us through the first verse of the national anthem," her voice sounded. "Girls, raise your hands. As you can see, these wonderful girls are sprinkled throughout the auditorium. Wherever you hear a voice, ladies and gentlemen, please keep up. If there's one thing I can't abide, it's a sloppy anthem!"

My father and I stood, followed by my mother and sister, which last ran her French-manicured hand through her brown hair before positioning it (her hand) above her heart. I prepared to mouth along as usual. Rachel Fish had arrived. She stood at attention, although not between her parents; a huge-eyed boy who had to be the math genius Hegel Fish clutched their hands while my friend stood apart, her dark head averted, and her face so pained and resigned and hopeful as she began to sing in her loud high voice that my heart, or what remained of my heart, flew out to her. As if she felt the warmth flowing in her direction, she turned her head and our gazes met and we smiled and I have always been glad of that smile and of our hands creeping to cover our beating hearts.

"That's enough," said Miss Bauer.

We retook our seats. Mr. Franklin approached the podium. He would speak, we knew, about the history of our town, its past and future, and then he would introduce Mrs. Glueck, PTA president, who would release us to the classrooms where we students had prepared science presentations. Mr. Franklin seemed unusually tall and impossibly benevolent. His white teeth flashed and I felt all the power of his affability, akin as it seemed to grace; itself akin, I think sometimes, to the assumption by one people or another—in his case, the White Anglo-Saxon Protestant—of an ascendant moral history. He has a moral center, his white teeth announce to this day, out of which he achieves a head-to-toes balance, a walking-on-the-balls-of-his-feet equilibrium.

But what is this bitterness, after all has been said and unsaid, done and undone?

If I had been asked, before that night, to compare Mr. Franklin to another person? I might have said Haywood Lofty: Haywood, who was and was not to the manor (as opposed to the manner) born; Haywood, whose deceased father and exhausted mother had made of him (although we were old enough to start making ourselves) a reluctant hero—witness his sober demeanor, his habits of bearing burdens and weighing justices and the determination with which, every day after school for some weeks now, he had punched at the five-hundred-pound bag hanging in the boxing corner of the boys' gymnasium.

Mr. Franklin wore eyeglasses that flashed in the stage lights. He "wore" a neat thick thatch of silver-gray hair. He slipped his speech from his breast pocket and smiled at Miss Bauer, as if to thank her for her forbearance. Meanwhile—was that a chuckle tripping light steps around the crowded hall? A flash of green? *A fringe of tropical shrubbery?* I shook my head to clear it. Mr. Franklin, we knew, always made the same speech: *Tradition AND! Progress.* The Speech began with the

Lenape Indian villages and ended with a few hundred more words about civic pride and a rather long glance at the Usable Future.

"Our town," Mr. Franklin said, clearing his throat.

We waited; the speaker maintained a steadfast silence. Was this a rhetorical gambit? It was almost eight o'clock. Elaine, holding the yellow suitcase, grunted. Hegel Fish squirmed in a mathematical sort of way. Susan Kolin cringed as if silence were another grease stain for which she would be held responsible. Rachel Fish kept winking at me; clearly Mr. Franklin's discourse couldn't deter my friend from our mission, the reunion of Elaine and Haywood. Beverley Carlsbad was still holding up what appeared to be a small white vial, until Charles grabbed at it and sent it spiraling over several rows of seats. "Chuck! Now look what you've done. Am I imagining this whole thing, and if so, what does that say about me?"

"Our town," Mr. Franklin said, "was founded on a dream of permanence. We call it 'tradition.' And yet, who among us"—he smiled so I thought his cheeks would crack—"has experienced the yoke of imperialism, the prod of colonialism? When you come right down to it, who can do more than conjecture as to the lives of people in other times?"

I was tempted—O hubris!—to raise my hand.

"Please, Chuck, sit still," called Beverley Carlsbad. "You lost your pills and now you're just going to have to control yourself. I don't even want to hear from hallucinations."

"We tell a certain story," Mr. Franklin went on, "until the afternoon light wanes." His hands lifted, Mr. Franklin looked almost hopeful, as if to say, *These aren't the words I intended, but you'll forgive me.* "Then something happens," he added, "and you start hating people. . . . I've been a widower for eight years. . . ."

"Where did you say Robert was, Alice?" whispered Mr. Wurner.

"He said he'd be back after checking on his hamster exhibit," whispered Alice Wurner. "I think he's all right."

"No one is ever all right," whispered Mr. Wurner. "There is no safety anywhere. We must all work at all times to maximum potential. Did you remember to empty the garbage in at least three different kinds of plastic bags?"

"Why would anyone do that?" she whispered. "They'll think we're strange."

My mother stood up abruptly. She whispered to my father and stepped into the aisle. "Where is she going?" I asked him. "I'll go see," Elaine said, and she slid from her seat and hurried, the yellow suitcase swinging against her thigh, after Rose. Where did Elaine think she was going? Or rather, with whom? I had often witnessed her natural complicity with Haywood Lofty, who got up now and also strolled out; and witnessed also her absorption into the subterranean sphere of Hugo and Sid's concerns. What would happen to her, to him, to them all? Beyond my father, Collette sat tall in her seat, and beyond her my friend Rachel sat gazing after Elaine and Haywood's retreating figures and I began to sense—O prolepsis!—that something was different about this evening, beginning and continuing with the fact of Mr. Franklin's speech being somehow altered.

It had a new, albeit recognizable flavor.

"The Lenape," said he, "were a darn bloodthirsty tribe."

Did he snigger? Did he fold his arms in smirking self-satisfaction or then again in extreme self-hating despair? Did he touch the hair on his head, and did said hair glide back and forth?

Collette's father and mine exchanged quizzical smiles. Many years ago, they had served simultaneously, if not side by side, in the army.

"They liked particularly," Mr. Franklin explained, "to drink from skulls. They had a thing about skulls, you see. Rather like the Elizabethans. Remind me to tell you about the skulls on London Bridge. Not to mention the dungeons beneath Versailles, the crimes against humanity of the colonial British, and the sheer homophobic bigoted viciousness of the Victorians. Tradition? Ha! As I was saying, not so long ago—three hundred years?—this delightful people dominated this territory."

Tunneling

He shook his head. "Had we time, ladies and gentlemen—members of the Augustus Franklin, excuse me, the *Benjamin* Franklin Junior High School Parent-Teacher Association, and their wonderful children—would the skinny kid in the third row please stop picking his nose"—for once, he couldn't have meant Robert Wurner, who, along with several bald boys, was at that moment lowering himself through a trapdoor elsewhere in the school building—"we might linger over an indomitable territory—the vast numbing beauty—ocean tide pounding the shoreline and pine trees standing tall and hills and innumerable changeling vistas—life! Inexhaustible life! Bison, elk, deer, rabbit, the inevitable and unvanquished raccoon—and intrepid beaver—and fish! What a subtlety of silvery fish! But there isn't time, this evening. Welcome to the future. You know"—for emphasis, he rocked his podium—"when you're Christian, everything looks different. God draws borders around every blessed thing. These days every class trip is a reconnaissance into my own gray matter. Hey, did you hear that?"

The audience stirred.

Mr. Franklin rocked his podium again.

Did the podium rock back?

"Progress!" Mr. Franklin barked. "Once upon a time, two Lenape villages prospered on the banks of the Hackensack. Until the Dutch, in time-honored Protestant money-grubbing fashion, razed them. We aren't talking about roots but rapine and bodies, dead bodies, live bodies, in-between bodies. War, the great mixer! Gross me out! No sooner have the Dutch covered their traces than the English arrive . . ." Mr. Franklin turned down his mouth. He reached into his pocket. He stilled his podium with a determined fist. "An odorous people, the English. You want my advice? What you need, ladies and gentlemen, is an ungodly night on the town. Matthew Arnold be damned."

"Excuse me," called out Mrs. Bigelow. "Where I come from, gentlemen don't curse."

"The agenda, Augustus," whispered Mrs. Glueck, who had freckles and eyes that had almost disappeared from years of smiling.

"We want to talk about the safety of the playing field," someone called out. "What if it isn't safe for children, all this Malathion
spraying?"

"Those signs . . ."

"The curfew . . ."

Mr. Franklin polished his bifocals on the end of his tie and cast
naked eyes about the auditorium. "Matthew Arnold be damned," he
barked. "Time marches on and the ocean may be vast but the spread of
our populations vaster. Have I got a surprise for you this evening—just
in over the wire. What did I mean by that, I wonder? From his perch on
Fort Lee Heights, Washington observes five thousand well-fed musketed
British soldiers as they boat up the Hudson. Permanence! Fleeing, his
men abandon tents, cooking pots, tattered smallpoxed blankets, whores.
Oh shut up, Bigelow. If you're leaving town, why don't you go already?
You wonder, my fine friends, where this is leading? Aha! Ha! I wake in
my widower's bed and a slant of light—moonshine, starshine, sun
through a big bay window—suggests not all is lost. Then the train that
divides one side of town from the other blows its tiresome whistle. Not
to mention, thirty-five years on the same job can get to a guy. If it weren't
for an occasional drink with a Mrs. Someone— Doesn't anybody hear
that?" he asked more plaintively. "Listen. I think it's under my podium."

Tap. Tap. We heard it now, all right. *Tap. Tap tap.* "Hoo boy," said
Mr. Franklin or whoever was impersonating Mr. Franklin. I inched forward in my seat.

"I don't feel myself," he sighed.

"Of course you don't," I hissed, very sotto voce.

It was clear to me now that the infiltration of our school had been
completed with the replacement of Mr. Franklin by none other than the
archvillain Laff Riot. The absorption in his own discourse and in himself—the urge to preach—the non sequiturs heaped helter-skelter—all
pointed to Laff Riot's presence. What that had to do with the spraying
of our neighborhoods and imposed, seering memories of a defoliated

nation (even as I write this, I shudder at those odors of *baked earth* and *jungle* and *detonation*) I might never know. Some further sign, some clearer hint as to the speaker's identity, and, S-Man or no, inner visions or no, I would act.

Tap tap. Tap tap tap. Tap.

"What a windbag," sneered Mr. Bigelow.

"I really can't wait to relocate to Birmingham, dear," said Mrs. Bigelow.

"How long does it take a kid to check on a gosh-darned hamster?" demanded Mr. Wurner.

"I think the podium is moving," said Alice faintly.

"Nonsense!" said Mr. Wurner. "Did you remember to wash out the toaster oven?"

"Perhaps we should get a move on, Augustus," Mrs. Glueck said, smiling. "I promised to take Mindy shopping tomorrow."

Mr. Franklin fumbled through the pages of his speech—his water glass seemed to dance—in fact it almost toppled—in reaching to steady it, he jerked his head and a neat mass of silver-gray hair slid onto the floor!

"Oh my," said Mr. Franklin, gazing down at what had been, what was, *a toupee.*

Tap tap tap!

"What I'm trying to tell you," Mr. Franklin said, skimming his hand along his bared pate, "what I'm trying to tell you"—in an abandon of academic decorum, he hitched his trousers—"is that all those lying, patriotic, ersatz-historical murals on your municipal walls don't amount to beans. Not beans! You have one chance in several hundred thousand of figuring out what's happening. There were dinosaurs for so long compared to you guys that it isn't funny. Progress? Have you ever sat and watched a clock tick? Do you think there is a snowball's chance of something or someone's flying to your rescue? Aha-ha-ha! Your children will be lucky if their ashes get saved. We're running out of room, boys and girls, and you go on pretending the self matters. *Boys and girls, the self does not matter.*"

By now a few teachers had risen. Mr. Foster stepped resolutely into the center aisle. Mrs. Wurner began to fan herself with her thick arms. "I forgot all about the toaster, Fred," she murmured. "We'll never forget," Fred agreed. Mr. and Mrs. Bigelow began shouting about a revote, about bringing the matter right now to a revote, at which Dr. Foster exclaimed, "What matter, for God's sake? Our children are our future!" and Mrs. Glueck took a dainty step toward the stage. Mrs. Bigelow clapped her husband on the back (he had a fit of coughing). Mr. Franklin bellowed, "PACK IT IN, you hypocrites! Pack it in!" and *"À bas la République!"* and Mr. and Mrs. Bigelow bellowed back, "Turn back the clock! Revote!" and I must have leaped onto my seat because I found myself clutching my father's shoulder and heard myself shouting, "Wait! Can't you see? That's not Mr. Franklin! Wait, everybody! That's an impostor!"

Can you blame me, for making this rather considerable mistake?

"He's an impostor! I know because I was there! I went back in time! I have a friend who takes me back in time!"

"Rachel?" asked my father.

"Let me go! He isn't really Mr. Franklin," I shouted.

An odd silence, having begun, endured. People's eyes swiveled to observe me, Mr. Franklin, me; I experienced the singular horror, one I have never forgotten, of telling my truth and not being believed.

"It's true, I don't feel at all myself," sighed Mr. Franklin, and he knelt to gather his toupee and to lay its white thatch tenderly on his pate. "There," he said. "That's better, isn't it?"

At which the toupee rose a few inches in the air.

"Fred?" asked Alice Wurner.

I'm not sure what would have happened then had not several things occurred. That is, the podium (to which Mr. Franklin was clinging) slid from stage right to stage left. Mr. Franklin was carried along (the toupee rose a few more inches, then several yards, then disappeared from view). In the space left by the podium—God hates a vacuum—a trapdoor was thrown open and a boy's head, ski-masked, and then a boy's khaki-garbed body and lastly his shiny military boots emerged.

"Hey Colin," called the boy. "You're kicked out because you missed tunnel practice. You're out and I'm in. What do you think of that?"

Still grasping his podium, Mr. Franklin stared at the boy, and then at the boy behind him and the one behind him as several boys (they looked like boys) emerged from beneath the stage floor.

"You always thought you were so special with your brothers and your one blue eye and all. Well, so there, Colin Duffy," said the first boy. "Uh, nobody moves."

"Okay, kids, I can take over now," said Mr. Carlsbad snappily.

At which Charles Carlsbad reached into his large plastic bag and took out what was later identified by the Teaneck Township Special Weapons Anti-Infiltration Squad—a squad that came into and went out of official existence in one evening—as an automatic MK-37. A gasp went up. Charles Carlsbad shoved past his wife and down the aisle. With a decisive leap he gained the stage and nodded to the bald boys as they took out smaller versions of the automatic rifle (LJ-24s) and waved them.

"This doesn't have to hurt," grinned Charles Carlsbad. "We just need a few volunteers. Because of the horrific nature of our mission, which I'm about to explain, we need kids. The older the better, but the smaller the better. So, math geniuses first. Hegel Fish, please come up here."

"Hegel?" asked his mother. "Won't Rachel do?"

"Where did that girl go, anyhow?" asked his father.

"Chuck," called Mrs. Carlsbad. "This is what happens when you don't take your medic—"

"Shut up, Bev," said Charles. "You just shut up or I really will shoot you this time."

"Oh," said Beverley. "That's not nice, Chuck. You're not allowed to talk to me like that in front of other people."

"Is that you, Robbie?" whispered Alice Wurner.

"No," said Robert, "it's Adolf Hitler. Of course it's me. Hey Colin, can you see me? Are you sorry you dropped out?"

"Not Hegel," cried Mrs. Fish. "Oh where is that sister of his?"

"Not Robbie," said Alice Wurner, more tentatively.

Where, I wondered, *was* that sister of Hegel's? At what moment had she managed to sneak out?

Charles Carlsbad, grinning, loaded a clip into his automatic rifle. He had several such clips hanging from his belt.

"Medication's wearing off pretty fast, I'd say," remarked Dr. Foster to my father.

"Foster," my father said quietly. "Just in case they ever come in handy, I have four gas masks in the trunk of my car. There's a spare key in a Hide-a-Key on the roof, near the antenna. I'm for making a move when and if we can. We don't want to take any unpremeditated action that might cost lives."

Dr. Foster nodded. "Good thinking, Finch. However, if we do see an opportunity, on the count of three, we'll rush the stage."

"Right."

Someone giggled, or I thought someone giggled, or I remembered someone giggling in a green sort of way.

"Okay, first him, then you other brats," Chuck called, his voice tightening like his fingers on the trigger and the front end of his MK-37 jerking up, down, down. "Okay, all of you, especially my wife, Bev, shut up. We got ammo. We got more than that. We got a plan: we're going to flood the network with trained children soldiers and get those gooks. Right?"

"One," my father said.

For emphasis, Charles Carlsbad let loose a round of automatic rifle fire at the overhead lights. Glass bulbs blazed, flew apart, then fell away.

Tunneling

"Hey!" squeaked a tiny amused voice.

"Hegel!" cried his mother. "Wait!"

But Hegel, ignoring her, began his slow ascent of the stage. He traveled toward Chuck and just stood there. My heart almost went out to him and then his mother cried out his name and I remembered how he had always made his sister's life difficult.

"Okay now, the rest of you brats, one by one, smallest first," Chuck said.

"Oh my," breathed Louise. "I guess that's me."

"I'm not quite ready," sighed Margarita. She laid a missive—it would be her last—on her seat. She smiled resolutely at Colin Duffy, who didn't seem to notice. "Okay, now I'm ready."

"I knew we should have left last summer," hissed Mrs. Bigelow.

"Two," said Dr. Foster.

"I tell you what," called the amused voice. "Yoo-hoo!" In the dim area above the stage I could just make out, sure enough, the little green man, sitting with his little legs crossed on the air. He had acquired Mr. Franklin's toupee—must have plucked it out of the air—and his eyes glowed with that strange intensity.

"You see!" I cried.

"See what?" my father asked.

"On three," whispered Dr. Foster.

"Wait, Dr. Foster," I said loudly. "And Dad. Please wait. I'm sure help is on its way."

"Hey," called out a voice. "The auditorium doors are locked!"

"I told you, Alice. This can happen anywhere."

Thus it was that one by one, as our parents trembled in various stages of fear and also loathing, we schoolchildren were instructed by the armed and dangerously insane war veteran Chuck Carlsbad to take what remained of the stage until we stood in size order (that meant Hegel Fish, Louise, me and so on) at the rim of the crater, as it were, from which we couldn't help but peer into the darkness of—the science laboratory. That subtle gleam represented, perhaps, Margarita's jaybird eggs; that other gleam no doubt Collette's illuminated display of Alaskan seals; that *eek-eek* could only have been a hamster's; that glint my Malathion exhibit replete with sample and, nearby, Colin Duffy's posters and his demonstrative specimen of TNT.

"What do you want with us, mister?" asked Collette, her voice cracking a bit. She steadied it. "Just tell us."

"I'm taking you hostages down into the tunnels," Chuck explained impatiently. "There's a whole network of gook tunnels in Vietnam only kids can fit into. American kids, I mean. Gooks have bones like cats. As for the adults here, well, the problem is, of course, that this operation has to remain top secret. So, as soon as we get the kids out of here, we're going to have to blow you all up. Sorry, guys."

"Cool," said Colin Duffy, peering down. "Wait'll my brothers hear. Hey mister. I know I didn't help dig, but I'd really like to be on your guys' team. Crime seems like so much fun!"

"Oh," said Margarita, her eyes watering.

"Hey, I went to all the practices," said Robert.

"Yeah, well, you're a putz," said Colin.

We heard Robert sniff from under his ski mask.

"Uh, I told you guys, absolutely no personal disputes," said Chuck. His eyes darted. His fingers on his automatic rifle were twitching like half-dead mice, or hamsters.

"Can't take conflict," whispered Dr. Foster.

My father nodded. "Conflict, ambiguity, anything could set him completely off his rocker."

"Okay, first the genius kid," said Chuck. "Then let's see," he went on, reading off names—from what looked a lot like Beverley Carlsbad's green Science roster. "Louise Bigelow. Right. Then Rachel Finch, Robert—no, we got Robert—Lester, Darin and Clarence. And who's this?"

He had stopped at Edward and Edwin Morse.

"Oh no," he said.

"Which one of you is you?" Chuck finally asked. He was smiling.

"I am," said Edward and Edwin, pointing.

"I can't stand ambiguity," shouted Chuck. "Ambiguity is the one thing that really makes me blow my stack! I know you don't want that to happen!"

"Ready, Finch?" Dr. Foster whispered.

"On three," my father said.

Charles Carlsbad aimed his automatic rifle. He would have fired at both boys, I think, just to relieve his sense of ambiguity.

"Oh Chuck," said Mrs. Carlsbad, letting out a sigh.

Was it the threat to her students that brought Beverley Carlsbad at last to her feet and her senses? Later she explained that it was all right for her to badger the twins, but not for anyone else to do it. "Oh Chuck," she said, in any event, tearing off her eyeglasses. Her eyes were red-rimmed but shone bluer than ever as she strode into the aisle, her face tear-streaked but resolved as she strode onto the stage. "I get it," she said, halting. "You're crazy, which means I'm sane. Which means, I want a divorce. Give me that gun right now."

"You don't know what you're talking about, Bev," said Chuck.

"They're my students, and whatever happens to them, happens to me. Hand me that."

"But Bev, I'm telling you, we're going to train these brats in the tunnels we built from your very own science laboratory while your back was turned, clear under the playing field to the underpass in one direction and to the New Jersey Savings and Loan bank vault in the other. After a few weeks in these tunnels, most of the brats will have died. War is hell. But the handful still alive will be ready for active duty in Vietnam's very worst White Zone."

"The White Zone," echoed Colin Duffy. "Wow. Give me that." And with a rather evil grin, he grabbed Robert's weapon from him. "Frontsies," Colin snickered to Louise, shoving Robert ahead of her. Robert sniffed.

"Just give me that gun and I'll ask Mr. Franklin to put in a good word for you," said Beverley.

"Nothing doing," snarled Chuck. "I hate your guts anyway and I don't care who knows."

"Oh," said Beverley, and her blue eyelids fluttered, but she stepped quietly into line behind me. "Men and women of tomorrow, we're in for an adventure, it seems. You first, Louise. Then Finch. Edwin and Edward, I'm sorry."

"Let's go," said Chuck.

"I guess this is it," said Louise sadly. She looked for a long moment into the darkness of the science laboratory below; then, holding onto the ladder, she turned and stepped onto its first rung. "I was looking forward to going home," she said in a sad clear voice. "When I was a little girl, I mean very little girl, we used to pick cherries in April. I loved that. And there was a smell to the earth, which was so red you could make mud pies without adding water. You just clapped at that red mud ball until it dried hard in your hands. And now I'm going to spend the last months of my life underground with dirt that doesn't ever become anything. It just seems so sad."

"Oh be quiet," muttered Cynthia. "Do you think I want to spend the last months of my life underground listening to you go on about dirt?"

"Yeah," said Mindy Glueck. "Just shut up and stop whining; you make the rest of us feel terrible. You and your racist parents should have gone home a long time ago."

"That's right," said Chuck uneasily. "This isn't ambiguous, is it?"

"That's the first intelligent thing I ever heard you say," said Cynthia to Mindy.

"We used to be friends," said Mindy. "Remember?"

"Huh," said Cynthia. "I guess."

"I'm sorry if you're sorry," said Mindy. "Since we're all going to die and all."

"Well, I'm kind of sorry about the staircase," said Cynthia.

"You should be," said Mindy.

"You started," said Cynthia, riling.

"Well, yes," said Mindy slowly. "I did. And what's funny is, I don't even like Steward Blumenthal that much."

"What'd you go and try to steal him for?"

"I don't know. You looked so happy together."

"It's true," said Cynthia. "He's a vain selfish White boy but I just love him to pieces."

"I feel sorry too," said Margarita.

She was looking at, of all people, me. "I wrote those terrible messages," she said. "I slipped one in your locker the first day of school, remember? And all because Colin Duffy kissed you once, and I was so jealous I thought I'd die. At least, I thought so until I realized just now what a dumb person he is."

"I guess girls have a lot to learn about backing each other up," said Collette.

"I'm sorry I was only interested in myself," said Steward Blumenthal, taking off his ski mask. "I see now that I should have picked one girlfriend and not let Mindy and Cynthia fight over me."

"Which one would you have picked?" asked Mindy, and then she caught herself and started laughing jerkily, and Cynthia put her arm around her and the two girls began to cry.

"Uh-oh," said Charles Carlsbad. He rubbed at his eyes.

"Gosh," said Susan Kolin. "I never realized you could cry, Mindy. I guess that means you're human, and I don't have to be afraid of you. That is, I wouldn't if we were all going to live. Maybe I wouldn't even bite my nails or mess up the laundry. But if my mother ever slapped me again, I don't know if this is right or wrong, but I would just slap her back."

"And I'm sorry to have been so disgusting in my personal habits," said Robert Wurner, from his place on line. "I realize now that my

Jewish self-hatred has expressed itself in three ways. One, I torture small animals. Two, I pick my nose and have other unhygienic personal habits. Three, all my life I've wanted to be Colin Duffy because he wasn't afraid of anything and I'm afraid all the time. Only now, faced with death, I'd rather die myself."

"You did?" asked Colin dully. "You wanted to be me? Do you know where I spent last Thanksgiving? At Bergen Pines, because my mother thought it would be nice if we could all be together. We didn't even have a turkey, because they wouldn't let us bring in anything for my brothers but tuna-fish casserole from the cafeteria."

"I don't love you anymore," said Margarita, "but I do feel sorry for you in a way that another girl might mistake for love."

"I feel sorry too. I'm sorry about that day in Miss Bauer's audition when I said I didn't like 'We Shall Overcome,'" Collette said, turning to me. "Actually I sing it all the time when I'm alone. We could sing it now, if you like, as we face certain death."

"That's a terrific idea," called Miss Bauer. "Breast cancer or no, I should have realized a long time ago that there's life after the national anthem."

"I'm even sorry I tore the nails off my guinea pig in nursery school," Robert added.

"I'm sorry I lied to you about where I go Saturday nights," someone called from the audience.

"I'm sorry I made my kids stay in when other kids were outside playing."

"I'm sorry I didn't up his allowance."

"I'm sorry I picked on Edward and Edwin. The more miserable I was, the more I wanted them to suffer. Their very difference from each other was a vulnerability, and their being vulnerable brought out a cruel streak in me. What's more, their *similarity* to one another, in spite of their apparent racial difference, stirred up my narcissistic sense of small differences, as Freud would put it. Thank God I'm in therapy now!"

"I'm sorry, Bev, but if you don't shut up, I really will blow your head off."

"I'm sorry I didn't contribute to more charities."

"I'm sorry to have put my career ahead of my family."

"I'm sorry to have gone on smoking cigarettes in secret."

"I'm sorry I snuck home from the office three times each week for seven years just so I could slip into your lace underpants, the ones with the days of the week embroidered by your mother, and parade in front of the hall mirror. I realize now that all that secrecy probably hurt our relationship, although I enjoyed it immensely."

"I'm sorry—hey, what gives around here? I can't tell who's good or who's bad. And I'm the one with the MK-37 automatic rifle, remember?"

"I'm sorry I claimed so many dependents on last year's income tax."

"I'm sorry to have covered all the furniture in our living room with plastic slipcovers as if it was a memorial to all the dead in Europe."

"I'm sorry to have visited my past on my children. Dear God, I'm so sorry."

"I'm sorry not to have moved into the house you wanted."

"I'm sorry not to have believed that Stalin was killing all those communists."

"I'm sorry . . ."

"I'm sorry I was always so sorry . . ."

"I'm sorry I didn't examine the origins of my racist feelings toward Jews, Black people and Chinese people more closely," said Mr. Bigelow. "I realize now that most of the world's evil stems from our way of valuing our own pain over other people's. So what if I don't get the promotion I want? So what if I never have a son? Other people's denigration can't raise me any higher. You have to see things not just personally but historically. As for certain culturally imbibed notions, notions of superiority or inferiority, well, those can be excised through intense psychoanalysis, as Bev Carlsbad's example shows, or, even better, through simple community actions, like the tending of community gardens, which bring all sorts of people together in an action-oriented way. Action is the way out of the mind. And if this American generation remains somewhat uncomfortable with questions of race, or gender, or class, there's always the next generation. I predict great things for America. I predict that America will be even better than a melting pot. America will be a tossed salad.

"Actually," he said, "I take all that back."

"Well, I'm sorry—" I began, but I never did get to say what I was sorry about, because at that moment Colin Duffy's face changed.

"Hey," said Colin. "Who's that?"

And he pointed the tip of Robert Wurner's LJ-24 (but he didn't fire) at the ceiling where the lithe green figure of Mr. Stick flitted from shattered lighting fixture to fixture before tumbling down to settle, legs crossed and eyes fiendish, just inches above our heads.

"Hi guys," he said.

He had planted the toupee rather sloppily across his own green locks.

"An Air-Delivered Seismic Intruder Device!" shouted Chuck, firing practically (or impractically) at random. "Holy God! Bev! This is really big news!"

"I'm not 'Bev' to you anymore," said Beverley Carlsbad. "You've gone too far and this relationship is over."

"I'm telling you, it's an ADSID! The enemy has developed superior technology!"

"Guess again," said the little man, grinning from green ear to ear.

"Holy shit," said Chuck, and he fired an automatic spray in the direction of Mr. Stick, who dove straight through the open floor, and another spray and *tat-tat-tat* another, which last must have connected with the TNT adjacent, dear God, to my Malathion project, and perhaps even the hamsters; in any event a hamster came flying through the blackened hole followed by a cloud of smoke and a cackling Mr. Stick as people screamed and began to pull and pull on the locked exit doors. Mr. Stick only dodged more willfully here, there, kicking his legs through the air as if swimming, and winking (at me?) and pointing at Chuck and slapping his little thigh—he seemed absolutely taken with himself and with the veteran's shots as they hammered: *tat, tat, tat-tat.*

"Down the chute and into the tunnels!" cried Chuck, pushing Hegel through the floor.

"Ick," said Hegel.

"I'm an impostor," the little man cackled, fleeing across the backs of our seats. *Ping!* A brick fell, followed *pang!* by another. People cowered. They cried out. They apprehended the very near future. Smoke billowed and another hamster shot through the floor.

At that moment, the roof of the auditorium was lifted clear off.

"S-Man!" I cried.

I saw sky, smoke above, smoke below and rising in an oddly intentional formation through what had been the ceiling. I heard an otherworldly oath—whose? "S-Man!" I cried again. On the sudden downdraft floated unimpeded not my flying companion but the terrible head of— Assemblage! Hegel Fish was seen to rise—not on the rungs of the ladder, up which Louise, face darkened with smoke, dashed past me toward Mrs. Carlsbad's outstretched arms, but through the air—until, over the open trapdoor, he hovered in telekinetic suspension. His figure twirled slowly in the electronucleic tide of Assemblage's intelligence collectors. "Gosh," Hegel said, eyes revolving. "Ouch. There goes another polynomial theorem. I just lost about a zillion cube roots."

"Not roots," called Assemblage (his voice hollow and loud). *"Rhyzomes."*

"Wow," said Hegel Fish. By now he was turning a little like a chicken on a rotisserie.

"This is it," said Charles, a bit uncertainly. "I warned you, Bev."

"Rhyzomes . . . ," said Assemblage intergallactically as he floated toward the math genius. *"We should stop believing in trees, roots and radicles."*

"Wow," said Hegel Fish. "E equals MC squared. The quadratic equation. Dirac's formula. Planck's equation. Bohr's theorem of the relativity of love. Gobbledygook. Middle Earth. Glugg. My brains feel like they're dripping out of my feet. Why am I always so mean to my sister?"

"There is no such thing as the self. . . ."

"I mean really wow. Ouch. Ouch."

"So stop whining."

Chuck Carlsbad, with a last confused glance, let his automatic rifle fall to his side.

Assemblage's collectors, like so many eyes, never left Hegel Fish's face. Any minute now, I thought, Assemblage would drop the child's sucked-out frame through the floor and, exponentially strengthened, turn his terrible apparatuses in our directions. And if Shakespeare himself had been nearly vanquished, what chance that a six-year-old could hold out against the otherworldly mind vampire? Where, for God's sake, was S-Man? What would he have done? What was it he'd told me once? *There's one thing Assemblage can't stand. . . .*

And then, for some reason, I saw not S-Man in my mind's eye but my friend Rachel Fish, and she was smiling at me and holding out her hand and warbling, *"Alms for the poor / Legs for the rich,"* and I knew.

"Ouch. Hey! You're hurting me!" cried Hegel.

"Collette," I said. "Is that you?"

"Yes," she said quietly. "I'm glad we used to be friends. And I am sor—"

"Would you sing it with me now?"

"I beg your pardon?"

"Sing it. Please."

"What? The national anthem?"

"No. You know. If we start," I told her, "other people might join in. You have such a beautiful voice. It's too bad Rachel Fish isn't here, but she's who made me think of it. I just asked myself, what would she do? She would always sing when she was upset, did you ever notice? There's just one thing."

"What's that?" she asked, a bit impatiently.

"I have to hum the part about the Lord. Because Collette, not only am I Jewish, which you probably knew before me, but I'm an atheist. Did you know that? I really believe in not believing."

"Shoot. I don't believe in God either, but I don't make a fuss," said Cynthia.

We stood there, contemplating the abysses above and below.

"We shall overcome," said a thin voice then. It belonged to Collette, who was trying hard, in spite of recent events, to sing. She went on for a moment or so. If the air hadn't been so cold or the night so present, she might have sung a little louder.

"We shall overcome," sang another lower, somewhat rasping voice; it was Miss Bauer, nodding brightly. "Very well, children! Sing whatever you please! I'm with you!"

"Huh," said Cynthia. "That old song!"

"Not that," said Assemblage. *"Please. Not that."*

"We shall overcome," sang Cynthia. "Huh."

"We shall overcome, so-ome day," sang Miss Bauer—and Dr. Foster, who joined in.

"We shall live in peace," sang Mrs. Glueck.

"We shall live in pea-eace," sang Mr. Wurner.

"Oh, deep in my heart," whispered Alice Wurner.

"Okay, everybody, here it comes!" cried Miss Bauer. "The refrain in two parts at least!"

"Oh, deep in my heart . . . ," sang Collette and Cynthia, and Floriana, and Mindy and Susan, their voices rising *precisely a fifth of an octave higher than my own or Miss Bauer's.*

"... Lord—"

"... mmmmm ..."

There was a sudden loud explosion. A terrible cry arose from Assemblage (only it issued, bizarrely, from Hegel Fish's mouth). Assemblage seemed suddenly to deflate, a little like a balloon, then he fled— I think he fled—through the open roof as Dr. Foster and my father leaped onto the stage and raced toward Charles Carlsbad, who allowed himself rather meekly to be relieved of his weapon.

"Oh Chuck," said Mrs. Carlsbad, not moving.

"Daddy," sighed Collette.

"S-Man," I said.

The individual so named, or so partly named, flew down now through what had been the ceiling, and proceeded to stand on the air a little like Mr. Stick, only with his arms folded in a way I knew so well I would have wanted to cry had I not already been doing so, what with his cape fluttering, and his chin held high, and his face full of the knowledge of the moment come at last.

"Who's that?" someone shouted.

"What's that?" asked Margarita, pointing. A piece of paper had fluttered to the floor near me; I picked the paper up and handed it to her and she read it aloud: "GOTCHA."

"That's not nice," she said resolutely. "Anonymous letters are not nice at all. Who *is* that?"

At which moment Mr. Stick zoomed closer and peered into my face and cocked his green head, and let out a sad snort (his breath terrible as ever), and then he darted through the open roof and wasn't ever seen again, I like to think, in Teaneck, New Jersey.

I would have been more relieved by his departure, had I not recalled that it was always the apprehension of death—D-E-A-T-H—that initiated it.

Chapter Nine

Sweetness and Night

IT WAS NICE AND COLD AND STARLIT IN THE AUDI-
torium, sans roof, and the air above our town filled with light: the
bright light of stars fixed and unfixed, and the softer light of a waxing
gibbous moon. The sky war was over. Indeed, it would have taken
S-Man much less time to conclude (he was eager to explain) had Laff—
the battle in the air had been waged by that technological fiend—not
made the rather brilliant move of front-loading the RiotPlane's guns
with a thinnish powder containing just enough Mother Planet Rainbow
Rock (he could never find enough to suit his evil purposes) to threaten
the individual to whom I have referred as "my flying companion."

"May I have your attention for a moment, folks?" S-Man asked, flying down. Within moments he had assuaged the crowd by using hyp-
notic techniques common among his Mother Planet ancestors. "It's
been quite an evening, folks," he added.

"You can say that again," said Dr. Foster, and he smiled.

"Who *are* you?" called my father.

Besides being a wonderful hypnotist, I realize, S-Man was this: a
born performer, charismatic and exuding, in spite of his musculature,
an aura of undeniable sweetness. Now that the auditorium (it had
become more of a Platonic idea of an auditorium) had grown almost

quiet, he offered his listeners as much explanation as he could; then, because he had brought with him several ingots—normal earthly gold ingots from among the hoard the U.S. government had seen fit, during the temporary reconstruction of its own Fort Knox vaults upriver, to store along with several ounces of plutonium and a single, all-important ounce of Mother Planet Rainbow Rock in our purportedly quiet NJ Savings & Loan—and because solid earthly gold has a sobering effect on people, he managed to relate the essentials.

Essentials!

Apparently—I tell you this in confidence, and ask only that you sanction the possibility that in spite of no one else's being able to verify them, my words might, in this universe or in some other, have a truth—apparently it had been for several months now the villains' plan to rob that quiet bank. Whether it was their desire to blow up the town (there was enough plutonium) or to eradicate or at least discredit the debuting superhero by tunneling from the underpass and beneath the railroad tracks into the bank vault itself, I don't know; perhaps each of the villains, greater and lesser, had his own idea of things. Sid, I imagine, only wanted the gold.

The construction of the tunnels would have been an overnight matter for Laff Riot with his technologically advanced tools, but in order to build them without S-Man's taking notice—sudden technological advancement being an instant tip-off to Laff's presence in any community—they had been obliged to proceed slowly, at night, and with the aid of ordinary townsfolk such as Hugo and Sid. The bald boys had served as diggers and lookouts and decoys throughout the weeks of toiling beneath the earth. Some had been let in on one version of the "scheme," others on another. They had suffered several close calls, including the weekly arrivals in the underpass of Mr. Bogardus and my mother, who had appeared again this very evening clutching the yellow suitcase that my sister and she had prepared and stored in Elaine's closet and which contained what my mother would need to elope, in a loose (very loose) manner of speaking, with my English teacher. (You will recall that I never liked him and may not be surprised to learn that I have never since spoken to my sister.)

To resume and then, thankfully, to conclude:

Because S-Man would have been on the lookout precisely for advanced technology, Laff and Mr. Stick had cleverly organized the most basic manual tunnel digging, based on the memories of Charles Carlsbad, whose mind lay open to their maneuverings. The sicker the mind (Carlsbad's post-Vietnam mind was very sick), the more it opened to that diminutive, terrible creature with his otherworldly sense of humor. So the tunnels that were dug beneath the railroad tracks and the football field and the science laboratory were modeled after the tunnel complexes of the beleaguered and central region of Vietnam known as Chu Chi, and it was the "ventilation shaft" (a foul crawl space) whose concealed entrance had lifted like another toupee that afternoon when I climbed the stairs with Mrs. Carlsbad's message for Mr. Franklin. There was a storage cache for weapons, explosives and foodstuffs (not just pizza), and even a sleeping chamber and a conference chamber and a firing post and a forward aid station for the wounded.

Only the strange thing about the tunnels, stammered Douglas Rothstein that evening, before S-Man had flashed the ingots in everyone's eyes and recited the old Mother Planet words that resulted each time in total (in this instance, near-total) amnesia, was that a terrible sorrow filled them from the beginning. Long before the tragedy—it was the tragedy, you see, that hurled Mr. Stick home again—the bald boys had sensed some ineffable truth, some encounter between an old and honorable relation with the soil and something more apparently successful and yet fatal to the natural world. So perhaps it was not so much of a surprise, although very much a shock, for their plans to go awry: first my mother and Mr. Bogardus appeared during the last meeting of the conspirators—certain of success, the latter had gathered at the trapdoor leading from the underpass storage room beneath the railroad

tracks, only to hear (I was dismayed and disgusted to learn) the passionate whisperings and embraces of my mother and her lover and then
to see their frightened but determined visages gleaming in the half-
light.

They were joined soon enough by Haywood Lofty.

Have I neglected, all this while, to account for someone?

Rachel Fish, upon hearing my cry of "Impostor!" and "I have a
friend who . . . ," had realized that the "plan" to reunite Elaine and
Haywood was factitious, an invention meant to blind her to the truth,
which was that I traveled through time; and so she had taken it upon
herself—stalwart soul!—to protect the would-be "lovers" from an
embarrassing subterranean encounter. Imagine her dismay when she
found Haywood in very dire straits, not bound and gagged like my
mother and Mr. Bogardus (who had begun to whimper) but engaged in
an ongoing altercation with Sid, who in spite of his height was no
match for Haywood. Haywood had always been (as you may have surmised) a pacifist, but on that occasion he seems to have relinquished his
beliefs. Rachel Fish called—shouted, rather—for Hugo and the bald
boys to stop the fight, stop it right now. Sid, who had said something
disparaging about the people we now know as African Americans and
also about my sister and her affections, had by then a rapidly swelling
left eye and a broken nose, and would have suffered more had Haywood
not been bodily restrained by all the bald boys at once.

There was no time, insisted Hugo, breathing heavily, for games;
whatever Sid was in the mood for, it was time for them all to move out.

Sid stepped back, then lunged and punched Haywood in the solar
plexus.

"Ooof," said Haywood and butting his head forward, he knocked
his assailant off his feet a second time. He managed also to land a punch
in Sid's other eye before the bald boys restrained him again.

"That is so unfair. Five against one? That is so monumentally, hor-
rifically unfair," shouted Rachel Fish.

Tunneling

"Oh yeah? I've been waiting for this a long time," snarled Sid.

"Come on. Come on," called Haywood.

"Okay. Right. We'll just take them all along as hostages," Hugo said quickly, stepping forward.

"And I've been waiting to tell you a thing or two," said Sid, to Hugo.

"A thing or two? You? Do tell," said Hugo. "Only not now, Sidney. Not when everything's set. All we got to do is get the gold and leave. That's all it takes. And then we split. We go our separate ways and you don't ever have to talk good again, not if you don't want, Sidney," said Hugo, whose own diction seemed in that moment (or so Haywood reported later) to slip.

Eventually, with those bald boys who had shown up (several, including Douglas Rothstein, had at the last been wise enough to stay home) and the four furious hostages, the group began to creep through the earth.

There was a tunnel, as I say, leading from the underpass to the bank and another that veered off toward the science laboratory (it had been the bald boys' practice, throughout that ill-attended season, to wait in study hall until Mrs. Carlsbad's back was turned and then to lift the trapdoor near Colin Duffy's experiment and continue their digging) and another *that led nowhere,* and it was into this tunnel that Rachel Fish, who must have been hoping since her arms were first bound and her mouth gagged to find a moment and an escape route in order to summon help and thus to rescue Haywood Lofty and the others (or, as she would have put it, "to die trying"), managed to "escape."

I cannot quite bear to consider what must have been her feelings when she realized—she must have realized—that the tunnel led nowhere (it had in fact been intended precisely to mislead the enemy) and then to realize that although she was no longer crawling in that pitch darkness, her skin was. She must have felt it slowly at first, then faster. She must have felt her skin erupting in a frenzy of eczematous reaction as a result of contact with various underground ingredients and insect bites and the inevitable mold and the fumes, even, of Malathion; whether that last had filtered (I fear it!) from the science laboratory upon the combustive fusion of Colin Duffy's and Robert Wurner's and my experiments or whether Laff Riot in inspecting the tunnels had left behind his telltale aroma, I cannot say. The tunnel was dark—pitch dark. It ended in a cul-de-sac. I see that much.

When she reached it, she must have cried out—surely she must have cried out. Behind her the others had already passed on. Had they realized her disappearance? She reversed her crawling—I know, because S-Man told me. She tried to find the way back to other people, to the world, to light. She made it to the juncture of two tunnels. There was no light but she could feel that the air was cooler, that the tunnel had widened. Perhaps she could hear people shouting and overheard the whir of—a helicopter?—and something else that she couldn't have identified but which would have been the sky battle between Laff Riot and S-Man. You will understand, I think, if I decline to render her demise any more real. Perhaps, familiar with the symptoms of anaphylactic shock—heightened perceptions, ringing in the ears, sudden pounding of the heart—you can imagine all this. I like to think that my best friend died still hoping; perhaps she managed even to remove the gag around her mouth and, if so, to call out in her lovely, loud, high voice. Who knows? She was, first and foremost, an A Cappella.

The defeat of Laff Riot took a little longer than expected, S-Man tried to explain, because Laff had managed to smuggle out a handful of rainbow-and-gold-colored Mother Planet rocks and had the brilliant idea of grinding them to a fine powder, which he then front-loaded into innumerable bullets, miniature warheads he sent spewing across the night sky at S-Man, who took them for a joke and then understood as his skin was pierced.

"I thought I was a goner," S-Man said, shaking his head, but I only gazed dully—it was mid-morning by then—at the bluish hair and excellent profile that had once been the marvel of my mortal eyes. His skin healed so quickly! He went on to explain—he never doubted himself and never apologized, but he did explain—that it was necessary to draw Laff away from the auditorium, to minimize danger to people there, and to keep an eye on Assemblage, although, he said, he suspected that I would find a way to hold off the latter.

I shrugged, having done so with such regrettable delay. If it hadn't been for my stupidity . . . if it hadn't been for Mindy and Cynthia . . . or Charles Carlsbad or Bev Carlsbad's ultimate courage . . . or Collette's singing or Miss Bauer's joining in . . . or if it hadn't been for the explosion in the laboratory . . . or Hegel Fish . . . Now the earth was gray and the air thick with the facts of life and death.

"S-Man," I said, tiring at last of explanation.

By then it had begun to rain, the gentle sort of rain that might have offered solace had my friend Rachel Fish not been on the verge that morning of being lowered one last time into the earth. There would be no exit—no light at the end of that last tunnel—or so it seemed to me.

My companion of some months ducked his head. I think he knew what I was going to ask—it was something, after all, that I had asked before.

"It can't be done," he said.

"S-Man," I whispered. Did I lay my hand on his arm? If so, his was a tough-skinned invulnerable arm.

"We tried in Stratford. It didn't work. It never will work."

"We only have to go back a day. One day, S-Man. She was still alive just yesterday. It isn't fair this way with her not knowing. We wouldn't have to stay long. I could tell her and then she wouldn't try so hard."

"I'll take you to Prague," he said suddenly. "We'll go now. We'll be back before lunchtime. No one will ever know."

No one would ever know; although his existence was now common knowledge, his future predictable. For an instant the Vltava River flowed beneath my mind's eye. I saw the Moldau and the bridges and the little path beneath which my mentor liked, in healthier times, to stroll with his favorite younger sister. I might stroll there with him. . . . I shook my head. The prospect of that colloquy was, is, ridiculous; the real writers of this world didn't and don't need help like that. They may need to read books, but they don't need to talk with their authors. If I still longed for tutelage, it was because the wrong Rachel had survived. It was my friend, my beloved friend Rachel Helda Fish (formerly Magdovitz), with her boldness of resolution, her lofty aspirations (no pun intended), her uncompromising demands for truth and justice, and her remarkably pure voice, who was the writer. I have never been more than a journalist, and a slanted one at that.

Of course the trip to Prague never took place; the funeral did. Rachel's mail-order rabbi was found to say a few meaningless words; Mrs. Carlsbad showed up without sunglasses and looking old; Hegel Fish seemed impatient for the service to end, and made such a fuss that his mother was obliged to walk him to the cemetery gates and tempt him with baubles and promised excursions; returning, she cast that apologetic look about, and her husband shook his head in a patronizing way as if to say, "We all understand what's happening here, don't we?" Then S-Man set about the by-now dreary business of hypnotizing everyone gathered by the little grave. His eyes may have flickered once upon meeting mine, because after the flash and whir of the diamond (he had squeezed it for the occasion) and the solemn repetition of the Mother Planet words, our two souls' union would truly have been dissolved; and it only wasn't because, at the moment of my townspeople's oblivion, the tiny key around my neck loosed from its chain (which had never seemed so very sturdy) and I felt it and looked down to find that key and chain had actually fallen in the shape of a little *S* into the still-open grave. I cried out; perhaps S-Man thought I did so in apprehension of the loss of memory; but memory was all I longed to lose that morning, and memory, reader, is what remains.

As the years pass, I remember everything and with increasing clarity. Sometimes it comes upon me as I am washing up in the evening—I have taken over the charge of this old house, now that Rose Finch Bogardus lives in that other domicile on that other hill overlooking a highway, and now that my father, who never remarried, has finally drifted off to a well-earned, eternal sleep ("Where is she?" he asked on a last drizzling morning), and now that Elaine, who never forgave me any more than I her, has been gone these many years. Elaine left Teaneck after high school and has never returned. From time to time Haywood and Collette Lofty hear from her—she is an actress, albeit not a singing one, and goes by a name you might recognize. Still she calls him, generally at night, when love or her agent has turned on her. Perhaps she is right to resent me; although she also has forgotten the events herein narrated, somewhere in her psyche must remain the experience of waiting by the roadside—she waited for hours, she said, after helping our mother and that Bogardus to elope, for Sid to come and take her away.

It comes upon me, as I say, in the evening.

Then a dog barks, or a last daylily refuses to close, and the feel of Laff Riot's hand in my chevelure (which means hair) or the infinite chill of the Planet Laff or the triumph he must have felt when the knowledge of my friend's death became his—"GOTCHA!" he scribbles again—all fades and I am not so much restored as returned to the moment. There remain, of course, the aspects of memory that do less harm. My menses never recommenced—doctors never could fathom why, and muttered about allergies to one's own flesh; I suspect the hardships upon the callow womb of excessive time travel—but I remember how once my blood did flow and how Anne Hathaway held me in her arms. I speak only a smattering of many languages, but I have still in my possession the remains of the shell, which I smashed into shards after S-Man had flown off for what has been, it turns out, the last time. Perhaps I expected him to return once more—to ask once more if I was at last ready for the journey to Prague. Who knows how many universes need him? Some hints of the events in our town got out before he hypnotized us all, but they have joined the general myth about him. Had the little key not slipped when it did, I might have led a more normal life. What of it?

What of it, indeed? I wanted to tell you something, namely this— and it was *this* that inspired me to sit down and narrate, however baldly, however self-servingly, the events of our youth. That is, I have found it at last: the bildungsroman. Or rather, I found the first draft.

I always knew that she had written it. In my mind it has looked a little like the NJ Savings & Loan—Grecian and well-lit from within. And it has plagued me—on those nights when the train's whistle deprives me of sleep. She had told me about it in those early days when our friend- ship seemed merely sufficient. At first I didn't think much about it—I mean the nubbly black-bound notebook she had clutched to her bosom that day. By the time I remembered, her school locker had been emp- tied and the library books returned. As I serve on the Board of Trustees of the Teaneck Public Library, I am in a position to know that she too had a way of not returning books—her bill that spring (somewhat dis- counted, in consideration of her demise) came to $52.41. Her parents took a long time paying—they seemed to forget all about her, once she was buried. By the time I would have asked their permission to look through her room another family lived there. The walls of that former home turned out to have been as white and nondescript as any walls (that season, standing between them, I felt a twinge of betrayal; now I consider exaggeration one of my friend's more charming traits), and there was no sign of the manuscript. The remains of her family were to move and move again, but tragedy would stalk them: Hegel Fish graduated as Bogota Township's high school valedictorian at the age of twelve, it's true, but then devolved the bleaker years of his on-and-off attendance of classes at Harvard University and the still-bleaker years of his lapse into schizophrenia. His has been perhaps the direst of fates suffered by the individuals who took part in the turbulent events of that spring; Charles Carlsbad was confined for some months in the Hackensack Rehabilitation Center, but he emerged much steadied, if subdued, by Lithium. By dint of his breakdown he escaped being tried with the perpetrators of that terrible event whose disclosure filled the newspapers soon after. I refer, of course, to the massacre of My Lai, which he had witnessed and perhaps helped to effect. None of us ever knew what Chuck meant by his oft-repeated words, "Mo, Mo," but we could guess at the meaning of *"all of them."*

As for Beverley Carlsbad—well! She recovered so rapidly from her arm wound and subsequent divorce that our communal heads are still spinning, and I will spare you the rest of that story, except to tell you that she never did remarry, but can be seen Friday afternoons at a certain dark bar at the end of town in the company of Mr. Franklin, whose hands may shake but whose gaze, since his early retirement, seems as blue-eyed and affable as ever. It's pretty clear that those two are in love with each other in a local sort of way. No one minds, just as no one recalls the occasion on which Mr. Franklin was so unforgivably not himself. Certainly Steward Blumenthal, who runs the bar (and is the father of four distinctly pudgy, cream-in-your-coffee-faced boys), welcomes their patronage.

So time passes, and the memory of my friend grows a little blurry, and then something happens and all memories converge. It was a gentle rain that fell the morning we buried her, but it was a harsh rain that dislodged the dead such a short season ago. No one mentions the corpses that flow through a town during such a disaster; our minds are bent, as they should be, on vital bodies' reaching drier ground. And if the aftermath may include rather haphazard reunion of these bodily remains with that gravestone, who wants to recall it? There are remains and remains. As a trustee of the Teaneck Public Library, one of my chosen duties is to attend to the physical safety of our books and, when necessary, their repair; once reluctant to serve, I have come to appreciate such a function and the library's continued importance to our town.

I have lived long enough, you see, to witness much that happened so fast that unnatural year happen all over again in its own time. Although the Malathion spraying, intended to keep us in our homes while the digging went on, was soon abandoned, it has since become common practice everywhere; the shaved heads, hirsute by June, have in decades since been newly shorn; the words of hate and divisiveness have returned; busing, to my amazement, has been halted. Laff and his cohorts, guilty of so much (including breaking and entering and the forging of town proclamations), could simply have waited for the secular to cede to the religious.

But that, as they are wont to say, is another story. Suffice it to say that with Catholic schooling with Catholic, and Jew with Jew, our public library remains the truly unified and central locale of intellectual endeavor. Its maintenance has become my pride and my chagrin—my only child, as it were. As a board member I have felt the common excitement (although not shared the common laughter) when an anonymous donor, someone who wished the library only well, contributed what purported to be a signed edition of the first folio of Shakespeare's *Collected Works*—a priceless document, had it not been published, someone (Mrs. Glueck's second cousin Ida Kolin, I believe) pointed out, after the playwright's death. How, Ida triumphantly asked the group at large, could Shakespeare have signed it? The signature, however genuine in appearance, could only have been forged. So we got nothing out of that contribution. But the signed edition of Diderot's *Encyclopédie* was verifiable and verified, and its use as collateral has permitted us to go about the total renovation of the library and the restoration of books that suffered in the flood.

Tunneling

For a brief moment, after the waters receded—how strange Town Hall looked with water flowing through its doors and windows!—a kind of unity reigned; through the dredging and discarding and wringing out and renovating, neighbor worked with neighbor regardless of creed or kind, and how quickly the children seemed to forget the trauma of their losses (mostly, it's true, of property), and to take advantage of the general bonhomie to romp together! With the passage of time and the return to a drier ground has come a return to business as usual; and so it is only in a very few places that on a given Saturday afternoon one can find everyone and his child engaged in the adventure of learning. And then the hours pass, and families return home, and I can let us in with my trustee's key and turn the lights back on—light, it seems, does go back on—and read in total tranquillity and silence, the dog lounging at my feet or watching me dolefully, expectantly!

The first time I came here alone, directly after the flood, my heart ached. Now I move swiftly to the stuffed chair by the old eagle-topped brass pole from which hangs a dusty American flag. We have kept some things and lost others—the capacious main entrance has been blocked off to make room for more shelves, and a new central staircase defies the original federalist decor. The paintings of our forefathers look odd amid such modernity! The computers lead the average reader to any destination with terrifying rapidity—I, who never pass the sign TRAVEL TO FOREIGN PLACES AND OTHER TIMES! READ! without trepidation, find such binary aids almost as frightening. Mine was and remains a certain generation; a sign assures its members of the continued, if no longer quite necessary, functioning of the Dewey decimal system. Who can say that I have not been blessed, when the recitation of those ancient numbers brings back so much? They are all around me in the silence and shadows and odd, bric-a-brac dignity of this dear municipal center: I mean Diderot and craggy Voltaire and sullen Rousseau; I mean Shakespeare, of course, and Achebe; and Confucius—why, I have failed even to mention our sojourn with that wise and courteous gentleman!—and as for Oscar Wilde, one cannot seem these days to avoid his telltale cloak and characteristic slouch. These are the men who taught me not to write, but to live in the service of words.

And then, of course, there is Kafka. But to say more on that subject would be, perhaps, to dilute the effectiveness of my friend's oeuvre. I found it—or rather, that rascal Boomer found it as it slid to the cool floor, and he would have carried it past me between his teeth—during the restoration of the library following the flood; for years the manuscript must have lain between the three library copies of Max Brod's biography, on whose title page I found these words, penciled in my friend's oddly wild handwriting: "MAX BROD IS MY FAVORITE WRITER." To think that my love was marred, tainted, by a reluctance to share a passion that wasn't mutual, after all! Life and death have at least one trait in common, it seems: a puerile, even slapstick sense of humor.

Initially I considered publishing the manuscript as I had found it—child's exclamations and boasting notwithstanding—then it seemed that I had been entrusted with a greater duty: I had been chosen, if only by time, to bring her text to maturity. And so I have endeavored this long winter (it has been a long winter, Boomer's company notwithstanding) to shape and to select and to privilege—in short, to edit. And now it is almost springtime again—doleful season!—and there remains little more for me to accomplish, other than a stroll to the old stuffed armchair, where I may claim my accustomed seat, and imagine that the faces on the wall recognize in me their habitual visitor. With what a confusion of sentiments, then, I open the folio and the very first lines of her *opus maximus* appear; whose contents, without further ado—reader, adieu!—I append.

APPENDIX A:
IN WHICH WE LEAVE FOR
PRAGUE

An Excerpt from a Novel-in-Progress,
by
Rachel H. Fish

(Edited by Rachel E. Finch)

"Please fasten your seat belts and make sure that all reclined seats are upright. Stewardesses, please take position for takeoff."

At last! I thought. We're on our way!

My father lifted his window shade and together we watched as the runway began very slowly, and then faster, to slip into the past. Soon we were racing toward the end of the asphalt and then the floor was tilting up and we were off!

After dreaming about it for months—for years—I was finally going to see the beautiful and inspirational city of Prague.

Prague! City of rivers and bridges! How the Moldau had grabbed my attention before I was even old enough to read (I was three and a half when I read my first word). How the name of the bridge that spans it—the Charles—made me thirst for its gently flowing waters! To be sure, I was not an ignoramus. I had heard of the defenestration of Prague. Nonetheless I was persuaded that certain cities give rise to genius; hadn't that sober, even somber city given us that ever-soaring talent whose magnificent chef d'oeuvre—which is not the same thing as hors d'oeuvres—went on being read the world over?

I refer, of course, to that magnificent study of a psyche done by that erudite and unbelievably generous friend of the friendless, supporter of the oppressed, reader of the unread, and not to mention REAL FAMILY MAN—

MAX BROD!

(I'm a girl, but he's still my favorite writer.)

"Well, well," said my father.

The no-smoking light had gone off and the stewardesses were moving about the cabin. Two men—they were extremely tall Swedish men with very blond hair—walked stiffly past us. A woman started hunting around in the overhead compartment. My father sat back in his seat and pushed the round silver button that would release it into an incline. I was glad to be traveling among other people with him. We were only traveling through space, of course, but in a manner of speaking, weren't we also traveling through time? Some of the buildings in Prague would look exactly the same. We knew, because my father had brought home for me a delightful red-velvet-covered book (probably it wasn't real velvet) that also contained a photograph of Max Brod's apartment at number 1 Schalengasse. Max Brod is dead now of course—he died last year in Israel, surrounded by his wife and their five children and seven grandchildren and all his best friends, none of whom he loved, of course, as much as he had loved K. (which in my experience generally stands for Kafka), but still. The other name for Schalengasse is Skorepka. That was something I looked forward to very much about Prague: all the streets would have German AND Czech names!

Speaking of which, my name is Rachel. I was named after my grandmother Rifka, who disappeared in Europe. They could only give me the "R" because they could never be quite sure she wasn't going to return from the dead. The "R" stands for hope, as you can see. So you can call me "R"!

"I just love airplanes," I told my father (which wasn't true).

"That's my girl," he said. He cupped his hand on my head, a favorite place of his. I leaned for a second on his shoulder. My father and I aren't just relatives; we're practically best friends. At least we were until I made a very special friend this year. She's mad at me right now, but that doesn't prove anything.

"That's my dad," I said. I didn't know what I meant by that, but it didn't matter, because we were on our way to Prague.

The funny thing was that I had sort of fallen in love with Max Brod the winter before, when his obituary appeared in the *New York Times*. I cut out the clipping and pasted it into my album along with other obituaries of important thinkers and artists and writers. A lot more people are dead than you realize! The obituary of Max Brod gave me the feeling that my stuffed animals used to give me, only more so. In the photograph of Max Brod's apartment you can see ornate murals of what looked like (they were) Greek gods. One was Dionysus. But there isn't time to tell you about them (or about the drawing of Max Brod, which shows how handsome he was) because just as I was settling into my seat—my father had opened his book, a history of the Czech Republic (it was a good book, he said, but it left out what they call "Prague Spring," which was the same spring Max Brod died)—two small people jumped out of the men's bathroom!

They were carrying blond wigs and stilts, and they weren't Swedish after all!

"This plane is hijacked!" they said.

"Hijacked!" everyone screamed.

"Please be quiet!" screamed the men. At first I thought they were Arabs, which was racist of me. (I'm Jewish but that's no excuse.) Then I realized that they were of course Vietcong, which is to say members of the fighting branch of the National Liberation Front. I could tell from the red-blue-and-yellow bandanas they wore around their necks and the way they kept checking in with their officers via two-way radio. I could also tell they weren't used to hijacking airplanes, which made me more nervous.

"No one gets hurt," they kept insisting. One of the men stuck out his tongue and fake-puked, as if he were "getting hurt."

"It's okay," my father whispered. "Just sit tight."

"I don't know what you mean by that," I hissed. "This is definitely not all right."

"Just sit tight."

Alas! My father may have been my best friend (until recently), but he couldn't stop the forward march of Destiny! This is what happened: we flew across the Atlantic. We turned south at Rome. The men, whose names I took to be Chu and Chi—unless that was the name of their neighborhood, I wasn't sure—kept talking into their radio sets. They seemed to be growing perturbed. They wore their shirts open at the neck and their loose black pants swam around their hips—they looked so hungry, so thin and hungry, and yet they wouldn't eat in front of us! They wouldn't take advantage of the situation to grab a bite, because we would have seen just how bad things were for their side! I disapproved of their methods but I had to admire their courage. They were very ethereal people.

Before long, they made clear their demands. They wanted ten million dollars and the release of eighty VC from the war compound in the Chu Chi (so it was a neighborhood) region.

"You'll never get it," sneered the pilot. He had put the plane on automatic, which also made me nervous. (The truth is that if it weren't for my father, I wouldn't fly at all.)

The pilot was right, of course; but no one could know then and there. The Vietcong were beginning to look a little crazed, perhaps from the odor of our dinners, which had been set to heat. I knew something bad was going to happen. You could just tell from the air, hot and moist—what you call "fetid."

Sure enough, they wanted to take some of us hostage!

"But why?" the pilot argued. "Let the passengers go. International opinion will be much easier to sway, I promise you, if you just let passengers fly on to their destinations."

"Very humanitarian," sneered the other Vietcong. "We tell you what. We want those two things. Maybe three. We want money and freedom for our men. We also want recruits. We're running out of tunnel runners."

"Tunnel runners?" asked the copilot—she was a dark-haired woman and hadn't said anything yet. I didn't particularly like the looks of her.

The Vietcong glanced at each other. The better speaker nodded slightly. The other one also nodded. Things were going to get better, their body language said. (All human beings have body language.) They were going to go home, and not die, at least not yet, and they would have recruits to show for their troubles.

"Small people. Young. Maybe children. The adult, especially American adult, he is too old already. Has fits. Also, threatens to litigate. Who you going to sue when the war is over? Sheesh! Anyhow. Got any volunteers? No volunteer, no return to city of destination! Aha!"

"Just sit still," whispered my father. I glanced at his face, which had paled. I felt an inward sense of doom. What if even my father, whose bravery I revered, was succumbing to the hijackers' powerful personalities?

"Please," my father went on whispering. "What would your mother say if she knew?"

"She's always liked H. better," I said. "You know that."

H., in case you're wondering, is my brother.

"Sibling rivalry is no reason to throw your life away," my father whispered. "What about your allergies?"

"You there. The big one talking. Stand up."

My father, realizing that he was the "big one talking," rose slowly. I say "slowly," but he didn't seem slow. He seemed solemn and graceful.

"Step into the aisle," the first man said. The second glanced at him as if to say, "Must we? Already?" But he didn't say anything, and I knew that I had about thirty seconds to create a diversion before they made "an example" of my father.

"I'll go!" I cried. "I volunteer!"

"R.!" my father said.

"It's all right, D.," I said. "I've always wanted to live in a tunnel for six months."

"Six months! One year!" the first man said proudly. He smacked himself on the chest and the hungry look vanished for a moment or so, as he recalled (and as he related to me later) the honor that had been bestowed upon him after one year's worth of living—not in one continuous period of time, but almost—beneath the ground with only the most rudimentary "Dien-Ben Kitchen" in which to prepare meals (and even then sometimes the smoke was so bad that cooking had to be abandoned). Imagine sleeping in a chamber eight meters belowground, and hearing every B-52 that whistles through the night sky, every explosion that shakes the earth loose all around you! Imagine—I don't have to imagine it, since it happened—your only food being a ball of rice twice each day, your only mattress the earth beneath you (which was very hard during the dry season) and your only entertainment the occasional visit of the Liberation Theater. I admit that I was moved by their performance and by the desire on the part of the playwright to improve his play, which was entitled *Primitive Weapons Can Overcome Sophisticated Weapons,* and which was much funnier than its title suggests. Even so, the playwright, Truong (that's his family name), was very depressed by the obstacles presented by his current employment—I like to think that I might have encouraged him. I think I did. I am a very patriotic American against the War and in favor of the Arts wherever I find them. Anyhow, by "occasional" visit I mean twice in the six months I lived underground. The rest of the time I had to crawl through communication tunnels—my special "assignment" was the delivery of important messages. Are you wondering how I managed to stay alive? Would you like to know more about life underground and the importance of freedom of opportunity to all peoples—whatever their race, religion or creed—everywhere? Well!

IF YOU WANT TO KNOW MORE, READ ON!

ABOUT THE AUTHOR

BETH BOSWORTH is the author of *A Burden of Earth and Other Stories* (Hanging Loose Press). Her short fiction has appeared in various journals and anthologies. She has taught at The New School for Social Research, CUNY's New York City Technical College, and for many years at Saint Ann's School in Brooklyn, where she is also founding editor of *The Saint Ann's Review*. Née Beth Finkelstein, she grew up in Teaneck, New Jersey. She lives in Brooklyn with her family.